# STELLA'S STORY

Eugene McEldowney was born in Belfast and educated at Queen's University. He enjoyed a long career as a journalist with *The Irish Times*, and began to write fiction in 1994. *Stella's Story* is his sixth novel. The companion novel, *The Faloorie Man*, was published by New Island in 1999. He lives in Malahide, County Dublin.

# EUGENE McELDOWNEY

# STELLA'S STORY

**NEW ISLAND**

STELLA'S STORY
First published November 2002
by New Island
2 Brookside
Dundrum Road
Dublin 14

The moral right of the author has been asserted.

ISBN 1 902602 84 6

British Library Cataloguing in Publication Data.
A CIP catalogue record for this book is available
from the British Library.

Typeset by New Island
Cover design by Slick Fish Design
Printed in Ireland by Colour Books Ltd.

**The Arts Council**
An Chomhairle Ealaíon

New Island receives financial assistance from The Arts Council,
(An Chomhairle Ealaíon), Dublin, Ireland.

10 9 8 7 6 5 4 3 2 1

*For my brothers*
*Gerry and Sean*

# BOOK ONE

# 1.

I was always attracted to good-looking men. They had to be handsome, and dark, like Clark Gable, who I sighed over on Saturday afternoons in the Regal cinema in Enniskillen. If a man wasn't handsome, I had no time for him. My mother used to laugh and say that good-looking men would be my downfall. Little did she know how right she was.

When I look back, I think I was aware of men for as long as I can remember. At first it was my father. He was tall, with broad shoulders and big, rough hands from the hard work in the fields. But he had a beautiful face, the bluest eyes I have ever seen, strong arms and black hairs along his chest like matted threads. I used to watch as he washed himself under the pump in the yard, on a summer's evening when he came in from work, the water splashing like silver pearls, and I would think I was looking at a god.

Later, there were boys who would tease me and try to kiss me in the schoolyard. I cut them dead, thinking them rough and awkward, even though their interest excited me. My time was only for my father. I loved the smell of him, the scent of machine oil and sweat, and I loved the way he would take me in his strong arms, hold me above his head and tell me I was his girl, the light of his life. I used to love his black hair that shone like coal in the light from the tilly-lamp. I think it was from my father that I learnt to admire handsome, dark-haired men.

His name was James Patrick Maguire. He was a farmer and we lived in Ballinaleck in County Fermanagh. I used to write at the top of my copy book in school: Estelle Maguire, Letterbreen Road, Ballinaleck, County Fermanagh, Ireland, the World, the Universe, God's Creation.

My full name was Margaret Estelle but I never used the Margaret part. Estelle was French. It meant 'star'. Mammy got it from a book she had been reading before I was born and she liked it and gave it to me. All the girls in school had common names: Mary and Theresa and Catherine and Bernadette. They were called after saints. But there was no one else called Estelle and that singled me out and made me special.

My sisters were called Kathleen and Bridget. I had two brothers: Michael and Martin. At the time I am speaking about, we were still children. We lived on a small farm and it was hard work. I had little knowledge of the world and I thought that everybody lived like us. But now I know that we were poor.

My father raised cattle. He bought them at the fair when they were calves, fattened them up and then sold them to the dealer. But the prices went up and down and the cattle would often get sick. Then he'd have to send for the vet and that cost money. Sometimes the cattle got so sick that they died and Daddy got no money at all.

He grew grass to feed the cattle, and vegetables – potatoes and cabbages and turnips – that we used to feed ourselves. What he had left over, he sold at the market, along with the eggs from the hens that Mammy kept, and the jam and scones she used to make. Every Friday he would take the pony and cart and travel the four miles into Enniskillen.

Sometimes, as a special treat, he would take me with him and I would sit beside him on the cart and hold the reins. When the market was over, we would go to Donnelly's pub where he would drink pints of black Guinness and buy me a glass of lemonade. The farmers would tickle my chin and say I was pretty as a picture, and I loved that. I loved the warmth of the pub and the smell of the beer and tobacco. Sometimes a ballad singer would come in and sing a song and people would put money in his tin. My father would drain his glass and a farmer would say: "Have one more for the road, Pat. Sure God knows, we could all be dead in the morning."

My father would look at me and say: "What do you think Stella? Have we time for another one?"

I knew asking me like this was only a game, because he would do what he wanted, anyway. But it made me feel important.

I would say: "One more, Daddy. For you know what Mammy said. We have to be home for our supper and bring the money with us."

The farmers would roar with laughter and push their caps back from their eyes and say: "Oh she's a right wee vixen, that one."

My father would put his big arm around me and cuddle me close.

"She's my wee angel, so she is, and when she grows up she's going to break some poor boy's heart."

Break some poor boy's heart. I always remember my father saying that. It sticks in my memory even now, after all these years. I can still see him leaning on the counter of Donnelly's pub with his dark hair and his big strong arms and the farmers standing around laughing. Break some poor boy's heart. How could he have known how true those words would be?

*

I was the second youngest child. Michael was the oldest, then Bridgie, Martin and me. Kathleen was the youngest and she was the baby.

I can remember the morning she was born. I was five years old. I knew Mammy was going to have a baby because she got fat from the baby in her tummy. That's what happened. Mammys got fat and that was a sure sign they were going to have a baby.

She used to let me stroke her fat tummy. Sometimes I could feel the baby kick and Mammy would smile.

"Did you feel that? It's going to be a boy. A big bruiser by the feel of him. Boys always make a fuss when they're coming. That'll be three. At this rate, I'll have a football team."

"Why do boys make a fuss, Mammy?"

"Because it's their nature, child. Boys are rough. Girls are gentle because they're ladies. Will you help me with him when he's born? Will you help me feed him and wash him?"

I said: "Yes, Mammy."

One morning I heard Mammy screaming from the bed next door.

11

"It's coming, Pat. Oh Jesus, it's coming. You'll have to go and get the doctor."

"Hold on, Annie. Hold on."

I heard Daddy clumping about in the bedroom, putting on his boots. It was a cold November morning and it was raining hard against the window pane. I held onto Bridgie in the bed we shared, while Mammy screamed and roared. The sound terrified me.

Then I heard Daddy rushing down the stairs and into the yard, and a while later he was back with Mrs MacConnell, the District Nurse. Dr O'Hare came after them in his motor car.

Mrs MacConnell started to boil kettles and pots of water in the kitchen and I could hear Dr O'Hare in Mammy's room trying to comfort her. He was saying: "There, there now, Mrs Maguire. Just push. Everything's going to be all right. Just push a wee bit harder."

But Mammy only screamed all the louder, like somebody was trying to murder her. The screams were awful. I thought she was going to die and I started praying to God to keep her alive. I covered my head with the blankets and bit the pillow while I tried to block out the terrible sound of her screams.

It seemed to go on forever before there was silence. Mrs MacConnell came into our bedroom and said: "Would you like to come and see the new baby?"

We went into Mammy's room in our nightshifts. She was lying exhausted on the bed, her hair matted with sweat. Daddy and Dr O'Hare were drinking glasses of whiskey by the window.

Daddy said: "You've got a wee sister. We're going to call her Kathleen."

I looked at my new sister. All I could see was a little head of black hair and pink cheeks and her mouth sucking at Mammy's big red nipple.

"Aren't you happy to have a wee sister?" Daddy asked.

I nodded yes. I was glad that Mammy was still alive and hadn't died. I looked at her again. She seemed to have gone asleep but I could still hear her screams ringing in my head.

I thought: It's all right for Daddy to be drinking whiskey. But what about poor Mammy? This is what babies bring. Trouble. Pain and suffering and trouble.

## 2.

"Stellie Maguire! Are you day-dreaming again?"

I came awake. I'd been thinking of the film I'd seen with Bridgie on Saturday afternoon. Clark Gable and Claudette Colbert. *It Happened One Night.*

Miss Brankin was staring at me with those big eyes of hers behind her thick glasses. She looked like an owl I had seen in a picture book. She was standing at the blackboard with a wooden duster in her hand. The class was silent.

"Well, Stellie Maguire? Have you lost your tongue?"

Stellie! She called me Stellie instead of Estelle. She did it to punish me.

"No, Miss."

"Don't lie to me, Stellie Maguire. I won't have a liar in my class. What was I talking about, just now?"

"Constantinople, Miss."

"Constantinople, indeed! That was five minutes ago. You were asleep."

She hurled the duster and it hit my desk and went skidding across the floor.

There was a hush as everybody kept their heads down.

Miss Brankin was in a temper now. She marched down the room and pulled me by the ear.

"I'll show you, you little madam. You get up there and stand in the corner. And put on the dunce's cap."

She dragged me to the top of the class, opened a cupboard and took out this long pointed cap like a witch would wear. She shoved it on my head.

I heard someone giggle.

Miss Brankin was still giving out. She was skinny and she wore this stupid cardigan with darning on the sleeve.

"I have myself worked to the bone trying to teach a bunch of good-for-nothing numbskulls. And the least I expect is that you stay awake and pay attention. I could be off in Enniskillen teaching the girls in the convent. Girls from good homes who appreciate the value of education. And instead, I'm stuck here with a class full of dunderheads. Now!"

She smacked her ruler hard against her desk.

"Repeat after me. Seven times seven is forty-nine. Seven times eight is fifty-six."

I stood in the corner with my back to the class and felt my eyes flood with tears. Miss Brankin hated me and my lovely name, Estelle. It was because she was jealous. Her own name was Philomena. She had it written on her books. It was an awful name. That's why she called me Stellie. Because she didn't have a lovely name like me.

I stood in the the corner and fought back the tears. I wouldn't let Miss Brankin see me cry. I wouldn't give her the satisfaction.

On the way home from school, Mary O'Connor put her arm around my shoulder to comfort me.

"Don't let that ould cow annoy you," she said. "Her nose is out of joint because she wants to be up there in the convent teaching the High School girls and the doctors' daughters. And they'd all be bowing and scraping and bringing her wee presents. And instead she's stuck with us and we haven't two pennies to rub together."

Mary O'Connor laughed. "You know what she needs, don't you?"

"What?"

She pulled my head close and whispered. "She needs a man to give her a good...."

I put my hands over my ears. "Oh, Mary. Don't talk like that. That's an awful thing to say. That's a sin. You'll have to tell it in confession to Father Kavanagh."

But Mary O'Connor just laughed louder. "Did you come down in the last shower or something? Sure they're all doing it."

*

Our house consisted of a kitchen and two bedrooms. Mammy and Daddy slept in a big double bed with a blue eiderdown in the main bedroom at the front of the house. Bridgie and Kathleen and I slept in the small bedroom off the kitchen. Michael and Martin slept in the loft of the barn. There was a privy out in the yard near the hen-house and it had a tiny snib so you could lock the door and be alone in there.

Mammy was always washing and cleaning and cooking. She would get up at six o'clock and light the stove and put on a big pot of porridge. She called it stirabout and that's what we got for breakfast. Stirabout and mugs of strong black tea. Daddy and Michael had bread and an egg because they had a long day ahead working in the fields. At the weekend, we had a fry as a special treat; eggs and rashers and fried soda bread that Mammy baked.

I would come home from school around four o'clock and Bridgie and I would help Mammy get the supper ready. She would have a pot of spuds and we had to peel them all and then wash them under the pump in the yard. I hated that job, the three of us sitting round the table slicing through endless spuds while Mammy quietly sang to herself.

*I know my love by his way of walking,*
*And I know my love by his way of talking,*
*And I know my love in his coat of blue,*
*And if my love leaves me, what will I do?*

Saturday was washing day. Mammy got out the big aluminium basin from under the sink and filled it with hot water. We would scrub the clothes with bars of yellow soap till all the dirt was gone. When that was finished, we had to take the clothes outside and wring them out in the mangle and hang them on the line to dry. Mammy's hands would be red and swollen from the washing.

My special job was feeding the hens. I had to make a pot of meal and oats and go out and go "Chuck, chuck, chuck", scattering the meal on the ground. The hens would come running from under doors and out of the barn, their beaks darting like lightening as they gobbled up the meal.

The big red rooster would come strutting into the yard and peck at the hens, and they would flap their wings to get out of his way. I had to make sure that the rooster didn't eat up all the food and that all the hens got fed.

Each season brought different jobs around the farm and we all had to help. We had two fields. The small field was closest to the house and was used for growing vegetables. Beyond it was the lower field. It was about two acres in size and this was where Daddy kept the cattle. Our fields were bounded by a stand of oak trees which gave way to more land. This was owned by an old bachelor called Daniel Turvey. He stayed inside his house most of the time drinking whiskey and his land was going to rack and ruin.

Early spring was planting time. Daddy would get the horse and hitch him up to the plough and he'd drive in lines across the fields to break up the earth. Michael, Martin, Bridgie and I followed behind, putting down seed potatoes and cabbage and turnip plants and covering them over again with soil.

The harvest was worse. It was back-breaking work, bending over the drills and picking all the spuds, even the tiniest ones that looked like little pebbles, and putting them into sacks to be stored in the barn.

Then the hay had to be saved and this was the hardest task of all. Daddy and Michael would get out the big scythes and Daddy would sharpen them on a whetstone till the blades shone like silver in the sun. I can still see the pair of them going down through the fields, swinging the scythes, with the tall green grass flying in the breeze behind them. We would gather it into rucks and leave it to dry, and then it would be stored for winter feed for the cattle.

Every night, when Daddy came in from work, he would wash himself under the pump. He would put on clean clothes and light the lamps and we would all kneel down and say the family rosary.

When we had finished praying, we would sit down at the kitchen table and eat our supper. Afterwards, Mammy would clear the plates away and wash them in the sink. Daddy would shake out the *Irish Press* and light his pipe and the house would fill with the lovely smell of tobacco. Bridgie and I would go to our bedroom to do our homework.

But I'd be so tired after all the work that I couldn't keep my eyes open. I would fall asleep with the school books lying on top of the bedclothes and my homework wouldn't get done.

That was another reason Miss Brankin didn't like me. That's why she called me a dunderhead and made me wear the dunce's cap.

# 3.

I came home from school one afternoon to find Daddy sitting at the kitchen table with the paper spread out before him. I was surprised to see him. Usually he didn't come in from the fields till supper time.

He looked up when I came in the door.

"Guess what?" he said. "We're at war."

"Who are we going to fight?"

"The Germans. They're after invading Poland and Mr Chamberlain told that Hitler fella that if he did that, there'd be hell to pay. So England has declared war on Germany."

I looked out the window. Everything seemed the same. I could see the cattle in the lower field lying out in the sun, their big black tails swishing back and forth to chase away the flies.

"What will it mean for us?"

"Oh, it will make a big difference. For a start they're going to have to raise an army. And then they're going to have to feed them. And what do you think they'll feed them on? Beef of course. So I suppose I'll get a good price for my cattle at last."

I could see that this war business had got Daddy excited.

"And there's another thing. It says here in the paper that the Free State is staying neutral. So there's going to be all sorts of shortages and that means great scope for the smugglers. I'll tell you one thing for nothing. There's some people's going to get rich out of this war."

That weekend, Daddy went into Enniskillen and bought a second-hand wireless in Burke's bicycle shop. We all crowded round to see this strange invention. It came in a polished wooden case with two big glass jars filled with coloured liquid that Daddy said was the battery. We watched in awe as he rigged it up. When he had finished, he told us to stand well back. Then he flicked a switch and a light came on, and the room was suddenly flooded with dance music.

Everybody clapped. Mammy grabbed Bridgie and me and waltzed us round the floor.

Daddy looked very important.

Martin wanted to know where the music was coming from.

"From London," said Daddy.

"And how does it get here?"

"It comes through the air."

"But how does it get into our house?"

Daddy scratched his chin.

"It comes down the chimney."

"And what if the fire is lit?"

"For God's sake, don't be asking so many questions," Daddy said, annoyed. "It's complicated. You wouldn't understand it."

Daddy was fascinated by the wireless. Nobody was allowed to touch it except him. Every night, after supper, he would fiddle with the dials and get reports about the war over in Europe, and the cattle prices, people speaking in posh accents. On Sunday afternoons, he would invite some of the neighbouring men and they would sit around the kitchen table listening to football matches.

I could see they were very impressed. Daddy would sit at the head of the table in his Sunday suit and his clean white shirt and his black hair neatly brushed. He would turn the dial on the wireless and the men would nod their heads and shout with excitement when somebody scored a goal. I would feel so proud as I watched the way the other men looked up to Daddy.

I was growing up pretty. I knew this because of the way boys were looking at me. I got to recognise that glance which told me they liked me. By now I was turning into a woman; I had breasts and wore an uplift and I was getting my periods.

One day, when we were alone, Mammy told me about babies and

how they got in your tummy. I could see she was embarrassed but I knew most of it already. Mary O'Connor had told me.

Mammy said that it was my duty to keep myself pure for my husband. She said that any girl who was free got herself a name, and no respectable man would have her. The worst thing that could happen to a girl was that she got herself pregnant before she was married. Girls like that ended up in a home and nobody wanted them. It sounded awful.

"Watch out for good-looking men, Estelle. Those ones are the charmers. They'll promise you the sun and the moon but if you're not careful, they'll lead you astray."

I thought of Daddy.

"You married one," I said.

Mammy sniffed.

"Daddy is different. Daddy is a good man."

*

Mary O'Connor was going with boys. She met them outside the snooker hall in Enniskillen on Friday afternoons and they would take her for walks into the country. They were older boys, about 16, and they smoked cigarettes. They were rough farm labourers and messenger boys for the big stores.

I was curious. One day, as we were coming home from school, I asked her what she did with the boys when they went walking.

"Oh, it's mostly kissing."

"Is it nice?"

Mary O'Connor shrugged.

"It depends. Some of them fellas don't clean their teeth and they smell like pig shit."

"Is it just kissing you do?"

"Well they try to feel me up. They would be grabbing at me and trying to put their hands up my dress, but I always keep my legs crossed."

I was really interested now.

"What else do you do, Mary?"

"They try to get me to feel them. Jackie Quinn took my hand and put it inside his trousers. And you'll never believe it. He had a thing on him as big as Cassidy's donkey."

"*That* big?"

"Sure. I nearly fainted. It reached down to his knee."

I was shocked.

"Mary, that's terrible. That's a mortal sin. You don't do the other thing, do you?"

I could feel my heart thumping like mad as I waited for her reply.

"Do you think I'm crazy. Jesus, I don't want to end up in the pudden club before I'm even out of school."

I was envious of Mary O'Connor and her boys, even if they were rough. At night in bed, I would think of Clark Gable. Our love would be pure. I would let him hold my hand and perhaps kiss me. But I wouldn't let him put his hand up my dress. Anyway, Clark Gable was a gentleman and Mammy said gentlemen didn't do things like that.

# 4.

Every Christmas, Uncle James sent us a big parcel in the post, filled with all sorts of lovely presents. They were mostly clothes; dresses for us girls and shirts and pullovers for Michael, Martin and Daddy. For Mammy, there was always something special, maybe a nice hat or a new coat.

Uncle James was Mammy's brother and he lived in America, in a place called Albany. He had no children but he had a big job as a manager over all these men, and he was rich. He owned a fancy house and a motorcar and he wore a suit to work. Daddy said: "One thing about Uncle James, he never has to get his hands dirty."

I knew all this because Mammy was always talking about him and, every year, he sent us photographs of himself and Aunt Eileen. They would be dressed up in their lovely clothes for a ball, Aunt Eileen wearing pearls round her neck and Uncle James smoking a cigar. You could tell they hadn't a care in the world.

I loved the clothes Uncle James sent. The dresses had fancy frills and ribbons and they came in pretty colours. The girls at school would be green with envy. I'd see them looking at me and wishing they had an uncle in America who sent them nice things. I used to count the days till that parcel arrived. It always came in the second week of December in a special delivery from Enniskillen. But one Christmas it didn't come.

Instead, Uncle James sent a Christmas card and a letter. Inside was a cheque for $100. Daddy read the letter and then he looked at the cheque. He held it up to the light and examined it, as if he didn't trust it. Then he scratched his chin.

"He says he's been told not to send the parcel because of the War. He says the boat that's bringing it over might get sunk, so he's sent us a cheque instead. What's a dollar worth, does anybody know?"

Michael said he thought a dollar was worth five shillings.

"Five shillings?"

Daddy took a pencil and did some scribbles on the back of a cigarette packet.

"That means he's sent us £25."

He looked at Mammy in amazement.

"My God, Annie, that's a powerful amount of money. You could buy an awful lot with £25."

"Well, let's not spend it before we've got it. Take it into the bank on Monday morning and get it changed and then we'll know exactly how much it is."

Kathleen began to cry.

"Does that mean we'll not be getting any nice presents for Christmas?"

I was worried too. A cheque for $100 was all very well, but it wasn't as good as the parcel with all the lovely things in it.

But Mammy just put her arms around Kathleen and said: "Shush, allanah. Of course you'll get your presents. I'll take you into Enniskillen myself and you can pick your very own thing."

*

I loved Christmas. It wasn't just because we got presents. There was something else, a magic that I couldn't put my finger on. It started on the first day of December. Miss Brankin would tear the date off the calendar, and clap her hands and say: "Now girls, we have entered the holy season of advent. Who knows what advent means?"

Hands would shoot up. We knew it off by heart. She asked the same question every year.

"Please Miss, advent is a time of preparation for the birth of Our Lord."

"Good girl, Eileen Brady. Remember what Christmas means. It's not

24

just having fun and drinking and stuffing ourselves with food. It's the birthday of Christ, our blessed Redeemer. What is Christmas girls?"

"The birthday of Christ, our blessed Redeemer."

"Good girls."

Around this time something would change. Miss Brankin wasn't cross anymore. She didn't pick on me and make me stand in the corner with the dunce's hat on my head. She stopped fussing about homework. Instead, she brought in rolls of coloured paper, gave us scissors and paste and showed us how to cut up the paper to make decorations. These she would string around the classroom.

She would say: "Miss Doherty says her class can make the best decorations, but I told her my class was better. So we'll just have to show them. Won't we, girls?"

We would chorus back: "Yes, Miss. Indeed, we will."

And the scissors would go snip, snip, snip as we all bent to the task of making better decorations than the class next door.

Next came the Christmas carols. Miss Brankin loved to sing. She played the organ at church. She had a piano in the corner of the room and every Friday morning we had Music. She would sit at the piano, stretch out her hands and flex her fingers, saying: "Now, girls. At the count of three. One, two, three.

*The first Noel, the angels did say,*
*Was to certain poor shepherds in fields where they lay."*

Miss Brankin knew lots of carols, even ones that nobody else had ever heard. My favourite was 'The Holly Bears a Berry'. I would find myself humming it on my way home from school.

*Oh, the holly bears a berry as red as the blood.*
*Just as Mary bore Jesus to be our sweet Lord.*
*Just as Mary bore Jesus, our Saviour to be*
*And of all the trees in the greenwood, I love the holly.*

At home, Mammy would be cleaning and scrubbing and getting things ready. She'd get a bucket of water and wash down the windows. She'd clean the chimney. She'd polish the floor and the lamps till they were gleaming. She'd put up clumps of holly behind the pictures. The house always got an extra going over before Christmas for Mammy said you wouldn't know who might drop in and you didn't want the place looking like a show.

When she had finished cleaning, she would begin the baking. She bought nuts and raisins and currants for the cake. When I came home in the afternoons, the house would be filled with this lovely warm baking smell. I would help her mix the ingredients in a big bowl and, as a treat, she would let me dip my finger in the icing sugar and lick off the lovely sweet powder.

A few days before Christmas, Daddy would say: "Time to get the bird." He would set off to see a man he knew who raised turkeys. He always got a hen because he said the meat was sweeter. Then he'd bring it home and spend a whole afternoon plucking it; the yard would be filled with feathers. He'd hang it up on a nail in the kitchen where it would stay till Christmas Day, its glassy eye staring accusingly at everyone who entered.

Christmas Eve was very busy. From early morning, Mammy and Bridgie and I would be getting things ready. There were potatoes to be peeled, vegetables to be prepared, clothes to be laid out, shirts to be ironed, boots and shoes to be polished. At four o'clock, as it was beginning to get dark, the postman would cycle up to the door with the last of the Christmas mail. Daddy would bring him in and pour two glasses of whiskey.

"My God, Mick," he would say. "There's another year nearly gone already."

The postman would knock back the whiskey.

"No point complaining, Pat."

"Have you time for another one?" Daddy would say and I'd see Mammy frown.

The postman would hold out his glass for a refill.

"Sure a bird never flew on one wing, Pat."

Then the postman would pull his bag on his back and cycle unsteadily down the road. Mammy would say: "For God's sake. Have you no sense, at all? That poor man has another twenty houses to go and if he gets a glass of whiskey in every one, he'll be scuttered before he's done."

But Daddy just laughed and said: "It's Christmas, Annie. And we mightn't live to see another one."

At half eleven, we'd set off for midnight Mass. The church would be packed with people. We'd see all our neighbours, and Miss Brankin sitting proudly at the organ. She would smile and nod when she saw us and at twelve o'clock she would press on the pedals and everyone would stand up and sing 'Adeste Fidelis'.

Afterwards, we'd go home through the fields. The moon would be out and there would be frost on the grass; in the darkness you would see the Christmas candles shining like stars in the windows of the farmhouses.

I couldn't wait to get home and cuddle up to Bridgie and Kathleen in the warm bed, to fall asleep dreaming of Christmas Day.

# 5.

Daddy was right about the War. It did put up cattle prices. The meat companies couldn't get enough animals. They sent men around all the farms in the district buying up everything they could lay their hands on and shipping it off to England for the soldiers.

He was also right about the shortages. One day I was with Mammy in Quinn's shop where she was buying her groceries. She went once a week to get the things we couldn't supply ourselves from the farm. It was a big shop which sold everything. It had sides of ham hanging on hooks from the ceiling and fat slabs of cheese. In the back, there was a little snug where the elderly farmers would sit and drink their pints of Guinness.

Mammy always wrote out her groceries on a list and gave it to Mr Quinn, who went around the shop getting the things she wanted. This day, he read the list and I saw him shuffle uncomfortably. He pushed his glasses hard against his nose. I could see he was embarrassed.

"I'm terribly sorry, Mrs Maguire. But there's some things here I can't supply you with."

"What do you mean?" Mammy said.

"Well, you have down here a pound of tea. I can only give you two ounces."

"Two ounces?" Mammy couldn't believe her ears. "Sure, two ounces would never do us. I have a husband and five children and they drink gallons of tea."

"It's not my fault," Mr Quinn said apologetically. "And I can only let you have half-a-pound of sugar and half-a-pound of flour. It's the War. We can't get the supplies. Everything's been rationed."

28

"What does that mean?"

"It means everybody has to put up with less."

Mammy went home and told Daddy.

"It'll get worse," he said. "I heard on the wireless the other night that the Germans are sinking all the Allied ships. They're trying to starve us into submission."

*

Daddy missed his tea. Mammy would make a big pot in the morning for breakfast and then she'd shake out the tea leaves, dry them by the fire and re-use them in the evening. In the end, the tea just tasted like bog water.

Everything got scarce and had to be used again and again till it was worn out, even things like soap and candles. Eventually, the Government gave everybody ration books so that it would be fair and people would get the basic things they needed.

We were lucky. Because we lived on a farm, we never went hungry, unlike some of the families who lived in the town.

Daddy missed his tobacco most of all. He tried different things to make it stretch. He would get his weekly ration and mix it with dried leaves and grass seed. Instead of the lovely fragrance that used to fill the house, there was this awful smell and Mammy would have to open the windows to let in fresh air. Smoking grass seed just made Daddy cross.

But the farm was going well and Daddy was raising more and more cattle. Michael and he were busy all day long. Michael was seventeen now, growing tall and strong like Daddy. The pair of them went about as pals. They worked the fields together and, on Saturday nights, Daddy took Michael with him to Donnelly's pub for his pint.

Bridgie was sixteen and had left school and got a job as a waitress in the Royal Hotel in Enniskillen. It was hard work but with her weekly wages and tips, she was able to save up to buy nice clothes across the border in Swanlinbar. Martin was fifteen and I was fourteen. Kathleen was nine.

Bridgie went with a boy called Charlie Kettles. He was an apprentice motor mechanic in Halliday's garage and he was the same age as Michael. Small and fat, he had a few tiny hairs of a moustache that he grew on his upper lip to make himself look older. I didn't like him, but Mammy would fuss over him whenever he called on Friday nights to take Bridgie to the pictures. She would make sure there was always fresh tea for him, as well as scones and jam.

I would watch Charlie Kettles stuffing his face with the nice things that we couldn't have because of the rationing and it would make me angry. He would finish everything on his plate and then Bridgie and him would go off into Enniskillen in a motorcar he had borrowed for the weekend.

I envied Bridgie her independence. Sitting in our bedroom, I would watch her getting ready for Charlie Kettles, washing herself and putting on lipstick and perfume, and wearing a nice dress to make herself pretty for him. I wished I had a job and money and nice things like Bridgie. But instead, I had to go to school and wear an ugly school uniform and stockings that were darned so many times they were nearly threadbare.

Martin was the quiet one of the house. He was pale and thin with long fingers that Mammy said were pianist's fingers. He was always reading books and studying. Because Bridgie was away all the time, I found myself drawn closer to him. Martin was very clever. I would go to him if I had a problem with my homework and he always knew the answer.

He was also gentle. He loved flowers and birds and animals, even the cattle that Daddy raised for the slaughterhouse. It used to make him sad to think that we only kept them for a while and then they would eventually be killed.

In the summer evenings when the work was done, Martin and I would go for walks across the fields. I asked him why he was studying so hard.

"Because I like books."

"But don't you want to finish school and get a job and earn money?"

"No. I want to go to college."

I couldn't understand this. College was for wealthy people, the children of the big landowners and shopkeepers. Nobody I knew had ever gone to college.

"What good would that do?"

Martin took my hand.

"Can you keep a secret?"

"Of course."

"I want to be a priest."

I started to laugh and he blushed.

"Why do you think it's funny?"

"I'm sorry. I just can't imagine you as a priest. They're all so old."

"There are young priests too. Where do you think the old ones come from? But they only take you if you pass the exams. And even then, you have to study hard for seven years."

"If you become a priest, you won't be able to get married."

"I don't want to get married," Martin said. "I want to go to Africa and help the poor people."

"Have you told Mammy?"

"No. You're the only one who knows. Don't tell her. If I don't make it, she'll only be disappointed."

*

Apart from the rationing and the demand for cattle, the War didn't have much effect on us. A few of the older boys went off and joined the army. Occasionally we'd see planes flying across the sky towards St Angelo airport and sometimes there'd be trucks with soldiers driving into Enniskillen. They always seemed to be happy. They would sound their horns when they saw us, waving and giving us the V for Victory sign.

But Daddy said the War wasn't going well. Hitler was proving to be a tougher nut than they thought. In fact, he said, maybe the Free State did the right thing staying out of the war altogether, for if the Germans won, they'd make us pay a heavy price. Daddy said the one thing that could swing it was if the Yanks came in.

One day, I came home from school to find George Armstrong

sitting with Daddy at the kitchen table. The pair of them were drinking stout together.

George Armstrong was the cattle buyer. He was a big heavy man with a red face and oily hair and he wore a smart crombie coat and shiny brown boots. As I came in, he gave me a sly smile.

"Is that the wee vixen used to come with you to the market, Pat? Hasn't she grown up fast? I suppose the next thing you know, she'll be getting herself married."

Daddy and he laughed. I poured myself a cup of tea, sat down beside the window and looked out over the fields. There was a mist rising from the grass. It hung like silver ribbons in the branches of the trees along Turvey's field.

I listened to the men. George Armstrong seemed to be doing most of the talking. I heard him say: "It's a damned disgrace, Pat. The country's crying out for food and the land is lying there idle. Anywhere else, the government would confiscate it."

"But would he sell?"

"Of course he would. Sure what use is it to him? He has neither chick nor child. All he's interested in is the whiskey bottle."

"Would the bank lend me the money?"

"They'd be delighted. I'll have a quiet word with Foster the next time I'm in and I'm sure he'll agree."

"I don't know," Daddy said.

"Oh come on, Pat. You know what the smart operators say? You have to speculate to accumulate. With this War on, there's never been a better time for farmers to make money. If you had that land you'd be able to raise twice as many cattle."

They talked for a while longer before rising. George Armstrong spat on his hand and held it out and Daddy shook it.

"It's agreed then?"

"It's agreed."

Armstrong was in good form. He clapped Daddy on the back and laughed. On the way out of the room, he stopped beside me.

"Are you going to the dances yet?"

"No," I said.

"Any day now. Any day now."

He tickled me under the chin and winked. I could smell the heavy scent of cologne. It made my stomach heave.

# 6.

We were going to buy Turvey's field. It was nearly as big as our two fields put together and it would double the size of the farm. Daddy was all excited, but Mammy wasn't so sure.

"How are we going to pay for it?"

"I'm getting a loan off the bank. George Armstrong has put in a word for me with the manager. They're thick as thieves, the pair of them. He's advancing me £300."

Mammy looked shocked.

"My God, Pat. That's a terrible lot of money. How are we going to pay it back?"

"From the sale of the cattle. With Turvey's field, I'll be able to raise twice as many animals. Sure, there's never been a better time to expand, Annie. They're crying out for cattle. George Armstrong will take every beast I can rear."

"It'll mean twice as much work."

"Michael and I will be able to manage. And there's Martin. He's fit and able. It's time he got his head out of those books and started earning his keep."

I thought of gentle Martin and his dreams of becoming a priest. But I had made a promise to keep it secret, so I said nothing.

A week later, Daddy got dressed up in his best suit that he wore to Mass on Sundays. He shaved himself and put on a clean shirt and tie. He took out a bottle of Jameson's whiskey and walked across the fields to talk to Daniel Turvey.

A few hours later and he returned in grand form.

"He's agreed. £300. We're getting the solicitor in on Tuesday to draw up the contract."

He took Mammy by the waist and held her tight.

"We're going to be rich, Annie. We're going to start living like the gentry. I'm going to buy you a fur coat and get a motor car."

Mammy went: "Tsk, tsk, tsk. It was far from fur coats I was reared, Pat Maguire."

But I could see she was pleased.

As soon as the deal went through, Daddy and Michael started clearing the extra field. It had become overgrown from lack of use, with weeds and briars everywhere. The fences were all broken. They got up at five o'clock before it was light and worked till it was dark.

One afternoon, the schoolmaster visited and I was sent down the field to get Daddy. Master McVey was a small man with grey hair who wore a tweed suit with a watch chain in his waistcoat pocket. He sat at the kitchen table and drank tea.

"Martin tells me you're taking him out of the school," he said.

"I need him," Daddy said. "There's an awful lot of work about this farm."

"I don't doubt it. And honest toil is no disgrace to any man. But Martin's a bright boy, Mr Maguire. He's the brightest boy I've ever had the pleasure to teach. And I've been a master for thirty years."

"But what good will it do him?"

"Dear man, you don't know what you're saying. The boy has the potential to become a doctor or a lawyer. I'd wager my reputation he could do anything he put his mind to. If you take him out of school now, he'll never be more than a farm labourer."

"Education costs money."

"I appreciate that. It's the curse of this system. Children with talent have no chance unless their parents have money. But there are scholarships, Mr Maguire. Let him stay on for one more year. I'll coach him myself personally for the scholarship. Take my word, he'll get it and go on to do great things. You'll not regret it. He'll be a credit to you."

35

I could see that the master's words were having a strong effect on Daddy. He screwed up his face. I was hoping he would agree for Martin's sake. Then I saw his eyes drop to the floor.

"I can't," he said. "I need him here."

In June, Martin left school and began work with Daddy and Michael. He wasn't as tall or strong as Daddy and Michael but he worked hard. I'd watch him stripped to the waist in the hot sun, his body pale and thin beside the other two, and my heart would go out to him. Eventually, they got the field cleared and fenced and Daddy bought new cattle.

This brought more work. The animals had to be tested by the vet. They had to be dosed for infections. As the winter drew in, they had to be given feed and bedding and the byres had to be cleaned.

Martin didn't complain about leaving school and no one spoke about the visit from Master McVey. But he continued studying. He joined the Carnegie library and, every Saturday, he would cycle into Enniskillen and come home with two or three books in the carrier basket. Late at night he would sit in the kitchen reading by the light of the tilly-lamp. When Daddy and Michael went off to Donnelly's pub for their pints, he would stay.

Daddy would shake his head and say: "Would you for God's sake give over them books and relax. You'll give yourself the head staggers."

But Martin would reply: "I *am* relaxing. This is what I like to do."

*

George Armstrong came to the house more and more. I'd find him sitting with Daddy drinking stout, the pair of them with their heads together.

He'd stare at me with that look in his eye and I knew what it meant. Whenever George Armstrong was in the house, I felt uneasy. I made some excuse to go out to the fields or into my bedroom.

But Daddy and he seemed to be getting very close. I'd hear him say: "Cattle are hitting two shillings a pound at Clones mart, Pat. That's the best price yet."

Daddy would say: "It's well for them in the Free State."

"There's no reason why you shouldn't get it too."

"How do you mean?"

"I know a man could bring them across the border for you in the back of a lorry."

"Ah no," Daddy would say. "That's illegal. If the customs caught me, they'd impound the whole damned lot and then where would I be?"

"There's ways round that, Pat. A few pounds to the right people and the customs will look the other way."

"No," Daddy would say. "I've invested too much to risk it."

George Armstrong had ways of getting things. Every time he came to the house, he would bring something.

"A present for you, Missus," he would say as he put a pound of tea on the table. Mammy's eyes would open wide with delight. Other times it would be sugar or flour, or tobacco for Daddy. George Armstrong was like one of those magicians in the story books, always pulling things out of his pockets.

*

Daddy was proved right again. One night in December, I found him hunched over the wireless. He was all agitated.

"It's happened," he said. "The Japs have bombed Pearl Harbour and now the Yanks have entered the War. This will put the tin hat on it, all right. Oh, Herr Hitler will be a sorry boy now."

By the following January, American airmen were a few miles away in Belleek. Word spread like wildfire and there was great excitement. Some of the older girls took a bus there to a dance and they came back with fabulous stories about the Yankee soldiers. They said that in their lovely uniforms they were as handsome as film stars and had the finest manners. Real gentlemen who said: "Thank you Ma'am," and spoke in cute American accents. Some of them got their pictures in the paper, standing beside their aircraft. Everybody thought they were wonderful.

*

One day, I was in Enniskillen on an errand for Mammy. It was a warm day and when I had finished, I decided to go into the Rio Cafe and treat myself to a lemonade. I was sitting at a table near the window when I spotted George Armstrong walking along the street.

I looked away but it was too late; he'd seen me and next thing he was coming through the doorway towards me.

"Well, if it isn't the wee vixen," he said, pulling up a chair beside me. "What are you doing here?"

I told him and he said: "And your Mammy lets you come here all on your own? Is she not afraid some big bad wolf might get you?"

"I'm well able to look after myself," I said coldly.

George Armstrong laughed. I could see him studying me, looking at my breasts. I wanted to get up and go away.

"You're getting very big. Have you got a boy yet?"

"That's my business," I said.

"What age are you now, Stella?"

"Fourteen."

"Oh fourteen's a grand age."

He moved closer. I could see the hairs curling from his ears and smell his Guinness breath.

"You're very pretty. You could easily pass for eighteen if you wore nice clothes. I could get them for you. I know the right people." He lowered his voice.

"How'd you like a pair of real nylon stockings?"

Before I could say anything, I felt his clammy hand on my knee. A shock ran through me. My face was red with embarrassment. I quickly pushed his hand away and stood up.

George Armstrong was laughing again. "What's the matter with you, girl? I'm only measuring you for the stockings."

I rushed out of the cafe. I wanted to get away from him as fast as I could. The whole way up the street I could hear his laughter ringing in my ears. With every step I took, it seemed to mock me.

# 7.

The farm was going well and Daddy was pleased. Every Sunday morning after Mass, he took out his black notebook that he kept in the dresser and did his accounts. In one column, he entered the money he had spent, on feed for the cattle, and vet's bills and repayments to the bank. In another column, he wrote down the money he received from the sales of the animals. His big concern was paying off the bank. Daddy was very cautious with money and hated to be in debt. He used to say that debt was like a millstone round a man's neck that could drag him under.

But the men had to work hard. I'd hear them moving about in the kitchen before it was light, getting ready to go out to the fields. They'd come back in again about eight o'clock for their breakfast. It wasn't so bad in the summer when the weather was fine, but in the winter it was cold and wet and I would hear the wind howling against the windows. I used to cuddle deeper under the blankets and feel sorry for them going out to the muddy fields.

Most of all, I had pity for Martin. He held his end up, working as hard as the others and never complaining. He liked working with the cattle. In the evenings, when the work was finished for the day, we would go walking in the fields. He would show me his favourite animals, stroking their heads and running his hands along their smooth flanks.

"Isn't she beautiful?" he would say.

Looking at the animal, all I would see was a cow.

"Yes."

"You know, they're just like people. Each one is different. They all have their own personalities. This one is always happy. That's why she's my favourite. I call her Daisy."

He would open a bag he brought with him and feed her fresh, newly plucked grass that he brought as a special treat.

But I knew Martin missed his studies. Any spare time he had, his nose would be stuck in a book. One day when we were walking, I asked him if he was sorry that Daddy had taken him out of school.

"He had no option, Stella. The family needs me, so my place is here."

"But now you'll never be a priest."

"You can't say that. Who knows what will happen when the War is over? Maybe I might get to college then."

"But you'll be too old to sit for the scholarship and you have no money."

Martin smiled.

"God moves in mysterious ways, Stella. If it's his will, then I'll be a priest."

If the farm was going well, the War wasn't. It had settled down to a bloody struggle between Germany and the Allies. Daddy's earlier optimism about the Americans had vanished. There were air raids every night on British cities. At Easter, there was a raid on Belfast, in which 1,200 people were killed and whole streets destroyed. The rationing got worse. Everything was scarce now. Tea, sugar, tobacco, clothes, petrol. People took on a washed-out look. Daddy got so depressed he stopped listening to the wireless. One night he said: "You know, these Germans are tougher than we thought."

"Do you think they might win?"

"It's possible."

"And what will happen then?"

He thought for a moment.

"We'll survive," he said. "They'll always need farmers. The Germans have to eat like everybody else."

*

40

By this time I had turned fifteen and was anxious to get out of the house to start earning money. Although I was doing fine at school, I had no ambition. I would do the very least to get me by. We had a new teacher now called Miss Larkin. She wasn't cross like Miss Brankin. She was always trying to encourage us. She would say to me: "You're wasting your talent, Estelle Maguire. God gave you a brain. Why don't you use it?"

But I couldn't see any point. My future seemed bounded by the small farmland around Ballinaleck and the county town of Enniskillen. The available jobs were all menial: skivvying or waitressing.

The war meant the linen factories were working overtime turning out uniforms and parachutes and war supplies, but the work didn't appeal to me. The better jobs for women, like nursing or teaching, were out of my reach. So I couldn't see why I should study hard at school.

Bridgie and Charlie Kettles were going strong now and there was talk of them getting married. Charlie had been offered a job as a civilian mechanic at the RAF base at Castle Archdale. The pay was good and there was accommodation on the base. But Mammy was against it.

"You're far too young," she said. "My God, sure you're only seventeen. You haven't lived yet."

"I'm in love with him," Bridgie replied, and I thought of Charlie Kettle's fat face and his stupid moustache and wondered how anybody could love someone like that.

"Love?" Mammy snorted. "Wait till you've got a house full of youngsters to feed and dirty nappies to wash and then talk to me about love."

"You were seventeen when you got married."

Mammy stared off into space.

"Things were different in those days," she said.

But Bridgie was determined. One evening when we were alone in our bedroom, she took a box out of her drawer and opened it. In it were lots of notes and coins.

"I've got eight pounds saved up. Charlie and me's getting married whether Mammy agrees or not. I'm old enough and I don't need her permission. Will you be my bridesmaid?"

I didn't know what to say. I was thrilled to be asked but I didn't want to go against Mammy.

"If you really want me."

Bridgie hugged me close.

"If it comes to the bit, we'll run away together. I love Charlie and Charlie loves me. There's nobody's going to stand in our way."

*

Bridgie got me a weekend job in the bar in the Royal Hotel. I worked Friday, Saturday and Sunday nights. I was a waitress; people would order their drinks and I would bring them to their tables on a tray and collect the empty glasses and clean the ashtrays. I got five shillings plus tips. I gave half of it to Mammy and put the rest into a Post Office savings book.

I had to wear a white blouse, a black skirt and black stockings. My figure was full now and I would see men giving me that same look I had received from George Armstrong. I would smile and try to be polite, but I didn't encourage them. I always got good tips.

The hotel staff were worse than the customers. I would catch the men watching me if I had to bend down or stretch for something. They would brush against me in the storeroom as if it was an accident.

But I kept thinking of what Mammy had told me all those years ago. I wasn't going to get a reputation. I was saving myself for the tall, dark man I would meet some day. I knew he was out there somewhere. I would keep myself pure for him.

# 8.

Mammy relented and Bridgie got married that June. It wasn't a fancy wedding. For one thing, we couldn't afford it. For another, the War had taken the goodness out of everything. The only people who could afford fancy weddings were the gentry and even they had to cut back.

She was married in the parish church by Father Kavanagh. I was her bridesmaid. A boy who worked with Charlie Kettles was best man. His name was Tommy Gorman and he was shy and nervous and couldn't find the wedding ring.

Bridgie wore a pink dress that she got run up by a dressmaker in Enniskillen. I wore a white blouse, a grey skirt and a navy jacket. The clothes were too big for me and I felt awkward and uncomfortable. The two men wore suits with sprays of heather in the lapels of their jackets. Mammy took pictures with a Brownie camera she borrowed from Mr Quinn, the grocer.

Afterwards, everyone came back to the house and we had a party. Somehow, Mammy had managed to get her hands on currants, icing sugar and enough flour to bake a wedding cake. Daddy had butchered half a dozen chickens and bought a ham. There were crates of porter and a couple of bottles of whiskey, and sherry for the women. For music, Daddy had hired a fiddler and a man who played the accordion.

Daddy drank too much and got tipsy. I think he was sorry to see Bridgie go. He made a speech and said he wanted to wish the young people well, starting out on life's great adventure. He said he wanted to pay a special tribute to the woman who had stood by his side all these years through thick and thin. The mother of his children and his best friend in all the world. He closed his eyes and pushed out his chest and began to sing:

*Shall we never more behold thee?*
*Never hear thy laughing voice again?*
*When the Springtime comes Gentle Annie,*
*And the wild flowers are scattered o'er the plain.*

Mammy started to cry and soon all the women were weeping. Somebody said: "Ah, for God's sake, cheer up. You'd think it was a wake we were at, instead of a wedding."

So Michael and Martin and a couple of the men moved all the furniture to the corner of the room and told the musicians to play. The dancing began.

The party went on all night. At five o'clock, as the dawn came streaming into the kitchen, Bridgie and Charlie Kettles put their suitcases into the motor car and drove away to Dublin for their honeymoon.

Daddy sat at the table and poured the last drop out of the whiskey bottle. He said: "There's my first daughter gone. The first wee chick to fly the nest. I suppose you'll be next, Stella?"

It made me sad when he spoke like that. It made me think that the family was breaking up. I was filled with a terrible sense of loss. I put my arms round Daddy's neck and kissed his handsome face.

"I'll never leave you, Daddy. I'll always stay here with you and Mammy."

I didn't know it then, but Bridgie's wedding was to be a turning point. Times would never be so happy around the farm again.

*

With Bridgie gone, Kathleen and I were thrown closer together. She was eleven and growing up. Bright and inquisitive, she was just like Martin. She would lie on the bed in our room and stare at the ceiling, asking me questions.

"Can you get a baby from kissing a boy?"

"For God's sake! Who told you that?"

"A girl in school."

"She's away with the fairies."

"So *how* do you get a baby?"

"Has Mammy not told you?"

Kathleen shook her head.

"You better ask her, so."

"No. *You* tell me."

I sat down beside her.

"You've seen the bull brought to the cow, haven't you?"

"Yes."

"Well, it's the same with people."

"You mean he sticks his thing into you?"

"That's right."

"And that's what Charlie Kettles is doing to Bridgie?"

I started to laugh and Kathleen laughed too. Soon we were both doubled up on the bed.

"Jeesus," Kathleen said. "There's no fear of me getting married, if it means all that carry on."

Other times she would say to me: "Are you going to get a job?"

"Eventually."

"What are you going to do?"

"I don't know yet. I haven't thought about it."

"I'm going to be a teacher. I'll wear a nice dress and the children will all stand up when I come in, and say: 'Good morning, Miss Maguire.'"

I couldn't help thinking of Martin and what had happened to his dream.

He had recently started getting headaches. Sometimes they were so bad that I'd hear him walking about in the kitchen when everybody was asleep, moaning to himself.

"You're run down," Mammy told him. "You're not getting enough rest. What you need is a good tonic."

She prepared nettle tea and honey for him to drink, but his headaches only got worse.

He was reading all the time. I would see Daddy looking at him as if

45

he felt sorry for taking him out of school and making him work on the farm. One day, Daddy came back from Enniskillen with a present for Martin wrapped up in brown paper. He opened it and inside was a book. *The Collected Works of W. B. Yeats.*

Martin's eyes lit up.

"That's a great book. How did you know I wanted it?"

Daddy looked pleased.

"I went into the bookshop and I told the man behind the desk I wanted a good book for a fella that was always reading and he gave me that."

"I hope you didn't spend too much money on it?" Martin said, cautiously.

"Yerra. It's a present for you. If it gives you pleasure what matter how much money it costs?"

Mammy said: "I've figured out what's causing these headaches. It's all the reading. You've given yourself eye strain."

Martin was sent off to Dr O'Hare, who tested his eyes. He told him he needed glasses. He got a pair with wire frames at a cost of five shillings. I laughed when I saw him wearing them.

"What's so funny?" he asked.

"Those glasses. They make you look like this funny professor I saw in a film at the Regal."

Meanwhile my older brother, Michael, had grown up tall and handsome like Daddy. He had his blue eyes and dark hair. Every Sunday night, he shaved himself in a bowl in the kitchen, put on his suit and tie, and went off to the dance.

One evening, Mammy said to me: "It's near time you were going to the dance as well."

"I don't want to go," I replied.

"But it's great fun. When I was your age, I would be out dancing half the night."

I thought of the awkward clodhoppers who'd be there. They wouldn't all be handsome like Michael. They'd be the sort of boys that Mary O'Connor used to go with, pulling and clawing at me and trying to kiss me and feel me up. The thought of it made me sick.

"I don't like the boys who go there."

"Don't get stuck up," Mammy said, "or you'll miss your market. If you're waiting for a good-looking man, you might be waiting for a long time and find in the end that he's not worth the trouble."

Martin didn't go dancing either. He seemed to have no interest in girls or drinking pints. He didn't even have any friends. He seemed to be content to work with Daddy on the farm and sit in the kitchen reading books after the day's work was done. On Sunday evenings, we would go walking through the fields. Martin would often bring a book and sometimes he would read to me.

His favourite poet was a man called Gerard Manley Hopkins.

"Listen to this," he would say as he opened the book to read.

*The world is charged with the grandeur of God.*

*It will flame out, like shining from shook foil.*

He paused and said: "Isn't that beautiful?"

"What does it mean?"

"It means that God is everywhere. In all the beautiful things we see around us. Most of the time we're blind to it. We get used to it and take it for granted. Just like we take God for granted."

It sounded very profound. I looked at Martin and he was smiling behind his stupid glasses. I thought he would make a wonderful priest. He was so kind and gentle.

"C'mon," he said. "Daisy will be wondering where I am."

One evening, after Michael had gone to the dance, Martin and I went walking down the lower field and onto the new land that Daddy had bought from Daniel Turvey. It was all properly fenced and cleared now and they had built a new byre for the cattle.

When we came to Daisy, she was lying on her side in the corner of the field, away from the other animals.

Martin hunkered down beside her and opened his bag.

"Here," he said. "Look what I brought you."

He took out a handful of grass and gave it to her, but she just turned her big, sad eyes towards us and made no effort to eat.

Martin stroked her head and then he pulled his hand away.

"There's something wrong. Feel her head."

I put out my hand. Her skin felt hot, like it was burning. Daisy tried to stand up but she fell down again and just lay there looking at us.

Martin turned to me. There was horror on his face.

"I think she's sick. I think we'd better get Daddy and the vet."

# 9.

The vet was called Mr McManus and he came in his motor car. He had a red face from being out in all weathers and he wore a mackintosh, trilby hat and wellington boots. He went down the field with us to see the sick cow, who was lying on her side, breathing heavily.

Mr McManus took one look at the cow and then turned to Daddy.

"How long has she been like this?"

"We just found her this evening. Is it bad?"

Mr McManus didn't answer. He bent down and felt the cow's head and then pulled the lid down from her eye and looked in. She just lay there and moaned. Mr McManus took out a syringe and drew blood from her rump. He stood up.

"We better talk about this up in the house."

We trooped back up the field, nobody uttering a word. When we came into the house, Mammy had the kettle on and poured cups of tea. We waited for Mr McManus to speak.

"I'll have to get this blood sample tested. In the meantime, I want you to isolate her from the rest of the herd. Have you got somewhere to keep her?"

"There's the old shed," Daddy said.

"Keep her there. Don't let any of the other animals near her."

I could sense that Daddy was afraid.

"What is it?"

"I'm not sure. I'll know when I get the results of the tests."

Mr McManus finished his tea, went outside and drove away.

We got a rope and dragged Daisy up the field to the shed. It was

49

hard work and the men were sweating. Martin and I stayed behind with her. Martin got a basin of fresh water and a cloth. He wiped her mouth and tried to cool her with the cloth. He talked to her in a soothing voice like you would use with a child. She just lay on a bed of straw in a corner of the shed, not moving. Martin put a blanket over her to keep her warm and we stayed with her till it got dark.

In the morning, her condition was worse. There was a great loop of white spittle dripping from her mouth and she could hardly breath. Martin tried to get her to eat, but she wasn't interested. We locked the door of the shed and went out into the field.

Martin kept his head down so I couldn't see his face.

"I think she's going to die, Stella," he said.

Mr McManus came back early the following day. He got out of his car and spoke to Daddy in the yard outside the house.

"I've got bad news," he said. "It's brucellosis."

I could see Daddy trying to calculate the loss of the animal and the cost of getting her slaughtered. Then Mr McManus said something that terrified us all.

"Have you got insurance?"

Daddy's face went pale.

"Why would I need insurance? It's only one beast."

Mr McManus took off his hat and wiped his brow with a large white handkerchief.

"Brucellosis is very infectious. The Ministry has strict rules."

"What is it, man? Say it out straight."

Mr McManus put his hat back on.

"I'm sorry, Pat. The entire herd will have to be destroyed."

*

That afternoon, two men from the Ministry of Agriculture came and shot the animals one by one, then piled the carcases onto a lorry and took them away to be buried.

I had never seen Daddy so distraught. After the men had finished, he went into the kitchen and took out the bottle of whiskey. He sat down at the table and sank his head in his hands.

"What's happened to us, Annie? What did we do to deserve this?"

Mammy sat, grim-faced, beside the stove.

"Can you not start again?"

"Och, woman dear. I owe the bank for Turvey's field. How am I going to pay them back with no cattle to sell?"

Mammy got up and put her arms round Daddy's neck and gently kissed his face.

"We'll manage, Pat. Surely to God, we'll manage."

Daddy went into Enniskillen and spoke to Mr Foster in the bank but he got no sympathy. Mr Foster told him the best they could do was defer repayments on the loan for six months. But if he didn't repay, they would have to foreclose.

Over the next few days, the neighbours came by and offered to help by giving Daddy some cattle to get him going again, but it was no use. He would still have to buy feed and fertiliser and he had no money. After what had happened, none of the suppliers would give him credit.

It was a terrible time for us. Michael went off and got work with a local farmer but nobody would hire Martin. Daddy got up as usual, before dawn, and walked the fields till supper time and then moped around the house. He slowly grew more desperate. One night when I was in bed I overheard him talking with Mammy in the kitchen.

"We're going to have to sell, Annie. I can't see any way out."

"You can't sell, Pat. That land's been in your family for over a hundred years."

"But what use is land, if I can't make it work for me? If I don't start making repayments on the loan, the bank will take it, anyway."

*

A week later, I saw the stocky figure of George Armstrong coming up the yard. He seemed in cheerful mood. He was whistling to himself. When he saw me he waved, but I hadn't forgotten the incident in Enniskillen and I frowned back at him.

He came into the kitchen, carrying a bag and wearing a bright new

51

suit. Opening the bag, he took out a pound of tea and a tin of tobacco and placed them on the table.

"My God, Pat. This is desperate news. You're the third farmer this month. There's two other men over by Lisnaskea had the same misfortune."

"That's not much comfort to me," Daddy said.

"What are you going to do?"

"What can I do? I've no money and the bank is threatening to foreclose."

"How much do you owe them?"

"Two hundred and fifty pounds."

"I could talk to Foster for you," George Armstrong suggested. "See if we can't come up with something."

"I've already talked to him. There's nothing he can do."

George Armstrong drummed his fingers on the table top.

"Pat, there's more ways than one to skin a cat. I've got a proposition for you."

"What?"

"You've got a big farm out there. It's a terrible shame to see it going to waste. What do you say if I put cattle on it and you work it for me? I'll pay you rent for the fields and I'll also pay you for your labour. You'll have enough to feed your family and some over to pay back Foster."

"But you'd get all the profit."

"I'm not a mean man, Pat. And I feel guilty because I got you to buy Turvey's field in the first place. I'll play fair with you. What do you say?"

I didn't want Daddy to work for George Armstrong. I didn't want us beholden to him. But I knew it was a good offer and that he shouldn't turn it down.

"I'd need Michael and Martin as well," Daddy said.

"Of course. I'll pay wages to the three of you. Is it a deal, Pat? It'll give you a chance to get back on your feet."

I could see Mammy willing Daddy to accept. For her, it was like a

Godsend. But Daddy still had his pride. What George Armstrong was proposing would turn him from an independent farmer into a hired labourer.

"I'll do it," he said, reluctantly.

George Armstrong spat on his hand and held it out for Daddy to shake.

"You're a wise man, Pat. You've made the right call."

Over the next few days, George Armstrong's cattle arrived on our fields. Daddy and my brothers worked hard. I could see they were glad to be back on their own land again. But Daddy's attitude seemed to have changed. He was no longer the happy man he used to be. He took to sitting by the window and staring out across the fields. One day, he took the wireless into Enniskillen and sold it and bought Mammy a new dress with the money.

When she protested, he said: "Annie, this damned War is going on too long."

# 10.

I left school the following June and got Bridgie's old job at the Royal Hotel. I had grown bored with school and the money was needed at home. The wages were twelve shillings a week plus meals and tips. I kept five shillings and gave the rest to Mammy.

Bridgie and Charlie Kettles were getting on well at Castle Archdale. Bridgie was working as a cook in the canteen and Charlie was getting plenty of overtime servicing aircraft engines. They were saving up so that Charlie could open his own garage when the War was over. Once a month, they drove over in a motor car and Bridgie would bring Mammy sugar and flour and other things she was able to get in the canteen.

I would see Charlie holding Bridgie's hand and smiling at her all the time. It was plain that he loved her. I began to think that maybe it wasn't such a bad match after all. He was a man who would care for her and provide for the children that I knew, instinctively, they were going to have.

I quickly discovered that real waitressing was hard work. The hours were long and I was on my feet all the time. Most nights, when I was finished, I'd be so tired I could hardly stand up. My shift started at 2 p.m. and ended at midnight. Sometimes, if I was lucky, I would get a lift home, but often I had to walk.

Serving tables was more difficult than I imagined. There was an etiquette about cutlery and glasses and the way the food had to be presented. The clients were businessmen and commercial travellers down from Belfast. They liked to eat in the hotel because we could get things that were rationed. At weekends, we would have parties of gentry in for dinner and they'd be drinking wine and whiskey and smoking cigarettes and the ladies would be all dressed up in their finery.

Sometimes a man would try to engage me in conversation but the manager had warned us not to get familiar with the guests. It was a sacking offence. If they asked my name, I would simply reply: "Estelle, sir."

"You're very pretty, Estelle."

"Thank you, sir."

"Have you got a young man?"

"No, sir."

"How'd you like to come to the pictures with me?"

"I can't sir. My father will be waiting to take me home."

"Oh well, it's your loss. I know how to show a girl a good time."

"Thank you, sir."

I would smile and make my way back to the kitchen as soon as I could.

But the women I worked with had no such scruples. They were older than me and their heads were turned with men. On their nights off, they went to Belleek to the dances with the American soldiers or Yanks. They returned with lurid stories.

"I met this Yank on Saturday night. Gorgeous, he was. He owns a ranch in Texas."

"And our Aggie's the Queen of China. Sure, they all say that."

"Honest, he does. He showed me pictures."

They would sit at the table in the kitchen drinking tea and swopping experiences and I would listen.

"You should have seen him in his uniform and his lovely American accent. And the *talk* out of him. Do you know what he called me? His little sweetie-pie."

"Get up the yard. Did you do anything?"

"He kissed me."

"Is that all?"

"Of course. What do you think I am?"

"A liar is what. Do you expect us to believe you sat all night holding hands? I know those fellas. They're all after the one thing. And it isn't a kiss and a cuddle."

"Well if we did, it's more than you got."

And they would fall about the table laughing.

One of the girls, Maggie Cameron, was seeing a commercial traveller who came down from Belfast once a week. He would take her to the pictures and afterwards they'd go for a drive in his car out the Irvinestown Road.

One afternoon, she took me aside.

"Stella. Can I trust you to keep a secret?"

"Of course," I said.

"I've just found out he's married. What do you think I should do?"

I was shocked.

"You've no choice. You have to give him up."

"But he says he loves me and he gives me beautiful presents."

"You don't want to wreck his marriage, Maggie. What about his wife and children?"

"She doesn't care for him. He says when the War is over, he's getting a divorce."

"Do you believe him?"

I saw the flicker of doubt in her eyes.

"It's wrong, Maggie. Give him up."

"I can't," she said. "I love him, too."

*

At home, the fields were filled with cattle again and the men were busy all day long. I was glad. It kept Daddy's mind from brooding. Gradually, he began to pay off his debt to the bank and his spirits improved at the prospect of being his own boss again.

A sense of solidarity settled over the house. But the carefree atmosphere I had known as a child was gone. It had been replaced with a nervous caution. What had happened had served as a warning that never again could anything be taken for granted.

George Armstrong held to his word and paid Daddy what he had agreed. But I hated being under his obligation. I would see him from time to time and he always had that look in his eye that told me what was on his mind.

One night, I was walking home along the Ballinaleck road when a motor car stopped beside me. A voice said: "Can I give you a lift somewhere?"

I was glad of the offer. I opened the door to get into the car when I saw it was Armstrong. He looked as surprised as me.

"Well, if it isn't Stellie Maguire. Hop in and I'll have you home in no time."

It was too late to refuse, so I got into the passenger seat and he started the engine. He began talking about work.

"You look tired. Did you have a hard night?"

I told him I'd been working since 2 p.m.

"Hard work never killed anyone. And think of the money you're earning. You'll be able to save up. A good-looking lassie like you won't hang around Ballinaleck too long. I'd say you'll be off to the big smoke any day now."

"I'm staying here, with my family."

"Oh, the Maguires were always a close lot. But you'd like Belfast. There's plenty to interest a young filly. All the dances and the fellas. Sure there's nothing round here for young ones except them Yankee Doodles over in Belleek."

He kept up a stream of talk as we drove along the lonely country road. I regretted taking the lift from him and couldn't wait for the journey to end. Eventually, he pulled up at the lane beside our house and stopped the engine. I thanked him and was opening the door when I felt his hand on my shoulder.

"Is that all I get for driving you home?"

"I have to go, now. Good night."

I moved to get out, but George Armstrong grabbed me and pulled me back. He tried to kiss me. There was a foul taste of whiskey and tobacco from his breath.

I struggled but he held me tight. I felt his fingers groping for the buttons on my blouse. I began to panic, and scratched wildly at his face until my nails drew blood.

He suddenly released me and wiped his cheek. His eyes were blazing.

"Fuck you," he spat. "Is that the thanks I get? If it wasn't for me, the whole damned lot of you'd be in the poorhouse by now."

I jumped out slamming the door behind me, and ran up the yard to the house. Mammy was reading by the fire.

"What's the matter with you?" she said. "You look pale."

"I'm just tired. I've had a terrible night."

I hurried to my bedroom and undressed in the dark. Kathleen was already asleep. I got under the blankets and lay for a long time staring at the ceiling. I could still smell George Armstrong, the stale odour of whiskey off his breath. It made me sick. I felt dirty and contaminated. But his words had hurt me even more. I couldn't get them out of my head.

"If it wasn't for me, the whole lot of you'd be in the poorhouse."

# 11.

Gradually, I grew to hate my job. The hours were long and the work was dull. The guests, when they weren't trying to flirt with me, were arrogant and rude. What kept me going was the fellow workers and their good-natured banter. But there were occasions when I thought perhaps George Armstrong was right and I should go to Belfast, where everyone said there were plenty of jobs because of the War. But something, perhaps a sense of duty, bound me to the family.

I never told a soul what Armstrong had tried to do. I was afraid that word might reach Daddy or Michael and that we would end up the worse for it. But any time he came to the house, I snubbed him. He grew wary of me and his attitude changed to cold formality.

I was taking my break one day when the manager, Mr Maxwell, asked to see me in his office. I wondered if I had done something wrong or if somebody had complained about my work. But I needn't have worried. He began by complimenting me on my time-keeping, appearance and general attitude.

Then he said: "How would you like to change your job?"

Immediately, I was apprehensive. I didn't want any kitchen or cleaning work, which was harder again than waitressing. I asked him what he had in mind.

"There's a vacancy coming up in the bar. One of the girls is leaving to get married. I was wondering if you might be interested?"

I said I was.

"Bar work is more demanding that waitress work. There's more interaction with the public. You're a bright young woman. I'm sure you'll fit in well. You can start on Monday."

I was delighted.

"What hours will I be working, sir?"

"Ten till six. You'll get an hour for lunch and every Wednesday off. Joe Gaffney will show you what to do. And Estelle ..."

"Yes, sir?"

"I'm sure I don't have to remind you. There are two topics of conversation that are forbidden in the bar. We don't talk about politics and we don't talk about religion."

I couldn't believe my good fortune. Bar work paid more and the tips were better. The hours were shorter and the work more interesting. It was a big step up from waitressing. Joe Gaffney was the head barman. He was a small, squat man and incredibly strong. His assistant was called Patsy O'Donnell and between them they did all the heavy-lifting work, like moving barrels and crates of beer. My job was confined to pouring drinks for customers and taking the cash and keeping the counter clean and tidy.

Normally the bar was quiet till 12 o'clock, when the customers would start to drift in. They were the same sort of people who used the dining room: businessmen, wealthy farmers and commercial travellers. They were mostly men, for women weren't encouraged to drink in a bar. It could get a woman a bad name.

Joe had written down all the prices and stuck them beside the till and I quickly learnt them off by heart. I got to know what mixers accompanied the different spirits. Over time, I even got to know what the regulars wanted to drink before they had time to order.

Some of the customers liked to talk while they had their drinks. They would tell you their troubles. The more they drank, the more they talked. I came to realise that many of them were lonely. They were bachelors and they liked talking to a woman.

Occasionally, one of the customers would ask me to have a drink with him, but this was forbidden. Joe said the thing to do was take the money and tell the customer you would have a drink when you finished your shift. That way, you got extra tips. We put them in a glass jar and shared them out at the end of the week.

I soon settled down and was very happy. I began to think that I had found a job that I could stick at and turn into a career. And then came the terrible day when I arrived home from work and found the household in turmoil.

It was a beautiful April evening. The cold winds of March had died away and there seemed a new energy abroad in the fields. The trees along the road where bursting into leaf. In the lane beside the house, I saw a fat thrush foraging for worms.

But when I came into the kitchen, I was met with a pitiful sight. Martin was lying on the sofa, moaning and clutching his forehead. Mammy was fretting over him. Kathleen had a cold facecloth and was wiping his brow. Michael stood nervously by the window, unsure of what to do.

They told me what had happened. Martin had been working with Daddy in Turvey's field when he began to complain of a pain in his head. He sat down to rest for a while but the pain only worsened. Daddy got concerned and brought him up to the house. By now, Martin was in agony. They got him to drink some whiskey and aspirin while Daddy hurried away for Dr O'Hare.

I went at once and and knelt beside my brother. His face was a terrible pale colour as if all the blood had drained from it, yet when I stroked his forehead it seemed to be on fire. I remembered what had happened with the cow and wondered if brucellosis could affect people too.

Martin turned his eyes to me.

I said: "It won't be long, now. Try to hold on. Dr O'Hare will know what to do."

He grasped my hand and we sat like that, Mammy holding one hand and me holding the other, till at last I heard the doctor's car crunching the gravel in the yard. He came into the house in his overcoat with his medical bag. The first thing he did was take hold of Martin's wrist and measure his pulse with his watch. Then he put a thermometer into his mouth.

He took out a little torch and examined Martin's eyes. Then he gently felt his throat. We all watched. Nobody dared to speak.

At last, Dr O'Hare said: "Tell me exactly what happened" and Daddy explained to him about Martin taking ill in the field and complaining about the pain in his head.

"He's running a temperature," Dr O'Hare said. "But his pulse is normal and he has no other symptoms of a fever."

He spoke to Martin: "Is this the same pain you had before?"

"Yes," Martin said. "It seems to be in the middle of my head. It's like a knife was stabbing in my brain."

Dr O'Hare looked worried. He said: "I'm going to give you something for the pain. It should also help you sleep. I'll come back and see you in the morning and if the pain is still there, I'll get you to the hospital."

He took out a syringe and injected it into Martin's arm. Then he took out a little box of tablets and gave them to Mammy.

"Use those if the pain comes back. Hopefully, he'll sleep and he'll be all right in the morning."

As he prepared to leave, Daddy drew him aside and I heard them whisper.

"Do you know what it is?"

"Not for certain."

"So maybe you should get him into the hospital right away."

"You don't understand, Pat. They won't have him unless it's an emergency. He'd be taking up a bed."

"But he's in agony. What worse emergency can there be?"

"I don't make the rules," Dr O'Hare said. "We'll give it another twelve hours, and if he's no better, I'll take him to the hospital myself."

We decided to keep Martin where he was rather than move him into the bedroom. Mammy covered him with a blanket and put a pillow under his head. Gradually, the pain eased and he got drowsy. Daddy and Michael hung around the kitchen till at last Mammy said: "Why don't the pair of you go off and have a pint? Stella and me will look after him."

Martin was still conscious. I put my hand on his forehead and felt the heat. I got a basin of cold water and Mammy and I took turns bathing his face.

"Would you like me to read to you?" I asked.

He nodded Yes. I went to the cupboard where he kept his books and got out the Gerard Manley Hopkins. I opened it at random.

"What about this one?"

I started to read.

*Glory be to God for dappled things,*
*For skies of couple-colour as a brinded cow ...*

A smile flickered across his tired face.

"Isn't that beautiful?" he said.

"I'll read you more. I'll stay with you and read all night if you want."

He squeezed my hand and I turned the page and read some more. Daddy and Michael came home from the pub and went to bed. Eventually I told Mammy to go too; there was no point everybody in the house being tired. I sat reading by the light from the tilly lamp till about four o'clock when Martin finally fell asleep.

I tiptoed into my bedroom. As I got undressed, I could hear Kathleen softly crying to herself.

"What's the matter?" I whispered.

She sat up. "I'm afraid, Stella."

"God forgive you," I said. "If you were a proper sister, you'd be praying for him."

"I *am* praying," she said. "But I can't stop thoughts coming into my head."

*

In the morning, the pain was worse. Now, Martin's speech was slurred and there was a wild look in his eyes.

We fretted about the kitchen till, at five past nine, we saw the doctor's car come chugging down the lane. He took one look at Martin and asked: "Is the pain still there?"

"Yes," Martin said.

"Better or worse?"

63

"Worse."

"Right. It's the hospital. We'll go in my motor."

He turned to Mammy.

"You'd better come as well, Missus. And pack a bag for him. He'll need pyjamas and his razor and soap and stuff."

Mammy said: "Mother of God. What kind of hospital is it that doesn't have soap?"

"I'll come too," I said.

We got into the car and made for the town. Mammy said very little but I knew what was going through her mind. Martin just kept staring out of the window at the fields rolling by. I suddenly realised that he had never been in a car before.

I said: "When Daddy gets back on his feet again we'll get our own motor and you can learn to drive."

Mammy said: "There's more important things than motor cars. And where are we supposed to get the petrol? Isn't it rationed too?"

"The War will end," said Martin. "Just like every war. And there'll be plenty of everything. And everybody will be wondering what all the fighting was for."

At the hospital, Dr O'Hare spoke to a nurse at the reception desk and she hurried off and came back with another doctor in a white coat. This one was tall and fussy.

He gave us a look and said: "Who are these people?"

"I'm his mother," Mammy said. "And this is his sister and we're here to keep him company."

"Well, only one of you can stay. This isn't a train station."

Mammy glared at the doctor.

"It's all right," I said quickly. "I'll go. I have to get to work."

I turned to Martin.

"I'll come again tomorrow. And I'll bring you books. You're going to get well. And when you come home again, we'll walk the fields and you can read me poetry."

I kissed my brother and walked out into the warm sunshine of a bright spring day.

# 12.

I kept myself busy all morning, trying not to think about the hospital. I washed glasses, polished table tops, scrubbed the sinks. I made work where none existed, just to keep my mind away from the terrible thoughts that waited to ambush me.

I was glad when lunchtime came, bringing with it the regular crowd. I welcomed the diversion. How eagerly I poured whiskey and sodas and ferried the crisp pound notes to the till to retrieve the change. How promptly I poured bottles of beer or measured out glasses of port.

Occasionally, I would stop to survey the happy drinkers at the bar, their heads close in conversation or thrown back in raucous laughter. Drink up, I thought. You may make the best of things for you have no worries. The little doubts that trouble you are nothing in the enormous scale of the world.

But, inevitably, the time came for them to drift back to their shops and offices, and the bar fell silent. At half two, Joe Gaffney came to me and suggested I take my break. I didn't want to go but there was no more work to do and I knew that if I refused they would ask me why, and I would be forced to reveal my terrible news.

Usually, we went to the kitchen and the cook would give us our lunch. But though I longed for the comfort of human company, I had no appetite. Instead, I went out to the garden. The last of the daffodils were fading now but the rose bushes were gathering strength, their long green shoots thrusting up towards the sun. I sat on a bench and thought of the fickleness of life, how quickly our luck had changed. A mere 18 months ago, we were on top of the world. The farm was thriving and there was more work than we could cope with. Then the brucellosis struck and wiped out our herd. And now, poor Martin had fallen sick.

I asked myself why God had allowed these tragedies to happen. Had we been too greedy? Too presumptuous? Had we attempted to rise above our station in life by buying more land and going into debt to the bank? But I felt guilty for entertaining these thoughts and asked God's forgiveness. I promised I would do anything he might ask of me, if only he would spare my brother's life.

I seemed to gather strength from these prayers and my spirits lifted. I went back into the hotel. The bar was empty. Joe Gaffney was stacking bottles on the shelves and he turned to look at me. Something in his manner told me at once that things were wrong.

He lowered his eyes.

"Mr Maxwell wants to see you," he said.

I left the room and went quickly along the corridor to the manager's office. I could feel my heart hammering in my breast. I knocked on the door and heard a voice telling me to enter.

As I came in, Mr Maxwell stood up from behind his big desk at the window. There was a pained look on his face. I remember the smell of cigar smoke in the air, the sound of blood thundering in my head. I closed my eyes and willed him not to speak. But through the noise and the tumult, I heard the words, plain as day.

"Estelle," he said. "I have bad news for you."

# 13.

Later, I was to learn the terrible events of that April morning; how they took x-rays of Martin's head at the hospital and discovered he had a brain tumour. How they rushed him immediately to the operating theatre and sent for the surgeon. How they opened his scalp and tried to cut away the malignant growth. But it was too late. Even though they worked for two hours, they couldn't save him. Martin died at ten minutes past one from a massive haemorrhage of the brain.

I don't know how we got through the next few days. It was like a nightmare from which we couldn't wake. I see it now in slow motion, as if it was a dream. Joe Gaffney drove me home and we waited till the hearse arrived from the hospital, the undertaker and his men in their sober overcoats and shiny boots. Daddy and Michael helped them carry poor Martin into the house and lay him out in the kitchen in his plain brown coffin. Father Kavanagh asked us to kneel and we said the rosary.

I think everyone was stunned, unable to comprehend the enormity of what had happened and the speed with which Martin was taken from us. They went around with white, shocked faces and staring eyes. They talked in whispers.

I sat beside Mammy as, one by one, the neighbours came. They brought food and drink. They crept into the house and offered their sympathy but their words washed over me like a wave. I kept thinking of the gentle boy who laid in the box. I thought of the walks we took through the fields. I thought of him nursing the sick cow. I thought of him sitting in the kitchen reading by the light of the tilly lamp.

It was the simple things that flashed into my mind: the childhood games we played; the time we bought the wireless and Martin wanted to know how the music arrived from London; the time Daddy told him he would have to leave school and work in the fields. He had never once complained. I saw his face trying to smile as I read the poem for him. Suddenly I was overcome with grief. I sank my head on Mammy's lap and cried and cried until I thought my heart would break.

All night long, the people came. A couple of neighbours took over the kitchen, making plates of sandwiches, pots of tea and slicing currant cake. There was porter and whiskey. People said a few prayers over Martin's coffin and left a Mass card; and then they had a drink and began talking about him.

I sat for as long as I could not wishing to show disrespect. But I was weary of it all. In the end, I slipped away to my room and fell asleep between the cold sheets.

In the morning, Bridgie arrived with Charlie Kettles. Kathleen made breakfast for them and we got ready to take Martin to the church for the funeral Mass. At nine o'clock I saw George Armstrong's car drive into the yard. He entered the house and shook hands with Daddy.

"My God, Pat," he said. "Nobody should have to bear this. He was a lovely boy. He was a credit to you."

I saw him take an envelope from his pocket and slip it into Daddy's hand.

"You're going to need money. Take that. It'll help with the expenses."

Daddy tried to refuse but George Armstrong pressed the envelope on him. He saw me staring at him and he lowered his head and turned away.

*

The church was packed with mourners – neighbours, boys who had been to school with Martin, people who knew Daddy. I saw Mr Maxwell from the hotel, Mr Quinn, the grocer, and his wife, Master McVey. Even Dan Turvey turned up in a long black overcoat and stood at the back of the church, shuffling uneasily throughout the service.

Father Kavanagh preached the sermon. He said Martin had been called home to God in the prime of his life and some people would find that hard to understand. But God's ways were not our ways and in the end, all would be revealed. He said this was a sad occasion but there was joy too, for Martin had left this vale of tears forever and would never again know pain.

Daddy, Michael, Charlie Kettles and a schoolfriend of Martin's carried the coffin out of the church to the adjacent cemetery. It was a beautiful morning, the sun high in a cloudless sky. A gentle breeze stirred the hedgerows. In a nearby tree, a linnet sang. I thought: If Martin had been able to choose his funeral, he would have picked a day like this.

The grave lay open, already prepared. Slowly they lowered Martin into the ground. The man who had dug the grave passed the shovel to Daddy. He scooped up some earth, then paused for a moment and lowered his head. I saw that he was weeping and I realised I had never seen him cry before. Then I heard the earth rattle on the hollow coffin lid.

I turned my face away, and stared accross the fields, green and brown like a patchwork quilt. I knew that everywhere I looked I would see Martin. Every tree and flower and blade of grass would remind me of him. As long as I remained at home, I would feel Martin's presence and know the terrible pain of his loss.

# 14.

After Martin's death, a melancholy settled over the house. It was as if no one could believe he was really gone. Mammy left his clothes hanging in the wardrobe; his Sunday suit, his good shirt and tie and the clothes he wore for working around the farm. His books remained stacked in the cupboard where he had left them. Even the cup that he used for drinking tea remained unwashed. I think she believed that if she got rid of his things, she would erase all trace of him.

Daddy and Michael worked the farm between them, but Daddy grew morose and silent. I never saw him smile again. He stopped going to the pub. I sensed that he blamed himself for Martin's death. Although there was absolutely no evidence, he somehow linked the brucellosis and Martin's brain tumour. One evening as we sat at the dinner table, I noticed that his black hair had become flecked with grey.

I returned to work in the hotel. People were very kind to me. Mr Maxwell said if I needed time off, I should ask him and he would arrange it. Instead, I threw myself into my job, as if the physical effort of work would obliterate the aching sadness I felt for the loss of Martin.

I thought about him all the time. Everywhere I looked, I saw traces of him. Objects and places, even snatches of conversation, reminded me of him. In the evenings, before sunset, I would walk the fields, hearing his voice in the murmer of a stream or the sighing of the wind as it moved through the trees. No matter where I turned, I couldn't shake him off. When I returned to the house, I'd find Mammy and Daddy sitting silent in the kitchen, the only sound the ticking of the clock. An awful depression settled over me like a cloak.

One afternoon, Joe Gaffney said to me: "You're very restless, Stella."

It was a quiet time of the day and the bar was empty. Joe and I were alone. He was washing glasses and I was drying them.

"I notice you're always on the go. You never stand still for a moment. It's a bad sign."

"I like my work," I said.

"Oh, you're a good worker, all right. But you never relax. You're all wound up like a piano string. Why don't you slow down?"

"I can't."

"You're still grieving for your brother?"

It was as if Joe could see into my heart. Suddenly, I began to cry. Joe left down the glass he was washing and put his arms around me.

"I can't help it. I miss him so much. I loved him and now he's gone and no matter how I try, I can't get used to it."

Joe gently stroked my hair.

"Stella, you must let go. Martin is dead. But you can't grieve forever. It's not healthy. Why don't you go to the dances with the other girls? Maybe you'll meet a nice boy?"

"I don't want to go to dances."

"Take my advice, Stella. I've seen it before. If you don't let go, you'll harm yourself."

In the days that followed, I thought about what Joe said. To stop grieving for Martin would be like a betrayal. But I wanted this terrible sadness to end and somehow I knew that if I stayed here, the grief would always remain. The more I thought about it, the more I realised I had to go.

The first opportunity I got, I spoke to Mammy alone. "I'm thinking of leaving," I said.

She showed no surprise.

"Where would you go?"

"Belfast."

"What would you do?"

"I don't know yet. But there's lots of work there. I'll easily find a job."

"Are you sure this is what you want?"

"Yes."

"It's your life, Stella. You're seventeen. Perhaps it's time for you to move on. The house is fairly emptying out. There's two of my children gone already."

I thought Daddy might try to dissuade me, but he just shook his head when I told him as if one piece of bad news was the same as another.

"I'll miss you, if you go. But maybe it's for the best. This place seems cursed now. Everything I touch is falling apart."

"Don't talk like that," I said. "Things will get better."

He looked at me with a dull emptiness in his eyes, as if he didn't believe it any more.

When Kathleen heard, she pleaded that I take her with me.

"How can I? You're only twelve. You have to stay in school."

"I don't want to stay in school. I want to go with you."

"I thought you said you wanted to get a fancy job. Didn't you tell me you were going to be a teacher?"

"If you go, I'll be here on my own. Who will I have to talk to?"

"Oh, for God's sake," I said. "You've still got Mammy and Daddy and Michael. I'll come back at weekends. And I'll write to you."

"Will you? I never got a letter before. Will you write to me and tell me all the exciting things that happen to you up there?"

"Of course. And when you're old enough, you can come and stay with me."

"I'd love that," Kathleen said, excited. "We can go shopping and to the pictures and ride on the trams and have a marvellous time. Promise you'll take me when I'm older."

"I promise."

Mr Maxwell said he was sorry to be losing me. He said he would write me a good reference that I could give to a prospective employer.

On my last night, the women in the kitchen organised a party for me. They baked a cake and Joe Gaffney let them have some drinks from the bar.

They dressed me up and put a bonnet on my head, making a big fuss like they did when a girl was leaving to get married. We sat around drinking beer and Madge Campbell sang: 'The White Cliffs of Dover.'

"For God's sake keep it low, a voice whispered. If Mr Maxwell hears, there'll be hell to pay."

Maggie Cameron sat down beside me.

"I wish I was going with you," she said. "I'd be closer to my man."

"Are you still seeing him?"

"Yes."

"Did he get a divorce yet?"

She shook her head. "He's waiting till the War is over."

"Come and see me, Maggie, any time you're in Belfast. We'll go out and have a good time together."

"You're lucky," she said. "They say it's marvellous up there. There's everything your heart could want. And they say the place is crawling with Yanks."

*

Mammy bought me a new suitcase and helped me pack it with clothes, books and photographs. She gave me scones she had baked for the journey.

"Stella. Promise me you'll be careful, she said. "You're very young to be in a big city on your own."

"Mammy, don't worry about me," I replied.

"I do worry," she said. "I worry all the time."

*

The following morning, after breakfast, I said goodbye to everyone. Kathleen looked so desolate that I kissed her and told her the first thing I would do when I got to Belfast was sit down and write her a letter.

Daddy drove me to the station on the cart, as he used to do when I was a little girl. I watched the fields go by, and the hedgerows, white with blossom. Although I wanted to go, now that it was happening, I felt regret. I thought: This is where I grew up and now I'm leaving.

When we got to the station, Daddy carried my suitcase out to the platform. The train was waiting. He took me in his arms but didn't speak.

I buried my face in his chest.

"I love you Daddy. I have always loved you and I always will."

I got on the train and the guard blew the whistle. Daddy stood waving as the train pulled away in a cloud of steam. I pressed my face to the window and watched as his lonely figure grew smaller and smaller until he was gone, and the train bore me away to my new life.

# BOOK TWO

# 15.

My first impression of Belfast was of crowds and noise. The train pulled into the station in a great whoosh of smoke and the clanging of bells and suddenly there were people everywhere. They appeared out of carriages and corridors, pulling luggage, slamming doors, shouting greetings. When I looked out, the station seemed to be packed with faces; soldiers and sailors and wives and sweethearts, all kissing and waving and making a great fuss.

I clutched my suitcase and struggled through the throng towards a sign that read EXIT. In my pocket, I had a piece of paper with the name and address of the woman who was going to give me digs. Bridgie had got it from someone she knew in Castle Archdale. I took it out and examined it. Lizzie McCrudden, 64 North Queen Street. I didn't know where it was, but Bridgie had assured me it was near the city centre.

I followed the crowds through the big hall of the station and out onto the street. Here, there were more people and more bustle. There were motor cars and horses, and a row of black taxis waiting to pick up the passengers. I went to the first one and handed the driver the piece of paper.

He was a small, pale-faced man with a black choker tied in a knot around his neck. Looking at my thin suitcase he said: "Is that all the luggage you've got?"

"Yes," I replied.

"Well there's no use putting that in the boot. You may keep it on your lap."

In the taxi I pressed my face to the window as the streets rushed past. I had heard so much about Belfast and here I was at last in the big city. I gazed at the shops and pubs, the fancy restaurants and churches. We passed a great white edifice and the driver said proudly: "That's the City Hall. That's the finest building in Northern Ireland."

It was the grandest building I had ever seen, surrounded by green lawn and statues of important people. A large, impressive union jack flew from the dome.

"Isn't that sticking out?" the driver said. "I'll bet you've never seen anything like that before."

"No."

"Where are you from?"

"Ballinaleck."

"Never heard of it."

"It's near Enniskillen."

"Och, sure I know where it is now," said the man.

We drove along by the docks. There were rows of ships tied up at the quay and gangs of men, stripped to the waist, unloading sacks of grain and bags of coal. After a few minutes, the taxi pulled into a long street of terraced houses.

"Here we are," the driver said. "That'll be half a crown."

I stared at him.

"How much?"

"Half a crown."

"That's ridiculous. Sure, you've only been driving for ten minutes."

"Do you think my car runs on fresh air? Do you know what petrol costs?"

"No. But I know when you're trying to rob me."

The driver grunted.

"God, you country ones give me the scunner. How am I supposed to make a living?"

"I'll give you a shilling and you're lucky to get it."

The man put out his hand and took the coin I held.

"A few more like you and I'll be out of business," he said and started the engine and drove away.

*

I stood on the pavement and examined my digs. It was a red-bricked house of three storeys, taller than the other houses in the street. There was a window with a potted plant, and the door had peeling paint and a heavy brass knocker. I felt disappointed. It had the look of a house that has seen better days. Reluctantly, I put down my suitcase and grasped the knocker.

A plump woman in a pinafore and turban opened the door. She had her sleeves rolled up and her beefy arms were still wet with soap suds.

"Are you Lizzie McCrudden?" I asked.

She folded her arms and examined me.

"And who might you be?"

"My name's Estelle Maguire. I was told you were going to give me digs."

"Och, sure you're my new lodger. I didn't think you were coming till tomorrow. Come in, come in."

She brought me into the front room. There was a small, timid-looking man in a cap and scarf sitting at the window reading a newspaper. He looked up when I came in but didn't speak.

"That's my husband, Tommy. He works on the docks but he's not well with the arthritis in his legs so he's off sick."

I started to say 'Hello', but the man shook out his paper and held it in front of his face.

"I'm just doing a wee bit of washing. Would you like a cup of tea and then I'll show you to your room?" Mrs McCrudden asked.

I said that would be nice and she went into a tiny kitchen. I heard the gas ring on the cooker go 'Pop'. I looked around. The room was sparsely furnished. There was a table and chairs, and a sofa. An oilcloth lay on the floor and on the mantlepiece sat a china dog, beside a picture of Mr and Mrs McCrudden on their wedding day.

From behind his newspaper, I could feel Mr McCrudden watching me. I looked up and he rustled the paper and buried his head again. Mrs McCrudden talked to me from the kitchen.

"Are you a nurse?"

"No."

"I thought maybe you were up to work in the hospital. I get a lot of nurses. They're all from the country."

I told her I hadn't got a job yet.

"So what kind of work are you going to do?"

"I don't know."

"Lindsay's mill is looking for stitchers. They're making parachutes for the War and they pay good wages. You'd easy get twenty-five shillings a week with a bit of overtime."

I said I didn't want to work in a mill.

"Well, you can check at the Broo tomorrow and they'll send you somewhere. There's no shortage of jobs. But don't be too fussy. That's my advice to you. You take whatever pays the best money."

She brought two cups of tea and sat down beside me.

"Estelle?" she said. "What kind of name is that?"

I said it was French and meant 'star'.

"I never heard that name before. It's very fancy. You're from Enniskillen?"

"Yes."

"Do you go to church, Estelle?"

"Yes. I go to the Catholic church."

Mrs McCrudden seemed to brighten up.

"Oh that's all right, then. We're Catholics ourselves. But everybody's entitled to their own views. Live and let live. That's my motto. I've a fella staying with me. Bill Dwyer. He's from Ballymena and he's a fitter in the shipyard. He's a Protestant and a finer fella you couldn't meet."

She sipped her tea.

"Dwyer's a strange name for a Protestant, don't you think?"

I said I didn't know.

"Oh it is. Somebody took the soup there, if you ask me."

I asked her what she meant.

"During the Famine, daughter. The Protestants went about giving the starving people soup if they would change their religion. I'll put my hat on it that's what happened in his family. Sure everybody knows Dwyer's a good Catholic name."

She sniffed.

"This street is mixed. At the other end, they're all Orangemen. There's some bad boys down there. They have a big bonfire on the 12th of July and they're out beating their drums and cursing the Pope. So, you be careful."

I said we had Orangemen in Enniskillen but they didn't behave like that.

"Oh, Belfast is different, daughter. This town is a black hole when it comes to religion. Believe you me."

We finished our tea and Mrs McCrudden took me up the stairs. My room was right at the top of the house. She pushed open a door and showed me in. I felt my heart sink. The room was tiny. There was a single bed with a big eiderdown and a wardrobe and a holy picture on the wall.

"Isn't it lovely and comfortable?" Mrs McCrudden said, waiting for my approval.

I said it was.

"And it's nice and quiet up here. There could be a bomb go off and you wouldn't hear it. The rent is seven shillings a week and that includes your breakfast. If you want your dinner as well, it's another two shillings. I charge a week in advance."

I opened my purse and counted out the money.

"The bathroom is down the landing. There's a queue in the morning, so don't be long. If you want to have a bath, it's sixpence."

"What for?" I asked.

"Hot water, daughter. You wouldn't believe what the Corporation charges me for gas."

Mrs McCrudden stuffed the money in the pocket of her pinafore.

"You and me's going to get on well, Estella. I can tell. I'm a great judge of people and I'm never wrong."

"Estelle." I corrected her. "My name's Estelle."

"Och look, why don't I just call you Stella? Sure Estelle's too much of a mouthful."

She laughed and I heard her feet padding back down the stairs. I stared at the tiny room. It was like a cell. There was barely space to turn. I opened the window and looked out. As far as I could see, there were black rooftops and chimneys and the spires of churches. In the distance, the green slopes of Cavehill brushed against the sky. Further out, I saw the sparkle of sunlight on the sea.

In the street below, a group of girls were skipping and singing.

*On the hillside, stands a lady, who she is, I do not know.*

*All she wants is gold and silver. All she wants is a nice young man.*

I closed the window and turned back into the room. I began to unpack, putting my clothes away in the wardrobe. Then I sat down on the hard bed, took out my notebook and began to write a letter to Kathleen, as I had promised.

# 16.

The sound of a mill horn woke me. I sat up in bed and wondered where I was. The horn was screeching and the sun was streaming in through the bedroom window. I rubbed my eyes. Outside my door, I could hear voices. I glanced at the travelling clock Mammy had given me as a going-away present. It was ten to seven. I got out of bed, put on my dressing gown and ventured out to the landing.

There was nobody about. I walked to the bathroom and turned the door handle. It was locked.

"Won't be a minute," a voice from inside said.

I didn't know what to do. I felt embarrassed, standing there on the landing in my dressing gown with my towel in my hand. But before I could do anything, the door opened and a young man came out.

He was about 23, tall and broad with dark-brown hair. I saw a little spot of blood on his chin where he had been shaving.

"Hello," he said. "You're new."

"I'm Stella Maguire."

"I'm Bill Dwyer."

I remembered what Mrs McCrudden had told me yesterday. This must be the Protestant from Ballymena.

"I'm pleased to meet you," I said.

Bill Dwyer grinned.

"We've no time to be talking. There's an ould fella called Billy Mack will be along in a minute. He's an overseer in the Corporation and he raises hell if he has to wait for the bathroom. I'll see you at breakfast."

I went into the bathroom and locked the door. I quickly washed myself and cleaned my teeth. Back in my room, I brushed my hair and put on a white blouse, jacket and skirt. I studied myself in the mirror and decided to apply a touch of lipstick. Then I went downstairs.

The smell of tea and toast met me as I descended. In the parlour, Bill Dwyer was already seated at the table. Beside him sat a small, middle-aged woman with mousey hair.

Mrs McCrudden came out from the kitchen with a big silver teapot. When she saw me, she said: "You're up early. I'd better introduce you. This is my new lodger. Stella Maguire."

"We've met already," Bill Dwyer said.

Mrs McCrudden looked at him suspiciously.

"Have you indeed? Well, you're a fast worker. I hope you work as fast in the shipyard."

She pointed to the woman.

"That's Bernadette McCloskey and she works in Woolworth's store in High Street."

The woman smiled shyly and bent her head to her plate.

"It's porridge and tea and toast," Mrs McCrudden said. "And there's marmalade as well. But go easy on it. It's rationed."

She went back to the kitchen.

"Are you up for a job?" Bill Dwyer said, pouring milk on his porridge.

"Yes."

"What do you do?"

I told him I hadn't found work yet.

"They're looking for stitchers in the mill. That was the hooter you just heard. They start at seven."

I told him I wanted to look around for a bit before making a decision.

"Where do you come from?"

"Enniskillen."

Bernadette McCloskey looked up.

"I've got friends in Lisnaskea. They're called McCoy and they have a hardware shop in Church Street. I go down to visit them every summer."

We chatted for a while and then Bill suddenly put down his cup and stood up.

"Have to be on my bike."

He winked at me and was gone out the door. Bernadette McCloskey followed.

I finished my breakfast. I wondered where Mr Mack was. I decided I would walk into town and visit the Labour Exchange as Mrs McCrudden had suggested. As I left the room, I almost collided with a plump man in a suit and waistcoat. He glared at me through horn-rimmed glasses.

"Why don't you look where you're going?"

"I'm sorry," I said.

"I should think so. Just take your time, young lady. It will suit you better than running around like a chicken with its head chopped off."

Mrs McCrudden gave me directions into town. Out on the street, I was suddenly aware of this loud rattling noise and a sweet, cloying smell of tobacco. It seemed to be coming from a large brick building with tall chimneys and rows of windows and a large sign that read 'Lindsay's Mill'.

I looked through the windows as I went past. Inside, it was dark, but I could make out rows of women in overalls crouched at machines. There appeared to be hundreds of them and the machines clattered and banged with movement. The noise inside the building must have been deafening. Right beside the mill stood another large building with a sign that read 'Gallaher's Tobacco'.

I made my way to the end of the street and came to a main road. There was a lot of traffic; cars and lorries and horses clipping along the cobblestones. I was about to cross when another loud noise made me step back again. A tram came clanging down the middle of the road in a shower of sparks. I watched, fascinated, as it sailed to a stop outside the church and people disembarked.

The Labour Exchange was in a dreary building on a street near Royal Avenue. It was crowded with people sitting on benches while they waited to talk to a clerk. The air was fetid with cigarette smoke and the smell of unwashed bodies. I took a seat and, when my turn came, I marched confidently up to the hatch.

The clerk asked my name, address and date of birth and wrote them down on a form.

"So, what can we do for you?"

I told him I had come up from Enniskillen and was looking for work.

"What are your qualifications?"

I said I had attended national school till I was 15 but I hadn't passed any exams.

"Do you have any experience?"

I told him I had worked as a waitress and a barmaid in the Royal Hotel in Enniskillen, and had a reference from the manager, Mr Maxwell.

The clerk didn't seem too impressed.

"Is it bar work you're looking for?"

I said I would prefer to work in an office, if he had any jobs like that.

I saw a smile play around the corners of his mouth.

"Och now, you'd need typing and shorthand for those kind of jobs. Sure everybody wants to be sitting behind a desk these days. Nobody wants to get their hands dirty. The Grand Central Hotel is looking for staff. Are you interested?"

"What kind of staff?"

"Waitresses."

"No," I said quickly. "What about a shop?"

"You need experience."

"Have you any bar jobs?"

"Not for women."

He tapped his pen impatiently on the counter.

"There's factory jobs. I've got plenty of them. It's good steady work and it pays well."

"I don't want to work in a factory."

"The City Hospital is looking for a trainee cook."

I shook my head.

He shuffled through a card index.

"How'd you like to work as a domestic? Five shillings a week and live-in?"

"No," I said, "Not that."

He was getting exasperated.

"You're very fussy for somebody with no qualifications."

"I expected something better."

"Then you should have stayed longer in school."

"The Grand Central," I said at last. "What's the pay?"

He checked the card index again.

"A pound a week and meals. Do you want it?"

I had come to Belfast with dreams of a bright future, a good job that would make Mammy and Daddy proud of me. But now I realised it wasn't going to be so easy. I thought of the six pounds I had saved and how quickly it would dwindle if I didn't find work soon. The job in the hotel would have to do until I had a chance to get something better.

"All right," I said, reluctantly. "I'll take it."

# 17.

The clerk gave me a card and told me to take it to the hotel and ask for the manager, Mr Watson. I found it easily enough. It was much bigger and far grander than the Royal Hotel in Enniskillen. I gave the card to the receptionist and she told me to take a seat and wait.

After ten minutes, a flustered man in frock-coat and pin-striped trousers came bustling up to the desk.

"My God," he said. "We've got fifteen American officers coming for dinner and now the chef's gone sick. If he's drunk again, he's fired. I'm taking no excuses this time."

The receptionist whispered something and he turned abruptly and stared at me.

"You've come about a job?"

"Yes, sir."

I had Mr Maxwell's reference ready to show him.

"Waitressing. Have you done it before?"

"Yes, sir."

"When can you start?"

"Whenever you like."

"Can you start right away?"

Before I could reply, he said: "Go down to the kitchen and they'll give you a uniform and tell you what to do. Now run along. Lunch will be starting in fifteen minutes. You can help get the tables ready."

I was surprised. I had been expecting a formal interview and, instead, I'd been hired on the spot. When I found the kitchen, it was like a madhouse. Enveloped in steam, there was noise everywhere.

People in white shirts and trousers were running around shouting and cursing, getting in each other's way. A woman who said her name was Minnie Roberts led me to a cloakroom, opened a cupboard and took out a black uniform with a white apron and cap.

"See if that fits you," she said. "You can leave your stuff here. Nobody's going to steal it. Then go immediately to the dining room and start setting the tables."

I changed into the uniform. I couldn't help thinking that the Belfast people were very unfriendly. They weren't at all like the people I had known in Enniskillen.

When I was ready, I went in search of the dining room. I found this vast space filled with tables covered in starched white tablecloths. Groups of women were moving from one table to the next, setting out cutlery and glasses.

Minnie Roberts spotted me and took my arm.

"Your section is tables one to ten. There's two other girls working with you. When the guests sit down, bring them a jug of water and a menu. Take their order and write it in your notepad. Bring the order to the kitchen. Keep the food coming. Don't leave them waiting. And for God's sake don't get the orders mixed up or there'll be blue murder."

She looked me over.

"You seem strong enough," she said. "Don't wilt."

For the next ten minutes, I helped set the tables and tried to remember everything Minnie Roberts had said. I didn't want to make a fool of myself on my very first day. But I was fearful of what might lie ahead.

At one o'clock, the doors opened and the diners began to come in. They were mainly businessmen and groups of soldiers in uniform. When the first group was seated, I grabbed a jug of water and a handful of menus and went to work.

Time passed in a blur. I took orders, ferried trays of food and carried away dirty dishes. I would barely have served one table when another was demanding attention. With all the running to and from the kitchen, I was in a sweat, and before long my blouse was soaked. My feet were sore and my legs and arms ached worse than I could remember.

At last, I had served desserts. A few stragglers remained, drinking whiskey and smoking cigars, but the worst of the work was over. I went back to the cloakroom, poured a tumbler of water and sat down to try and catch my breath.

Another girl sat down beside me and took out a packet of cigarettes.

"Jaysis," she said. "I have the feet run off myself. Is this your first day?"

I told her it was.

"You'll get used to it. The tips are good. The only thing you have to watch out for is when they try to grope you."

"What?"

"The officers. They feel your bum when you're serving the table. They think it's a big joke."

She blew smoke out the side of her mouth.

"And what do you do when they grope you?"

"Just keep smiling and try to move away."

"Do you not complain?"

"Oh God, no. You can't speak to the guests unless they speak to you first."

She stubbed out her cigarette.

"Don't worry. It doesn't happen very often. It's mainly at dinner when they're drunk. And the good thing is, when they grope you, they usually leave a big tip."

After lunch, we cleared away the tables and prepared them for the evening. Then it was time to eat. I was starving. I hadn't eaten anything since breakfast, ten hours earlier. I went into the kitchen and sat down to a plate of potatoes and cabbage. I was just about to start when a phone on the wall rang. I lifted it and pressed it to my ear. It was Minnie Roberts again.

"Room service for 43. They want the silverside of beef, roast potatoes, turnips and the roly-poly pudding."

"What am I supposed to do?" I said, helplessly.

"Are you kidding? You get the order from the kitchen and bring it up to their room. *Immediately!*"

I finished work at nine o'clock and had to walk home, as the trams had stopped running on account of the Blackout. I was exhausted and my head was spinning. Everything was in darkness. All the street lights were out and people had their windows covered up in case of air raids. Occasionally, you might see a little chink of light coming from behind the curtains. When I arrived in, Mrs McCrudden was sitting at the table in her apron listening to the wireless.

"Och daughter dear, you look worn out. You just sit down there and I'll get you a wee mouthful of tea."

She went into the kitchen. I noticed her husband was still in his chair by the window reading by candlelight. He glanced at me slyly from under his cap.

"Did you get a job?" Mrs McCrudden asked.

I told her I was a waitress in the Grand Central Hotel.

"Ooooh. That's high and mighty, now. That's where all the posh people go. Between you and me, Stella, that's a better job than the mill. You'll meet a much better class of people working in the Grand Central Hotel."

I didn't tell her about the soldiers groping the waitresses and everybody cursing and swearing in the kitchen.

"I suppose they feed you there?"

"Yes."

"So you won't be needing any dinner, then?"

"No. Just breakfast."

I finished the tea and wearily climbed the stairs to my room. I got undressed and went along the landing to the bathroom. I wished I had given Mrs McCrudden sixpence for a bath but I was too tired now to go back downstairs again.

I washed myself in the basin, then soaked my clothes and hung them in front of the window to dry. I got in under the sheets and thought about my day. I hadn't landed the fancy job I had hoped for. Instead I was back waitressing again. It was worse that the Royal Hotel and, on top of everything, I had to pay for digs.

I began to think that perhaps it hadn't been such a good idea to come to Belfast after all. But I could hardly go back now. It would make me look stupid. I closed my eyes and, a few minutes later, I was fast asleep.

# 18.

I slept late the following morning because I was so tired and, when I woke, it was after nine o'clock. I could hear sounds drifting up from the street below; the rattle of the mill and the hum of traffic.

As I got out of bed, I noticed a letter lying on the floor. Somebody must have slipped it under the door while I was asleep. I picked it up. It was addressed to me but I didn't recognise the handwriting. There was no stamp. I quickly tore it open.

It was a note from Bill Dwyer.

Dear Stella,

I hope you won't think I'm too forward but I wonder if you would like to see a flick with me on Saturday afternoon? We could go and have tea afterwards. I could show you round the town. Let me know if it's okay.

Yours sincerely,

Bill

I stared at Bill's lovely, neat handwriting and felt a flush of excitement. A formal invitation, no less. I had never been asked out in such a polite way. I was flattered. Bill was quite handsome. I thought it would be nice to go to the pictures with him and get his advice about the city.

Then I remembered I was due to work on Saturday. My hours were 11 a.m. till 9 p.m. and Wednesday was my day off. Disappointed, I hid the note at the bottom of my suitcase, put on my dressing gown and hurried along the landing to the bathroom.

*

The pace at work was relentless. Lunch was the busiest time and most days the dining room was crowded. In the evening, at dinner, the guests were mainly people who were staying at the hotel and parties of British and American officers who were stationed in Belfast. They would come in once a week, just to get a break from their mess halls, and order the best things on the menu, drinking whiskey and brandy and sitting till late, chatting and laughing.

Despite my original impression, the staff turned out to be friendly. They were mainly working-class women and they had a strong sense of solidarity. They would look out for each other and cover up if someone was late or got into trouble.

Minnie Roberts was the supervisor. She was married with three young children, but her husband had been injured in an accident on a building site and couldn't work any more. So Minnie was the breadwinner. At break time, we would drink tea and Minnie would tell me all about her family and how the children were doing at school.

She had a little boy, Liam, who was very bright and wanted to be an engineer. But he would have to study at the Technical College and that cost money. So Minnie worked all the overtime she could, to save up for the fees.

She would say: "Stella, education's the only way for the likes of us. You just have to look at some of the galoots we get in here with their fancy clothes and their big jobs. They haven't got the intelligence of a flea. But they've all been to college and that's what counts. It's no good people like us having the brains if we don't have the education."

The head chef was a man called Tucker Magee. He had a big belly that hung out of his trousers and a red nose pitted with black spots that resembled a ripe strawberry. He was a kind man, and I would see him slipping Minnie Roberts and the other women parcels of meat when the manager wasn't about. Most of the time he worked hard and everybody in the kitchen looked up to him.

But, once a month, he would start drinking whiskey and then he'd go mad. Pots and pans would be thrown around the kitchen and people would scramble to get out of his way. He would take off his apron and offer to fight the manager. He would roar at the top his voice: "Where's that bollix, Watson? If he shows his sleekit beak in my kitchen one more time, I'll shove his pin-striped trousers so far up his arse, he'll need an operation to get them out again." The staff would have to lock Tucker in the cloakroom till he sobered up. Other days he'd be so drunk he wouldn't come into work at all and Mr Watson would threaten to fire him. But he was such a good chef when he wasn't drinking that Mr Watson always kept him on.

Some evenings after work, I would sit in the cocktail bar with one of the girls. Mr Watson didn't like us going in there. He was afraid that the bar staff would give us free drinks. But we would just sit in the corner with a glass of lemonade and watch all the activity around us.

The clients were army officers in their smart uniforms and young men in sharp suits and women with jewellery and necklaces and fancy frocks. I would watch them tip the barman, the ten-shilling notes and the silver half-crowns passing smoothly across the counter. I would envy them, thinking how nice it would be to sit up at the counter with a handsome officer buying me martinis, instead of skivvying in the dining room.

*

Gradually I got to know the other guests in Mrs McCrudden's digs. Bernadette McCloskey was from Dungiven in County Derry and she had come up to Belfast 15 years before to take a job in Woolworths. She had never married. Every morning she went out to work at 8 a.m. and every evening she came back again. She had her dinner and then spent the evening reading in her room.

One night a week she went to play bridge with some friends on the Antrim Road. Every year, in July, she spent her two weeks holidays with the McCoys in Lisnaskea. At Christmas she stayed with relations in Dungiven for a couple of days. That was her life. She was shy and withdrawn, rarely speaking. I felt sorry for her but she seemed content enough.

Mr Mack had a big job in the corporation. His wife had died of cancer and they had no children. He couldn't bear to live alone in the house after his wife died, so he sold up and moved in with Mrs McCrudden.

He had the best room in the house, a big double bedroom with his own wash basin. He dressed smartly in a suit and waistcoat and his boots were always polished. He never smiled. He had the seat at the head of the table and got his meals served first. I think Mrs McCrudden was afraid of him.

But I discovered that Mr Mack had a soft side. One afternoon, when I was on my break, I met him coming out of a flower shop on Royal Avenue with a big bouquet of roses. When he saw me, he tried to hide them.

"Hello," I said. "Is it somebody's birthday?"

He stared coldly at me.

"That's none of your business, young lady."

"I'm sorry. I was just trying to be friendly."

I turned to walk away but Mr Mack reached out and held my arm.

"Forgive me. I was rude. I apologise."

"There's no need to apologise. I shouldn't have been so nosey."

"The flowers are for my wife. Once a month, I leave roses on her grave."

I looked at Mr Mack and saw the sadness in his eyes. He took out his handkerchief and blew his nose.

"You remind me of her," he said. "She was just like you. So full of life. When I first met her, she was so giddy and high-spirited. She was like a young mare. I miss her terribly."

I said: "I think it's nice of you to leave flowers for her. I'm sure you must have loved her very much."

Mr Mack shook his head.

"You've no idea," he said. "No idea at all."

The only one I didn't get to know was Mrs McCrudden's husband Tommy. He moved about the house like a ghost. He never spoke to me but I knew he was watching. I tried to ignore him but it was impossible. He was like a spy. The very thought that we lived under the same roof gave me the creeps.

# 19.

I began to see Bill regularly. The routine was always the same: I'd meet him somewhere in town and we'd have a drink, then go and see a flick. He would walk me home in the Blackout and, at the corner of the street, he would kiss me Goodnight and I would return to the digs alone. Having smoked a cigarette, he would follow ten minutes later. This way, we managed to keep our romance a secret from Lizzie McCrudden and the residents of 64 North Queen Street.

After a while, I wrote to Kathleen.

I have met a nice man. His name is Bill Dwyer and he is a fitter in the shipyard. It's a good job and he earns good money. He's very handsome. He is about six feet tall and has dark eyes and brown hair. He is very kind to me and buys me nice presents. I think he fancies me, but I don't know if I fancy him.

I also wrote to Mammy every week but I didn't tell her about Bill. I just told her about my job and the people in the digs and all the exciting things that were happening in Belfast. She would write back in her crooked handwriting and pass on the gossip about the farm and the neighbours. Cattle prices were holding up well and Daddy seemed to be getting back on his feet. With only four mouths to feed, there was more money to go around. She always signed off by telling me to say my prayers every night and make sure to go to Mass on Sunday and pray for them all.

Although Mammy never said it in her letters, I think she was disappointed that I hadn't found a grander job than waitressing. She had this idea that everything was better in the city, that there were endless opportunities. I was getting fed up myself, growing desperate to get out of the Grand Central Hotel. It wasn't just that the work was hard and I was always tired. I had no social life. While other girls were out dancing, I was serving tables. I couldn't even see the one man I had met, except for our weekly trip to the pictures on a Wednesday night.

One evening, as we were walking home along Royal Avenue, Bill said: "Could you not get Saturday off and we could go away for the day somewhere? We could get the train down to Bangor and have a good time. Have you ever been to Bangor?"

"No."

"Och, you don't know what you're missing. It's a wonderful place and the sea air is great for the chest."

"But Saturday is the busiest day of the week. They'd never let me have Saturday off."

"They're taking advantage of you," he said. "Somebody should start a union in that place and demand proper conditions."

Keeping our romance secret was a source of great excitement for us. We never spoke to each other when any of the other lodgers were around except to say 'hello'. If we passed on the landing, Bill would make a grab at me and try to kiss me. But at breakfast, we would just make innocent small talk about the weather.

Bernadette McCloskey was too naive to notice anything and Mr Mack, after our encounter with the flowers, had softened towards me. Once a week, he got a half pound of pork sausages from somewhere and Mrs McCrudden fried them specially for his breakfast. The delicious smell of cooking sausages would fill the house and make us all hungry. Mr Mack would sit up to the table and lick his lips in anticipation while the rest of us contemplated our simple porridge and toast.

But one morning, he did something extraordinary. While we were waiting for Mrs McCrudden to bring in the teapot, he speared a big juicy sausage and passed it on to my plate.

Everybody stared in surprise.

"Take it," he said. "You're working hard and you need your strength."

He didn't offer a sausage to anybody else.

"The ould divil's after you," Bill said later.

"It's his wife."

"What about her?"

"I remind him of her."

*

Because of the hours I was working, I never got an opportunity to look for another job. Finally, one morning, I went back again to the Labour Exchange.

"I'm looking for a change," I said to the clerk. "Have you anything else?"

He gave me a queer look.

"What's wrong with the job you've got?"

"There's nothing wrong with it. I just want to do something different."

"The Grand Central Hotel is the finest hotel in Northern Ireland. Is it not good enough for you?"

"That's not what I said."

"You should be grateful to have a job in such a place. A job in the Grand Central is a calling card for a job anywhere."

I was getting annoyed. The interview was going nowhere.

"Look, you don't understand. I don't want to be a waitress for the rest of my life. In the Grand Central or anywhere else. I want to do something different."

He took out his filing cards and made a pretence of running through them.

"There's mill jobs, there's cleaning jobs, there's munitions work. What would you like?"

"No," I said. "Nothing like that."

"Well, if you're not happy in the Grand Central, I can't force you to stay. But I have to warn you. If you leave of your own accord, you won't qualify for unemployment benefit."

"Surely you must have a job in an office somewhere?" I said in desperation.

99

He smiled indulgently and put away his cards.

"I told you the last time. You need qualifications for a job like that. Your trouble, Miss Maguire, is you're getting above your station."

Despite the clerk's lack of encouragement, I was to leave the Grand Central, and sooner than I expected. It was a Saturday afternoon and we had been busy all day. At lunch, there was an excursion group from Dublin. All of my ten tables were occupied and, to make matters worse, one of the girls had called in sick.

After lunch was finished and we had re-set the tables, I went for my meal. They usually let us have whatever was on the menu, except for the expensive things like salmon and steak. I had chicken and potatoes, then headed to the back of the kitchen where the other women sat smoking. I was already feeling exhausted and dinner was yet to come.

Minnie Roberts sat down beside me. "You look knackered," she said. "You look like a washed-out rag."

"I'll bet she was up half the night with that man of her's," one of the women said. "I hear he's a real micky-dazzler. I hear she had him in the cocktail bar the other night."

I felt my face go red.

"Tell us about your man, Stella," another woman said. "Is he passionate?"

Someone sniggered.

"He's not my man," I said. He's just a friend. He was taking me to the pictures."

"And when the lights went out did his hands start roaming?"

There was more sniggering.

"You need to watch them fellas, Stella. You wouldn't know what they'd get up to."

The tiredness overwhelmed me and, suddenly, I felt my temper crack. This kind of banter was all right while they confined it to their own boyfriends. But it seemed so grimy and dirty when they applied it to Bill.

"I don't know what you get up to with *your* men," I snapped. "But my friend is a gentleman. And what's more, I think you've got filthy minds, the whole lot of you. You should be ashamed of yourselves."

I got up from the table and stormed out. Minnie Roberts came running after me.

"For God's sake, Stella, don't pay them any heed. It's just a bit of banter. They don't mean any harm."

"I'm sick of this place, Minnie. This isn't a job. It's a slave camp. If I could get something else, I'd be out of here in the morning."

"Never mind the morning, darlin. Just hang in for tonight. We've got thirty officers for dinner. British *and* Yankees."

I went into the cloakroom, washed my face and drank a cup of tea. I was annoyed with myself for snapping. I knew Minnie was right. There was no harm in the way the women talked. It was just something to add a bit of excitement to their lives.

Dinnertime arrived and I went back to the dining room. The guests were already seated and, to my dismay, I saw that some of them were already tipsy. They had been drinking in the bar beforehand. They were laughing loudly and making jokes and ordering bottles of wine.

There were four of us on duty and we served the soup course. Just as we were finishing, the American officers arrived. Thankfully, there were only eight of them. We got them seated and took their orders.

Halfway through the main course, one of the British officers started to sing. It was a song I had heard them sing before.

*The German generals crossed the Rhine, parley-voo.*
*The German generals crossed the Rhine, parley-voo.*
*The German generals crossed the Rhine,*
*Raped the women and drank the wine.*
*With your inky-pinky parley-voo.*

The table exploded in laughter and I saw the American officers smiling. I began to get worried. When they started celebrating like this, they never wanted to leave, and that meant we could be working till after midnight.

We kept going, rushing between the two groups, trying to keep the food served. As the night progressed, the Americans began to relax and eventually they joined in the singing with a chorus of 'Shenendoah'. Mr

Watson came in at one stage to see what was going on, but they just ignored him, so he hurried away again.

At last it came to the coffee. The officers had taken off their jackets and were lighting cigars. I felt relieved. At this stage, we usually cleared away what dishes we could and then withdrew and left them alone.

I took the heavy coffee pot to the table. There was much laughing and back-slapping. I could see that some of them were pretty drunk by now. A brandy bottle had appeared. I bent across the table to pour and suddenly I felt a rough hand slide up between my legs and pinch my thigh.

For a second, I froze in terror. Then I screamed and dropped the coffee pot. It crashed onto the table. I turned and saw a fat man smirking at me. Without thinking, I drew my hand and smacked him hard across the face.

I heard a gasp and then an embarrassed silence. People stared at each other but nobody spoke. The spilled coffee was spreading across the table cloth like a black lake. Out of nowhere, Minnie Roberts was at my side.

"You better go, Stella. Leave it to me."

She signalled to another girl and between them they started to clean up the mess. I left and went down to the cloakroom. I took off my uniform and put on my coat. Outside, there was a big yellow moon in the sky and it lit up the darkness all the way home.

# 20.

It was with a feeling of trepidation that I reported for work the next day. The receptionist met me in the lobby and told me I was to go at once to the manager's office. I knew by the way she looked at me that I was in trouble.

Mr Watson was sitting behind his desk surrounded by account books and lists and bits of paper. He was on the telephone, but he put it down at once when I came in.

"I've had a complaint. From an army officer who says you assaulted him last night."

I couldn't believe this.

"I assaulted *him*?"

"He says you slapped his face. He has witnesses."

"I did slap his face."

"So you admit it?"

"Of course."

Mr Watson could barely restrain himself.

"Were you out of your mind? What in God's name possessed you to attack a guest? Particularly such good guests as those officers who spend so much money here? Have you no thought for the publicity this could bring? I have never come across such behaviour in all my years. It cannot be tolerated."

"Can I speak?"

"No, you cannot."

He opened a drawer and took out a sheet of paper.

"The gentleman in question is very upset but thankfully, he has agreed not to take matters any further. *Provided* he gets a letter of apology from you. I have told him this will be forthcoming. I have the letter typed and ready. You will sign it."

He pushed the letter across the desk and stiffly handed me a pen.

I looked at the letter. It was written in the most abject terms.

*Dear Sir,*

*I beg your forgiveness for my disgraceful behaviour last evening. This was a regrettable aberration for which I most humbly apologise. I am filled with remorse for my action and for the shame it has brought on my employers and colleagues and on the fine reputation of the Grand Central Hotel.*

*I trust you will accept this apology in the contrite spirit in which it is offered.*

*Yours sincerely,*

*Estelle Maguire*

I handed back the letter.

"I can't sign this."

Mr Watson's face turned livid.

"Have you gone mad? I'm offering you an opportunity to salvage the situation. You realise he could sue you? And the hotel? Now sign at once."

"*He* should be apologising to *me*."

"I beg your pardon."

"He assaulted me first. I was defending myself. He interfered with me."

"I'm warning you, Miss Maguire. Do not make matters worse by wild allegations."

"They're not allegations. He did assault me. I have witnesses too."

"Who?"

"Minnie Roberts. She knows what happened."

"Right. We shall see."

He lifted the telephone and dialled.

I waited for what seemed like an eternity before hearing a knock at the door. Minnie Roberts came slowly into the room. She glanced nervously at me and then at Mr Watson.

"Mrs Roberts, you were present last night when this outrageous incident occurred. Did you see this gentleman interfere with Miss Maguire in any way?"

Minnie Roberts lowered her head.

"Well, Mrs Roberts. What have you got to say?"

"I ..."

"Speak up, woman."

Minnie swallowed hard.

"No, sir."

I felt my heart give a little jump. I couldn't believe she was denying me.

I blurted out: "But, Minnie. You saw what he did. You saw him put his hand up my skirt."

Mr Watson stood up.

"That will be all, Mrs Roberts. You may go now."

Minnie glanced at me again as she left and I could see the shame in her eyes. Then she hurried out of the room.

"Now, Miss Maguire. I am losing patience. Will you sign this letter?"

Again I entreated: "But I did nothing wrong. Why should I apologise?"

"Will you sign the letter?"

I took a deep breath.

"No."

Mr Watson gathered up the letter and put it in a drawer.

"Very well. You leave me no option but to dismiss you. You may collect your wages at reception. Less the cost of breakages and repair for the damage done to table-linen."

I bit my lip.

"And Miss Maguire. Do me the pleasure of never darkening the door of this establishment again."

On my way through the lobby, I ran into Tucker Magee. He drew me aside and thrust a parcel of meat into my hands. As he went away, he whispered: "Good on you girl, for standing up for yourself. It's about time somebody put manners on those ignorant bastards."

I left the hotel with a burning sense of injustice. I had been dismissed because I wouldn't apologise to a drunken officer for assaulting me. My treatment was so unfair that it filled me with impotent rage.

Most of all, I was angry at Minnie's betrayal. I knew she was terrified about losing her job. She was the breadwinner in her family and she wanted to give her son an education. But surely she could have stood by me and told the truth?

After a few days, my anger receded and I began to face the harsh reality that I was unemployed. Worse, I had no reference and if I went looking for another job, the first thing they would ask was where I had been before and why I had left. The thought of going back to the Labour Exchange filled me with dread.

I sat in my room and counted my money. I had almost nine pounds saved. But I had to pay rent and buy food and clothes. It wouldn't be long before my money ran out and then what would I do?

I didn't tell Mrs McCrudden I had lost my job. I was worried that her attitude towards me might change if she knew I was no longer earning money. Nor did I tell Bill. For the next few weeks, I carried on as if nothing had happened. I got up for breakfast and then left as though I was going into work as usual.

Instead, I went to the public library and scanned the 'Situations Vacant' column in the newspapers. I still had hopes that I might find a good job in an office. I bought fancy notepaper and, in my best handwriting, applied for several positions. I hoped that if I could at least get an interview, I might persuade them to employ me. But though I waited for weeks, no reply ever came.

I began to grow desperate. I took to spending my days scouring the city looking in shop windows for vacancies. I ate in cafés and took long tram rides to the outskirts of town. Killing time became my main occupation. I considered Lindsay's mill, but the thought of joining the ranks of those poor huddled women I had seen, relentlessly tending their machines, made me recoil.

Bit by bit, my little store of money shrunk away till I had only three pounds left. It began to look as if I would have to return home. But pride made me hang on. I had come to Belfast to escape the grief I felt for Martin and to make my way in the world. I was determined to remain until my last shilling was spent and all hope was gone.

One morning, as I was leaving the digs, I saw this smart car waiting at the pavement. I knew at once it was a Yankee car because the steering wheel was on the left. There were two men in the front seat and as I approached, the door opened and one of them called my name.

"Miss Maguire? May I have a word with you, please."

I stopped. The man who had called me was dressed in a US army uniform and he had the close-cropped hair that the soldiers wore. I went closer. He looked about 40 and his face was vaguely familiar.

"Do I know you?" I asked.

"Maybe. You served me dinner recently. My name is Ed Costigan. I'm a Major in the 168th Infantry Battalion, United States Army."

I knew him now. He had been one of the party of American officers on the night of the incident.

"Forgive me for intruding, Miss Maguire. But I was concerned about you. I hadn't seen you at the hotel recently and when I inquired, one of your colleagues told me you'd been fired."

I felt my cheeks flush.

"I saw what happened that night. I saw that man assault you. I spoke to the manager about it but he wasn't interested. So when I heard you had lost your job, I thought an injustice had been done and I should do something about it."

"That's very kind of you," I said.

"If you want to make an official complaint, I'm prepared to act as a witness for you," he offered.

"I don't think it would do any good. They won't take me back."

"Have you got another job?"

"Not yet."

"So what are you going to do?"

"I have some prospects," I said.

"Look. It's none of my business. But we have a social club. It's called the American Eagle. It's just up the street from the hotel. It's a club for service personnel. We have a bar. Have you ever done bar work?"

"Yes," I said eagerly. "I worked in a bar in Enniskillen."

Ed Costigan reached into his jacket and took out a card.

"Captain Bukowski is the officer in charge. Go and talk to him. He'll be there this evening. Tell him I sent you. I think he might have an opening for you."

He started the engine.

"How can I thank you?"

"You don't have to thank me. Good luck, Miss Maguire. Maybe I'll see you in the American Eagle some night."

"Wait," I said. "How did you know where to find me?"

"The supervisor lady. Mrs Roberts. She gave me your address. She asked me to to tell you she was sorry."

# 21.

The American Eagle was to change everything. Just when I was at my lowest ebb, it provided a lifeline. It was more than a job. It quickly became a venue to meet interesting people and make new friends and enjoy myself. The American Eagle became a social club, not just for the GIs who frequented it, but also for me.

It was run by two older officers – Pete Bukowski and Bob Ruffino – and they took a fatherly interest in the young soldiers who passed through the doors. After the regime in the Grand Central Hotel, with it's relentless parade of people demanding to be fed, work at the Eagle was a pleasure. The Americans had a relaxed, egalitarian attitude to the job. I didn't have to start until six o'clock and I finished at eleven. By that time, the trams had stopped running but somebody always gave me a lift back to my digs, or the club paid for a taxi.

I had two days free and the pay was thirty shillings a week. To me, it was a fortune. On top of that, I got tips, which often came to another pound a week. I was very well off, much better than I could ever have imagined.

On my first evening, I was introduced to Paul Brady, who was the head barman. He showed me how the system worked. I was to take the orders for drinks and ferry them to the tables. Occasionally, when things got busy, I was to help at the bar. Paul taught me how to make the different cocktails and what they cost.

On my second evening, Pete Bukowski took me aside and said: "Stella, our mission is to make our guests as comfortable as possible. Try to remember that they have left their families behind in America to come and fight this war in Europe. And some of them won't be going home."

Officially, I was known as a 'hostess'. It was an American term and I thought it sounded quite smart. Tess O'Neill was the other 'hostess'. A small woman with dusty-brown hair and a big bust, she had the energy of a sparrow. Tess was very proud of her bust and always wore a tight blouse to show it off. When she served the floor, she walked with her back straight so that her breasts stuck out and the soldiers stared.

She was 25 and married with two small children and lived in a house on the Falls Road. Her husband, Gerry, was a milkman and looked after the children while she worked at the club. Tess was always jolly and she liked to banter with the soldiers.

She would say: "Poor guys. I feel sorry for them. Sure, it doesn't cost much to make them happy."

*

Few of the soldiers had been away from home before and they were lonely for their families. They would open their wallets and show me pictures of their parents and their girlfriends. They would boast about the great places they had left behind in America.

They reminded me of the old bachelor farmers who used to tell me their troubles in the bar of the Royal Hotel in Enniskillen. They had cute American names like you would hear in the films: Chuck and Buzz and Dean. They were clean-cut and handsome. I would just get to know them when one day they wouldn't show up any more, and when I inquired, I would be told they had been 'shipped out'. This meant they had gone to the War. People would just shake their heads and change the conversation. That was the sad part.

The highlight of the week was the Friday night dance. The club had its own professional dance band. They played swing music by Glenn Miller and Tommy Dorsey. Women soldiers came to the dances, and some of the officers. But the women were always in a minority and there was great competition to dance with them. They spoke in that smart American way that I quickly came to admire. I enjoyed observing them.

If a soldier was tipsy and they didn't want to dance with him, they would say: "Get lost, Buster." They could do the jitterbug and the new American dances. I thought them very sophisticated and would secretly practice talking as they did.

Because there were so few women, the soldiers would sometimes ask Tess or me for a dance. They would say: "May I have the pleasure of your company, Ma'am?" and, as they lead us out onto the floor, their friends would clap and shout encouragement.

Nobody minded if we danced with the soldiers and often, after work was finished, there were parties. One Friday night, Tess said to me: "There's a gang of us going back to somebody's flat on the Antrim Road. Why don't you come too, Stella?"

I was intrigued, but I wasn't sure if it was right.

"What about Gerry? Won't he mind?"

"Get away with you. Your head's full of feathers. What he doesn't know won't do him any harm. I'll tell him I was working late."

"I don't know."

"Och, c'mon. It's only a few drinks. Sure nothing's going to happen."

I went in the end and it was an enjoyable party. We sat around drinking and dancing to records and I didn't get back to the digs till 3 a.m. In the morning, I felt guilty and I couldn't get the thought of Bill out of my mind. By now our romance was blossoming. My new job meant we could see each other more often. It suited Tess to let me have Saturday and Sunday off, as her husband was off work and could look after the children. So, on the weekends, Bill would take me all over the city on the tram and afterwards we would go to a restaurant and have a nice meal.

One Saturday, he took me to the Zoo at Bellevue. It was a beautiful sunny afternoon and the trams were packed with day-trippers. Bill bought ice creams and we walked through the fields below Cave Hill till we came to a quiet place. We sat down and I waited for him to put his arms around my shoulders and kiss me.

I loved it when he kissed me. I got this beautiful warm feeling. I closed my eyes and thought of Clarke Gable and Claudette Colbert. He put his hand on my breast and squeezed my nipple. I didn't stop him. I knew it was wrong but it felt nice. I could feel him hard against me and I knew he was excited and that made me excited too.

"I think I'm falling in love with you," he said. "I think about you all the time. Even when I'm at work, hammering rivets in the shipyard, I can't help thinking about you."

I kept my eyes closed. It was just like the films.

"Tell me you love me too," he urged.

"I love you," I said.

His breath was hot against my cheek. I felt his hand on my leg, gently pressing the flesh above my knee.

"Let me show you how much I love you," he said.

His hand moved higher and suddenly I was afraid.

"No," I said. "Please don't do that."

I sat up quickly and brushed away his hand.

Bill sat looking sorry for himself.

"You can be so cruel, Stella. You lead me on and then you stop."

"It's not right."

"Oh to hell with that. We could be killed any day. What about all those poor people who died in the Blitz? Don't you think if they had known, they would have made love every chance they got?"

I leaned forward and kissed him gently on the lips.

"What you're asking is very special. I can only give it to one man. And that man is you. But you have to wait."

"Do you mean that, Stella?"

"Yes," I said. "Of course."

It was getting more difficult to carry on a romance in Mrs McCrudden's house. Some nights I would go to Bill's room. We would lie on his bed and kiss, but I could never relax. Mrs McCrudden didn't allow guests in each other's rooms and I was terrified she would find us.

I used to catch her sometimes, listening at the bottom of the stairs or along the landing. And it was almost impossible to come or go in the house without passing her look-out post in the front room. Her husband was worse. He still had not spoken to me and his eyes continued to follow me everywhere I went.

In the end, it was him who drove me out of the house altogether. It happened one Saturday afternoon. I had arranged to meet Bill in a bar downtown – we were going out dancing – and I was taking a bath. I got undressed in my room and slipped on my dressing gown and went down the landing to the bathroom.

Standing up to dry myself, I became aware of a moaning sound. I stopped and listened. It was a low whimpering and seemed to be coming from the room next door.

I pressed my ear to the wall and the sound got louder and then I noticed a small round hole in the plaster. I had never seen it before. I put my eye to the hole and felt my heart stop. Another eye was staring back at me.

I screamed and struggled out of the bath. I got into my dressing gown and ran from the room. Tommy was standing on the landing. There was a mad look in his eye. He held his penis in his hand and was rubbing it furiously.

"Whooaa," he said. "Isn't that a beauty? How'd you like that fella right up you?"

I couldn't believe this was happening. I closed my eyes and pushed past him and got to my room. I locked the door and sat on the bed, trembling with shock.

# 22.

I left Lizzie McCrudden's house that evening. The thought of spending another 24 hours under the same roof as Tommy gave me the creeps. I didn't tell her why I was going. I knew she wouldn't believe me and it would only cause trouble. I just said I had found somewhere else that was more convenient. Tommy kept out of my way and I never saw him again.

I told Tess what had happened and she said: "Well, chicken. You can move in with us. You can have the spare room and sure I could do with the money."

Number 28 Iveagh Place was another red-bricked house in a long terrace that seemed to shelter in the lee of a tall mill chimney. It was smaller than Mrs McCrudden's house but my bedroom was bigger and I was mercifully free from Tommy's prying eyes.

Now that we were living together, Tess and I grew closer. She had two little boys called Damien and Terry, and they were aged three and four. She said Damien was named after a priest who used to care for the lepers in Africa. Terry was named after her brother.

The boys had nice brown hair, like their mother, and were very good-natured children. They accepted me at once, calling me Auntie Stella. They loved me to read them stories out of a big picture book that sat on a sideboard in the parlour and they used to fight over who could sit on my knee.

Tess was the boss in her house. Gerry was quiet and he always did what she said. Sometimes she would bully him and it used to embarrass me. It made me think of Daddy and the way he was the centre of our household in Ballinaleck. But Gerry was different. He seemed content to let Tess make all the decisions. It made me uneasy to see a man so weak. I felt there was something not right. When I mentioned it to Tess, she just laughed and said: "Men need to know who's in charge, Stella. You have to humour them. Most of all, you have to put your foot down. If you don't, they just have no respect for you."

I often wondered if she really loved him. At the club, I would see her flirting with the soldiers and sometimes, when we went to parties, I would catch her kissing her partner when they were dancing. Once or twice, she even went off to a bedroom with a soldier and they would come back half an hour later, laughing and joking. I tried to think it was innocent, but something told me it might not be.

One evening, she said to me: "What about this fella you're going with?"

I told her all about Bill and she said: "Is he the first?"

"Yes," I said.

"Do you love him?"

"I'm not sure. Sometimes I think I do. I know he loves me."

"What age are you, Stella?"

"Eighteen."

"For God's sake, you're only a child. Take my advice and see a bit of life. Why do you want to tie yourself to one man?"

"Because he's kind and generous and I like him."

"Stella, all that can change. Don't make the mistake I did. I got married at nineteen and now I'm stuck with a husband and two kids. You're an attractive girl and the men like you. I see the way they look at you. You could have your pick of any of them. Go out and have a fling. Sure we could be all dead in the morning."

But I didn't want to see other men behind Bill's back. Even if Tess O'Neill thought it was okay, I thought it was a treacherous thing to do, that a woman who could do that to a man couldn't amount to much.

*

Bill wanted to know why I had left North Queen Street and moved in with Tess. He had never met her, but I think he suspected she was a bad influence on me. When I told him about Tommy, he said: "I'm going to break that swine's neck."

I said: "No, Bill. If you do that, you'll get arrested and then the whole business will have to go to court. It will be just my word against Tommy McCrudden's."

"A bastard like him should be locked up. He's dangerous."

I had never seen Bill so angry. He smashed his fist into the table of the cafe where we were sitting.

"I always knew there was something strange about him. The way he sits in the corner watching everything that's going on and never speaks a civil word to anyone. And this business about arthritis. It's all a cod. He's never done a day's work since I've been in that house. The man's a pervert."

I said: "Bill, if I'd known you were going to react like this, I wouldn't have told you. Promise me you'll let matters rest."

"I can't, Stella. The idea of another man looking at you like that drives me crazy."

"Promise me."

He buried his head in his hands.

"I promise," he said.

Over time I had noticed that Bill was growing more jealous and moody. If another man smiled at me or looked at me in the street, it would make him angry. The thought of me working in the American Eagle with all those Yankee soldiers really upset him. He began to pester me to give up my job.

"And what am I supposed to live on?"

"You'll easily get something else. They're crying out for people."

"That's not what happened the last time."

"The last time was different."

"No, Bill. I can't give it up. It's a good job. The pay is good and the people are nice to me. I'd never get another job like this again."

He held me tight.

"Give it up Stella and marry me."

I stared at him in amazement.

"What did you say?"

"You heard me."

"You're asking me to marry you?"

"Yes. I love you. I've loved you ever since I set eyes on you. Remember? Your first morning in the digs when you were waiting to use the bathroom? Marry me, Stella. I'm earning good money and I could earn more if I worked overtime. I've got some put away. We could get a house somewhere. We'd be so happy. You'd never have to work again."

I heard Tess's warning voice in my head.

"But I'm only eighteen."

"That's old enough. There's plenty of girls getting married younger than that."

"And I'm a Catholic and you're a Protestant."

"Oh to hell with religion! It doesn't matter."

"It does to some people."

"Not to me. I'll turn Catholic, if it makes you happy. Mrs McCrudden says I've got Catholic blood anyway."

I felt a storm of emotions surge in my breast.

"Bill, it's lovely of you to ask. I'm really flattered. But I can't give you an answer right now. I need time to think."

"That's all right," he said. "Take your time. But I won't give up. I'm not going to lose you, Stella."

*

Bill's proposal had caught me by surprise. It had never crossed my mind that he might want to marry me. I regarded our relationship as just a romance. When I told him I loved him, I said it to please him. It was like a game. I didn't think he would take it seriously. And now that he was talking about getting married, it made me panic.

I wrote to Kathleen and swore her to keep it a secret. I wondered what Mammy and Daddy would say, if they knew. They would surely disapprove. People frowned on mixed marriages. But Kathleen wrote back and said it sounded wonderful, and if I married him, she wanted to be my bridesmaid.

I knew there was no point asking Tess for advice. I knew what she would say. She would tell me to go out and enjoy myself and let Bill go. But apart from Tess, I couldn't think of anyone else to ask.

I spent days deciding what to do. Bill was a decent man and he would make a good husband. I knew he had faults like everyone else, but I could learn to accept them. In the end, it was my very indecision that convinced me. I told myself that if I really loved him, I would have no doubts. I would jump at the chance to marry him. But I had doubts and therefore I would have to turn him down.

I steeled myself to tell him, knowing how he would be. I picked an evening the following week when we were going out to the Ritz cinema to see a film. I had arranged to meet him for a drink in Robinson's hotel. Since my dismissal, I had never again set foot in the Grand Central.

He was waiting at the bar in a nice suit and tie. I could see at once that he was in a good mood. He kissed my cheek and called out to the barman for drinks.

I said: "Bill, I have something to tell you."

But before I could proceed, he interrupted me.

"And I have something for you."

He took a little box out of his pocket. It had been wrapped in fancy pink paper and tied with a bow.

"Here," he said. "Open it."

I untied the bow and opened the box. Inside was a gold locket and chain. I undid the clasp and the locket sprang open. There was a picture of Bill inside. I was astonished. No one had ever bought me a present like this before.

"It's beautiful," I said. "It must have cost a fortune."

He took the locket and placed it round my neck.

"I want you to wear it always. To remind you of me."

I felt my earlier resolution melt away.

"Oh Bill, you're far too good for me."

# 23.

Tess wanted to know where I got the locket, and when I told her, she said: "My God, chicken. It's beautiful. He must be cracked about you."

"He wants to marry me."

"Well at least he's putting his money where his mouth is. Not like some of these chancers that's going about turning young girls heads and when the babby comes along they can't be found. What did you tell him?"

"I said I needed to think about it."

"You did the right thing, Stella. It's none of my business, but it's not like he's the only fish in the sea. You'll have plenty of fellas chasing you. You just take your time and see a wee bit of life before you settle down, because you might be a long time regretting it."

"But I like him, Tess, and I don't want to hurt him."

"Chicken, you listen to me. Not wanting to hurt a man is just about the worst reason to marry him."

I agonised for weeks but I could never get up the nerve to tell Bill. I just had to see him waiting for me in a bar or a cafe, all spruced up and smiling, and my courage would fail. He was always kind, always considerate. He was generous and good-hearted. He made me laugh. Hurting Bill would be like hurting myself.

His biggest fault was his jealousy. He kept pestering me to leave the American Eagle, and grew hostile to Tess and suspicious of any man I came in contact with. And he kept pressing me for a decision to marry him.

One evening, in the Unicorn bar, he said: "I'm going home to

Ballymena this weekend. Would you like to come with me and meet my family?"

I felt my heart jump.

"Why would they want to meet me, Bill?"

"Because I've told them all about you and they're dying to see you. We'll have a great time. I can get the loan of a car and take you up to Portrush."

I began to panic. Meeting Bill's family would move our relationship on to a new plane. It would enmesh me further. It would make it even harder to break with him.

I said: "Bill, I don't think that's a good idea."

"Why not?"

I summoned all my courage.

"Because I've decided not to marry you."

I saw his face crumble and his smile wither away. Immediately, I felt sorry for him.

"Is it because of our religion?"

"No. It's nothing like that. It's just that I don't think I'm ready. Marriage is a big responsibility."

"I told you I'd wait. I'm in no hurry, Stella. We could get engaged. As long as I know you're going to marry me in the end, I'll be happy to wait."

"No, Bill. I don't want to get engaged."

At this, he began to get angry.

"You've found someone else. One of those flash Yankees in that damned club. You think I'm not good enough for you, any more."

"No. I'm very fond of you. Why do you think I keep going out with you?"

"Then it's Tess O'Neill. She's turned you against me. This only started when you met her."

"It's got nothing to do with Tess O'Neill. Or the club. It's me. I'm not sure. And when I decide to get married, I want to be absolutely certain."

"You've led me on," he said, bitterly. "All that kissing and cuddling.

And you told me you loved me. What was I supposed to think? I'm only flesh and blood. You've led me on and all the time, you were never serious."

His remark stung. I said: "Bill. That's not true."

"Yes it is. You're a schemer, Stella. You used me when you had nobody, and now that you've found fancy new friends, you don't want to know me any more."

I could see he was on the verge of tears. I reached out and put my arms around him.

"Bill. Let's not say anything we'll regret."

He pushed me away.

"I'll say what I damned well like. You don't want to hear the truth. You're a scheming bitch, Stella, and I curse the day I ever met you."

He got up and stormed out of the bar and left me sitting alone. I could see people staring at me, but I didn't care. I had finally broken the news to Bill. It was as if a great weight had been lifted off my shoulders and, even though his words had hurt me, finally I was free.

I went back to Iveagh Place and took off the locket and chain. I put them in an envelope and posted it to Bill. I didn't enclose any note.

When Tess saw I was no longer wearing the locket, she asked: "Did you have a wee row? Did you fall out with him?"

I told her what had happened.

"The cheek of him!" she said. "These fellas think they can take you out to the pictures and buy you some jewellery and then they own you. You did the right thing, Stella. You're better off without him."

The following night at the Eagle, I saw her flirting with some officers. She called me over and introduced me.

"This is Glenn. We're going to a party after the club closes. Why don't you come? Glenn has a car and he can drive us home."

I looked at him. He was about thirty. He had blond hair and nice blue eyes. He pulled a silly face.

"What do you say, Stella?"

"Sure," I said. "Why not?"

*

A few weeks after we broke up, Bill wrote to me at the club. He apologised for what had happened and begged me to forgive him. He pleaded with me to see him. He promised that he would never again raise the question of marriage.

I thought about the letter for several days, but I never replied. I knew Bill wouldn't change, no matter how much he promised. I knew we would only argue again. I realised something else. Tess had been right. I was too young. I hadn't lived life. And now that I had my freedom, why should I surrender it?

# 24.

On Tess's advice, I threw myself into a wild social whirl. Every night now it was parties. The cast kept changing. Young men would be around the American Eagle for a few weeks and then they'd be gone overseas. For me, these parties were just a bit of fun, a chance to relax and enjoy myself. We'd drink, play records and dance. Sometimes, if I liked the man I was with, I would let him kiss me and maybe we would have a cuddle.

But Tess was less restrained than me. She had the attitude of a lot of people during that time: you never know when you're going to die and therefore you should get the most out of life while you can. I would see her kissing passionately and occasionally disappearing into a bedroom with a soldier.

When I asked her about it, she just shrugged and said. "Chicken, you've only got one cherry. And when it's gone, it's gone. All you're left with is the box that the cherry came in."

She nudged me and laughed.

Occasionally, a man would take my fancy and I would let him bring me out to lunch or for drives in his car. I accepted presents. They bought me perfume and nylons and chocolates and clothes. I saw no harm in it. I knew it was only for a while and then they'd be gone.

Before Christmas, I went home to Ballinaleck. Outside the station, there was frost on the ground and the fields had a sad, empty look. Beside the ditches, I could see the cattle huddled together for warmth and their breath hanging like steam in the air.

Daddy met me and we drove along the twisting road to the house.

He brought me up to date with the news. The farm was going well and he was paying off the bank. Soon, he would be a free man again. Kathleen was getting good results at school and Michael was going out with a local girl called Molly Teeling.

I remembered her. She was a frumpy young woman about twenty and she worked as a shop assistant in Mooney's drapery store in Enniskillen. Daddy said he was worried that Michael might marry her and give up the farm altogether and then how would he manage on his own?

"Why would he want to do that?" I said. "Won't he get the farm when you retire?"

"He may not want to be a farmer. That young hussy has his head turned with notions about a factory job. She's telling him the work is easier and the pay is better. That's all right while the War lasts. But what's going to happen when it's over? Land is land, Stella. And people always have to eat."

Mammy and Kathleen were waiting for us at the house. Mammy fussed over me and made me sit up to the fire while she made the tea. She had already put up the Christmas decorations and stuck clumps of holly around the pictures in the kitchen. She produced a cake and wanted to know all about my job and how I was getting on in Belfast. I had put on a little suit with a lace frill around the collar and a white blouse and scarf, specially for the occasion. Mammy looked me up and down and said: "My God, Stella, but you look like a film star and you dressed up to the nines. How do you afford all those lovely clothes?"

I laughed.

"I work hard."

When we had drunk our tea, I gave them their presents. I had got a dress for Mammy, tobacco for Daddy and an expensive silk scarf for Kathleen. It had been a gift from a boyfriend. She shrieked with joy when she saw it and put it round her neck and ran to the mirror to admire herself. It made me happy to see the simple pleasure the presents gave.

Mammy said: "And I've got a great bit of news for you. Bridgie's pregnant. She's expecting in May. She's been to the doctor and it's all confirmed."

I wasn't surprised. It was what I knew would happen. But now, I felt no envy for her. Bridgie had chosen a different life to me. She had settled down and naturally she wanted children. I was too busy enjoying myself to think of marriage and family.

The person I most liked talking to was Kathleen. When she got me alone, she demanded to hear all about the excitement of the big city.

"Is it true they put the lights out and everybody has to go around in the dark?"

"Don't be silly. It's just the street lights. You can still keep the lights on inside the house if you keep the curtains drawn."

"And why do they want to do that?"

"In case the Germans come back to bomb us. If there's no lights they can't see what they're doing."

"I don't think that will work," she said. "It just means they'll bomb something they didn't mean to bomb. Tell me about this place you work in. Are there lots of lovely Yankees?"

"Loads."

"Are they glamorous?"

"Very."

"And do they ask you up to dance?"

"All the time."

"Do they ask you for a date?"

"Of course. I have them driven mad with passion for me."

"And is Bill not jealous?"

"I broke it off with him," I said.

Kathleen jumped on top of me and started to box my ears.

"Whaaat? You scab you. You never told me. What happened?"

*

The weekend passed quickly. Outside Mass on Sunday, all the neighbours came to talk to me and ask how I was getting on. I could see the younger women admiring my clothes and my hair. It reminded me of the time before the War, when Uncle James used to send us parcels from America.

After lunch, I went for a walk through the fields. Daddy and Michael had done a good job. The farm was tidy and neatly fenced and the cattle looked fat and healthy. Unbidden, Martin came into my mind. I realised that nobody had talked about him since I had come back. It was as if they had made a pact not to mention him in case it made me sad. I thought of the happy times we had here when we were young and my eyes filled up with tears. Unable to walk any further, I turned back to the house.

The morning I was leaving, Mammy cooked a big breakfast of ham, eggs and fried bread.

When I protested, she said: "I don't think you're looking after yourself, Stella. You're far too skinny."

"That's the fashion now. All the women want to be thin."

"Rubbish. Any man with any sense would want a woman with a bit of meat on her bones."

Daddy drove me to the station and waited till the train pulled in. As I went to board, he held me close and said: "It was lovely to see you again, Stella. You know, things haven't been the same since you left. We all miss you."

"I miss you too."

He held my hand as I turned to go.

"There's something I want to tell you. This is your home. Whatever happens to you, I want you to remember that."

I got on the train and sat beside the window. But there was none of the sadness I had felt before. This time, I was glad to go. I couldn't wait to get back to the city and the excitement. I didn't know it, but it would be a long time before I would return. And when I did, everything would be changed.

*

One evening in the club, somebody said: "I think it's only a matter of time now till the War is over. We're going into Europe and Hitler's on the run."

The wireless and the papers had been full of it for weeks. I didn't pay much attention. The fighting had been going on for as long as I could remember and sometimes it seemed it would never end.

But I began to notice a new confidence among the officers and soldiers in the American Eagle. They had an optimism that I hadn't seen before. The thought occurred to me that maybe the War really was coming to end and I began to consider what I would do when it happened.

A couple of evenings later, Pete Bukowski came rushing into the bar about nine o'clock. I had just taken an order and was standing at the counter while Paul Brady got it ready.

Pete went up onto the stage and stopped the dance music. Then he took the microphone. The conversation died away. People waited expectantly to hear what he had to say.

"Everybody listen. I've just heard some great news on the radio. General Eisenhower has announced that the allied troops have landed in France."

The room burst into clapping and whistling. People stood up and cheered.

"The general says our armies landed this morning on the coast of Normandy. You know what this means? The invasion of Europe is under way. And if I know Ike, we'll be in Berlin faster than the Führer can whistle Dixie."

The place went wild. People jumped up and hugged each other. A young soldier at the bar put his arms around me and kissed me.

"Isn't that the best Goddamned news? I can't believe it."

"It's great," I said, laughing.

"I just feel so happy."

He held out his hand.

"My name's Bud. Can I get you a drink?"

"Maybe later."

"Oh, c'mon. We've got to celebrate."

He turned to Paul Brady and slapped some money on the counter.

"Give the lady a Blond Bombshell."

The room was going mad. The dance music had started up again and people were jitterbugging. There were more men than women, but that didn't seem to matter. On stage a groups of soldiers had linked arms and were singing: *Ma, I miss your apple pie.* I saw Tess caught in the middle of them and she waved.

The excitement gripped me. I lifted the Blond Bombshell and drained it, and a warm glow swept over me.

The celebrations went on till after midnight. Nearly everyone was tipsy. People kept buying me drinks till my head was light and I felt unsteady on my feet.

At closing time, Tess came to me and said: "There's a gang has ordered taxis and we're going to somebody's flat for a do. You have to come."

I felt myself sway.

"Stella! Are you all right?"

"I'm fine. We're going to kick Hitler's ass."

Tess wrapped her arms around me.

"Atta girl, Stella. You only live once."

The flat was packed when we arrived. The men had brought bottles and everyone was drinking. Couples were dancing to records. I took off my coat and someone put a martini into my hand. I felt a tap on my shoulder and turned to see the young soldier from the bar.

"It's me again. Bud. Mind if we dance?"

"Why not?"

He took me in his arms and we moved to the music. All around us, people were laughing and singing. I felt incredibly happy and relaxed. At the back of my head, a voice told me I was drunk, but I didn't care.

Bud's lips were moving and I realised he was speaking to me.

"What's your name?"

"Stella," I shouted, above the noise.

"You're very beautiful, Stella."

"Thank you."

I looked at him. He was quite handsome. He had lovely dark eyes and black hair and a strong face and chin. I thought of Clark Gable.

"Can I kiss you, Stella?"

I leaned my mouth into his warm lips and felt a shiver run along my spine. I closed my eyes and he kissed me again.

Bud took my hand and led me across the room. All I could see were faces and they were laughing and happy.

We were on a bed in a room. Bud was kissing me again. It was beautiful. I felt his hands moving along my breasts, undoing the buttons on my dress. I didn't try to stop him. I didn't care. I pulled him down and kissed him hard. His tongue pushed past my teeth and into my mouth. I closed my eyes and he entered me. I felt a dart of pain and then a surge of pleasure.

I wanted it to go on and on and never stop. The feeling built to a climax and then I heard Bud moan. I bit his shoulder and felt this warm explosion filling my body with wave after wave of pleasure.

# 25.

I don't remember getting home, or what time it was when myself and Tess did arrive. All I remember was standing in Tess's kitchen and Gerry in his pyjamas demanding, in an angry voice, to know where we had been.

Tess brazened it out.

"Did you not hear the news? Sure the Yankees have landed in France and the War's nearly over. Everybody was celebrating. The club was like a madhouse tonight. We're only just finished."

"Stella looks drunk," he said.

"Your head's cut. She tired, that's all. Sure, the cratur's been run off her feet. Just like me. I'll get her to bed and then I'm going myself."

Tess took my arms and guided me up the stairs to my bedroom. She undressed me and tucked me under the sheets.

"My God, Stella. You're a dark horse," she whispered. "That was some glamour-puss you were with tonight."

"Bud ..." I said.

"What, Stella?"

"His name is Bud."

I closed my eyes and everything went dark.

*

I woke with the worst headache I have ever known. My stomach felt sick and my tongue seemed stuck to the roof of my mouth. I stared at the bedside clock and saw it was twenty past ten. I covered my eyes with the sheet as the events of the previous night filtered through.

Then, I remembered what had happened in the bedroom and was immediately filled with remorse.

The remorse quickly gave way to fear. I got out of bed and hurried to the bathroom. I got into the bath and scrubbed myself all over. I remembered reading somewhere that you should always wash after sex and wondered if it was too late. I washed myself thoroughly and then I got dried and went back to my room to dress.

Downstairs, Tess had prepared tea and toast but I couldn't eat. She sat across the table and studied me.

"You look like something the cat dragged in. How do you feel?"

"Rotten. I'm never going to drink again."

"You were langers, Stella. Sure you were knocking back the Blond Bombshells like they were going out of fashion. Drink up your tea and you'll feel better."

She took a bottle of asprin out of the cupboard and gave me two tablets.

"Get them into you. They'll help the headache, anyway."

Damien and Terry were watching me silently from the sofa. I couldn't bear to look at them.

Tess lowered her voice.

"Did you do anything with that fella?"

I shook my head.

"Well, thank God for that. I had an awful job convincing Gerry we were working late. He's not an eeejit, you know. He can put two and two together. We'll have to be more careful the next time."

I drank the tea and then felt ill. I rushed back to the bathroom and was sick into the bowl. I vomited till there was nothing left and my throat felt raw. The bathroom was filled with the smell. I flushed the toilet and opened the window to let in fresh air. Then I sat on the toilet seat and felt a cold sweat break across my forehead.

I hadn't prayed for a long time but I got down on my knees beside the bath and begged God that I would be all right. I knew the hangover would pass. It was the other thing that worried me. I swore to God that I would never do it again. I heard Tess knocking on the bathroom door.

"Are you all right in there, Stella?"

"Yes," I said. "I'll be out in a minute."

*

That night in the club, I felt jittery. I could barely concentrate on my work due to embarrassment. I kept waiting for people to come in and talk about the party. I thought they would all know what had happened. I thought they would be looking at me and whispering behind my back. "There's Stella. She got loaded last night and went to bed with Bud." But if they knew, nobody said. All they were interested in was the invasion and the fighting in Normandy.

I dreaded Bud coming in. I didn't know how I would look at him or what I would say. I was consumed with shame. All night long I watched for his dark, handsome face to show up in the crowd, but he didn't appear. I was relieved. At twenty past eleven, Tess and I got into a taxi and drove through the darkened streets to her house. I was grateful to get into bed and pull the bedclothes tight around me.

Bud didn't show up the following night or the night after. The thought occurred to me that he was avoiding me for the same reason that I dreaded meeting him. He was ashamed of what had happened. I began to wonder if I would ever see him again. But as the days passed, other events pushed him out of my mind. Normality pressed in and I had little time to think about him. Tess's little boy Terry got sick and she had to take time off work. I had to cover for her so I was busier than usual.

The mood in the club changed. Now, there was a whiff of victory in the air. Everybody was talking of getting to Europe and kicking Hitler's ass. People couldn't wait to go. The allied forces were pushing through France and the Germans were in retreat. I wrote to Daddy and told him what I heard in the club; that the Americans were confident of success and the War was definitely coming to an end.

One night, I heard a familar voice at my shoulder. I was at the bar, waiting for Paul Brady to fill an order. I turned and Ed Costigan was by my side. He was with another officer, a plump, fair-haired man with a small moustache.

"It's Stella, isn't it? You remember me?"

"Of course. Major Costigan."

"So you took my advice. I hope they're looking after you?"

"Yes, indeed. I'm very happy here."

Ed Costigan smiled.

"I'm glad things worked out for you, Stella. You're a plucky young woman. You deserve to succeed."

"Did I ever thank you?"

"What for? All I did was make an introduction. You did the rest yourself."

He took his drink and sat down at a table near the door. I wished I could have talked longer to him. There was a quality about him, a solidness and a decency that reassured me. But I was busy serving tables and when I looked for him again, he was gone.

Terry recovered and Tess returned to work. There seemed to be more soldiers and more parties. Almost every day, men were leaving for France and there were farewell celebrations. I threw myself into the festivities but I was careful now about how much I drank.

A couple of weeks later, we were at a party on the Lisburn Road. A soldier was miming to a Bing Crosby record and a bunch of colleagues were in a circle around him offering encouragement. A few couples were dancing. Everybody was drinking and having a good time.

A young private came and sat beside me.

"Excuse me. Don't I know you from somewhere?"

I looked into his face but I didn't recognise him.

"I don't think so."

"I've seen you before."

"I'm a Hostess in the Eagle. Maybe that's where you've seen me."

"No. It wasn't there. Some place else. Weren't you at a party a few weeks back? Weren't you with Bud?"

At the mention of his name, I felt my heart skip.

"That's right."

"Bud always had an eye for a good-looking woman. That's how I remember you."

I picked up my courage.

"How is he?" I said.

"Didn't he tell you?"

"Tell me what?"

The young man looked embarrassed.

"He's gone. He was shipped to Europe two weeks ago."

# 26.

I'd been waiting for my period, counting off the days in a little diary I kept in my handbag. It was always regular, so when the day arrived and it didn't come, a cold anxiety began to creep over me. I tried to busy myself so I wouldn't think about it, but as the morning slowly passed into the afternoon, I became distracted with worry. Where was my period? Why didn't it come? By the time evening came round, the worry had given way to panic.

I told myself it was sure to arrive the next day. Before I got into bed, I prayed to Our Lady and St Jude. I felt it wasn't right to be praying for something like your period to come. If I had behaved myself in the first place, if I had followed the advice that Mammy and my teachers and even stupid Mary O'Connor had all given me, I wouldn't be in this situation. Down on my knees on the cold oilcloth in the bedroom praying to Our Lady. If I hadn't got drunk and given into my own lust, I wouldn't be here now, unable to think because I was terrified I might be pregnant.

There was no sign of it the next day either. I got up at seven o'clock and had a hot bath. I had heard somewhere that this sometimes caused your period to come. I made the bath as hot as I could bear and lay in the water and examined myself, hoping to see blood. But there was none. When the water was cold, I got out of the bath, dried myself and went down to the kitchen to see Tess.

She said: "You're up early, chicken. Could you not sleep?"

I wanted to tell her. I wanted to tell somebody. I wanted to hear reassuring words. But I was afraid that Tess would only laugh at me and tell me my head was full of feathers. So I just pretended everything was all right.

"The sun woke me," I said. It's such a nice morning that I thought it would be a waste to lie in bed."

"Well suit yourself. I'm going out to get some messages, so you can come with me."

She was getting Damien and Terry ready, combing their hair and washing their faces. I ate some toast and watched her fussing around the house. She was happy and carefree. I thought what pleasure there was in simple things when you had nothing to worry you. We went out to the shop at the top of the street where Tess bought her groceries, then we went for a walk in Falls Park. The boys fought over who could hold my hand. They played on the swings and Tess and I sat on a bench and watched.

"You're not yourself, Stella," Tess said. "You seem very quiet. Are you sure you're all right?"

I told her I was tired.

"Is something bothering you? Maybe that's why you can't sleep?"

"No."

Tess began to smile.

"You're still thinking about Bill. You're still fond of him. Is that what it is?"

"Yes," I lied.

She nudged me and laughed.

"Och, for God's sake, chicken. Never lose sleep over a man. Put him out of your head. You'll soon forget all about him."

*

I knew they had medical books in the Central Library on Royal Avenue. They had a reference section that had books on everything; encyclopedias and dictionaries. So in the afternoon, I told Tess I was going into town early to look around the shops. The library was quiet as a church, just a few old pensioners getting a free read of the papers. The light was streaming in the big windows as I climbed the stairs to the reference section. I went to the desk and told the woman what I was looking for and she got me to fill out a card.

I was so nervous that I put my home address on the card and then I had to tear it up and fill out another one with Tess's address. I thought the woman would be suspicious, able to read my mind, but she didn't pay any attention. She just took the card and told me to find a seat and, a few minutes later, a porter with a cart brought the big medical dictionary to where I was sitting.

I opened the pages. There was a dry, musty smell off them. They were shiny and filled with pictures and diagrams. I didn't know where to start and I was afraid to ask. I thought there would be a section on periods but there wasn't. I went to the front of the book and looked at the contents and found the page for the human body.

It was called 'menstruation'. It said it was the monthly discharge of blood from the vagina in women of childbearing age. Vagina meant down there. I knew that much. It said the cessation of the period was the first indication of pregnancy. I felt my skin grow cold when I read that. It said sometimes the period was irregular. This could be caused if a woman was unwell or had suffered a shock. Even a common cold could cause it. It said the cessation of the period alone was not a definite indicator that a woman was pregnant. A medical examination was also necessary.

I closed the book and stared across the silent library floor. I could feel my heart beating in my breast. My periods had always been like clockwork. Nothing had ever disrupted them before. But it was a straw and I clutched at it. Maybe I'd been working too hard and was run down.

I told myself I was stupid for worrying like this just because I was a couple of days late. What were the chances of getting pregnant the first time? They must be a thousand to one. Women were married for years and having sex all the time and they didn't get pregnant. The thought gave me hope. I told myself my period would come. If it didn't come this month, it would surely come next.

I got up and left the book on the desk; immediately I felt better. I went down the wide stairs and out to the busy street. I made up my mind to put the whole notion right out of my head and get on with my business. But just for insurance, I went round the corner to St Patrick's chapel and lit a candle before the statue of Our Lady of Lourdes.

But by the next month, when my period still hadn't arrived, I was in terror. I stripped naked before the mirror in the bathroom and stared at my body. I had been proud of it and now I hated it because it was letting me down. I willed my period to come. I had always hated it, all the messing with sanitary pads. Now I wished for it more than anything else in the world. The sight of blood would have been the most joyful thing to me. It would have been a cause of celebration. But there was no blood and no period and now I was certain I was pregnant.

After a week, I could no longer bear it. I had to talk to someone and the only person I could turn to was Tess. I remember it was a hot morning in August. It had been hot for days, and the wireless said we were having a heatwave. After she had fed the boys, I said: "Tess. There's something I need to talk to you about."

I think she must have seen it in my face, for she gave the boys slices of bread and jam and told them to go out and play in the yard.

"What is it, Stella? You can tell me. I've noticed for weeks you're worried about something."

"I think I'm pregnant."

For a moment, she didn't speak.

"Why do you think that?"

"Because I've missed my period."

Tess tossed her head.

"Och, chicken. That's not unusual. That doesn't mean a thing."

"I've missed two. And I've never missed before. I'm worried sick. What am I going to do?"

I began to cry and Tess cuddled me close. I could feel her hand gently stroking my hair.

"It's not the end of the world, love. We'll get you to Dr McNamee and he'll find out for sure. Let's just cross one bridge at a time."

I was in floods of tears now, but Tess's words were like balm.

"It's happening all the time. There's half a dozen girls in the district in the same boat. It's the War, Stella. People are only human. McNamee has his surgery in half an hour. Get your coat and I'll take you."

I got up and wiped my eyes.

"Who do you think it might be?" she said.

"Bud. He's the only one."

"That nice-looking guy at the party?"

"Yes."

"And he's gone, isn't he?"

"Yes."

Tess slowly shook her head.

"Och, God help you, chicken. You're having lousy luck."

*

Dr McNamee was a young man in a white shirt and tie. He looked not much older than me and he was nervous and embarrassed when he came to examine me. He started by asking me about my last act of intercourse. His face was crimson. I had the date imprinted on my mind and I told him and he wrote it down.

"When you say, last. There was only the once," I said.

He looked at me.

"Right."

He scribbled again in his notepad.

"When was your last period?"

I told him. I could see him noting the lack of ring on my wedding finger. He asked me to undress and get up on his couch. I felt ashamed taking my clothes off, even in front of a doctor. Maybe it was because he was so young. He felt my breasts and stomach and gave me a little bottle and told me to go into the bathroom and take a sample. I didn't know what he meant, so I stood there with the bottle in my hand, looking like a fool.

"A urine sample, Miss Maguire. I want you to pass water into the bottle."

I was mortified. I went into the bathroom and tried to pee but it wouldn't come. I could hear Doctor McNamee scribbling in his note-pad outside and it only made it worse. I closed my eyes and tried to forget where I was. I counted to ten and suddenly the pee began, a dribble at first and then a rush so that the bottle overflowed and I wet my legs.

Dr McNamee took the bottle and put a seal on it and wrote my name on a little tab. He looked as relieved as I was that it was all over.

"I can't say for definite, Miss Maguire. But the sample will be conclusive one way or another. I should have the results back in a couple of days. Come back and see me then."

I couldn't sleep. I shifted in bed. I lay on my back and my side but the terrible worry weighed on my mind like a stone and kept me awake. Tess gave me a nightcap of whiskey and hot milk and I dozed off and had awful dreams. Mary O'Connor and Miss Brankin were pointing at my fat stomach. All the class were laughing. Miss Brankin sat at the piano and said: "Now girls, sing after me. Stellie Maguire is going to the home." I woke with the sheets drenched in sweat.

The day came for the results. I got up early and helped Tess with the boys. I kept busy so I would stay calm. I didn't want to break down and make a fool of myself. On the way out the door, Tess said: "Remember, Stella, whatever happens, you're not the first and you won't be the last. And I'll be here to help you."

In that moment, I loved Tess.

I knew the result as soon as I went into Dr McNamee's surgery. He kept his head down and wouldn't look me straight in the face. His words were no surprise to me. He just spoke as if I wasn't in the room at all.

He said: "The results have come back and they're positive. You're ten weeks pregnant."

# 27.

My first thoughts were for Mammy. She was the one I felt sorry for. She was the one who would suffer. I was pregnant and it was my own fault. In my mind, I had already accepted the truth, even before the doctor told me. But poor Mammy was innocent. She had done nothing wrong and she would have to carry the terrible shame.

I couldn't bear to think about it. If word got out at home, I wouldn't be able to show my face around the place again. The only ones who ever got pregnant like that were skivvies, and some of the others who weren't right in the head. It just didn't happen to respectable girls like me. It meant you were no better than a slut and your child was a bastard.

On the way back from the doctor's, Tess called into an off-licence and bought a bottle of Manley's South African sherry. They wrapped it up for her in soft tissue paper and put it in a brown bag. When we got to the house, she took off her coat, got two cups and filled them with wine.

"Either this is a celebration or else it's a wake. Whatever it is, I need a drink," she said.

I took a sip of the stuff. It had a sweet, cloying taste and it made me feel sick.

Tess said: "Stella. We've got to talk about this. What are you going to do?"

"I don't know."

"Can you go home to Fermanagh?"

"Oh God, no. I couldn't do that. If my parents found out, it would destroy them."

"Do you want to keep it?"

"How do you mean?"

"Well there's ways of getting rid of it. There's a woman in Sandy Row. She's a retired nurse ..."

I stared at her. I couldn't believe she was talking like this. It made me angry. I said: "How could you even suggest such a thing? You're talking about abortion. That's murder. This child is a living human being inside my body."

Tess got all excited and waved her arms.

"For God's sake, calm down. I'm not suggesting anything. I'm only giving you the options. If you want to keep it, bully for you."

"Of course I want to keep it."

She drained her cup and filled it up again.

"Well, it's not going to be easy, Stella. But if that's what you want, I'm right behind you. I suppose the first thing we should do is try and find the father. What's his name again?"

"Bud."

"What's his surname?"

I couldn't look at her. I turned my face away at the terrible shame of it.

"I don't know."

"Jesus Christ, Stella. Don't tell me you let this guy screw you and you don't even know his name?"

Suddenly, I realised how people would see it. I wasn't just a slut. I was a whore. I had sex with people I didn't even know. If someone like Tess was shocked, how would others react? I felt lost. My predicament was hopeless. I sunk my head in my hands.

"I know you won't believe me, Tess. But it was my very first time. I never did it before."

Tess wrapped her arms around me.

"There, there," she said. "Of course I believe you. It's always the same. Sure, the ones who've had practice never get caught."

*

142

I had to go back to see the doctor. He told me I would have to go for check-ups at the Maternity Hospital, and that I'd have to take orange juice and cod liver oil supplements to build me up. Handing me the prescription, he asked:

"Can you afford to pay for these?"

"How much will it cost?"

"A month's supply is ten shillings."

"I can afford it," I said.

He wrote me a letter and made an appointment for the hospital. When he was finished, he said: "You're a healthy young woman. You should have a normal pregnancy. Just take care of yourself. Try to get plenty of rest. Avoid stress and eat properly."

"How much do I owe you?"

His face coloured and I saw he was embarrassed again.

"You don't owe me anything."

"But I've had three visits. I have to pay you."

Dr McNamee pretended not to hear.

"You're going to need your money, Miss Maguire. You'll have to buy things for your baby. The visits are free."

In my anxiety, I hadn't even thought of money. But what the doctor said forced me to consider it. If I managed to keep my condition secret, I could work for another four months before it would show. I had about £15 saved and I could probably save another £10 if I tried hard. But once it became obvious I was pregnant, they would let me go.

I would have to buy baby clothes and a pram and lots of other things. There might be medical bills. I would have to feed myself and pay my rent. I would have to do all this out of the money I had saved because I wouldn't be able to work. I thought that if I could find Bud, I might be able to persuade him to contribute in some way. But I didn't know where he was. I didn't even know where to start looking for him.

It all seemed too much for me to cope. I sunk into a depression, moping around the house and going for long walks. I grew listless and distracted at work. At night, I lay in bed and cursed myself for what had happened. I had made one simple mistake and God had punished me. Why me, when so many others got away? In my distress, I blamed everyone. Bud, myself, Tess. The only one I didn't blame was the unborn child in my womb.

Eventually, Tess said: "You've got to snap out of this, Stella. You've got to stop feeling sorry for yourself. You're not the only girl found herself in the puddin' club and no man."

"It just seems so unfair."

"That's as maybe. But moping around the house isn't going to help. You've got to start living again."

I sat down and wrote a long letter to Mammy. I tried to be as cheerful as possible, telling her again about all the wonderful things that were happening to me in Belfast. I wanted to allay any suspicions for I realised I wouldn't be visiting my family again for a long time. At all costs, I had to keep it secret. Nobody at home must ever know. I knew if Mammy found out, it would break her heart.

I tried to find Bud. At work, I dropped hints about him in a casual way, hoping to discover more. But the crowd was constantly changing and no one could tell me anything. Soon, there was nobody who even remembered him. I asked Pete Bukowski and he said: "What does this guy look like?"

I described Bud.

"Does he have a second name?"

"I don't know it."

He gave me a quizzical look.

"Have you taken a shine to this guy, Stella?"

I blushed and made up a story about borrowing a record from him and wanting to give it back.

"I'd keep the record, if I was you. He could be anywhere. Sure, half the men in the US army are called Bud."

My next step was to contact Ed Costigan. He was a Major and I thought he might be able to help. He took down the scant details I could give and said he would get back to me. A week later he called to say he had checked the lists of men serving in Northern Ireland but, without a surname or an army number, the task was hopeless.

Tess tried to find out too. She asked around, even checking with the people who owned the flat where the party was held. But it turned out that it was rented and the people who lived there had gone. Bud seemed to have vanished. In the end, I gave up asking about him. It was only drawing attention.

Slowly, my body changed. My breasts became fuller and the nipples grew dark and hard, the little ring around them spreading wider. I had to buy a bigger bra. My stomach didn't show much in the beginning, but finally it changed too and I began to put on weight. Every week I weighed myself on the scales in Dinan's Chemist on the Falls Road and wrote down the weight gain in my diary.

I never got cravings. Tess said she got cravings when she was pregnant, a different thing each time. With Terry it was coal. She got a passion for coal and tried to eat it. Even when the doctor told her to stop, she still kept doing it. With Damien, it was tomatoes. She got the worst cravings in the middle of winter when there was hardly a tomato to be found and Gerry had to hunt all over the city for them, just to satisfy her.

I bought a book about pregnancy which said that morning sickness was common in the early months. But I didn't get it. What I got was a bigger appetite. Tess encouraged me.

She slipped me extra portions at lunch time. She was very particular about vegetables, especially carrots, which I hated. But Tess swore by them. She said they were full of Vitamin A which was very good for the skin. She would force me to eat them, sitting across the table and staring at me till I gulped down every one.

I got my cod liver oil and orange juice. They came in bottles and I took a tablespoon every morning like the label said. The orange juice was nice but the cod liver oil tasted vile. I was very healthy. I wore loose clothes to disguise my condition. It worked for a while, but I couldn't hide it for ever. One day as I was getting up from the lunch table, Gerry looked at me and said: "My God, Stella. You're fairly putting on the beef. Anybody would think you were pregnant."

# 28.

The time was fast approaching when I could hide my condition no longer. I spoke to Pete Bukowski and told him I had to leave. He seemed surprised. It was a good job, the sort of job people wanted to hold on to. To leave without a good reason appeared strange.

He said: "Are you unhappy? I thought you looked a bit distracted. Like your mind wasn't on your work."

"Oh, no. I'm happy. But my mother has taken ill. I have to go back to Fermanagh to look after her."

The lie just jumped out of my mouth and, immediately, I regretted it. After everything that had happened, it seemed like blasphemy, as if I was tempting God.

Pete looked concerned.

"I'm sorry to hear that. I hope it's not serious?"

"Oh, no. But she needs me. My father has to work."

"Okay. When your Mom's better, you just give me a call and we'll have your job waiting for you."

He put out a hand and pinched my cheek, like I was a baby.

"We're going to miss you, Stella. You sure brightened things up around here."

*

The birth was scheduled for March 3rd, 1945. On one of my visits to the hospital, I asked the doctor when I would have to come in to have my baby. He gave me a strange look.

"You won't be coming here, Miss Maguire."

"Why not?"

"Has no one told you?"

"Told me what?"

"About your situation?"

I felt my cheeks burn with embarrassment.

"You'll have to go elsewhere. There's a place. Stranmillis Court. It's a home for unmarried mothers."

He saw the look on my face and hurried to reassure me.

"You don't have to worry. The services are very good. You and your baby will be perfectly safe."

"But why can't I have it here?"

He lowered his eyes.

"Because it wouldn't do. All the mothers here are married. The truth is, people would complain."

When I told Tess, she got very angry.

"Jesus Christ. I don't believe it. You're as good as any of them, Stella. And your baby will be as good. What do they think you're going to do? Steal the bedclothes or something?"

"They won't have me. They said the other women would complain."

Tess was furious.

"They're nothing but a bunch of bloody hypocrites! I'll tell you something. There's more churches in Belfast than you could shake a stick at. But there isn't one real Christian among them."

*

One day, Tess said to the boys: "I have a secret to tell you. Auntie Stella is going to have a baby."

They looked puzzled.

"Where is it?"

"In her tummy. It'll be coming in the next couple of weeks. And when it arrives I want you to be nice to it."

Damien said: "But Auntie Stella has no daddy."

"Yes, she has. Her daddy is down in Fermanagh."

"No. I mean a real daddy. Like our daddy."

He pointed to Gerry.

Tess said: "Not every baby has a daddy. This baby is special. It's going to be one of our family. I want you to promise me you'll treat Stella's baby like it was your own wee brother or sister."

Damien put his tiny arms around me

"Don't you worry, Auntie Stella. When your baby comes, we'll love it just the same as we love you."

I looked at his little face, the innocent eyes devoid of any shame or judgment. I fought back the tears.

"Thank you, Damien. That's the nicest thing you could have said."

*

I had to buy baby clothes and things for my confinement. Tess got Gerry to go up to the attic and he came back down with a battered old pram that had belonged to the boys.

"I'll do it up for you," Gerry said. "All it needs is a wee lick of paint and it'll be good as new. Sure it'll save you a few shillings anyway."

Tess took me shopping for baby clothes. I didn't have much to buy. Just a couple of baby gowns and a shawl and nappies. One of Tess's neighbours had knitted two white cardigans. White was a neutral colour and would do for a boy or a girl.

Tess wanted to take me to the Variety Market where they sold second-hand clothes. But I refused. I wanted new clothes for my baby, not clothes that some other child had worn.

When we had finished shopping, we went back to Castle Street to get the tram. It was a Saturday afternoon and there were crowds everywhere. Since the invasion of Europe, people had become more relaxed. The Blackout had been abandoned. There was a new optimism abroad. Everyone seemed impatient for the War to end, so they could get back to their normal lives.

As we walked onto Royal Avenue, I heard someone calling my name. I turned instinctively. Mr Mack was puffing along the pavement towards us. He had on a thick overcoat and scarf against the cold and his glasses seemed to be steamed up from the exertion.

"Miss Maguire. I thought it was you."

I stopped.

Mr Mack stood beside me and tried to catch his breath. I introduced him to Tess and he shook her hand.

"I thought it was you, Miss Maguire. From the back. You look so distinctive. How are you getting on since you left us?"

"Very well, thank you."

"Yes, indeed. You look fit and healthy."

His eyes were looking me over. He couldn't miss the fact that I was pregnant. But he made no comment.

"North Queen Street isn't the same since you left. We still talk about you. You brought a touch of gaiety to the house. Maybe you'll pay us a visit some day?"

I told him I might do that.

"We'd love to see you again. I think Mrs McCrudden misses you. And Bill. Bill certainly misses you. I can see that from the change in his demeanour."

"I must be going," I said. "We have to catch our tram."

"Of course. Well good luck, Miss Maguire. It's been so nice meeting you again."

He pressed my hand and looked into my face.

"And remember. Life's trials are but a passing moment. There are always good people who will help you, if you ask. Don't be afraid to ask, Miss Maguire."

He turned and was gone into the passing crowds. We walked to the tram stop. Meeting Mr Mack had made me sad. It reminded me of the time when I had first come up to Belfast to work. It reminded me of the innocence I had lost. It was only eighteen months ago, but it seemed like a lifetime away.

# 29.

I will never forget my first impression of No 31 Stranmillis Court. It was a cold morning in February and there was a bitter wind blowing. It had been cold for weeks and there was a threat of snow. There were icicles hanging from the gutters of the houses and frost misting the window panes.

I had everything ready. My suitcase was packed with a nightdress, baby clothes and a change of underwear. In a smaller bag, I had soap and washing materials.

Tess came with me. She said: "Don't you be worrying your head about anything. There's a lot of nonsense talked about having a baby, most of it by people who've never had one. I'll come and see you every day. Sure, before you know, it will all be over."

I was nervous, but Tess's presence reassured me. We got the tram into town and then another one for the Lisburn Road. It was a fancy part of the city with big detached houses set well back from the road.

I looked at the houses as we passed. They had neat lawns and flowerbeds and trees, their empty branches pressing like fingers against the dark winter sky. I thought of the people who must live here. They would be wealthy, wanting for nothing. They would have servants to wait on them and good food and coal to warm their homes. If the women had babies, they would have them in the maternity hospital where there would be no unmarried mothers.

Stranmillis Court was a small street off the main road. Number 31 was a bleak, Victorian building with a grim, forbidding air. Even from the outside, it seemed to radiate menace. The moment I walked through the door I smelt disinfectant. A group of women were down on their knees scrubbing the floor with buckets and brushes.

When we entered, they glanced at us for a moment and then bent again to their task. No one spoke a word. I felt fear flutter in my breast. A thin, middle-aged woman was sitting behind a desk writing in a ledger. When she saw us, she stopped writing and examined me with small, beady eyes.

"Miss Maguire?"

"Yes."

"We've been expecting you. You were supposed to be here at nine o'clock. What time is it now?"

She pointed to a big clock over the hallway door. It was twenty past nine.

I started to apologise.

"We had to wait for the tram."

"Belfast Corporation's transport problems are not my concern. When we say a time, Miss Maguire, we mean it. What have we here?"

She pulled open my suitcase and took out my night dress. It was pink with a little white bow at the throat. I saw her sniff.

"You won't be needing this. Or this."

She pulled out my dressing gown.

"In fact, you won't be needing any of this. You will be issued with a set of clothing and regulation washing materials."

She put the clothes back into the suitcase, along with the soap-bag and gave it to Tess. Then she turned her attention once more to me.

"My name is Miss Baxter. I'm the matron. You'll be confined here till your baby is born. You are not allowed to leave this building. If you do, we will no longer be responsible for you. You are not allowed to receive visitors."

"But ..."

She stopped speaking and her eyes seemed to bore right through me.

"Yes, Miss Maguire?"

"Does that mean Tess can't come to see me?"

"That's exactly what it means. There are no exceptions. Have I made myself clear?"

"Yes."

"Yes what?"

"Yes, Ma'am."

"Breakfast is served at seven o'clock sharp, after which you will be assigned your duties for the day. Lunch is at one o'clock. The doctor will be in attendance from two o'clock till three to carry out medical examinations. You will be called when you are required. There is an evening meal at six o'clock and lights are out at nine."

She pushed a piece of paper and a pen across the desk.

"Can you write your name?"

"Yes."

"Sign where the 'x' is."

I tried to read the paper, but Miss Baxter was impatient.

"Where the 'x' is, Miss Maguire."

I scribbled my signature and gave the paper back.

"Right. Come with me."

She came out from behind the desk, placed her hand on my shoulder and propelled me forward. I turned to look at Tess and I could see tears standing in her eyes.

Miss Baxter led me down a long, narrow corridor till we came to a dormitory. There were twelve beds stacked in rows. Each bed had a pillow, sheet and a grey blanket. They were neatly made, the blankets tucked it at the ends. There were no eiderdowns.

She stopped at a bed with a bundle of clothes laid out on top.

"This bed will be yours. You will be responsible for keeping it tidy. You will wear these clothes. You have a locker for your toothbrush and soap. There is a washroom at the end of the dormitory. Have you any questions?"

"No, Ma'am."

"You will have a medical examination this afternoon. In the meantime I will assign you to your duties. Let me see your head."

I bent my head and she parted my hair with the end of her pen.

"That seems clean. Nevertheless, you'll have to undergo a thorough disinfestation. I'll send the nurse along immediately. Report back to my desk when you have finished."

She turned and left. I watched her march down the dormitory and slam the door shut behind her. Sitting down on the bed I buried my head in my hands.

I was sick with misery, lonely, afraid and already missing Tess. I thought: This is my punishment for breaking the rules. I have got pregnant outside of marriage and I will be made to suffer. I'm not fit to have my baby with other respectable mothers in case I give scandal, so they hide me away here where no one can see me.

My thoughts were interrupted by the arrival of the nurse. She wore a starched blue uniform with white cuffs and soft shoes, so that I didn't hear her approach.

She said: "Miss Maguire?"

"Yes."

"My name is Nurse Larkin. Get undressed and come with me."

If I expected kindness, there was none. She stood over me while I got out of my clothes, then gathered them and put them in a brown paper bag. It already had my name on a little tag.

Naked, I walked behind her to the washroom. Above the door was a large sign in capital letters. It read: CLEANLINESS IS NEXT TO GODLINESS. Nurse Larkin pushed open the door and I followed her in.

There was a row of six toilet stalls open to the wider room and four gleaming aluminium baths. Nurse Larkin put a plug in the first bath and turned on the taps. A cloud of steam rose up. She tested the water with her finger, then emptied in the contents of a little container. I smelt the pungent disinfectant fumes fill the room.

"Get into the bath."

The bath was hot. I sat down and Nurse Larkin scooped up water with a jug and poured it over my head. She took a bar of soap and scrubbed till I could feel my skin burn. The disinfectant made my eyes weep. I wanted to cry out but I didn't dare. I just sat there obediently till my body stung with the pain of the scrubbing.

She stood up and released the plug.

"You can get dressed now and go and see Matron."

I dried myself and put on the clothes she had brought. Grey knickers. White ankle socks. A shapeless grey gown. I looked exactly like the poor creatures I had seen scrubbing the floor when I arrived. I left the washroom and went down to Miss Baxter. With each step I took, I felt my spirits sink.

# 30.

Miss Baxter assigned me to laundry duties. There were two others working with me: a young girl called Betty Saunders from Ballynahinch and an older woman called Bella McGookin who came from the Shankill Road. Like me, this was Betty's first time in Stranmillis Court and she was terrified. Bella was a veteran. She had been here on two previous occasions.

The work involved washing the bedlinen and the clothes. There were two big tubs burning on gas rings and we had to keep turning the washing with wooden ladles. It was hard work and the heat in the laundry room was stifling. After a few minutes, the sweat was pouring from me. I could see it running in streams from Bella's face. She kept wiping it away with red, calloused hands.

She asked me: "When are you due?"

"The third of March."

"Say your prayers that it's premature. The sooner it comes, the sooner you'll get out of this kip."

Betty watched with open mouth. She was no more than a child, a simple country girl, clearly overwhelmed by what had happened to her.

"This place is worse than jail," Bella said. "I've been there and I know. At least in jail you know what you're in for."

"What happened to your other babies?" Betty asked.

"They took them off me."

"And where did they go?"

"They gave them away to people that couldn't have their own kids.

At least they got decent homes. Sure what chance would they have with me, the life I have?"

"What sort of life is that?" Betty asked.

I listened intently.

"A no-good life, child. They say I'm not a fit mother. Maybe they're right. My trouble is, I'm too fond of the Tony wine. And when I get a bellyful of wine, I just lose the run of myself. I can't say 'no' to any man that asks me."

She stirred the tub like it was a giant pot of soup.

"But these ould ones in here, Baxter and Larkin, they've never seen the colour of a man's micky. And they're jealous as hell of us that have. That's why they're down on us. Spite! Baxter told me the last time, if I got up the pole again, she'd have me locked away for my own good. She said I had no morals and any man could take advantage of me and if I didn't take care of myself, then they'd have to do it for me."

"What were you in jail for?" Betty asked.

"Misdemeanours."

"What does that mean, Bella?"

"It means whatever they want it to mean, child."

"Would you not keep your baby, this time?"

Bella stopped turning the ladle and gazed into the distance.

"Och, they'd never let me. Not with my record. They'll just take it off me, like the other ones, and give it away to somebody else."

Betty had got pregnant with the first boy she ever knew, a farmhand called Johnny Spade. He ran off when she told him and now the police were looking for him. She was only fifteen at the time. In the two weeks I spent in Stranmillis Court I got to hear all their stories. There were twelve of us altogether, but women kept having their babies and leaving and new ones would come and take their place. Eliza Bowen was the only permanent one. She was simple-minded and had three babies. The word was, they were fathered by her own brothers. The authorities had decided the best thing was to take her out of the family home for good.

Eliza was a poor, harmless soul. She was thin, about thirty-five and carried a big black bible with her all the time, even though she couldn't read. She would sit in a corner and look at the pages and nod sagely to herself. At meal times she would often burst into a verse of a hymn and Miss Baxter would fly into a rage and try to quiet her.

*I've got the joy, joy, joy bells, down in my heart,*
*Down in my heart, down in my heart.*
*I've got the joy, joy, joy bells, down in my heart,*
*Since Jesus, came into my soul.*

She was the only inmate who ever had a visitor. Each Sunday afternoon, a clergyman came to see her and they would sit and talk in the reception room that was reserved for important guests. No one from her family ever came.

Some of the women were prostitutes and worked out of Amelia Street beside the railway station. One woman, Rosie McCoy, liked to talk about the clients she had.

"I've got a judge comes to see me regular. Randy ould divil, he is. You wouldn't believe the antics he gets up to. Pays me fifteen shillings to smack his bare arse with a stick."

She would laugh and slap her thigh at the thought and the rest of us would smile. The prostitutes were raddled creatures with red, coarse features, and tough as boots. They weren't afraid of Miss Baxter or Nurse Larkin. They gave them cheek and made faces when their backs were turned.

Nobody cared what other people had done. Nobody passed judgement. We were all in Stranmillis Court together and that was the tie that bound us. Most of them seemed content that they were pregnant. It was accepted as natural. We were all women and getting pregnant was part of our lot.

One day, Betty Saunders said to me: "I've made my mind up, Stella. I'm going to keep my baby when it comes. I'm not giving it away to nobody. What about you?"

Giving my child away had never even entered my head. The thought filled me with horror.

"Me too, Betty," I said. "I'm keeping it, no matter what happens."

*

The food was dreadful. For breakfast, there was porridge, bread and tea. For lunch, cabbage and tinned bully-beef. For dinner, toasted bread and baked beans. And always the orange juice and cod liver oil supplements. The diet never varied. I don't think I ever saw an egg the whole time I was there.

We rose at 6.30 a.m., washed, and went down to the refectory for breakfast. On Monday mornings we were given our work assignments for the week: cleaning, cooking or washing. Women who were near to labour were excused work but had to stay in bed.

There was no radio and the only reading material was a bundle of religious tracts that had been donated by some charity. The stories were all wholesome and uplifting; tales of poor women overcoming the odds to build a better life for themselves. But most of the women in Stranmillis Court couldn't read, so even this poor diversion was denied them.

We worked till meal-breaks and in the afternoon, if you had a medical appointment, you went to see the doctor. His name was Fraser. He was a middle-aged man with a thin, ascetic face, who worked full-time at the maternity hospital and filled in at Stranmillis Court for bonus money.

On my first visit, he examined me and said: "You're an intelligent young woman. How did you get yourself into this pickle?"

I resented his question.

I said: "What pickle is that?"

"In the puddin club and no man in sight."

I could see from his attitude the way he regarded me: as a giddy fool who had gone and got myself pregnant. It made me angry.

I said: "I don't see that it's any of your business. Your job is to examine me. How I got pregnant is my own concern."

He wasn't used to being answered like this and I could see he was put out.

"You were glad enough that we were here for you."

"I wouldn't say glad. I had no choice. The maternity hospital wouldn't take me."

"Can you blame them? The women there are all respectably married."

His remark infuriated me.

"Are you implying we're not respectable?"

I saw his face grow red with embarrassment.

"I've seen your type before, Miss Maguire. A few weeks out in the real world and you'll soon know your driver."

*

I fell into the routine of the place but all the time I was thinking of what was happening outside. There was a garden at the back of the home and we were allowed to walk in it after lunch to get fresh air. It was the only glimpse I had of the sky.

On my second visit to Dr Fraser, he said my labour would begin soon and he was taking me off work duties. I was confined to bed. I worried about my family. We couldn't make phone calls or write letters. I knew they'd be thinking about me and wondering why I hadn't been in touch. I prayed that word hadn't reached them about what had happened.

One morning, before dawn, I woke with a sharp pain in my gut. I could feel myself all wet. I knew from my conversations with the older women what was happening. My waters had broken and the baby was coming.

I struggled to sit up in the bed but the pain now was terrible. It came in spasms, rolling over me and then rolling away again. I cried out to Betty Saunders, who was in the bed next to mine. "Betty, get Nurse Larkin. Quick. I think it's coming early."

Other women were waking and soon the place was in uproar. Betty ran down the dormitory in her night-shift, waving her hands and shouting in excitement.

"Stella's baby's coming. Stella's baby's coming."

She came back with Nurse Larkin. She took one look at me and said: "Right. It's the delivery room for you."

She returned with a trolley and Betty Saunders and Bella McGookin helped me up onto it. Somebody whispered: "You'll be all right, Stella. Everything will be all right."

I began to pray to Our Lady and St Jude to help me through the ordeal. Nurse Larkin wheeled me into the delivery room and lifted me onto the table. She began filling the sinks with hot water, laying out instruments. I could see them gleaming in the light. I was in agony now.

Suddenly, I had a flashback to Mammy in the big bedroom of the house in Ballinaleck, the morning Kathleen was born. The screaming had terrified me and made me think she was dying. I closed my eyes and bit the towel Nurse Larkin had given me.

The pain seemed to last forever and then I felt myself slipping out of consciousness into a black tunnel where the pain slowly ebbed away.

I was brought to by a new voice. It was Miss Baxter.

She said: "You've given birth to a healthy baby boy. I have to register the birth. What do you want to call him?"

I didn't have to think. I had long ago decided on a name.

"Martin," I said. "I want to call him Martin."

# 31.

Martin was a handsome baby. He had a little pink face and a snub nose and a thick head of black, curly hair. I loved him from the moment I saw him. All the women crowded round to have a look when they brought me back from the delivery room.

Bella McGookin said: "My God, Stella. That fella's a dream-boat. Would you take a look at him. What weight is he, anyway?"

"Nine pounds," I said, proudly.

"*Nine* pounds? He's a bruiser. No wonder you had a hard labour. Look at the lovely long eyelashes he has on him. You mark my words. That fella's going to be a hunk."

Betty Saunders tugged at my sleeve and whispered: "Was it sore, Stella? Did it hurt you when he was getting born?"

I thought of the agony I had endured in the delivery room. I looked at Martin lying peacefully in the iron cot beside my bed.

"No, Betty," I said. "It wasn't sore at all."

The women fussed over us. They tickled Martin's chin and made him gurgle. They went: "Googa, googa, googa," right into his face. Somebody gave me a bar of chocolate they had smuggled in. Somebody else gave me an orange. It was dry and wrinkled like it had been kept a long time for a special occasion. I knew it was an important gesture, so I peeled it and ate it, sucking the last juice from the fruit.

I slept for most of the morning, exhausted after the delivery. In the afternoon, Dr Fraser came with Miss Baxter. He seemed to be in a hurry to get away. He examined Martin and me. He said: "Your baby is perfectly healthy and so are you. You should be able to leave in a day or two. Have you some place to go?"

"Yes."

"I suggest you take it easy for a while. Nursing mothers are entitled to vitamin supplements and orange juice for six months. I'll write the appropriate letter for you and you can take it to the dispensary. It's free, Miss Maguire. It won't cost you a penny."

I heard the heavy stress he laid on the word free.

When he was gone, Miss Baxter looked at me sternly and said: "What do you propose to do with your child?"

"Why, keep him, of course."

"You gave no name for the father on his birth certificate."

"No."

"Is he supporting you?"

I thought of Bud, far away in Europe, if he was alive at all.

"No," I said.

"What about your parents?"

I shook my head.

"So how do you propose to care for your child?"

"I'll work. I have a job I can go back to."

"And what if you can't find work?"

"I'll claim social welfare."

Miss Baxter's thin lips parted. It was the first time I had seen her smile.

"Are you out of your mind? Social welfare indeed! Do you expect the honest tax-payers to subsidise your fornication?"

"There must be some benefits I'm entitled to."

She had stopped smiling. Her face was a grim mask.

"There are no benefits, Miss Maguire. And it would have served you better to have thought of that before you got yourself in this situation."

Her tone alarmed me.

"What do you mean?"

"We have a responsibility for you and your baby, even if you have none for yourself. Your position will be assessed by the authorities. I have to tell you, Miss Maguire: If it's deemed that you're not a fit person to bring up your child, he'll be taken from you."

I glanced at Martin, lying peacefully beside me.

"No," I screamed.

Miss Baxter ignored me.

"Where is this place you'll be staying?"

I gave her Tess's name and address.

"We'll check it out. We have good people who will be happy to take your baby and care for him. They'll give him a better life than you can ever hope."

Her remarks upset me. I became possessive of Martin and wouldn't let him out of my sight. I worried that they might take him in the night when I was asleep. I even brought him with me when I went to use the bathroom for fear he might be gone when I got back.

Miss Baxter returned a few days later with a small man in a shabby grey suit. He sat silently making notes while she talked.

"We've checked the address you gave us. The place looks decent enough. Mrs O'Neill says she's prepared to take you and your baby and vouch for you. Have you any money?"

"I have £25 in a savings account."

"That won't last long," Miss Baxter said.

"I can work."

"And who'll look after your baby while you're working?"

"Tess will."

"But Mrs O'Neill is working herself."

"We'll come to some arrangement," I said hastily. "You don't have to worry."

I saw her glance at the man in the suit.

"What do you think, Mr Coulter?"

He shifted uncomfortably in his seat.

"As a rule, I believe it's best if the child can stay with the mother. All things being equal of course. I think Miss Maguire is capable and I can arrange for the District Nurse to visit."

He turned to look at me. His eyes were sad and melancholy.

163

"But I must be blunt with you," he continued. "We will monitor your situation. If there is any indication that your baby is being neglected or if you should get pregnant again, then there would be no question. We would be obliged to take the child into care."

When the women heard the news, that I was to keep Martin, they cheered. They saw it as a victory over Miss Baxter and Nurse Larkin. Betty Saunders asked: "How did you do it, Stella?"

"You have to convince them. Mr Coulter is the one who decides. You have to convince him that you can look after your baby."

"I'll convince him all right. I'll make up a story. I'll tell them my father has plenty of money and he's going to buy me a house."

"But it has to be true. They check."

"They're not getting my baby," Betty said, firmly. "He's mine and nobody's going to touch him."

I glanced at Bella McGookin. She just shook her head but didn't say a word.

That afternoon, Tess came for me. She brought my clothes and waited till I got dressed. I had to sign a form to discharge myself. Nurse Larkin took it in silence and gave me back a bundle in brown wrapping paper. I peered inside. It was second-hand baby clothes. There were no words of farewell.

I turned to leave. I wanted to get away from Stranmillis Court as quickly as possible. As we reached the door, I heard a voice call my name. It was poor, demented Eliza Bowen. She came hurrying along the corridor and caught up with us.

"Take me with you, Stella. Take me with you and your wee babby."

"I can't, Eliza. They wouldn't allow it."

"Please take me."

She clutched at me and held my coat. I saw Nurse Larkin come rushing towards us. She grabbed Eliza's waist and pulled her free. As we parted, Eliza tried to press something into my hand.

It fluttered to the ground. I bent to pick it up. It was a religious tract.

"The Lord is My shepherd," it read. "I shall not want."

# 32.

Tess was excited. She seized Martin and held him up for inspection.

"He's a smasher, Stella. The very spit of you. My God, this guy's going to be a film star."

She looked into my face.

"It's great to see you."

"You too," I said.

"You must be delighted to get out of that kip. That ould one who was in charge. You'd think somebody had stuck a poker up her arse."

"But the women were great."

She returned Martin and hugged me close.

"Tell you the truth, I missed you, Stella. But now that you're back, everything's going to be the way it used to be."

She pushed out her chest and I could see her breasts straining against the white fabric of her blouse. She raised her fist and punched the air.

"Yes Siree! Happy times are here again!"

Tess's infectious gaiety made me smile. But I knew she was wrong. Now I had a child. Things would never be the same again.

*

I came to an arrangement with her. She wouldn't charge me any rent but I would pay her ten shillings a week for food. In return, I would mind Terry and Damien and keep the house for her when she was at work.

"It's just for a few months," she said. "Just till you get back on your feet again. Then we can take another look at it."

165

It seemed to work well. I was so relieved to be free from Stranmillis Court that working in Tess's house was a pleasure. Each morning, I got up at seven o'clock after Gerry had gone out on his milk round. I would dress and feed Martin and get breakfast ready for Damien and Terry. Tess would get up about nine o'clock unless she had been to a party the night before, when she might not rise till noon.

Gerry had fixed up the pram like he promised and, after breakfast, I would take the boys for a walk in the park. They loved to push the pram with me. It gave them a sense of importance. Terry would roll up his sleeve and show me his muscles.

"Am I getting strong, Auntie Stella?"

"Yes," I would say.

"When I grow up, I'm going to marry you and then I'll be your daddy."

"I'm not going to get married."

He would pull a disappointed face.

"But everybody has to get married."

"Not everybody. Anyway, I'll be too old for you."

"No, you won't. You'll still be lovely. I don't care what age you are, I'm going to marry you."

*

The first chance I got, I wrote home. I hadn't written for about a month and I didn't want Mammy worrying about me. I made up a string of lies about my life and what a good time I was having in Belfast. I told them about all the exciting people I was meeting and the money I was saving. I told them that everybody was saying the War would soon be over and the Germans couldn't hold out much longer.

But I felt guilty as I wrote. Lying to them made me feel cheap. I kept thinking that Mammy and Daddy had a grandchild they didn't know about and would probably never see. I wondered how things would be in different circumstances. If I was married and had a child, there would be joy and celebration. I wouldn't have to hide and lie. I would be able to acknowledge my son to my family instead of denying him, as I was doing now.

A few weeks after I came back to Tess's house, she said: "You'll have to get him christened, Stella. God forgive me, but the child's a wee pagan. You'll have to get him signed up to the one, true church. I'll go and talk to the priest about it."

She organised it. The baptism was arranged for the following Sunday after twelve o'clock Mass. Tess and Gerry were the sponsors and she loaned me the christening shawl she had used for Terry and Damien.

Father Ogle was an old man with soup stains on his soutane and grey hair that hung in rats' tails over his collar. I remember feeling sorry for him and thinking he was too poor to get his hair cut. He didn't ask any questions about Martin's father. Perhaps he thought he was away in the War. Or maybe he just didn't care. He had the look of a man who is weary with the world and can't be surprised any more.

He said the prayers and anointed Martin with the oils, then poured the water over his head till he bunched up his face and squirmed with discomfort. Then he shook hands with us all and wrote down Martin's name in a big ledger they kept in the sacristy.

We all trooped back to 28 Iveagh Place for a party. Tess had bought bottles of lemonade and a bottle of Manley's sherry, and she made sandwiches. Gerry had got hold of a camera somewhere. He took pictures of me with Martin and me with Tess and all of us together with the boys. He took a special picture of Martin in his christening shawl.

He said: "It's a special day, Stella. When the picture is developed, you can get it framed and it will be a memento."

Tess filled her glass with wine and offered a toast.

"Here's to us. Who's like us?"

I stared blankly at her.

"Och, c'mon Stella. Surely, you know the rest of it?"

"No, I don't. I never heard it before."

"It goes: 'Very few and they're all dead.'"

She laughed and filled her glass again.

"Jesus," she said. "I wish this bloody War was over."

*

Soon after, the District Nurse came to call. She was a big-bosomed woman with a jolly face and a smell of carbolic soap.

"Well now," she said, taking off her coat and hanging it behind the door in a businesslike fashion. "Where's this champion of yours? I hear he's the biggest baby born in Stranmillis this two years. Nine pounds they tell me. God Almighty, the child must be a marvel."

I had been dreading this visit, but her breezy manner reassured me. Hearing her talk like this about Martin filled me with pride. He was sleeping in the pram. I took him in my arms and he began to cry.

"He's got a healthy pair of lungs on him, anyway," the District Nurse said. "Would you take a look at the size of him. This fella looks like he eats nails for his breakfast."

She laid him across her knee and examined him. She took his temperature and listened to his chest with a stethoscope. She had brought a set of scales with her and she weighed him. I watched as the little arrow swung round.

"Nine and three-quarter pounds. Well he's certainly gaining weight. Are you still breast-feeding?"

"Yes."

"Mother's milk is the best food of all, Miss Maguire. But in a few months time, you could wean him on to a bottle, if you wanted."

"I'll do whatever you think is best."

I saw her smile.

"Then just continue with the breast. Now, what about yourself? How are you keeping?"

"Well, I think."

"No complaints? Bowels regular?"

She spoke so plainly that I felt no embarrassment.

"Yes."

"Appetite?"

"Fine."

"You're taking your supplements?"

"Yes."

She had taken out a chart and was ticking off items.

"Sleeping all right?"

"Like a log."

"Good. You need plenty of rest. Giving birth is a very exhausting business. You've been carrying that bruiser around for the past nine months. No wonder you're tired. Let me tell you something, Miss Maguire."

She leaned towards me conspiratorially.

"They call us the weaker sex. But in my opinion, women are far tougher than men. If men had to go through half the trials that we endure, they'd be falling like flies."

The thought seemed to amuse her. She started to laugh.

"Like flies. Can you imagine it? The hospitals would be working overtime. We'd never hear the end of their complaints."

She stood up.

"Well, time to go."

"Can I make you a cup of tea?" I offered.

"Thanks very much, but I've got six more visits before I'm through."

She began to put on her coat. I wanted to ask if she was satisfied, if I had passed whatever unspoken test the authorities had set for me. But I was afraid.

At the door, she turned and smiled.

"I understand from Stranmillis that they were concerned about your circumstances?"

I didn't dare to look at her.

"Yes."

"Well, I don't know what all the fuss was about. You're healthy. Your child's healthy."

"So, I'm a good mother?"

She turned and stared.

"My God, child. What are you talking about? What have they put into your head? Of course you're a good mother. If half the mothers I see were as good as you, I'd be able to retire."

169

# 33.

The War ended on May 13th. It had been ending for weeks. The radio and the newspapers had been full of reports of German defeats and surrenders all over Europe. But on May 13th, it ended for good.

I learnt the news as I was bathing Martin in the big tub in the kitchen. Tess came rushing in, all excited, and said: "It's over, Stella. I just heard Mr Churchill on the wireless. He's been to Buckingham Palace to have lunch with the King and he says the War is over."

She sounded out of breath.

"Isn't it great news? Now we can all start living again. The first thing I'm going to do is buy some decent clothes. Jesus, I'm sick to death of this bloody rationing."

"Yes," I said. "It's great news. Thank God it's over."

It seemed unreal though. I thought of all the things that had happened to me since that autumn day, six years ago, when I had come home from school and Daddy had told me that Britain had declared war on Germany. It seemed like a lifetime had passed.

There were celebrations and victory parades. In London, thousands of people took to the streets and danced and sang all night. In Belfast, there were street parties and the pubs stayed open late. People were overjoyed that the long years of fighting had finally ended and they could look forward to a bright future.

But it wasn't all good news. One night a few weeks later, Tess came back from the Eagle looking dejected. I knew at once that something was wrong. She slumped down on the sofa and kicked off her shoes. When I asked her what it was, she said: "The club is closing."

"What?"

"It's closing, Stella. Pete Bukowski told us tonight. He said with the War over, the boys will all be going home."

"Did he say when?"

"In a couple of months."

She shrugged.

"I should have known it couldn't last forever. The gravy train is pulling out of the station, chicken. Now it's back to porridge."

*

I was busy now keeping house for Tess and looking after Martin. I prepared meals and washed dishes. I polished and scrubbed and cleaned. I did the weekly laundry. I read stories to the boys and took them for walks. For a long time, we were happy, but then things began to change.

It happened almost without warning. If I was to pinpoint a moment, I would say it began around the time I scorched Gerry's shirt. It was a Friday afternoon and Tess had gone into town. Martin was dozing in his pram, and the boys were playing in the little strip of garden in front of the house. I was ironing clothes by the window, where I could keep an eye on them.

I heard Martin cough. I was always alert for any sounds he made. As I listened, the cough got worse. I heard him struggle for breath, as if choking. At once, I put down the iron and rushed to pull him out of the pram. His face was already red.

I began to panic. Laying him on his tummy, I thumped his back till he coughed up a piece of bread and he began to breath again. I stared at the bread. Where had he got it? I hadn't given it to him. Where had it come from?

It was then I caught the smell of burning cloth. I turned in horror and saw that I had left the iron on Gerry's shirt. Smoke was already rising from it. I put Martin back in the pram, whipped the shirt away and tossed it in the sink. I put the iron down on its stand. By now I was angry. I went to the door and called the boys into the house.

"I want to know who gave Martin bread to eat?"

They looked nervously from one to the other.

"Well? Can nobody talk? Martin almost choked on a piece of bread and I want to know where he got it."

They looked away and tried to avoid my eyes. I could feel my temper rising. I took them by the arms and shook them.

"DO NOT GIVE HIM BREAD! Do you understand? He's only a baby. He's got no teeth. He can't chew. If you give him bread it will stick in his throat and he could die."

The boys were frightened now. Damien started to whimper, then Terry.

"I thought he was hungry," Terry said. "So I gave him a crust. I didn't mean any harm."

I felt my anger melt away. I put my arms around them and held them tight. I was close to tears myself.

"Please, boys. Don't give him anything to eat. Promise me."

"We promise," they chanted.

*

Naturally, Gerry was furious when he saw that his shirt was scorched. It was his good Sunday shirt and now it was ruined. I apologised and promised to buy him a new one but he brushed it aside and said it didn't matter, but deep down, I knew he was annoyed.

Worse was to follow. A few days later, when the house was quiet, Tess came to me and said: "Stella, you and me's got to have a talk."

Her face had a dark look that should have warned me. I followed her into the front room and she closed the door.

"The boys tell me you shook them the other day."

I was shocked.

"That's right. I did."

I tried to tell her what had happened with the crust and Martin, but she silenced me.

"Stella, I don't want you laying a finger on my children. If they do something that needs chastising, tell me and I'll do it."

"I didn't hurt them, Tess. I was upset. Martin nearly choked. I just wanted to impress on them that they shouldn't give him things to eat."

"You scared them. Now they're afraid of you."

"I didn't mean any harm. I'm sorry."

"Sorry isn't good enough."

"For God's sake, Tess. It was nothing. Why are you making a big thing out of it?"

Her eyes flashed rage.

"You may think it was nothing. How would you react, if I was to attack *your* child?"

I couldn't believe she was talking like this.

"I didn't attack them. I shook them, that's all."

"And who gave you the right to do that?"

I lowered my head.

"No one."

"That's right. No one. Don't touch them. I'm warning you, Stella. Don't ever abuse my children again."

She turned and left the room. I sat alone and watched the evening shadows lengthen in the street outside and the rain begin to beat against the window pane.

# 34.

Tess apologised to me the following morning. "Och, chicken, I lost my dander," she said. "But I'm just so protective of those wee divils, there's times I want to wrap them up in cotton wool. I think I feel guilty because I'm away so much."

This was the old Tess and I felt so relieved.

"I'm sorry too, Tess. You've been such a good friend to me and Martin. You took us in when we had nowhere else to go. I wouldn't do anything in the world to hurt you."

"I know that. So let's just put the whole thing behind us and start afresh, like it never happened. Do you know what it is? I think you're too cooped up here, Stella. I've got next Wednesday off. Why don't we have a treat? Why don't I take you to the flicks?"

"But who'll mind the kids?"

"Gerry. I'll have a wee word in his ear. And maybe a wee promise of something nice when I get him to bed."

She winked and laughed.

It was all forgotten. And yet, somehow, it wasn't. The incident had brought instability into our relationship. I was careful now of everything I said and did with Damien and Terry for fear of offending Tess. I think they sensed this too, for they grew bolder and more boisterous in the knowledge that I wouldn't chastise them.

At the same time, I came to distrust them. They had frightened me once and now I was wary of them. I wouldn't allow them near Martin unless I was present. Gerry, too, began to change, his attitude towards us growing cooler. I think he resented our presence. He was a man marooned in a house with two women and three children. And one of the children wasn't even his own.

But the incident had a more lasting effect. It made me face the truth. Martin and I were in Tess's house on sufferance. Even though she treated us generously, the balance of power was all in her direction. I had no independence. I couldn't afford to upset her or her husband. At any time, if our relationship changed, she could turn us out.

So far, I had managed to survive on the £25 I had saved. Tess gave me baby clothes so I didn't have much to buy. But gradually, my money was running out. It went on small things: stockings and underclothes, baby toys for Martin, little presents for Damien and Terry. The drip, drip, drip of expenditure wore my savings away. One day, I checked my money and got a nasty shock. Only £8 remained.

I was filled with panic. How long would £8 last? And when it was gone, what would we do? I couldn't expect Tess to keep us for nothing, especially since she was going to lose her job when the Eagle closed. And always, hanging over me like a black cloud, was the terrible threat of having Martin taken away if the authorities should learn about my plight.

I thought of finding work; something that would pay me enough to move out and get a flat and hire some girl to mind Martin. I began to scan the newspapers again hoping to find something that would suit me. But with the War over, jobs were becoming scarce. Men were being demobbed and the mills and factories were working short-time.

I began to grow desperate. I hoarded my remaining money like a miser. I spent nothing that wasn't absolutely necessary. And I kept my worries bottled up inside myself, afraid now to confide in Tess in case I revealed just how vulnerable I had become. At night I lay in bed, listening to the measured rise and fall of Martin's breathing, my mind filled with terror.

One Saturday afternoon, I was peeling potatoes at the kitchen sink when I heard someone knock at the front door. I paid no attention, assuming it was a neighbour or a delivery man. I listened to Tess's footsteps as she went to answer. A few minutes later, she was back.

There was a puzzled look on her face.

"It's for you."

I was amazed. No one had ever called for me since I had lived here.

"For me?"

"Yes."

"Who is it?"

"Go and see for yourself."

I took off my apron and tried to fix my hair. I went cautiously out to the hall. A tall man stood in the afternoon sunlight, his back towards me. A wild thought seized my imagination. It was Bud. He had heard about our child and come back to rescue me.

As I approached, the man turned around and my heart leaped into my mouth. It wasn't Bud. It was Bill Dwyer.

He smiled. "Hello, Stella."

"Bill! What are you doing here?"

"I came to see you. I checked with the people in the American Eagle and they gave me your address. I wanted to talk to you."

"I ..."

"Can we go for a stroll somewhere? There are things I want to say."

I was caught unawares and felt flustered.

"Wait here," I said.

I went back into the house to tell Tess, and she said: "Go and have a talk with him. What harm can it do? I'll mind Martin. He's a nice-looking fella, I'll say that for him."

I ran up to my room and put on my best dress and shoes. I quickly brushed my hair and added a touch of lipstick before coming downstairs again.

Bill had brought a present. He gave it to me, neatly wrapped in gift paper and tied with a ribbon.

"It's just some chocolates. I know you like them so I saved my ration coupons."

"You shouldn't have done that," I said.

"Why not? It gives me pleasure."

We walked to the Falls Road and along to the park. Bill told me about his job. He had been promoted to foreman and now had a gang of men working under him.

"And I've bought a house, Stella. I decided to get my own place. I didn't see why I should pay rent to make Lizzie McCrudden rich."

He laughed.

"It's a nice house on the Antrim Road. It's got three bedrooms and a garden. There's lots of room. Much more than I need."

We came to a bench and sat down. Bill was wearing a smart blue suit and a white shirt and tie. His hair was neatly groomed and his cheeks were smooth where the razor had shaved. I thought he looked quite handsome.

He cautiously took my hand.

"I've tried to forget you, Stella. I've tried to put you out of my mind, but I can't. You told me once you loved me. Is that still true?"

I felt a knot tighten in my chest.

"Bill, there's something you should know. Things have changed."

"You have a child."

I looked up quickly.

"How did you know?"

"Mr Mack told me. He said he met you one day in town and you were pregnant. He was very concerned about you, Stella. He cares for you a lot. Just like me."

"I have a baby boy. He's five months old. His father is an American soldier. I think he was killed in the War."

Bill squeezed my hand.

"It doesn't matter to me. The last time we spoke, you said I was too possessive. I've tried to work on that, Stella. Marry me. I can give you a good life and a good home. And I'll leave you alone. I promise I won't try to run your life."

"You'd take another man's child?"

"He's your child. And, therefore, I love him too. I would accept him as my own."

"But people will talk."

"To hell with them. I don't live for other people. I live for myself. And for you, Stella. And your wee boy."

177

I looked at Bill. I realised how good and kind and generous he was. I thought how foolish I had been to cast him away.

"This is a shock," I said. "I need time to think."

"That's all right. I didn't expect you to answer at once."

He took a piece of paper from his pocket.

"That's my address. Write to me if you want to see me again."

He walked with me to the gates of the park. As I turned to go he reached out and held me.

"Can I kiss you, Stella?"

I turned my mouth towards him and felt his lips, soft and gentle. A warm feeling passed through me. It had been so long since I had been with a man that I had forgotten how good a kiss could be.

# 35.

Tess was waiting for me when I got back to the house. She could barely contain herself.

"Tell me all about him," she said eagerly, as soon as I was seated. "Is that the old boyfriend?"

"Yes."

"The one that works in the shipyard? The fella who bought you the locket?"

"That's right. His name is Bill Dwyer."

She looked impressed

"He's not half bad, Stella. What did he want?"

"He wants to marry me."

"What?"

"Yes."

"My God. Does he know about ..."

She motioned with her thumb towards the pram where Martin was sleeping.

"Yes, he knows. Do you remember the man we met when we were shopping in town? Mr Mack? He told Bill."

Tess stood up.

"I think I need a drink."

She went into the kitchen and came back with a bottle and two glasses.

"Stella, are you sure this fella's right in the head?"

"Of course he is."

"And he's prepared to marry you with a child and everything?"

"Yes."

"Jesus, I've heard it all now," she said and took a swig of wine. "What did you tell him?"

"I said I needed to consider."

Tess almost choked.

"Are you crazy or something? What is there to consider? This guy could be your lifeboat. And you're going to keep him waiting?"

"I need time, Tess. You don't expect me to make a decision on the spot?"

"I expect you to see sense. How many men do you think would marry a woman and take on another fella's baby? And him with a steady job and such a good-looker as well. Stella, I'll tell you straight. If it had been me, I would have handcuffed him in case he tried to escape."

I found myself smiling.

"He's also got his own house. He just told me."

"Mother of God. You've won the jackpot."

She downed the wine and poured another glass. My head was in a whirl. I was still struggling to come to terms with what had happened.

"Stella, listen to me. You have to take him. There's no two ways about it. A chance like this only comes along once in a blue moon. If you turn him down again, somebody else will grab him for sure and then you'll never see him again."

"There's something you're forgetting," I said. "You told me yourself not to marry him. Do you remember?"

"Och, that was then and this is now. You didn't have a youngster then. You were a single woman with the world at your feet and he was trying to buy you with his presents. I'll tell you the truth, Stella. You didn't do yourself any favours when you got pregnant. I'm afraid that changed the whole game."

She reached out and held my hand.

"Let's be honest with each other. I can see the way you're scrimping and saving. Look at you. When's the last time you spent a penny to buy yourself something nice? And that wee fella, Martin, is getting bigger by the day. Soon, he'll be eating solid food and growing out of his clothes and the bills will start mounting up. What are you going to do then?"

Tess's words seemed to crystallise all my fears.

"I don't know."

"You can stay here as long as you want, but that isn't going to solve the problem. I'm expecting the Eagle to close any day now, so that will mean only one pay-packet coming in to feed the whole lot of us."

"I'm looking for a job."

"And who'll mind Martin?"

"Maybe you could do it and I could pay you?"

She slowly shook her head.

"Face reality, chicken. It's not that I wouldn't be willing. But you'd need to get a *very* big job to be able to pay all your bills *and* feed and clothe yourself, not to mention the wee fella."

I turned to look at her. I was close to tears. Everything she said was absolutely true.

"What am I going to do?"

"Would your parents not take you in?"

"Oh God, no. It would kill them."

Tess gave a weary sigh.

"Well then, I don't think you've got any choice. If you want to hold onto Martin, you've got to marry Bill Dwyer."

*

I knew Tess was right. All the evidence had been gathering like a storm. I was almost penniless and I had no chance of finding a decent job. I faced a future living from hand to mouth, constantly counting the pennies, a stigma forever hanging over Martin and me.

I thought of him, sleeping in his cot. He was innocent and deserved better. He was entitled to a proper home, maybe brothers and sisters to keep him company as he grew up. Bill Dwyer would provide all that if I would marry him.

I spent days agonising over my decision. No matter how I looked at it, it came down to a stark choice: Take Bill or lose Martin. Bill was offering something that few men would. If I married him, my life would be secure. I would become a respectable married woman. He had offered to accept Martin as his child, so I could become reconciled to my parents. The future would be rosy.

But it would be a loveless marriage, a marriage with no heart. It would be an empty husk with nothing at its core. For all his good nature, all his decent qualities, I knew I could never love Bill. I knew I couldn't give my life to him, even if it meant saving my child.

A few nights later, when Tess was working at the club, I took out the pen and ink that she kept in a drawer. I sat down and wrote to Bill. My hand shook as the pen moved slowly across the page.

I thanked him for his offer of marriage and his generosity to me. But, regretfully, I had to refuse. I tried to make it easy for him. I said I would always remember him and the good times we had together.

I sealed and stamped the letter and took it to the post box at the top of the street. It dropped with a heavy thud into the box. I had crossed a line in my life and there could be no turning back. I returned to the house with leaden steps and went to bed.

Closing my eyes, I cried myself to sleep.

# 36.

I knew now I would have to surrender Martin and it made me cling to him all the more. With the few pounds I had remaining, I took him into town and bought him new clothes. I bought a teddy bear with brown button eyes and a tartan bow. I bought toys for Damien and Terry. I was like a drunken sailor but it gave me comfort and I felt better for it.

When Tess discovered I had turned Bill down, she sat me at the kitchen table and said: "You know what this means?"

"Yes."

"So what do you propose to do?"

"I'm going to talk to Father Ogle at the chapel and see if he can find a home for Martin. One thing's for sure, Tess. He's not going back to Stranmillis Court."

"You're determined?"

"Yes."

"Well God help you, darlin. At least the pair of you will have a new start in life. But I know if it was me, it would break my heart."

"It's breaking mine too," I said. "Don't think it's not."

*

I summoned my courage and spoke to the parish priest. Now that I had my mind made up, I wanted it done quickly. He listened patiently, his tired old eyes taking in everything I told him.

When I had finished, he said: "There's a man up in Ardoyne called Father Ambrose and he specialises in these situations. I'll give you a

183

letter for him and your baby's baptism lines. I'm sure he'll be able to help you."

I thanked him and took the tram up the Crumlin Road. I had never been to Ardoyne before. It was almost out in the country, a nest of small terraced houses and tall mill chimneys snug in the shadow of the mountain.

Towering over the streets were the twin spires of Holy Cross church; beside that stood the monastery were the priests lived. I was shown into a parlour to wait.

As the minutes ticked by, doubts began to creep in. I thought, maybe I'm doing wrong. Perhaps I'm being selfish. Maybe, if I made an effort, I could hold on to Martin. We could go away some place where no one knows us. I could find a job and we could build a life together.

The more I thought of it, the more attractive it seemed. If I got up now and left this room, I could still keep my baby. I could escape, get the boat to London and find a place to live. Tess would lend me the money.

I was convinced now. The very moment I stood up to leave, the door opened.

Father Ambrose came slowly into the room. He was a plump man with fair, scanty hair and bright, sparkling eyes. He took my hand.

"You're Stella?"

"Yes, father."

"What can I do for you?"

I gave him the letter from Father Ogle. He took his glasses out of a case and began to read. Then he put the letter down on the table, turned to me, and said: "This is the hardest thing you will ever do, Stella. The hardest thing in your life. But you have come to the right place and I will help you."

When he spoke these words, it was like a dam had burst in me. My chest heaved and I felt all the pain of the last fourteen months come flooding out. I buried my face in my hands and sobbed uncontrollably.

Father Ambrose took out a big white handkerchief and gave it to me. He waited while I composed myself, then rang a bell and ordered tea.

"Stella, I know this is painful for you. No mother should ever have to give away her child."

I was still weeping, my eyes red with tears.

"I don't want to, but I've no money and I can't provide for him."

"Tell me, where is his father?"

"I don't know. He was a soldier. He went to Europe."

"Does he know he has a son?"

"No."

"Do your parents know?"

"No."

"Stella, how did you manage to keep Martin for five months? Most women in your situation give up their babies at birth."

I told him about my arrangement with Tess.

"But now it's no longer possible?"

"She's losing her job."

Father Ambrose shook his head.

"We live in a cruel time, Stella. So cruel that generations to come will not easily forgive us. I know a couple who are desperate for a child. The woman has had several stillbirths. These are good people and they will give your baby a good home."

"What are they called?

"McBride. Sarah and Isaac McBride. Would you like to meet them?"

"Yes."

"Can you bring your son here this afternoon and I'll arrange for them to be here?"

"Yes."

We drank our tea in silence and then it was time to go. Father Ambrose walked with me to the door.

"Stella, you must never reproach yourself. What you are doing is very brave. You are giving your baby another chance. These people will care for him and love him. And love is everything. It's worth more than position or wealth. Always remember that."

I returned to Iveagh Place where I fed Martin and dressed him in his new baby clothes. I filled a bag with the few small things that he owned in the world: the rattle and the teddy bear and the toys that Tess had given him. I wrapped him in his shawl and brought him back to Ardoyne.

I remember every minute of that journey: waiting for the tram to arrive and the big black clouds that came scudding across the sky with the threat of rain; the look on the conductor's face as he helped me onto the tram and found a seat for me near the door.

I knew this was the last journey Martin and I would take together. I knew that I would never again go to sleep with the gentle sound of his breathing in the cot beside me; that I would never see the light of recognition in his eyes; never feel his hungry mouth as it searched out my breast.

I looked at him as he slept in the shawl, his face peaceful, his tiny fists balled tight against his head. I prayed that when he grew up, he wouldn't think I had abandoned him, that somehow he would understand I had no choice.

The McBrides were waiting. They were a working-class couple, dressed expectantly in their Sunday clothes. Isaac was small and thin. His wife, Sarah, was taller, and I remember she wore a camel-haired coat that had seen better days.

Father Ambrose introduced us and we shook hands.

"Stella, these are the people I told you about. The people who'll be looking after Martin."

Mrs McBride smiled, shyly. She craned her neck to look at the bundle in my arms.

"Can I hold him?" she said.

Without thinking, I handed him over and she clasped him tight. That's how it happened. That's how easily I gave my child away.

She cradled him in her arms and gently withdrew the shawl from his face.

"Och, he's beautiful, so he is. Would you just look at him, Isaac."

Isaac peered at Martin and I saw a smile of contentment spread across his face.

"Well boys a boys," he said. "Boys a boys."

They were cooing and chucking and making a fuss of him. I stood alone untill Father Ambrose drew me aside and asked me to sign the consent forms.

I looked at the McBrides and saw the joy that Martin had already brought them. But it didn't seem to matter to me. It didn't seem to count against the pain that was tearing me apart.

I went to Mrs McBride and gave her the bag with Martin's things.

"Can I come and visit him sometimes?" I said.

"Sure, you can. Sure. We'll always be glad to see you."

I thanked her and left the church. There was a fine rain falling and it covered the mountain in a blanket of mist. As I walked down the Crumlin Road to get my tram, a thought kept hammering in my head: "Why did I thank her? I have just given her my baby. She should be thanking me."

# 37.

I rose early next morning and went back to the Labour Exchange. I needed to work. I needed the money, but most of all, I needed something to distract myself from what I had done.

The arrogant little clerk was still there but the place seemed to have changed. It had grown greyer and more depressing and the queues of people waiting on the narrow benches had got longer. I waited till it was my turn to approach the window.

The clerk glanced at me.

"Yes?"

"I'm looking for work."

I had already filled up the necessary form and he read it quickly. He examined me more closely.

"I know you. Didn't I send you for a job in the Grand Central Hotel?"

"Yes."

"So, why did you leave?"

"I got sick."

"Did you supply a medical cert?"

"No."

"Why not?"

"Because I didn't see a doctor. It wasn't that kind of sickness."

He frowned.

"You're not supposed to do that. When you go sick, you're supposed to tell us. Now, you're looking for a job again?"

"Yes."

"Well, the situation's got very bad. There aren't so many jobs now."

"I'll take anything."

He looked up sharply.

"You've certainly changed your tune," he said. "Last time you were here, nothing would do you but a fancy office job."

He quickly leafed through his sheaf of cards and selected one.

"The River Restaurant is looking for a waitress."

I knew the River Restaurant. It was a rough working men's cafe on a street near the docks.

"Okay," I said.

"The wages are twelve shillings a week."

"I'll take it."

He stared at me for a moment and then his face broke in a tight little smile of triumph.

"You're making the right decision, Miss Maguire. No doubt about it. Jobs are getting scarce. And people like you with no qualifications or nothing, sure you can't afford to be choosey."

Damien and Terry wanted to know where Martin had gone. Ever since the incident with the crust, they had grown cautious around him. But I could see they missed him now. I had agreed a story with Tess, so I told them he was staying with people who were minding him for a while.

"Did he not like living here?"

"No. It's got nothing to do with that."

"Is he coming back again?"

"Maybe. In a wee while."

Damien tugged my sleeve.

"Has he got a new mammy and daddy, Stella?"

Tess and me exchanged a glance.

"Sort of," I said

"But you're still his real Mammy, aren't you, Stella?"

I felt my heart give a tiny thump.

"Yes," I said. "I'll always be his real Mammy."

*

189

I couldn't wait to see Martin again, so the first Sunday I was free, I went up to Ardoyne. I was filled with excitement. Since I had parted with my baby there had scarcely been a moment when he had not been on my mind.

The McBrides lived on Brompton Park. It was a long street of small houses that stretched from the Forum cinema down to the tall mill chimneys on Flax Street. Their house was easy to find. It had a small strip of lawn and clumps of lupins in purple flower. The windows were newly washed and the heavy knocker shone in the bright afternoon sun.

Mrs McBride came to the door. She seemed surprised to see me. She brought me in to the small front room and invited me to sit down. The walls were festooned with holy pictures: the Virgin Mary and the saints and Jesus with his sacred heart.

"Isaac's gone out for a wee walk," she said by way of explanation. "He always goes for a walk after his Sunday dinner."

I could see no sign of Martin, so I asked where he was.

"He's sleeping."

"Would it be all right to see him?"

Mrs McBride looked uncertain, but she got up and left the room and I heard her climbing the stairs. A few minutes later she was back, with Martin wrapped in a fancy new shawl.

I looked at him. His skin was pink and healthy and he laughed when he saw me. I reached out to take him in my arms but Mrs McBride pulled away.

"Can I not hold him? Just for a minute?"

Reluctantly, she gave him to me. I held him close to my breast. I wanted to hold him forever and never let him go.

Mrs McBride must have sensed my feeling. She seemed to get nervous. She reached out and plucked at the shawl.

"You're only disturbing him," she said. "He needs his sleep."

She took him from me and fussed with the shawl, tucking it in and wiping his chin. He began to cry and she rocked him in her arms and went: "There, there, there," till at last he stopped. I saw the tenderness in every move she made. She looked at me but didn't speak and I knew in that instant that she had taken possession of him and he would never be mine again.

*

The new job was hard. At 7 a.m. I started serving breakfast to the labourers from the nearby docks. They were rough, working men who drank mugs of black tea and smoked endless cigarettes so that a thick blue fog hung permanently over the place.

Everything they ate was fried in a great pan of sizzling lard and the smell got everywhere; into my hair and my clothes and even under fingernails. I worked ten hours a day, six days a week. I was waitress, cook and kitchen maid. I served tables and washed plates and peeled potatoes till I barely had the strength to stand.

But in those first weeks, I clung to that job. In a strange way, I welcomed it. I relished the noise and the heat and the company. It diverted me from the terrible loneliness that plagued my mind. There were times when I think it was all that stood between me and insanity.

Every Sunday, I went to visit Martin. With the little money I was able to save, I bought him presents I could ill-afford: teddy bears and stuffed clowns and baby clothes edged in blue. It was as if I was compensating for giving him away. Each time I left him, I felt the guilt weighing on me like a stone.

It couldn't go on. The end, when it arrived, was quick, brutal and infinitely painful, and I didn't see it coming. It was a cold day in September, eight weeks after I had given Martin away. The wind scattered the leaves in the park as I waited for the tram. I wore my winter coat and brought Martin a cardigan that Tess had knitted.

Mrs McBride came to the door in answer to my knock. I thought her face looked odd and stiff. She folded her arms and barred my way to the house.

"He's sleeping," she said.

"Maybe I could wait till he wakes?"

She seemed to summon her strength to say something she had been considering for a long time.

"No. It's no good. All this calling is upsetting him. It's upsetting you too. You have to let him go."

I felt a panic seize me.

"But he's my child."

"No. He's *my* child. He can't have two mothers. If you keep calling, he'll only get confused."

"Please? Can I see him one more time?"

Slowly, she relented. She held the door open and I walked into the room. Mr McBride was there with another man I hadn't seen before. He kept his head bowed as if he was embarrassed.

Mrs McBride brought Martin to me. He was smiling. That's the memory I carried with me. Martin's beautiful face smiling at me as I said goodbye. Without speaking, Mrs McBride held him out for me. I took him in my arms and kissed his cheek.

At last, I gave him back, then turned towards the door. Mrs McBride was speaking again.

"It's for the best. Everybody says it's for the best."

I barely heard her words. I walked down the path and up the long street. Every few yards, I stopped and looked back, my eyes blinded with tears. I knew that a chapter was closing in my life and I would never see my child again.

# BOOK THREE

# 38.

When I gave away Martin, something inside me changed. I built a shell around myself to make me tough to the world. I also became a liar. The lies began as small untruths. I had to explain a gap in my life. I had to hide things from my family. My motives were good. I lied to avoid pain and embarrassment. But eventually, lies became easier and they slipped off my tongue without a thought.

I knew now that I had to leave Belfast. When Mrs McBride barred me from her house, she removed my last reason to stay. I counted my money and found I had almost ten pounds. I collected my wages and left my job, returning to Iveagh Place to tell Tess about my decision. She was sorry to see me go. Since the American Eagle had closed, she had come to rely on the money I paid her for rent. But it was much more than that. Tess and I had been good friends and had seen happy times together. And my departure was a signal that her own life was changing too. I packed a suitcase and gave Tess the things I didn't want. I gave the boys ten shillings each as a going-away present. I knew Tess would probably take the money from them and that's why I did it. I said goodbye and caught the train to Dublin.

This was a new city where I knew no one, and that seemed like a good reason to go. I wanted to start afresh, to put the past behind me and begin anew. The only memento I brought from that period in my life was the picture of Martin in his christening robes. I had it framed and kept it always beside my bed.

I remember the feeling I experienced as the train pulled out of the station in a clanging of wheels and panting steam. It was the same feeling I'd had when I left Ballinaleck three years earlier: the sense of embarking on an adventure which could take me anywhere. But I was older and wiser now and events had hardened me. I no longer saw life with the dewy eyes of innocence. I knew that it was going to be a struggle, that it could be brutal and harsh. Experience had made me cynical. I took nothing on trust and questioned everything.

Dublin was different to Belfast. The War had barely touched it. The buildings were grander and the streets were wider. There were more shops, more churches, more pubs, more people. The skyline was dominated with spires and domes and glistening rooftops. When I got off the train, I looked across the river and saw the mountains. They seemed to reach right into the heart of the city, as if I could stroll out there in an afternoon and be among them.

Outside the station, a taxi-driver asked if he could take me somewhere. I told him I was looking for digs but didn't want to pay too much. He put my case in the back of his car and drove me to a house in Ranelagh. It was a big, solid house with a garden and an iron gate, and two stone dogs guarding the front door. The woman who answered my knock was small and wore a hairnet and glasses that were stuck together with elastoplast.

She inspected me, her eyes taking in my clothes and my shoes and my battered suitcase.

"You want a single room?"

"Yes."

"I can give you a room and breakfast for ten shillings a week."

She said it with the air of someone who wasn't too pressed. It seemed reasonable, so I accepted.

"One week's rent in advance. No drinking in your room. No male visitors. Laundry is extra. Breakfast served from seven till nine. Front door is locked at eleven o'clock. My name is Mrs Bolger. I'm a widow."

She stuck out her hand and I grasped it.

"Stella Maguire. I'm pleased to meet you."

"Come in, Stella. I'll show you the room. I'm sure you'll like it. It's nothing fancy, but it's comfortable. I'm known as a plain dealer. You play fair with me and I'll play fair with you. Do we understand each other?"

She spoke in a rapid, staccato voice, with an accent that I found difficult to follow.

She led me into the house. There was a coat-stand and a table and mirrors. Off the hall was a parlour and kitchen. I saw a skinny servant-girl in an apron slicing vegetables. She looked at me shyly but didn't speak.

Mrs Bolger took me up the stairs, pointing out things as she went.

"The bathroom's in there. I expect it to be kept clean. If you want to have a bath, tell me in advance. Guests are allowed their own wireless sets but noise must be kept down. Wireless sets to be turned off completely at eleven o'clock."

She came to a room and pushed open the door. It was a nice bright room with a single bed and a wardrobe and a writing desk beside the window. There was a dressing table with a mirror and a vase holding imitation flowers.

Mrs Bolger folded her arms and waited for my response.

"Well?"

"I like it."

She brightened at once.

"You're very wise, Stella. You won't get better digs than this. I have commercial gentlemen travel up to Dublin several times a month and they go out of their way to stay with me. Word of mouth. Best advertising."

She held out her hand and I opened my purse and took out a ten shilling note. I watched her squirrel it away in a pocket of her cardigan.

"You're from the North?"

"Yes, Enniskillen."

"I knew by your voice. I've never been there. Dublin's fine by me. Never want to leave."

"It's not so bad. You might like it," I told her.

"Maybe, but it's too late now. Your name? Stella? Is that a Northern name?"

"No. It's French. It's short for Estelle. It means 'star'."

Mrs Bolger was impressed.

"My, my. It's a beautiful name. Your mother gave you that name?"

"Yes."

"She must be a very discerning woman. Yes indeed. Discerning. A woman with taste, I'd say."

Next morning, after breakfast, I set out to find a job. I dressed in my best clothes: a dark jacket, white blouse, grey skirt, and nylon stockings I had been given by a soldier in the American Eagle. I'd been saving them for a special occasion. I got out my shoes and polished them with a cloth till they shone. Finally, I applied a thin line of lipstick and studied myself in the mirror.

I looked presentable. I had made up my mind. This time, there would be no more dead-end jobs. I was determined to get something good, something with position that paid well. It would be a career. But I had no illusion that my lack of formal qualifications narrowed my options.

Mrs Bolger had told me how to get into town. I walked down Ranelagh Road to Charlemont Street bridge and turned right along the Grand Canal. It was a bright October morning with just a touch of cold in the air. People went by on bicycles. Occasionally, a tram went clanking past, or a motor car phut-phutting its way into the city. I walked briskly along the banks of the canal, past the ducks feeding among the tall rushes at the water's edge, till at last I came to a newsagent's shop.

A bell tinkled as I entered and a pasty-faced man in a brown shop-coat looked up from the counter.

"Good morning."

"Good morning," I replied. "I need your advice. I'm new to Dublin. Which paper is best for employment advertisements?"

The man beamed, as if welcoming the challenge.

"That depends on the type of job you're interested in. If it's professional vacancies, *The Irish Times* is best."

"No, it's not professional."

"Clerical?"

"No."

"Hotel?"

I shook my head.

"Domestic?"

He was enjoying the game.

"Definitely not."

He laughed.

"I said that for a joke. I can see you wouldn't be interested in domestic work. You're much too … refined. What you need is the *Independent*. It carries all the employment vacancies. If it's a job worth having, it'll be in the Indo."

I paid him and went and sat down on a nearby bench. Opening the paper, I turned to the 'vacancies' column and began to scan the adverts.

There were long black columns of type advertising jobs as clerks and secretarial assistants but I paid them no attention. There was no point wasting my time. I knew they would demand typing and book-keeping skills that I didn't possess. My eye sped past requests for domestics and cooks and waitresses till I came to a category headed SHOP ASSISTANTS.

I thought, this is something I could do. I could sell things. It would mean standing behind a counter and talking to customers. Most of the time, they would know what they wanted and it would be a matter of wrapping it for them and taking their money. It would be an interesting job. I would be meeting people. One advertisement particularly caught my attention. It read:

> Young lady required for busy cosmetics department. Must be smart and well-groomed. Punctuality and diligence essential. Must have previous experience. Apply: General Manager, Brown Thomas, Grafton Street, Dublin.

I circled the ad with my pen. This was the one. It said smart and well-groomed. I thought of my hair. It needed a cut. I was running low on money, but this was an emergency. I would have to get to a hairdresser's. By now I was excited. I could see myself at the cosmetics counter advising the ladies on lipsticks and perfumes. Another thought came hurtling into my head. The ad stated: MUST HAVE PREVIOUS EXPERIENCE.

There and then, I decided I would bluff. I wasn't going to let this opportunity slip from my grasp. I rolled the paper in a ball and tossed it in the first bin I found.

Two hours and one haircut later, I presented myself at the store and asked to see the General Manager. It was a grand place with long, shiny counters and carpeted floors. It was grander than any store I had ever seen before. While I waited, I fingered my hair again. Now, it was soft and silky, where it had recently been washed and set.

At last, a tall woman approached.

"You've come about the cosmetics vacancy, Miss ...?"

"Maguire."

"Have you experience?"

I looked her straight in the eye.

"Of course."

"Follow me, please."

She led me to a glass-panelled office and knocked respectfully on the door before entering.

"Miss Maguire to see Mr Henderson."

She left me and an older woman took charge.

"Please take a seat. Mr Henderson will see you in a while."

She proceeded to ignore me, turning to a large typewriter and hammering on the keys. I looked around the office. On the wall, hung a picture of a man with a bushy moustache looking stern and important. Calendars advertised men's overcoats and ladies' umbrellas, and the ticking of a clock seemed to fill the small room.

Eventually, a phone rang and the woman answered.

"Mr Henderson will see you now," she said to me.

I followed her. Mr Henderson sat behind a huge desk with his back to the window. He was a well-fed man of about fifty with plump, red cheeks and grey, close-cropped hair; dressed in a neat striped suit with shirt and tie. He stood up as I came in and shook my hand.

"Please sit down, Miss Maguire."

I gave him my best smile. As he pointed to a chair, I saw him examining me, checking my looks and my clothes, but his face gave nothing away.

"Where are you from?"

"Enniskillen."

"Ah, a Northerner. Northerners know the value of a shilling. And they're not afraid of hard work. What experience do you have?"

I cleared my throat and plunged ahead.

"I worked in Anderson and Macauley's store in Belfast for three years."

"Which department?"

"Millinery."

"Not cosmetics?"

"No. But I'm willing to learn. I believe selling is the same whichever department. It's a matter of satisfying the customer and sending her away happy."

Mr Henderson seemed pleased with my reply.

"Very good, Miss Maguire. My own sentiments entirely. We expect our staff to be courteous and helpful. We expect them to be ambassadors for the company. Shop work can be very stressful. How would you cope with that?"

"By keeping busy."

"Excellent. Stress is a mental condition. People who are busy don't have time to get stressed. Miss Maguire, from time to time, this job will involve advising ladies on which cosmetics to purchase. It requires a good eye and excellent taste. And diplomacy. What suits one lady may not suit another. Do you think you would be able for that?"

"Certainly. I would regard it as a challenge. And if I have any doubts I will consult my superior."

Mr Henderson sat back and smiled.

"Well, I think there's little more to say. When can you start?"

I struggled to hide my excitement.

"Whenever suits."

"Tomorrow morning. The hours are nine to six, Mondays to

Saturdays. Wednesday is a half day. Pay is thirty shillings a week. We provide a staff canteen where you can have a nourishing lunch at subsidised prices. Do you have any questions?"

"No, sir."

"Very good."

He leaned across the desk and shook my hand again.

"Welcome to Brown Thomas. We need your references for our files. You can leave them with my secretary on the way out."

I felt my heart stop.

"I ... I don't have them with me."

Mr Henderson gave me a startled look.

"No references?"

"They were destroyed in a fire. It burnt down my flat in Belfast. I lost all my personal possessions. I just had the clothes I stood in."

"My God, that's terrible. Was anybody injured?"

"No. The flat was empty at the time. The fire brigade think it was something to do with the electricity."

Mr Henderson was all concern now.

"That must have been a terrible shock, Miss Maguire. Never mind. Put it all behind you. Report to Miss Burgess in the morning and she'll show you what to do."

As I stepped into the crowds of shoppers swirling along Grafton Street, I could scarcely contain my joy. At last, I had managed to secure a decent job, something with promise and potential, something I would be proud to write home and tell my parents about. I had lied and bluffed to get it but I told myself I had no choice. I had been given another chance and I made a silent vow that I would allow nothing or no one to take it from me.

# 39.

Emily Burgess was a thin, nervous woman with a worried face and narrow, suspicious eyes beneath a pale complexion. She was in her mid-forties and lived with her older, unmarried sister in a small flat in Clontarf. I think her parents were dead. From the very beginning, she took a dislike to me. She was my supervisor, in charge of six young women assistants and responsible for dealing with the representatives of the perfume and cosmetics companies who called once a month to take orders.

She was extremely conscientious. Although the store didn't open till nine o'clock, Miss Burgess insisted we be at our posts at 8.45 a.m. for a general inspection. This involved standing in line like schoolgirls while Miss Burgess examined our stockings, uniforms and even our fingernails.

She would march up and down and deliver her lecture: "Remember girls. Brown Thomas is the premier store in Dublin and you are its ambassadors." She parroted Mr Henderson's words exactly. "Our customers expect to be attended by an assistant who is neat and well-groomed. They don't expect to be served by someone looking like a scullery maid."

It didn't take me long to discover that the cosmetics counter was regarded as the top counter in the store and the women who worked there were the envy of the other staff. To work in Brown Thomas at all, you had to be bright and intelligent. But to work on the cosmetics counter, you needed something more. You needed a touch of class.

Our uniform consisted of blouse, skirt and scarf. Miss Burgess

checked that the blouse was freshly laundered and the seams of our
stockings were straight. She made sure our make-up was properly
applied and our hair was washed and brushed. She even checked that
we had cleaned our teeth. When she was satisfied, she snapped her
fingers and we hurried to our posts, smiling and ready for the first
customers.

Miss Burgess was a martinet, but I quickly detected an insecurity
behind the bluster. She had been in charge of cosmetics for ten years
but her long experience hadn't given her confidence. Quite the reverse.
The cosmetics counter was the one area in the store where youth was
prized and Miss Burgess was constantly on the lookout for a rival
among the younger staff coming behind. Many of our customers were
seeking glamour. They wanted to look young. Miss Burgess was getting
old and she knew her days were numbered.

For the first week, she put me working with a young woman called
Connie Campbell, so I could learn the job. The most difficult part was
getting to know the range of products we sold. We had scores of
lipsticks and mascaras; dozens of make-ups; different types of
shampoo; various shades of hair conditioner; diverse brands of
perfume.

I enjoyed the work and quickly adapted, but the first few weeks were
difficult. I had to work a week in lieu which meant it was a fortnight
till I got paid any wages. So I harvested my meagre cash. I budgeted
tightly and spent only on essentials: rent, tram fares and meals. Mrs
Bolger's breakfast was porridge and toast, exactly like Mrs
McCrudden's, but it carried me through till lunchtime and the staff
canteen where, for a shilling, I ate roast beef and boiled potatoes or
chicken and stuffing followed by bread and butter pudding and
custard.

With the few pounds I had left, I bought a supply of stockings and
blouses. I washed my hair several times a week, making sure to always
look smart. At last I had got a decent job and I was determined to hold
on to it. I certainly impressed Mrs Bolger. One morning, I overheard
her tell Miss O'Leary, a gangly young woman from County Clare who

worked in the Department of Lands, that I had secured a senior position in Brown Thomas.

"Of course, she comes from a very well-to-do family in the North. Her mother is a most refined person. Speaks French, she does. Oh Yes. Speaks it like a Frenchwoman."

*

It wasn't all work. I quickly became friends with Connie Campbell and, one evening, she invited me to her family's house for tea. She lived in Raheny and we got the tram from Nelson's Pillar after work. The tram ran out through the northside of the city, past Fairview and Killester, and Connie took great pleasure pointing out places of interest.

I was introduced to her mother and father, two brothers, and a younger sister. We crowded round the big family dinner table and waited for Mrs Campbell to serve us eggs and rashers.

She was a large woman with a jolly face and a blunt, no-nonsense attitude to life. She peppered me with questions.

"How do you like Brown Thomas?"

"I like it very much," I replied.

"I think you and Connie are very lucky. There's plenty of girls would give their right arm for a job like that. Such a swanky store. They only take the cream. Of course, Connie was always clever. She got the best marks in Holy Faith school in her Inter Cert. The nuns always said she'd do well."

Connie groaned and rolled her eyes. The smell of the food was making me hungry but I tried to remember my table manners. Mrs Campbell encouraged me. She kept piling more onto my plate.

"Go on. Eat up. You've been on your feet all day. An empty sack can't stand."

"I'm full," I protested.

"Get away out of that. Sure you poor creatures in the North must have been starved these last few years. I read all about it in the papers. Everything was rationed. I believe the people couldn't even get a cup of tea for love nor money."

She bombarded me with questions about Belfast and the War while the rest of the family watched with awe as if I was some rare exotic bird. When I was leaving, Mrs Campbell pressed a parcel of apple cake into my hands.

"That's for when you get hungry. I know what it's like living in digs. Some of them landladies would expect you to exist on the skin of a herring."

\*

Connie was going out with a young man called Gabriel Doyle and one evening she suggested we go on a foursome to the pictures with his friend, Jimmy Rickard. The two men were clerks in Guinness's brewery and Connie was planning to get married, even though it would mean giving up her job in Brown Thomas.

I hadn't been to the pictures for months, so I agreed. We met the men at Clery's clock in O'Connell Street. They were dressed up for the occasion: blazers and slacks and hair oiled with Brylcreem. Connie's man was small and thin with pale blue eyes. He seemed unsure of himself. He grabbed her hand and held it tight as if he was afraid she might run away.

Jimmy Rickard was tall and broad-shouldered, with sandy hair that stood up in spikes, despite the Brylcreem. He held open the cinema door for me and dusted the seat with his handkerchief before I sat down. We watched *Objective Burma* with Errol Flynn and afterwards went to Cafolla's Café for ice cream.

Gabriel seemed happy to sit gazing into Connie's face but Jimmy was full of chat.

"It must have been dire living in Belfast."

"How do you mean?"

"With the War and everything. Were you there when the Germans dropped the bombs?"

"No, that was earlier."

"I'm glad we stayed out of it. If we'd been in, Hitler would have bombed us too. Anyway, I don't see why we should be fighting England's wars after all she did to us for six hundred years."

"It wasn't just England's war," I protested. "It was everybody's war. If Hitler hadn't been stopped, he would have taken over the entire world."

Jimmy was shocked.

"Are you a Protestant?"

"What's that got to do with it?"

"Stella's a Protestant name, isn't it? And you look like a Protestant."

I laughed.

"What does a Protestant look like, Jimmy?"

"Well-bred and healthy. And good-looking. Just like you."

A few days later, Connie approached me once more. She told me that Jimmy was very taken by me and wanted us to go out together again. But I knew that one thing would only lead to another. I wasn't ready for romance. I was still grieving for Martin, so I turned Jimmy down.

I threw myself into the job, learning the names and prices of all the different products. I studied the brochures and the promotional material. I bought the latest fashion journals in Easons bookstore and read them from cover to cover. I was quickly becoming an expert in style.

At work, I put on my most cheerful face. I was willing. I was considerate. I was punctual. I was always neat and well-groomed. I worked hard and made myself pleasant to colleagues and customers. I took on extra tasks. I was the perfect employee.

But always, I was aware of Emily Burgess. She watched me all the time, waiting for me to make a mistake. She counted the minutes when I went to the washroom or for my tea break. She never offered me encouragement or advice. Something had turned her against me and at first I didn't know what it was. Then the reason dawned on me. She had singled me out as a potential rival.

# 40.

One day, a few weeks later, I looked up to see a tall, thin woman smiling pleasantly at me. She was dressed in a smart tweed suit and a string of pearls nestled against the pale skin of her throat. To my unpractised eye, the pearls looked real.

"I wonder if you could help me? I'm looking for a fragrance."

I gazed into the well-preserved face and tried to guess her age. It was difficult. She could have been anything from thirty to fifty.

"Certainly, Madam. Do you have anything in mind?"

"I thought you might be able to advise me. I've been wearing La Rose, but now I'm tired of it."

She lowered her voice and whispered conspiratorially.

"It's becoming too popular. I thought I might try something else."

"Yes, Madam. I understand. Have you tried Reve by Danielle?"

I had a tray of perfumes ready and I brought them out and set them on the counter.

"Reve is new. I don't think you'll find too many people wearing it. Would you like to try it?"

I sprayed some scent on my wrist and held it out for her approval. She lowered her nose.

"Too loud. I want something more discreet. I believe a fragrance should be subtle. It shouldn't assault one."

"Of course, Madam. There's Diamanté by Corsair. Perhaps that might suit?"

I produced the bottle and sprayed again. She sniffed and shook her head.

"Too bland."

I tried several more without success. She was proving a difficult customer.

"What about Gigolo?" I said at last.

"Gigolo?"

I watched an eyebrow shoot up.

"It's for the younger woman," I said quickly. "A delicate scent but with a strong sensual undertone. It might not suit every lady, but I think it would suit you."

It was straight from the sales catalogue with a large dollop of flattery thrown in. I saw at once that she was interested.

She sniffed and smiled.

"Intriguing."

"This scent combines subtlety with distinction. It was launched just last week at Cannes and by all accounts it was a big success. This batch only arrived today. I can safely say you'll be the first lady in Dublin to wear it."

She was hooked.

"I'll take it."

"Would Madam prefer the large or small bottle?"

"Oh, the large, of course. I'm rarely in Dublin these days. I find travelling so tiresome. My husband is having a business lunch at his club and God knows when I'll be back."

While I wrapped the purchase, she opened her handbag and took out her cheque book.

"Thank you. You've been most helpful."

When she was gone, I looked at the cheque.

Lady Cynthia de Vere, Rathmore House, Co Wicklow, was printed at the bottom, below her illegible signature.

*

In my next pay packet, there was a note from Mr Henderson to say the company was very satisfied with my performance and the reaction from customers had been extremely positive. It urged me to continue in the same vein. I felt a thrill of pleasure to know that my efforts were not going unnoticed.

We were heading into the Christmas season. It was the first Christmas since the War and the company was expecting heavy trading, particularly from British visitors to Dublin; while rationing still continued in Britain, it was practically non-existent in the Free State.

Miss Burgess seemed to be in a state of constant panic, unsure how many goods to order, worried in case she ordered too few and the store lost sales or too many and we were left with unsold stock. I sympathised with her. It was a difficult task calling for fine judgement but she made it worse by continually changing her mind. I could see the representatives from the cosmetics companies getting exasperated.

To make matters worse, she took out her frustration on the staff, nit-picking about time-keeping and fussing over appearance and service. The women could only suffer in silence and pray that things would improve when Christmas was over. But the constant petty criticism was affecting their morale.

For some reason, she left me alone. Perhaps she was saving me for a major confrontation, waiting for me to make a blunder of such proportions that it would damn me without reservation. Sure enough an event occurred towards the end of November which set us on a headlong collision.

It was a Saturday, the afternoon of our busiest day. I was working beside Connie Campbell when an elderly lady approached the counter. Connie began to serve her. I heard the lady say she wanted to purchase a lipstick for her niece. Connie showed her several samples and, eventually, the lady picked one. She took her purse out of her handbag and paid. Connie wrapped the lipstick and I saw the lady slip the purse and the present together into a black shopping bag and move off through the crowded store.

I was distracted by a customer wanting to be shown some face make-up. I helped her decide and then another customer asked to buy soap. I was kept busy till the sound of raised voices drew my attention. The elderly lady was back and she was arguing with Connie.

"I tell you it was here. I must have left it on the counter."

"I'm afraid I didn't see it," Connie replied, politely.

"But you must have seen it, girl. You were the last person I was talking to. I didn't realise it was gone till I was in the bookshop next door."

"If you left it here Madam, I'm sure I would have seen it."

The lady was distressed and beginning to get agitated.

"Don't contradict me. I always keep it in my handbag and it's not there. Now, where else could it be?"

At that moment, Miss Burgess appeared. She walked quickly to the head of the counter and brusquely moved Connie aside.

"I'm the supervisor, Madam. Can I be of assistance?"

The lady appealed to her.

"I've lost my purse. The last time I saw it was here, when I bought a lipstick. This young lady served me and now she says she didn't see it."

Miss Burgess turned to Connie.

"Well, Miss Campbell. What have you got to say?"

Connie looked helpless.

"I did sell her the lipstick but I didn't see her purse."

"You must have seen it," the lady insisted.

She was very excited now. Around the store, heads were beginning to turn. She pointed a finger at Connie and demanded: "I want the police called. I believe she stole it."

Connie gasped. This was the most serious charge anyone could level against a shop assistant.

I was loath to get involved but I knew I couldn't stand aside and let my friend be accused like this. I walked quickly to her side.

"Maybe I can help," I offered.

Miss Burgess gave me a frozen look.

"Please stay out of this, Miss Maguire. This is none of your business."

"Connie's just been called a thief. Someone has to defend her."

Miss Burgess bristled.

"I'm ordering you to return to your post. *I* will deal this."

I ignored her and spoke directly to the customer.

"Have you looked in your shopping bag?"

"My shopping bag?"

"Yes. I think you put your purse in your shopping bag along with the lipstick."

"I couldn't have. I never do that."

"Why don't you check?"

I glanced at Connie and she was trembling with fear.

"It'll be all right," I whispered. "Trust me."

The lady opened her bag and her expression changed. She now looked crestfallen. She slowly drew out the purse.

"Good Lord. I don't know how it could have got there. I always put it in my handbag."

She turned to Connie.

"I'm dreadfully sorry. I must have got confused."

Connie took a deep breath.

"That's quite all right, Madam. We all make mistakes."

Miss Burgess spoke through clenched teeth.

"Well if everything's in order, you may return to your duties, Miss Campbell."

She glared at me through narrow eyes, a look of pure hatred.

"You too, Miss Maguire."

# 41.

From this point on, Miss Burgess's enmity was out in the open. I had challenged her authority in front of a customer and, worse still, in front of a member of staff. And I had been proved right. Miss Burgess's loss of face was enormous.

Word of what had happened spread like wildfire. By closing time, it seemed that everyone in the store had heard the story about Connie being accused of theft and how I had come to her rescue. It made me a kind of heroine, but it wasn't what I wanted.

I could see now that Miss Burgess would have no option but to have me removed: I posed too great a threat to her. I also knew she would go about her task in a surreptitious way. A direct attack would be too obvious. I would have to be constantly on guard. But I had little idea what she would ultimately unleash.

There was a tradition of going for a drink after work on Saturday in the Bailey pub on Duke Street. It was the end of the week, everyone had got paid, and Sunday was the Sabbath Day.

When I walked into the pub that evening with Connie, the place erupted in applause. I blinked in the dim light of the bar. It seemed that half the store was there standing up and clapping. I hadn't realised just how unpopular Emily Burgess really was.

People crowded round. Someone pressed a gin and tonic into my hand. Paddy Kinsella, the elderly commisionaire, leaned close and whispered: "Well done, Stella. I wish I'd been there to see that ould wagon's face when you told her to shag off."

"I what?"

"Told her to go and have a good hump to herself. That's what I heard anyway."

"I never said that. Did I, Connie?"

She was laughing.

"Not in so many words. But it amounted to the same thing in the end."

"As for that other ould biddy," Paddy Kinsella continued, speaking to Connie. "Accusing you of stealing her purse. The cheek of her. You know you could sue her for that? You know that's slander? And you've got plenty of witnesses."

Connie shrugged.

"What's the point?"

"Well it might just teach her to button her lip in future before she goes firing off allegations about people."

We had one more drink before it was time to go. Outside, there was a bitter wind blowing up from the Liffey. I pulled my overcoat close around me as Connie and I walked towards the tram.

"How do I thank you, Stella?"

"For what?"

"Saving my bacon. I hadn't a clue where that woman had put her purse."

"She would have found it eventually."

"I suppose you're right. But it was very decent of you, nevertheless. You know Miss Burgess will never forgive you? You realise you've put your head on the chopping block?"

"Of course. But I had no option."

It sounded brave but privately I was afraid. I had crossed Emily Burgess and I knew I would have a fight on my hands.

*

Every Saturday night, Mrs Bolger played poker in the parlour with four of her cronies. They gathered at eight o'clock, after the evening meal was served, the dishes had been washed, and Maggie Skillen, the skivvy, had been given the night off to go to the pictures with her boy. The women enjoyed their poker and, if I went past the parlour door, I would hear them cursing like troopers. In the morning, the place would stink of cigarette smoke and Mrs Bolger would open all the windows to let in fresh air.

That night, as I came in from the pub, Mrs Bolger was waiting.

"This evening, Stella? Are you booked?"

It took me a moment to catch her drift. She was asking if I was going out again. I was feeling tired and I had planned to read a book and get an early night.

"No," I said.

"Good. You ever play poker?"

I shook my head.

"It's easy. I'll teach you. Rosie Callender's not well. Her angina's playing her up. We're short a player. You'll do."

Before I had time to argue, she swept me into the parlour and dealt out the cards.

"Everybody gets five and you can buy three more. Best hand is a royal flush, then four aces. I'll show you."

We spent half an hour practising and then she let me go.

"Eight o'clock. You be down here. And bring money," she shouted as I climbed the stairs to my room.

Even though I was tired, I felt compelled to attend to Mrs Bolger's demand. She was my landlady and I had grown fond of her. Besides, I didn't feel like making two enemies on the same day. So, at the appointed time, I went down to her parlour. Mrs Bolger and three crones sat around the card table. They stared at me silently like the witches from Macbeth. One of them reached out and pushed the deck across the table.

"Put a penny in the middle and deal."

*

At work, the pace was hectic. Miss Burgess had stopped speaking to me now, except to give orders. It was difficult to stand all day in the same company and not exchange small pleasantries. This was a tactic I had witnessed at school, when a girl had fallen foul of the pack and was

215

effectively shunned and sent to Coventry. It was cruel and I never agreed with it. But, at least here, I had the company and support of the other women.

So I was surprised when Miss Burgess came down the counter one morning to say there was a telephone call for me. It was rare to receive calls at work. I had never had one before and I was intrigued. I walked to where the phone lay beside its cradle and picked it up.

A plummy voice came down the line. It sounded like it was coming from very far away.

"Hello. Is that Miss Maguire?"

"Yes."

"Cynthia de Vere speaking. I must say that fragrance you sold me went down a treat. All my friends are desperate to know what it is and where I got it. But, of course, I won't tell them."

"I'm very pleased."

"Yes, well. I'm glad I took your advice. Look here. I'm coming up to Dublin today to do my Christmas shopping. I'm calling in to Brown Thomas to see you. Will you be there?"

"Certainly."

"Very good. Twelve o'clock. Freddie's giving me lunch so I must be finished by one. I'll see you then. Goodbye."

I assumed Freddie must be her husband. I got on with my duties while I waited her arrival, but Lady de Vere didn't come at twelve o'clock as promised. She came at twenty to one, accompanied by a burly man in a chauffeur's uniform who was loaded with boxes and parcels. He put them down and took out a handkerchief to wipe his red face. Lady de Vere peeled off her gloves.

"We've been delayed. Never saw such crowds. People behaving like absolute savages. No consideration. Now then, I need the following."

She gave me a handwritten list of items: perfumes, mascaras, lipsticks, powders. There were about twenty articles. It would take me at least half an hour to find them all.

"Chrsitmas presents for my friends," Lady de Vere explained. "And I need each item individually wrapped."

216

She turned to the chauffeur.

"What time is it, Casey?"

The man took a large watch out of his overcoat pocket.

"Quarter to one, Ma'am."

"Good God. We're going to be late. Freddie'll be drunk as a skunk."

"Yes, Ma'am."

I could see her getting agitated.

"Damned crowds. I told Freddie we should come earlier. Bloody fool wouldn't listen."

I had an inspiration. I said: "Lady de Vere, would you trust me to select these items for you? You could go and have lunch and, when you come back, I'll have them ready."

She beamed.

"What a wonderful idea. My husband is such a child. The minute I let him out of my sight, he starts straight into the McClennan. Come along, Casey. You can drive me to Jammets. I could do with a pink gin myself."

They were back at four o'clock, an unsteady Freddie supported by a weary-looking Casey. I had the presents wrapped and tied with ribbon and placed in a large box that Casey could easily carry to the car.

Lady de Vere was delighted. She looked at the bill which I had stuck on the top of the box, then took out her cheque book and wrote a cheque for the amount. She was about to put the book away when she changed her mind and opened it again. She quickly scribbled another cheque and handed it to me.

"A Christmas present, Miss Maguire. For all your help. You've been a darling."

I glanced at the cheque. It was for five pounds.

I looked up and saw Miss Burgess watching me. She had a look on her face that seemed to say: Enjoy yourself while you can. I have the measure of you and you won't last long.

# 42.

I didn't go home for Christmas. I couldn't face them after all that had happened in Belfast. The wounds were still raw. I didn't trust myself with all the lies it would have called for. So I wrote a long letter explaining that we were too busy at the store, and enclosed money for presents. I told Mammy I was having a wonderful time in Dublin and wished them all a happy Christmas.

Only two other guests remained with Mrs Bolger over the holiday period: Miss O'Leary from the Department of Lands, and a middle-aged bank official called Mr Pender, who had no relatives except an old aunt in a nursing home in Blackrock. Everyone else had returned to their families.

On Christmas Day, after Mass, we gathered around the big table in the parlour and Mrs Bolger served turkey and ham with Brussels sprouts and roast potatoes.

Mr Pender brought a bottle of Italian wine. It came in a little wicker basket and he popped the cork and poured glasses with the air of a sophisticate. Miss O'Leary protested that she didn't drink, but Mr Pender coaxed her and reluctantly, with much blushing and fluttering of eyelids, she agreed to have a splash.

"I do hope this doesn't go to my head, Mr Pender", she said, nervously sipping at her glass.

"Not at all. It's good for you. The Mediterranean people swear by their wine. They have a saying: A meal without wine, is like a day without sunshine."

"Oh that's beautiful, Mr Pender. So poetic. Of course, they are a poetic people."

"Yes, indeed, Miss O'Leary. The cradle of Dante and the Renaissance. Not to mention Michelangelo and the wonderful operas. Have you ever visited?"

"Not yet, Mr Pender."

Mrs Bolger caught my glance across the table. I heard her sigh and roll her eyes to heaven. We clinked glasses and toasted each other's health. Afterwards, we had plum pudding with custard and Mrs Bolger put on the wireless and tuned into a programme playing Christmas carols. She suggested poker but none of the others knew how to play. So we just huddled together in the parlour as darkness fell and pretended to enjoy ourselves, while outside, the wind shook the window frames and hurled raindrops against the glass.

I had been invited to spend St Stephen's Day with Connie and her family. The following morning, I indulged myself. I lay in bed till ten o'clock, and then had a luxurious bath and a cup of tea, and strolled into town.

It was a cold morning and the streets were empty. Nothing stirred. In the windows of the houses, the Christmas candles burned. At the bridge, I turned onto the canal path. It was deserted, the only sound the wind whistling drearily through the leafless trees.

As I walked, I felt a sadness settle over me. I thought of all those people at home with their families while I was alone in this empty city. I thought of Martin. This was his first Christmas. I wondered if he missed me, or even remembered me. My heart filled with grief. I stood for a while staring into the dark waters of the canal and the realisation came to me that all my Christmases would be like this; that I would always wonder about my child and never be able to forgive myself for giving him away.

*

At the Campbell's house it was difficult to remain sad. I got the tram from the Pillar and arrived at Raheny in time for lunch. There was a gaiety around the dinner table that quickly drew me in. Mrs Campbell wrapped her beefy arms around me and gave me a big hug and then I handed her the present I had bought – a set of kitchen knives which I got at a discount in the store. She tut-tutted about spending my hard-earned cash, but I could see she was pleased.

As the guest of honour, she made me sit at the head of the table, while her husband carved the turkey. Everyone had to wear paper hats. Mr Campbell said Grace and we all tucked in.

Mrs Campbell kept a maternal eye on me as we ate. Every time my plate got low, she forked food in my direction.

"Have more turkey."

"Have more ham."

"Have more potatoes."

I protested, but she would brook no refusal. In the end, I was glad when the dishes were cleared away. Then the chairs were pushed into the corners of the room, and the fire was stacked up.

Mr Campbell produced bottles of stout and glasses of hot toddy. The neighbours began to drift in at five o'clock; Gabriel Doyle arrived with Jimmy Rickard, carrying more parcels of stout. Gabriel found a seat beside Connie and Jimmy sat down beside me.

Mr Campbell said it was time for a song. He stood up and sang 'Danny Boy'. Everyone applauded and someone else sang: 'Biddy Mulligan, the Pride of the Coombe'. Eventually it was Jimmy Rickard's turn. He looked at me and took my hand.

*Oh, love is pleasing and love is teasing;*
*And love is a pleasure when first it's new.*
*But love grows colder as love grows older;*
*And fades away like the morning dew.*

He had a beautiful tenor voice and the room fell silent. I could feel that everyone knew he was singing this song for me. At the end of the evening, when it was time to go, Jimmy came with me into the hall.

"How are you getting home?"

"I'll get the tram."

"But the last one's gone. It's only a limited service today."

"Then I'll get a taxi."

"You'll be lucky. I'd say all the taximen in Dublin are safely tucked up by their own firesides tonight. C'mon, I'll drive you. I've got the jalopy outside."

We made the journey through the empty streets in half an hour. Jimmy drew up outside my digs and turned off the engine.

"Why did you sing that song?" I asked.

"Because it's the way I feel about you. Everybody thinks love makes you happy. But sometimes it doesn't. Sometimes it just makes you sad."

He put his arm around my shoulder.

"Do me a favour, Stella. Make me happy."

I looked into his eyes. They were almost pleading.

"Okay," I said. "If that's what you want. But I can't give any guarantees how it will turn out."

"That's fine. I'll take my chances."

He drew me close and I felt his warm lips embracing mine.

*

At work, the hectic pace continued. When we reopened after Christmas, it was to face the stampede brought on by the sales. If anything, the atmosphere was more frantic than before, as people clawed their way to the counters, fighting and arguing over bargains. We endured a week of stress before the sales ended and business returned to normal.

It was the second week in January when Emily Burgess's plans for me became clear. One morning as we were engaged in stock-taking, Mr Henderson approached the counter and asked to see me in his office. He was a rare sight on the shop floor, preferring to direct operations through his army of managers and supervisors, so I knew at once the matter was serious.

I followed him into his office and closed the door. He cut straight to the point in a cold, formal voice of authority.

"Miss Maguire, I have to tell you that certain facts have been brought to my attention which make me most unhappy."

I thought he was going to raise the incident of the lost purse, even though it had happened weeks before and I had assumed it was forgotten. But it was something else entirely … his words hit me like a thunderbolt.

"You might recall at your interview, you told me you had worked in the millinery department of Anderson and Macauley's store in Belfast?"

"Yes."

"You told me that your references had been lost in a fire?"

"That's right."

"Well, I have been in touch with Anderson and Macauley's, and they tell me they have no knowledge of you working in their millinery department. Indeed they have no knowledge of you ever working there at all."

I was stunned.

"Did you work there or not?"

I hung my head.

"Well, Miss Maguire?"

"No," I admitted at last.

"So you told me an untruth at our interview?"

"Yes. But I was desperate to get the job and I told you I would work hard. I've done that. You sent me a note yourself to say that you were pleased with my performance."

"That may be so, Miss Maguire. But you gained employment here under false pretences. To put it bluntly, you lied to me."

"I couldn't see how else to get started."

"Miss Maguire, the company takes a very dim view of an employee lying to us. You leave me no choice but to terminate your employment."

I felt weak. I saw my job, my career, and my life in Dublin disappearing before my eyes.

"I have no option, Miss Maguire. You may work to the end of the month. But I have to transfer you from the Cosmetics counter. You will work out your time at the Lingerie department. You may go now."

I stood up and walked to the door. Then I turned back.

"You said this information had been brought to your attention. Someone informed on me. It was Miss Burgess, wasn't it?"

Mr Henderson didn't reply. He had bent his head now and was busy writing on a pad.

"It was Miss Burgess who told you?" I persisted.

He looked up and I saw the truth in his eyes.

"That will be all, Miss Maguire."

# 43.

I was devastated. Everything I had striven for had been reduced to ashes, my dream of a new life shattered. I was right back where I started. I left Mr Henderson's office and walked unsteadily onto the floor. With every step I took, I was aware of Emily Burgess. When I turned to look at her, she stared back, a tight smile of triumph on her face.

I kept telling myself: You must be strong; you mustn't show how hurt you are. But I felt anything but strong. I felt like the liar I was and, worse, a liar who had been found out and exposed. I wondered how many other people knew, and imagined them, watching me now, aware of my guilt. I approached the Lingerie counter and asked to see the supervisor.

Betty Evans – a small, energetic woman with a plump, friendly face – was obviously expecting me. Patting my hand she said: "There, there, now. You just come with me Stella, and we'll have a nice cup of tea."

We went to the canteen and she ordered scones. But I couldn't eat anything. I was still in shock.

"Look, dear," she said "I don't know what this is all about but it can't be easy for you. So, for the rest of your time here, I'm not going to put any pressure on you. You just turn in for work and I'll be happy. I won't pretend it's difficult. You could do it in your sleep and, if you have any problems, just come to me."

The kindness of her words was like balm.

"Thank you, Miss Evans. I won't let you down."

"Call me Betty, dear. And of course you won't let me down. But try to cheer up. It's not the end of the world."

But it was for me. I sat quietly sipping my tea till at last Betty Evans said it was time to go back to work. She patted my hand again, like a mother soothing a child who has bruised her knee.

"You can observe for today till you pick up the hang of it. Just behave as if everything is normal. And try to look on the positive side. You've got another two weeks and sure who knows what might turn up?"

Of course, everyone at the Cosmetics department was desperate to find out what had happened. When I left the store that evening, Connie was waiting for me. We walked together to get our trams.

"What in the name of God is going on, Stella? Burgess has been going about all day like all her birthdays have come at once. She was even humming a song this afternoon. I can't remember when I saw her so happy. She's beside herself with joy."

"I've been fired."

"*What?*"

"Mr Henderson is letting me go at the end of the month."

"I don't believe it."

"It's true, Connie."

"Has it got something to do with your run-in with Burgess?"

"In a round-about way."

I acutely felt the shame of my situation, having to explain to my best friend that I had lied to get the job. I told her about my interview with Mr Henderson.

Connie stood ashen-faced.

"Is that all it is? My God, you'd think you'd robbed the place or something. It's your ability to sell they should be thinking about, not whether you've got proper references. Everybody knows you're a bloody good saleswoman."

"But I told them a lie, Connie."

"It wasn't a big lie. Sure, we all lie every day, telling women they'll look beautiful if they buy our products when we know it's a new face some of them need."

"Mr Henderson says I got the job under false pretences."

225

"Oh, to hell with it. The real reason you're getting fired is because Burgess is afraid of you. She knows you'd make ten of her. She can see the way the staff look up to you. I'll tell you something I've never said before. *You* should be the supervisor. You've got a way with people that makes them loyal to you. And that's the secret of being a good manager. Treat people decently and they'll lie down in front of a train for you."

Connie's insight surprised me. I had never considered that she even thought about these things.

"What are you going to do, Stella?"

I squeezed her hand.

"God knows."

Apart from Connie and Betty Evans, no one knew my secret. I certainly didn't tell Mrs Bolger and she continued in ignorance of my plight. If I was going to be unemployed, I wanted the security of a roof over my head while I tried to find another job.

*

Rosie Callendar's angina hadn't improved and I had now been coralled as a regular player in the Saturday night poker school. What's more, I had become quite expert at the game and often came away winning four or five shillings, much to the chagrin of the other players I found that I would lose some of it again the following week, so, on balance, the money seemed to go round each player in turn.

I spent my free time looking out for job opportunities. But I was back at the impasse that had always faced me: I could apply for interviews but I couldn't tell a prospective employer that I had worked for Brown Thomas. They would be bound to ask why I had left such a prestigious store. What's more, they were certain to check with Mr Henderson.

In giddy moments, I wondered if I should throw myself on his mercy and beg him at least to provide me with a reference so that I could obtain another opening. But then cold reality would grip me and I knew it was useless: his sense of rectitude would never allow him to recommend someone he had dismissed for lying. The more I thought about it, the more my avenues of opportunity closed down, till in the end I was forced to recognise that my situation was bleak indeed.

My anxiety must have shown. One evening when we were in Cafolla's after watching a film at the Savoy, Jimmy Rickard said to me: "What's the matter with you, Stella? You're very irritable tonight."

Without thinking, I blurted out: "So would you be in my situation."

"Why, what's wrong?"

I quickly tried to recover.

"Oh, it's just my time of the month."

There was a silence round the table.

"Time of the month?" Gabriel Doyle asked with a stupid look on his face. "What does that mean?"

Connie hit him a dig with her elbow.

"It's a rash she gets. Once a month. Regular as clockwork."

"Jaysis," Gabriel Doyle said. "Sounds rough. There's stuff you can get for that in the chemist's."

\*

The days ticked down to my departure. Connie had given up asking what I was going to do. I had told her so often that I had no success that she feared embarrassing me. Then, a few days before I was due to leave, I came back from the canteen to hear a familar, high-pitched voice.

"Look here. I simply have to see her. I will deal with no one else, so there's no point trying to fob me off."

Lady de Vere was standing at the cosmetics counter and berating Miss Burgess. Wearing a long black overcoat that reached almost to her heels, a fox fur was slung carelessly across her shoulder. On her head sat an outrageous hat with a trailing ostrich feather.

As I approached, she turned round and spotted me.

"Ah! There you are, Miss Maguire. They've been trying to tell me that you weren't available. I need your advice with some hand cream."

I looked from Emily Burgess to Lady de Vere.

"I'm afraid I don't work at Cosmetics anymore. I've been transferred."

227

"Transferred? Where to?"

"Lingerie."

"Good Lord. What idiot was responsible for that?"

She rounded on Miss Burgess.

"Was this your decision?"

"No, Madam."

"Then who was it? I demand to know."

"It was the General Manager, Madam."

"Dickie Henderson? Tell him I wish to see him immediately. Tell him Cynthia de Vere is waiting."

Miss Burgess hesitated. But there was an imperious tone in Lady de Vere's voice that warned she would brook no argument. And the use of the General Manager's first name hinted at familiarity. Miss Burgess quickly hurried away and returned a few minutes later with a beaming Mr Henderson. He rubbed his hands together as he approached.

"Why Cynthia, how good to see you. How is Freddie?"

"Cut out the claptrap, Dickie. I demand to know why this young person has been transferred from the Cosmetics counter and exiled to Lingerie?"

The smile faded from Mr Henderson's face. He glanced at me and then back to Lady de Vere.

"Exiled? Who said anything about exiled?"

"I did. Why isn't she on Cosmetics?"

Mr Henderson cleared his throat.

"It's an internal staff matter."

"My God, man. What are you talking about? Miss Maguire is the best assistant you have. Why, at Christmas she chose all my presents for me totally unaided. She has unerring taste. My friends were delighted. I insist you put her back on Cosmetics at once."

Mr Henderson bit his lip. Lady de Vere's shrill tones were attracting attention. People were beginning to stare.

"Well, Dickie. Are you going to do as I say, or do I have to bring this matter up with the board?"

"No, no, no. Of course."

Mr Henderson turned to me.

"Miss Maguire, you will return at once to Cosmetics."

"Yes, sir."

"I really don't know what you've been thinking about, Dickie. Miss Maguire is invaluable and you bury her in the Lingerie department. I expect to find her on Cosmetics from now on. Do I make myself clear?"

Mr Henderson's face had gone deep purple. He squirmed with embarrassment within his neat pinstriped suit.

"Certainly, Cynthia. That's exactly where she'll be."

# 44.

Through Lady de Vere's intervention not only was my job saved, but I had gained a powerful protector. I was later to discover that her husband, Lord Frederick, was a director of the company and sat on the board. Now, I understood the alacrity with which Mr Henderson had acceded to her demand.

I settled back at work. Emily Burgess could barely conceal her unhappiness but there was nothing she could do. At the same time, I was loath to reopen hostilities with her. I had glimpsed once again the hard, lonely life of the unemployed and it had given me a scare. All I wanted was to get on with my job.

But something Connie had said kept rattling round in my head and I couldn't shake it off. *You should be the supervisor. You've got a way with people that makes them loyal to you.* The idea was very tempting. I recognised the truth in her words. People *did* trust me and I knew I could easily do Miss Burgess's job. But I wasn't about to cross swords with her again.

But, in the unlikely setting of Mrs Bolger's smoky parlour, the hand of fate was to intervene at one of the Saturday night poker games.

By now I was totally engrossed in the game, and eagerly awaited our weekend sessions. That evening I had run into the worst kind of luck: good hands that led me to bet recklessly against even better ones.

The main beneficiary of my misfortune was Mrs Dragg. She was a heavily built woman in her late-fifties, addicted to snuff, and with dyed black hair and a florid complexion. I suspect she had been a striking woman in her day, but, like Mrs Bolger, she was a widow, or at least I took her to be a widow, for her husband was never mentioned. She did have a son called Cyril who I had heard her speak of occasionally when she was in the mood to talk.

That Saturday night, Mrs Dragg was in very good form. She had already relieved me of the best part of five shillings and had a stack of cash sitting in front of her on the green baize cloth that Mrs Bolger used to cover the card table.

"Heh, heh, hch," she cackled as she spread out a flush to top my three queens. "Filled it from the inside. Only bought one card. You took me for two pairs, didn't you, dear?"

She scooped up the pile of pennies and sixpences to add to the stack of coins she had already won.

"Always be respectful of a one-card buyer," Mrs Dragg advised, opening her snuff box and taking a large pinch between stained fingers. "One-card buyers have a nasty habit of surprising you."

I waited for the cards to go round the table again.

"Did I tell you Cyril's coming home?" she said to Mrs Bolger. "Got a letter from him this morning. He's being transferred to Dublin. They're even giving him a motorcar. What do you think of that?"

"Shut up and deal," Mrs Bolger snapped.

"What does your son do, Mrs Dragg?" I asked, politely.

Mrs Dragg flashed her dark eyes at me.

"He's a traveller, dear. He's got a very senior position."

"A traveller in what?"

"Ladies' cosmetics. He works for a big company in London. They're promoting him. Making him manager for the whole of Ireland. If you don't mind!"

My interest picked up.

"When's he coming home?" I asked.

"Next week."

"Would you mind giving me his telephone number?"

Mrs Dragg looked me up and down and then her face broke in a knowing grin.

"Cyril's not spoken for yet, dear. But I've no doubt he's looking to settle down."

Beside me, I heard Mrs Bolger groan.

"Oh, for God's sake. Are we playing cards or talking about Cyril's love life? Anybody got openers?"

*

Cyril Dragg looked exactly like his mother. He was a big, well-fed man with a pink complexion and a head of tight, black curls. He wore a demob suit of grey flannel with turn-ups in his trousers, a blue striped shirt and a red tie with horse-shoes printed on it. He had a gold ring on the little finger of his right hand and a chunky wrist watch with a silver strap.

We met for afternoon tea in the Hibernian Hotel. It was a Wednesday afternoon and I was on my half-day.

"Why don't you have a cake, Miss Maguire?" Cyril indicated the plate of pastries he had ordered to accompany the tea.

"No, thank you. I've just had lunch."

"They're very good." He sliced into a fruit tart. "Much superior to the rubbish we've had to put up with across the pond. Do you know, yesterday I had my first real egg for six months. Powdered eggs is what they feed you over there. Can you believe that? *Powdered eggs?*"

He stared at me while he ate, his tiny eyes fixing on my legs without any trace of embarrassment.

"We've had to put up with an awful lot because of the War. You people in Dublin don't know how well off you were. Bombs. Every bloody night, we had air-raids. People sleeping on top of each other in the tube stations. You'd wake up in the morning and you wouldn't know who would be lying beside you."

"We had bombs here too."

Cyril waved his hand.

"That was nothing. A complete accident."

"People were killed."

"Well, I'm sorry about that, of course. But I'm talking about a *blitz*. Hundreds of tons of bombs. Night after night. Thousands killed. And the rationing! You couldn't get a decent bite to eat for love nor money. And it's still going on. It's one of the reasons I agreed to come back here."

He started into a cream cake and now transferred his gaze to my breasts. I began to feel uncomfortable.

"Why did you want to see me?"

I cleared my throat.

"Your mother told me you're the representative for a cosmetics company."

"Managing Director, Ireland," Cyril corrected me. "Pompadour Ladies' Accessories. It sounds French, but that's just for effect. We're totally British."

He handed me his business card.

"What can I do for you?"

"I work at the Cosmetics department in Brown Thomas. Do you know it?"

"The big store in Grafton Street?"

"That's right. I might be interested in your products."

"What do you do, exactly?"

"I'm an assistant buyer. I thought we might be able to do business."

My lie was prepared; I had been working on it since the night I heard about Cyril coming back to Ireland.

I watched as he sniffed the bait.

"Well now." He licked his fingers clean of jam and cream and snapped open a bulky leather briefcase. "Let me show you our catalogues."

He produced a bundle of brochures and handed them to me.

"What sort of budget are we talking about, here?"

"That depends. You appreciate that we have our regular suppliers. For Brown Thomas to do business, you would have to be competitive."

"Pompadour can compete with anyone," Cyril boasted. "Our products are top of the range. We supply all the major stores in Britain. I can provide testimonials. I guarantee that anything your suppliers come up with, we will undercut."

"Did you bring samples?"

"Of course."

Cyril delved once more into the briefcase and took out handfuls of

233

products, which he set out on the table between us. I was impressed. The samples were imaginatively packaged in slender bottles of bevelled glass and elegant pots tied with ribbon. They weren't at all the tacky merchandise I had been fearing.

I unscrewed one bottle and raised it to my nose. The aroma was subtle and fragrant. I tried the creams. They were delicate and light with just a hint of perfume. The face powders came in smart little boxes, the lipsticks in shiny silver cartridges, the mascaras and eye-liners in chic containers. The products were of the highest quality. I knew I could recommend these to Mr Henderson with no fear of embarrassment.

I studied the prices and made a quick calculation.

"To do business, I would expect a fifty per cent discount."

"What?"

Cyril sat up straight as if someone had kicked him. "At that rate, I would be giving the stuff away."

"No you wouldn't. You'd still be making ten per cent profit. I know the margins."

"Thirty-five per cent."

"Fifty. I'm giving you an opportunity to get in on the top floor. If Brown Thomas stocks your goods, the other stores will follow. You would have the Irish market sewn up in no time."

Cyril's tiny eyes bulged.

"I can't go fifty. I'd be sacked."

"Then we'll have to stick with our existing suppliers."

I stood up and took my coat from the chair beside me.

He reached out quickly and laid a hand on my shoulder.

"Sit down. You drive a hard bargain. Jesus, you're like a dealer at a cattle fair."

"I was raised on a farm," I said, coolly.

"Then it must be in the blood. I'll give you fifty per cent on orders over £200."

I took a deep breath.

"Let me keep these catalogues and samples. I'll have to discuss this matter with my colleagues. I'll get back to you in a few days time."

Cyril put the items in a bag and handed it to me. He appeared to have relaxed. His eyes were now fixed on my face. His little pink tongue shot out and licked his lips.

"Let me buy you dinner tonight, Miss Maguire. I know a smart place where we can get a delicious steak."

"I can't," I said. "I'm seeing my boyfriend. He's a rugby player."

*

The following morning, I made an appointment to speak to Mr Henderson. He saw me at ten. He was sitting at his desk in his shirt sleeves. When I came in, he put his jacket on.

"I trust you've settled down again, Miss Maguire? I trust you're happy now?"

There was no hint of irony in his voice. He watched me warily, as if suspecting that I was about to unload more trouble on him.

"What can I do for you?" He asked.

I began the sales pitch that I'd rehearsed for days.

"I've got a proposition to make. I have a contact who is the director of a cosmetics company. Yesterday, I took the liberty to talk to him about his products. They're very good products, the sort we could carry in our store without any concern about quality."

I opened the bag and put the samples on his desk. Mr Henderson examined them, one by one.

"Hmmm. I see what you mean."

"I think our customers would be keen to buy this range. I know we could sell them."

He looked at me suspiciously.

"But we have our established suppliers. Miss Burgess deals with them."

"If you forgive me for saying so, the range is old-fashioned. Since the War, women are looking for more exciting products. If we don't supply them, they'll go elsewhere. I know what I'm talking about."

Mr Henderson was nervous now.

"I really think this is something you should discuss with Miss Burgess."

"No. Hear me out. Miss Burgess is the last person I would talk to. She wouldn't listen to me. She barely speaks to me, anyway. I'm thinking about the company, Mr Henderson. I'm thinking about our future. Things are changing and nowhere faster than in women's fashions. We have to move with the times or we'll get left behind."

I saw his eyes flicker. He leaned forward and examined the samples again.

"They *are* impressive. Imaginative design and packaging. You think our customers would go for this?"

"Certainly."

He stroked his chin.

"Once a market is lost, it's damned difficult to recover it."

"Sometimes, it's never recovered," I said.

I could see he was worried. I delivered the clincher.

"I can get this range at a fifty per cent discount. The best discount we have at present on cosmetics is thirty per cent. That's a gap of twenty. That's profit for us. If we stock this range, we're not only keeping our customers happy, we're making money."

"What's this chap's name?"

"Cyril Dragg."

Mr Henderson made up his mind.

"Tell him to come and see me tomorrow. You come with him."

# 45.

Cyril got the contract. What convinced Mr Henderson was the fear of being left behind. It was true, events were changing rapidly now that the War was over. People wanted new things. There were more motor-cars on the roads and there was even talk of a firm in Britain producing television sets. They already had them in America and you could see them from time to time in the films.

The Pompadour cosmetics range was a big success and it reflected well on Mr Henderson. In turn, he rewarded me. I got a £15 bonus at the end of June – more than a month's wages –and a strong letter of commendation. Cyril was happy too. As I predicted it gave him an entry to the market, and his business grew.

He sent me a couple of bottles of champagne and myself, Connie and her friend Majella Pike got tipsy with them one night in Majella's flat in Sandymount, and played loud records till the neighbours banged on the ceiling to complain.

But it was a bitter blow for Emily Burgess. I had undermined her. I had usurped her authority and instead of being disciplined, I was encouraged. It was clear to everyone now that she was becoming irrelevant. On those rare occasions when Mr Henderson appeared on the shop floor, it was to me he addressed his remarks and his small chat.

I had never known her to be sick, but now Miss Burgess began to take days off. In June, she was ill for three weeks and, in her absence, I was asked to take charge. When she returned to work, she looked dreadful. Her skin had an ugly grey pallor and she had developed a nervous tic which made her left eye blink uncontrollably.

I had never forgotten what Miss Burgess had tried to do to me. But, if I felt any guilt about my behaviour, I told myself it was for the good of the company. She became increasingly erratic and forgetful. Representatives would turn up for appointments and she wouldn't be there. She forgot people's names and the price of things. From time to time, the till didn't balance at the end of the evening – something unheard of – and we would spend hours checking the register.

As Miss Burgess' personal appearance began to deteriorate, she became paranoid, suspecting conspiracies everywhere. She accused people of talking behind her back. For a woman who had once lined us up to inspect our teeth, her decline was painfully striking. She began to turn in with snags in her stockings and stains on her skirts and her blouses smelt of body odour.

The end came on a day in August, in the middle of Horse Show week. It was always a busy time for the store. The city was crowded with people up from the country and many of them used the occasion to do their shopping. But, as chance would have it, I wasn't there. I had some shopping of my own to do and I had arranged to take a late lunch.

When I returned, it was to a scene of chaos. Glass and broken bottles lay scattered around the floor. A cabinet was smashed and Paddy Kinsella was busy sweeping up the mess. The staff were rearranging the displays. Miss Burgess was nowhere to be seen.

I took Connie aside and got the story from her. It seemed that Miss Burgess had grown increasingly distracted as the busy afternoon wore on. She began snapping at staff and even at customers. She got prices wrong and gave incorrect change. One of the girls suggested she take a break but she became abusive and eventually, half an hour later, exploded into violence.

The incident that tipped her over the edge involved a plump farmer's wife who accused her of being impolite. Miss Burgess had been attempting to sell the woman a bottle of perfume.

"Impolite?" asked Miss Burgess.

"Yes", said the farmer's wife. "You should remember who's paying your wages. I find your attitude plain rude."

"Rude, is it now? Jesus, I'll show you what's rude."

Miss Burgess took the perfume bottle and hurled it at a glass cabinet, which smashed into tiny pieces. The result seemed to excite her. She swept her arm along a tray and sent the contents spinning along the floor. She grabbed a heavy decanter and hurled it against the wall.

All the time, as she went about systematically destroying the cosmetics counter, she kept up a stream of abuse.

"Impolite! Rude! I've worked here for thirty years and this fucking bog-trotter has the cheek to tell me I'm impolite."

Eventually, it took Paddy Kinsella and a couple of his colleagues to restrain her and lead her away.

\*

Emily Burgess was never again mentioned officially. Except once. But that didn't stop the rumour mill grinding out lurid tales. In the version most favoured by the messenger boys, she had been jilted by a secret lover, a married man who wouldn't leave his wife to run away with her, and it had driven her mad.

But I knew what had caused her to crack and behave the way she did, and I was surprised no one ever referred to it. The closest it came to a mention was a week later when, once again, I found myself sitting across the mahogany desk in the General Manager's office. Mr Henderson leaned back in his chair and brought the tips of his thin fingers together.

"Dreadful business. Dreadful. In all my career, I can never remember anything like it. And the damage to our reputation! We had to move heaven and earth to keep it out of the newspapers. If I may speak to you in confidence, Miss Maguire. Miss Burgess has had a nervous breakdown. It appears she's been suffering from the impression that her job was under threat."

"Really?"

He nodded gravely.

"Apparently she blames you. She complained to me once or twice that she felt you were undermining her. Of course, I appreciate that nothing could be further from the truth."

He paused and looked at me intently.

"I think the reality is that the work got too much for her and she wasn't able to cope. She has been under a lot of strain recently. You must have noticed her appearance. And her personal hygiene had gone to the dogs. You know, she isn't a young woman. She's fifty-two."

"That old?" I said. "I wouldn't have guessed it."

"Oh yes. The job needs a younger hand. Someone with more energy. Someone more in tune with the times. Privately, I can tell you that Miss Burgess is in a nursing home and won't be coming back. Which leaves a vacancy. I was wondering if you would like to take up the position of supervisor?"

I had waited a long time to hear words like these, but strangely they gave me no pleasure. I thought of Emily Burgess in the nursing home, and the role I had played in putting her there, and all I felt was remorse. But this was too big an opportunity to turn down.

"I'd be happy to discuss it with you," I said.

# 46.

The following Monday morning, I took up my position as supervisor of Brown Thomas Cosmetics department. My salary was £5 a week plus bonus. It was my first step up the corporate ladder and I felt proud of my achievement. I carried my head high and, in the beginning, I think I took myself a little too seriously.

The remorse I felt about Emily Burgess's breakdown didn't linger for long. I knew when I left Belfast that I would have to fight for recognition. I had no advantages except my own intelligence and determination to succeed. On those few occasions when my conscience bothered me, I comforted myself with the knowledge that, if I hadn't supplanted her, someone else would. It was only a matter of time.

As part of my negotiations with Mr Henderson, I had secured his agreement to hire another two staff, bringing the complement up to eight. I also got approval to introduce new products and new suppliers. Our sales had slipped during the last months of Miss Burgess's reign and I saw it as my mission to re-establish Brown Thomas as the leading store in Ireland for what we now called "Ladies' Accessories".

It was a busy time, selecting staff, interviewing reps, eating lunch with suppliers and, in the middle of it all, moving out of Mrs Bolger's digs.

I had calculated that I could now afford to have my own flat and, after weeks of searching, I found the perfect place – a small two-bedroom apartment in an old house on Leeson Street. It had been empty for more than a year and was badly in need of repair, but there was a charming garden and the place had definite potential. At an asking price of only £250, with the aid of a mortgage, I could afford it.

I was sorry to leave Mrs Bolger. I had become fond of her during the two years I had lodged in her house, grown used to her odd ways. She had a kind heart. I think she believed I added a touch of sophistication to her establishment; she never stopped talking about me and my job to the other guests till I'm sure they grew sick of hearing it. And, of course, she was once again short of a poker player.

Jimmy Rickard helped me move my belongings and Connie came round in the evenings to help me with the redecoration. We stripped the walls and painted them in nice bright yellows and reds and whites.

I got a plumber to install a new bath, and a shower, which was a novelty then. We gutted the kitchen and installed a sparkling new cooker and sink. We built cupboards and a breakfast bar from a design I had seen in an American magazine.

I trimmed and weeded the garden, planted roses and geraniums and put down daffodil bulbs for the spring. Within two months, the flat had been transformed. I opened a bottle of wine and Connie and I sat on the balcony and watched the traffic move slowly down Leeson Street towards St Stephen's Green.

It was one of those late September evenings when it seems that summer is hanging on by its finger tips. The air was warm and the birds were chattering in the trees along the road; and one or two lights were coming on in the city.

"You know, I envy you," Connie said. "You've got everything."

"Oh, Connie, don't be foolish."

"Well look at you! You've got a good job and plenty of money. People admire you. And now you've got this lovely flat. You must be mad happy."

I sipped my wine and watched the last rays of the sun spread shadows across the rooftops.

"*You've* got Gabriel," I said.

Connie put down her glass and turned to look at me.

"And you could have Jimmy if you wanted. He's crazy about you. He worships the ground you walk on. And yet you treat him so cold."

"I don't love him, Connie."

"Love grows. But you have to give it a chance. I don't believe in this love-at-first-sight business. That only happens in the films."

"You don't understand. I don't want to encourage him and then have to hurt him. I've already hurt too many people in my life."

Connie put her arm on my shoulder.

"I've watched you, Stella. You can't relax. You drive yourself too hard. You always want to be in control. It's as if you're afraid to leave anything to chance. Why don't you just let go and see what happens?"

Her words struck a chord in me. But I had seen what could happen when I lost control of my own life. I had been forced to give my baby away.

"Everybody is different, Connie," I said. "Everybody is moulded by her own experience."

*

Connie was married the following Easter. Jimmy Rickard was best man and her sister Angela was bridesmaid. It meant she had to give up her job. There was a practice at that time; no married women were allowed to work. I didn't want to lose her and I made representations on her behalf, but Mr Henderson was adamant. He couldn't change the rules just for Connie. Where would it end?

The wedding was at Raheny church and the lunch was held in a lovely old hotel in Howth, right at the water's edge where the waves came rolling up onto the shore. It was a beautiful spring day; the primroses were out and the trees beside the hotel were bursting into leaf. You could see clear up the coast as far as Skerries.

Jimmy Rickard stood beside me and pointed.

"See that blue shape in the far distance?"

I could just make it out through the haze that hung on the sea.

"That's the Mountains of Mourne. County Down. That's your neck of the woods. You didn't know it was so close, did you?"

"I'm from Fermanagh, Jimmy. It's nowhere near the Mountains of Mourne."

"Well, it's all the North, isn't it?"

"That's like saying Cork and Dublin are the same."

243

"No it's not. Northerners are different. I don't know what it is, but there's something about you lot."

"Yeah, we've got fangs that come out at night when it's dark and we go looking for young virgins to despoil."

Jimmy started to laugh.

"Is that what it is? I often wondered. Now I know."

We had a lovely meal: Wicklow lamb, new potatoes and garden peas, and afterwards, apple-tart that Mrs Campbell had baked specially. We toasted the bride and groom with wine and Mr Campbell made a speech.

I think he was a bit drunk. There had been a lot of drinking at the bar before the meal, the men buying each other black pints of porter while the women sipped decorously from slim sherry glasses. He told everyone what a wonderful girl Connie was and how they'd all miss her but he said Gabriel had a good, solid job in Guinness's brewery so he wouldn't be losing a daughter but gaining a regular supply of beer.

About nine o'clock, I needed fresh air, so I went out and walked along the beach. There was a big yellow moon hanging over the sea. Everything was still, the only sound was the gentle rise and fall of the waves against the shore. As I walked, I thought of Connie. She believed I had everything, but she was wrong. There were things she had that I lacked. She was secure and content and she was in love. I had my job but there was an emptiness in my life.

Eventually, I heard footsteps behind me and turned to see Jimmy. He took me in his arms.

"You look tired. Stella. Let me take you home."

We drove in silence, my head resting on his shoulder. As soon as we were inside my flat, he took me in his arms again. I was hungry for his kisses. I felt his hands on my breasts as slowly he undressed me. He kissed my body, long lingering kisses that made me mad with desire.

When we were finished, Jimmy lay on the bed and smoked a cigarette. He lifted the picture of Martin in his christening robes that I kept on the bedside table.

"Who's the kid?"

I quickly took the photograph from him and replaced it.

"It's my sister's child. I'm his Godmother."

Another lie had slipped off my tongue. But this was no small untruth. I didn't know it, but this was a lie so big that it would follow me all the days of my life, even to my deathbed.

# 47.

Jimmy and I became lovers. He was good in bed and always made me happy in a sexual way. I used to look forward to our lovemaking. It was mostly on Saturday nights. Jimmy would meet me for a drink in the Bailey after work, then we'd go and eat somewhere and catch a film. We would get back to my flat after eleven and I'd have a shower and get in under the cold sheets. Jimmy would already be there waiting, a cigarette hanging from his lips. That's one of the things I remember: Jimmy smoking. He smoked Craven A cigarettes. They were tipped and had a picture of a black cat on the box.

When it came time, Jimmy would put on a Durex, which he got from some man he worked with. I think he told me once they were smuggled across the border from Belfast. I know you couldn't get them in Dublin.

He was slow. He took his time and it made the pleasure last. I've had other lovers who were more passionate, men who rutted like a goat so that our bodies would be sticking together with sweat. But I always remember Jimmy's lovemaking with affection; his head resting on my breast when it was over, his laboured breathing, the little brown mole on his back, right between his shoulder blades. It's funny the things that remain in your memory.

In the morning, we'd lie in bed and listen to the church bells ringing out across the silent city and we'd do it again. Eventually, I'd get up and cook rashers and eggs and, after breakfast, Jimmy would drive home to Artane where he lived with his mother.

He kept asking me to marry him but I always found some excuse. The more he pursued me, the more I fled. I didn't want to tell him that I would never marry him because I didn't love him. I was a coward. I had hurt Bill Dwyer and I didn't want to do it again. So I kept putting it off, hoping that somehow the affair might peter out without recrimination and we would remain friends.

That was my life with Jimmy. Saturday nights and Sunday mornings. And occasional mid-week visits to the cinema or to a party. The rest of the time, I was busy at my job, taking papers home with me and working long into the night on catalogues and order sheets. I didn't see so much of Connie once she got married and left the job. In a short time, she was pregnant. I went to the christening; a little boy. And then, soon after, I heard she was gone again. I had never considered Gabriel Doyle to be a sensual man, but you never know what goes on in a marriage.

I stayed with Jimmy for over twenty months. It might have been longer except that two events conspired to change the course of my life once more. The first happened at work.

I had succeeded with my mission to make our Cosmetics department the best in Dublin. There were other stores that were cheaper and had a wider range. But we had quality. People paid more in Brown Thomas because they got better goods. I worked hard to maintain that reputation. With the staff, I stressed the importance of service, of always being polite and well turned-out. We were an advertisment for our products. On that point, Emily Burgess had been right.

I was constantly on the look-out for new lines. I travelled to trade fairs and exhibitions. Gradually, I built up a stable of regular customers who, in turn, brought their friends. Lady de Vere, for instance, despite her obsession with exclusivity, soon introduced her wide network of confederates. It became like a club. They asked for me specially and relied on my advice. In less than two years, I had doubled the revenue from the department and firmly established the reputation of the store.

Of course, I was well remunerated. I got regular bonuses and pay rises. And I loved the life; the lunches and the drinks parties and the busy round of executive meetings. I enjoyed the status of being a manager, the respect and the power that it conferred. And, through it all, I retained the confidence of my staff. I trained each new recruit personally. I encouraged them. I rewarded them. I defended them. I always made time to listen to their problems. In return, I secured their loyalty.

But slowly, I began to notice that the buzz was going out of my career. What had once been exciting now seemed routine. I felt myself grow restive again, ready for fresh challenges.

One morning over coffee, Betty Evans inclined her head, which was always a signal that she had some news to impart. I bent my ear to listen.

"I hear Dickie is on the move," she whispered.

"Dickie Henderson?"

"Who else? I hear he's being kicked upstairs. Executive General Manager. Big title and no authority. Stand by for an announcement any day soon."

This *was* news. Indeed it was a shock. Mr Henderson had been General Manager for over twenty years. I asked the obvious question.

"Who's getting his job?"

"Answer that and you win the cigar. There's Mr Donovan in Men's Outfitting and Mr Spiers in Furniture. They'd be the likely candidates. But you never know who might pop out of the woodwork. My guess is, it's already spoken for. I've been around here long enough to know the way they do business. They don't make a move as big as this without having everything nailed down and secure."

I thought for a moment.

"They'd never appoint a woman, would they?"

Betty Evans began to laugh.

"My God, Stella. You're not thinking of yourself?"

"Why not?"

She stopped laughing and became serious.

"Why not indeed? Except it's never happened. Never in the history of the store."

\*

In due course, the rumour became fact, and it was public knowledge that Mr Henderson was moving to what was described as a senior position with an overview of strategic planning and development. I could find nobody who could tell me exactly what that meant.

He held a farewell drinks party in his office for heads of department; debonair in his well-cut suit and shirt as he made small talk amid the clinking cocktail glasses. His secretary had stripped a banner across the ceiling which read: *Bon Voyage.* Mr Henderson shook each guest warmly by the hand and thanked them for their support over the years. People wished him well in his new appointment. The question of who might succeed him was politely avoided.

But out on the floor, there was talk of nothing else. For whoever became General Manager would wield immense power over the lives and careers of many people, not to mention the fortunes of the company. The position was never advertised, which confirmed Betty Evans's suspicion that it was already agreed. Neverthless, I decided to apply.

I spent nights preparing my application. I listed my achievments, detailing the improvements I had made in the Cosmetics department, citing sales figures and turnover and profits. I outlined my vision for the future. I set out strategies to improve the service to our customers and see off our competitors.

When I was finished, I took the application to a stationer's shop and had it typed up and bound in a nice presentation package. I had ten copies made and sent one to each member of the board.

For days, I waited for an acknowledgment, none was forthcoming. From time to time, Betty Evans would ask if I had any news and I would shake my head. I began to doubt the wisdom of submitting the application at all. I tried to keep myself busy with work but the application became an obsession. Every morning when I awoke, it was the first thought that popped into my head. Maybe today! Maybe this is the day I will hear!

Eventually, about a fortnight later, a letter did arrive at my flat. My hands shook as I tore it open. It was a terse two sentence response. It thanked me for my application and said that the board had decided to appoint Mr Paul Arthurs, chartered accountant of Stanley and Sons as General Manager of Brown Thomas with immediate effect.

I stared at the letter in disbelief. I had never heard of Paul Arthurs. He didn't even work in the store. He was an accountant with no experience of sales or management. And despite the hard work I had put in, they had preferred him over me. They hadn't even given me the courtesy of an interview to put my case.

I told myself I had been naïve to ever think I had a chance. Betty Evans had warned me about the way things were done. Nevertheless, I couldn't help feeling bitter as I made my way into work that morning. Paul Arthurs was already installed when I arrived. A tall, lanky, arrogant man about thirty years of age who already looked as if he owned the place.

He was being shown around by Mr Henderson's secretary, who fawned and grovelled as she introduced him to each departmental head.

I nursed my disappointment for another week and then the second thing happened. I decided to pay a long-overdue visit to my parents in Ballinaleck.

# 48.

It was four years since I had been home. At first, my pregnancy and the birth of Martin made it impossible. Later, after I came to Dublin, I kept putting it off. I always seemed to be busy. Of course, I kept up a correspondence with Mammy and Kathleen but, somehow, I never found the time to visit. Now I felt guilty that I had neglected them so long.

I brought presents: an expensive coat for Mammy, a pure wool cardigan and a tin of tobacco for Daddy, a fancy silk tie for Michael and, for Kathleen, a couple of smart dresses that I knew she would like. She was seventeen now and at Teacher Training College in Belfast.

Daddy met me at the station. The old horse and cart had been replaced by a car, a second-hand Ford that Michael had found for him at a garage in Enniskillen. He flung his arms around me and clasped me tight and then held me at arms length and gazed into my face.

"My God, Stella, how you've changed. You look so smart. How have you been keeping?"

"Fine. Fine. You got my letters?"

"Of course. Mammy's been showing them round the district. She's never done boasting to the neighbours about the big job you've got and all the money you're earning up in Dublin. C'mon, give me your bags. I've got the motor waiting."

He led me to the dusty old Ford and piled my luggage onto the back seat. I used the opportunity to sneak a look at him. He had aged terribly. He had lost weight and his fine black hair had been replaced with grey. I noticed, as he lifted my bags, that his joints seemed stiff and awkward and his face winced in pain.

"Are you all right?" I asked, anxiously.

"It's nothing. Just a touch of arthritis. This damned weather sets it off."

He got into the front seat and started the car. He had never learned to drive properly and his steering was erratic, but he seemed ignorant of his defects and proud of his new-found skill.

"You're nobody now unless you've got a motor. They've all got them. Did I tell you Michael's running the farm now?"

"What happened to Molly Teeling?"

"Och, that all fizzled out. I can't say I'm sorry. That young hussy was too big for her boots. She was filling his head with nonsense. He's got another girl now and she's more sensible."

We chatted as the car bumped along the road to home. As we approached, he turned to me and said: "I've got a surprise for you. We have visitors."

"Who?" I asked eagerly.

"Bridgie and the kids."

I hadn't seen my sister since Martin's funeral. She had three children now, two little boys and a baby girl. I would need to get them something, so I asked Daddy to stop at Quinn's shop and got the girl to fill two brown paper bags with chocolate bars and bullseyes.

They were waiting expectantly in the yard, two plump little tousel-heads two and three years old. They watched me shyly as I got out of the car and helped Daddy with the bags. I stretched out my hand and they shook it politely.

"What have we got here? Two handsome young men. I'm your Aunt Stella. Now tell me your names."

The eldest boy was more confident. He pointed to his brother. "He's Gerard and I'm Charles."

"Well, I'm delighted to meet you. Do you like sweets?"

The eldest boy nudged his brother and they both giggled.

"Of course you do. And that's just what I got you."

I gave them the bags and they greedily tore them open.

"Thank you, Auntie Stella," they chorused and ran laughing into the house.

I followed. Mammy was busy at the cooker. It was where I always found her and always remembered her. She had got a new one, a big shiny range with dials and knobs. She wiped her hands on her apron and took me in her arms.

"Och it's great to see you. Come in, come in."

"You too, Mammy."

"And look who's here."

Bridgie was sitting at the kitchen table feeding a baby, with Charlie Kettles beside her. He had his arm flung casually over the back of the chair and was smoking a cigarette.

"Bridgie. Is this your new baby?"

"That's wee Annie," Bridgie said, proudly. "We named her after Mammy."

She held her out for my inspection, a big, healthy bundle with a pink, chubby face. I took her in my arms and rocked her and suddenly I thought of Martin. The last time I held a baby it was him, the day I left Mrs McBride's house for good.

"She's beautiful, I said. "How old is she?"

"Six months," Bridgie replied. "And already she's got an appetite like a horse."

"You can never feed a child too much," Mammy said, putting down a plate of scones and a pot of tea.

Daddy came in with the bags and we all sat together round the kitchen table. I could feel the anticipation in the room.

"They've got news," Mammy said. "Go on, Charlie, tell her."

Charlie Kettles stubbed out his cigarette.

"We're going to live in America."

"America?"

"Uncle James is sponsoring us," Bridgie put in, eagerly. "Charlie's sold the garage. He's going to start a new business in America."

I was dumbfounded. As far as I knew, Charlie's garage was thriving and they were happy. I had no idea they were contemplating anything like this.

"I have it figured out," Charlie said. "The trouble with running a business in this country is: nobody wants to pay you. They expect you to do everything for nothing. I was busting my ass fixing cars for people and waiting months for my money."

"When are you going?"

"In six weeks," Bridgie said proudly. "We've got everything signed. And Uncle James is putting us up till we get on our feet. Sure everything's different in America. They don't care who you are so long as you're prepared to roll up your sleeves and work."

"Uncle James went to America with barely an arse in his pants," Charlie added. "And now he's running a steelworks in Albany."

"That's not quite true," Mammy put in. "He had a good suit on him when he left. I remember that."

"Well, you know what I mean, Mrs M. There's no discrimination. It's not like here. Who you know, not what you know. Over there, the only thing that counts is whether you're willing to get your hands dirty."

"There's poor people in America too," Mammy said.

"Not if they work. In America, hard work gets it's reward."

"That's why it's the greatest country in the world," Bridgie said.

I noticed that Daddy sat quietly drinking his tea, not saying anything.

*

Over the next few days, I visited old friends and neighbours. I went back to the Royal Hotel in Enniskillen, but of all the people who had worked there with me, only Joe Gaffney remained. He told me that trade had fallen away when the War ended and staff had left. I asked about Maggie Cameron and he said she had married a local boy and was working in the mill in Lisbellaw.

Before I knew, it was time to return to Dublin. As the train pulled out of the station, I couldn't stop thinking of what I had learnt. Charlie Kettles's words echoed in my head. I thought of the country I had seen in films and read about in books, where people rose from humble beginnings to be rich and successful.

I thought of my job and where it was going. Nowhere. In the male world of Dublin business, it wouldn't matter if I quadrupled the revenues of Brown Thomas. I was a woman and I had reached the pinnacle of my career. If I stayed, I would remain as head of the Cosmetics counter till a younger woman came along and displaced me, just as I had displaced Emily Burgess. But I would never be allowed to rise any higher.

I could marry Jimmy Rickard, but it would be a loveless marriage, just as it would have been with Bill Dwyer.

Or I could take my chance and go to America. Perhaps Uncle James would sponsor me too. I had experience now and could get a reference. America would give me the chance to to leave the past behind me and start afresh. The more I thought of it, the more convinced I became. By the time the train came panting into Amiens Street station, I had made up my mind.

I was so excited that I went immediately to a nearby hotel and rang Uncle James. It would be morning in New York. After about ten minutes, the operator connected the call and then Uncle James's voice was echoing down the line.

We chatted for a while. He wanted to know all the news. Then I came to the point. I told him I was thinking of joining Bridgie and Charlie and asked if he would sponsor me.

I heard his laughter coming from miles away across the ocean.

"My God, Stella, at this rate of going, there'll be nobody left over there."

"Will you?" I pressed.

"Of course. I'd be delighted. You'll love it here. Do you know what the temperature is right now? It's seventy-five degrees and it's only May. When's the last time you saw seventy-five degrees in Ireland?"

"I can't remember," I said.

"That's because it never happened."

The following day, I went to the US Embassy and applied to Immigration. I was interviewed by a young man in a neat business suit and a shirt with a button-down collar. He wrote down all my details, including Uncle James's address, and told me I would hear within two weeks.

Ten days later, the acceptance letter arrived in an envelope with the US seal in the corner. I had already worked out my finances. With over a hundred pounds saved, the sale of the flat should push that up to four hundred. It was a fortune. I wrote to Mammy and told her the news. Then I booked my passage and handed in my resignation.

It did not take long to find a buyer for the flat, and I decided it was time to break the news to Jimmy Rickard. He sat stone-faced while I told him. He said he would follow me if I wanted but I said no, I needed time to settle in. I promised to write but, in my heart, I knew it would never happen.

I visited Mrs Bolger and Connie to say goodbye. Mrs Bolger gave me a chain with a St Christopher medal and said it would keep me from all harm. Connie sat in the kitchen of her house in Killester with her two babies bawling and screeching, and looked miserable. When it came time to take my leave, she clung to me and said I was the best friend she ever had and she would never forget the wonderful times we had together in Brown Thomas.

The night before I left, I brought my colleagues for drinks in the Bailey. They gave me a set of suitcases as a farewell present. People kept asking me how I had managed to secure an immigration visa. They said I was the lucky one to be getting out and starting a new life among the skyscrapers of New York. My last memory was of Paddy Kinsella, propped against the bar with a pint of beer, singing 'We'll Meet Again'.

I got a taxi back to Leeson Street and immediately fell asleep. The following morning, at nine o'clock, I caught the train for Cobh, and the liner that would carry me to New York.

# BOOK FOUR

# 49.

How shall I describe the magnificent sight that greeted us as the RMS *Mauretania* steamed into New York harbour on that morning in June 1950? My first vision of America. We stood on the arrivals deck and watched Liberty sail past and the sun reflect in a million spangles of light on the glass and steel of the Manhattan skyline.

My heart danced with excitement, my spirit swelling with a tremendous sense of freedom as America drew near. I was twenty-four years old, and I was arriving in the Land of Opportunity. I had left Ireland with its sad memories and bitter disappointments. Here, everything was possible. I stood on the threshold of a new life and I was eager to begin.

We gathered our possessions and made our way down the gangplank and onto American soil. Bridgie clutched the baby and shepherded the two boys and Charlie and I struggled with the suitcases as we made our way into the vast arrivals hall.

It was packed with people, pushing and shouting in a hubbub of strange accents. A burly policeman in blue tunic with gun and billy-club struggled to keep order; black porters pushed trolleys loaded with luggage; carters plied for business. A man in a trilby hat eating a hotdog at the barrier smiled at me, tipping his hat as I smiled back.

I glanced at the two boys, timidly clutching their mother's coat. They were strangely mute, their eyes wide with wonder.

"Welcome to America," I said, "Isn't it marvellous?"

At last, we got through Immigration and Customs and out into the harsh sunlight of the ferry terminal. Charlie had taken charge now and quickly organised a yellow taxi. We got in and sped through the hot Manhattan streets. I pressed my face to the glass and watched the sidewalks rush past. They seemed to vibrate with life. I stared at the fruit vendors, the honking traffic, the skyscrapers, the flashing adverts for strange beers and cigarettes. I could feel the energy and I couldn't wait to be part of it.

The taxi left us at the Port Authority building on 40th Street. We bought our tickets for Albany and climbed aboard the bus. Bridgie had brought a bag of doughnuts for the journey but I wasn't hungry. I was too busy watching the countryside as we drove north through New York State, past rolling pastures and picturesque towns with white-gabled colonial houses. Finally, we arrived at our destination, where Uncle James and Aunt Eileen were waiting at the depot.

Uncle James was a tall man with a thin, angular face, who wore a dark business suit and bow-tie, despite the summer heat. Aunt Eileen was a small woman with permed hair and a flowered summer dress.

Charlie had phoned ahead from the Port Authority to tell them we were on our way. They welcomed us, helping carry our luggage to a blue sedan parked nearby. We set off for their house, which was on the edge of town, and set back from the road by a winding drive lined with chestnut trees. It was like a mansion; a big old structure of brick and wood with pillars and flower beds and a sprinkler system that sprayed water in silver beads on a perfect lawn.

I had never seen a place so grand. We were met at the front door by Noreen, Uncle James' Irish maid. She brought us inside and led us to the dining room. She had set out dishes of cold meat: turkey, ham, roast beef, along with plates of salads, a pot of coffee and juice for the boys. A handy-man in blue dungarees carried our suitcases into the hall.

"You must be famished," Aunt Eileen said. "So you just tuck in there and then we'll show you to your rooms and you can have a wash."

I waited politely for her to begin, but she waved her hand.

"Uncle James and me have already eaten lunch."

Bridgie and I fixed plates for the boys and then for ourselves. Uncle James came in, sat down on a sofa and lit a cigar.

"So, how's everybody back home?"

Bridgie filled him in on all the news about the farm and the family. He asked about Mammy and Daddy and then said: "I guess nobody in Ireland ever got rich from farming."

He turned to Charlie: "What are you planning to do? I can give you a start at the steelworks, if you want."

"I was thinking I'd go into the garage business," Charlie said. "That's what I did back home. I'm a qualified motor mechanic. I thought I'd look around and see if there's any opportunities."

"There's opportunities all right," Uncle James said. "If you build a reputation for good work and people can rely on you, you'll do okay. But always remember – anything you get in this country, you have to earn."

"I'm ready to work," Charlie said. "Tell you the truth, I can't wait to get started."

Uncle James smiled.

"You keep that attitude Charlie, and you'll be just fine."

"What about you, Stella?" Aunt Eileen ventured.

I looked around the lovely room with it's fine furnishings: rich drapes and thick carpets, and the delicate chandelier that sparkled above the dining room table.

"I want to find a big job and get fabulously rich. I want to meet a handsome man and get married. And I want to have lots of children."

They all thought it was very funny. Uncle James threw his head back and laughed. Even the two boys came out of their shells and giggled.

*

I woke early next morning with the sun shining in my bedroom window and the smell of fresh coffee wafting through the house. I showered and went down to the kitchen.

It was 7.05 a.m. Noreen was already there. She had the skillet going and was cooking eggs.

"Good morning, Miss Stella. Did you sleep well?"

No one had ever spoken to me so formally and it sounded strange.

I said: "Noreen. There's no need for you to address me like that. Just call me Stella."

"Oh, no. I couldn't do that. You're family, Miss Stella."

I watched her as she busied herself at the stove, a thin, determined woman of about fifty years of age.

"How do you like America, Noreen?"

"I love it."

"Where are you from?"

"Donegal. A place called Killybegs."

"And when did you come out?"

"In 1920. I was nineteen years old. My father died and there was no work back home so I decided to come here. I've been working for your Uncle James for twenty-five years now and I'd never leave. He's the kindest, most generous man I've ever met. He's so good to me, Miss Stella and he's been so looking forward to you coming."

"I've been looking forward to it, too. Have you ever been in New York?"

"Oh yes. I worked there for a while when I first came over. I didn't like it. Too much noise and too many people. All they want to do is make money."

These were the very things that attracted me.

I said: "I think I'll go and live there."

The others arrived down and we gathered around the kitchen table and ate a big meal of ham and eggs and fried potatoes.

When we had finished, Uncle James spoke.

"I want you to know you can stay in my house till you get settled. I'm delighted to have you, so just make yourselves at home. When I first came to America, people helped me and now it's my turn to help you. That's the way the Irish work in this country. We all look out for each other."

He opened his wallet. I saw it was stuffed with crisp green notes. He took out six bills and gave one to each of us. I looked at the note. It was a hundred dollars.

"That's a present," he said. "So you'll always remember you're first day in America."

I was astonished.

"That's an awful lot of money."

Uncle James smiled and waved his hand.

"Let's hope it's the first of many."

# 50.

Despite his hearty exterior, Uncle James was a hard taskmaster. He had a study off the hall and I used to hear him on the phone giving instructions to his foremen at the plant. He got up every morning at 6 a.m. and read the business papers that were delivered specially by the local newsagent.

He would read the stock market reports and then ring his broker and give orders to buy and sell shares. I got the impression that he had a big portfolio of stocks in properties and mining companies. He never raised his voice when he was on the phone, but he spoke in a way that told you he wasn't a man to argue with. Listening to Uncle James on the phone impressed me.

Over the next few days, they showed us the city and introduced us to American customs. Everybody seemed to drive and you'd rarely see people walking. They drank coffee instead of tea. They ate hamburgers and bagels. They tipped everyone who provided a service, from the waitress to the cab driver.

I found it all new and exciting. The clothes were smart, the women were neatly groomed, the people seemed healthy and well fed. Noreen had a radio in the kitchen and it played music all day long and spilled out adverts for toothpaste and haircream, in these smooth American voices. And all the time, the sun shone out of a cloudless sky. A voice in my head kept saying: This is magic, Stella. And you're right here in the middle of it.

But I soon became restless. I wanted to find a job and start working. One evening, Uncle James brought a man to the house. He was short and squat, his hands calloused from rough work. Uncle James took him into the kitchen, gave him a beer from the fridge and introduced him to Charlie.

"I want you to meet a friend of mine," he said. This is Mike Shanahan. He runs a motor business downtown. Mike, this is Charlie Kettles. He's married to my niece. He's just come out from the old country. Can you give him a job?"

The three men sat drinking beer and talking for about half an hour exchanging information. When he left, Charlie had a job working as a mechanic at a dollar an hour.

Later he said to us: "This is just to get me started. It's good money but I won't stay forever. I'll use the opportunity to learn the business and then I'll start up on my own."

Already he sounded like he knew his way around.

Uncle James went off to work and, with Charlie gone, the house was quiet. Bridgie seemed to have quickly settled down. She nursed her baby and took the boys for walks in the park and, in the afternoons, she read magazines in the sitting room while they played in the back yard.

I spent a lot of time in the kitchen with Noreen.

"Tell me about New York."

"It's just a big place, Miss Stella. Like I said, too many people and everybody rushing around like there's no tomorrow. I prefer Albany. Things are quieter here."

"But it must have been exciting?"

"Oh it was. Too exciting for me."

"You must have seen the sights. The Empire State Building and Times Square and the New York Public Library?"

"They're just buildings. Miss Stella. That's all."

But I wasn't going to be put off.

"Is it easy to get a job there?"

"I'd say so. What kind of a job do you want?"

"I don't know. I worked in a big store in Dublin. Brown Thomas. Did you ever hear of it?"

Noreen shook her head.

"I was in charge of the Cosmetics department."

"Well if it's shop work you want, then New York's the place to go.

265

There's plenty of stores. Streets and streets of them. There's more stores in New York than I ever saw in my life."

"What about some place to live?"

"You can rent an apartment. I don't know what it costs, but you can easily find out. Next time you're in town, get the *New York Times*. There'll be pages of adverts. Job adverts too."

I spoke to Aunt Eileen.

"There's no need to move all the way to New York. You could get a store job here, Stella. In fact, Olson's are looking for staff. I saw a notice in their window just last week."

But it was the big city I craved. Already, Albany was losing its appeal. It was a nice place and there were lots of interesting things to see but it didn't have the energy I had sensed in Manhattan. New York was smarter and faster. There was a buzz that Albany lacked. And besides, New York was bound to have better opportunities.

The following day, I bought a copy of the *New York Times* and eagerly turned the pages to the Appointments section. Noreen was right. It was crammed with adverts. But now, I wasn't sure if I wanted to work in a store again. I sensed there were new openings to be explored, fresh challenges.

As I scanned the paper, one particular job caught my attention. It was for an office manager in an advertising agency called Brazil Bros. I had learnt a little about advertising in Brown Thomas and I had good management skills. The job sounded interesting. I sat down at the big Remington typewriter in Uncle James's study and typed out my letter of application.

The mail man came every morning at nine o'clock in a little blue van. About a week later, the letter I was waiting for arrived. It was from a man called Jack Morrison and it asked me to present myself for interview at the offices of Brazil Bros, Advertising and Promotion, in two day's time. I looked at the address on the letter head. Madison Avenue. It was in the heart of Manhattan.

I felt elated. I had secured a job interview at my very first attempt. I quickly got out the bus schedule and checked times. There was a bus leaving at 8 a.m. which would get me into the Port Authority terminal by ten. From there, I could catch a cab to Madison Avenue.

I had a better idea. Why not travel the day before, stay over in New York and get to the interview bright and fresh? It would also give me an opportunity to check out the city. I was excited now. I got the phone number of the YWCA and booked into their house in East 47th Street.

Aunt Eileen drove me to the depot and wished me good luck as the bus bore me away. I arrived in New York shortly after midday and got a cab to the Y. It was a big old brownstone building on a street off Eighth Avenue. I checked in and went upstairs to my room.

I was fiddling with the key when the door to the next room opened and a young woman came out. She was about my age, small and plump with blond hair cut short and a face dappled with freckles. She was wearing a dressing gown and had a towel draped over her arm.

When she saw me, she stopped.

"Pardon me. Can you tell me how I get to the bathroom? I've just arrived and I haven't got the hang of this place."

"Neither have I," I said. "But I think I saw a sign down there."

I pointed to the end of the corridor and she thanked me and went off. I opened the door and entered.

The room was small and neat, furnished with a single bed, a dressing table and wardrobe. There was a writing desk beside the window, but I didn't think I would need it. I planned to change into slacks and loafers and get out and explore the city.

I sat down on the bed. From the window, I could hear the roar of traffic. I felt my heart beat faster. I had arrived at last and I couldn't wait to get on to the streets of the most exciting city in the world. I opened my case and began to unpack.

# 51.

The refectory of the YWCA was a bright airy room with trestle tables and a self-service counter that ran the length of one wall. At 8.30 a.m., it was packed with noisy young females munching and chatting and smoking cigarettes. I had a tray which held my breakfast – a mug of coffee and a muffin – and I had nowhere to sit.

I looked out over the sea of faces and wondered what I should do. I couldn't bring the food back to my room. There was a list of instructions behind the door which said that food was strictly forbidden. Just then, I saw someone waving at me. I looked closer and recognised the young woman I had met the night before.

She squeezed along the bench to make room for me.

"Isn't it crazy?" she said, as I sat down. "Where did they all come from?"

"Beats me," I said. "They weren't here last night. At least, I didn't see them."

"Me neither," the woman said. "Maybe it's a high school group or something. Anyway, now you've got somewhere to eat."

She stuck out a pudgy hand.

"I'm Kathy Brewster."

"Stella Maguire."

I noticed she had a plastic folder opened in front of her.

"I've got a job interview this morning. I was just running over my notes."

"That's a coincidence," I said. "I've got an interview too."

"Where?"

"Brazil Bros. It's an advertising agency on Madison."

"Wow! You're in advertising?"

"Not really. It's a job as office manager."

"Handling people! I'm not sure I'd be able for that."

"I've done it before. And you?"

"I've got an interview with the *New York Post*. I'm a reporter. I work for the local paper in my home town of Curtis. It's in Indiana. Do you know it?"

I shook my head.

"Don't worry. Nobody else does. Tell you the truth, I feel like a country hick in New York. But if I get this job, it'll be a big break for me. How long have you been in the city?"

"I just arrived yesterday. Like you."

"Where are you from?"

"Dublin."

"Ireland?"

"Well, I'm not actually from Dublin but I've been working there for three years."

We talked for a while and then she suddenly looked at her watch.

"Got to run. My interview is at ten o'clock. Don't want to create a bad impression."

"Good luck," I said.

"You too. You know, it's been great talking to you. I don't know anyone in New York. You're the first person I've actually held a conversation with in two days. Isn't that something else?"

She grabbed her folder and was gone.

*

Jack Morrison turned out to be much younger than I expected. He was a tall, good-looking man of about thirty, with dark, close-cut hair and brown eyes. He led me into his office and offered me coffee.

"No thanks," I said.

Now that I had got here, I was suddenly nervous. So far, everything had gone too smoothly. But I was also determined.

He began by asking me about my previous experience. I told him about my work for Brown Thomas. I had already enclosed a glowing reference from Mr Henderson with my job application.

"But this job isn't selling."

"I know. It's management. But I ran the Cosmetics department of the biggest store in Dublin."

"How many staff?"

"Twenty-five," I lied.

"The staff here is much smaller. Only a dozen."

"That should make my task easier."

"Why should selling cosmetics equip you for running an office?"

"Because it demands the same skills. I presume you want the place to run efficiently? You want your staff to be happy and work hard?"

"You got it in one."

"Then give me the job."

Jack Morrison smiled.

"You're a woman. You're only twenty-four. Some of the staff here are twice your age."

"You think that's a problem?"

"It could be."

"Then why don't you put me on probation? Say three months. If you're not happy, I'll go."

He leaned back in his chair and laughed.

"You've sure got some chutzpah, Miss Maguire."

"What does that mean?"

"It's Yiddish. It means you've got ... Well it means, you've got a brass neck."

"So, are you giving me the job?"

"When can you start?"

*

I was to begin the following Monday. The job involved drawing up work schedules, organising office supplies, maintaining the equipment and arranging holiday rosters. The salary was fifty dollars a week, which was more than Charlie was getting for fixing cars. I couldn't believe I'd swung it.

I found a pay phone and rang Aunt Eileen to tell her my good news. I explained that I was spending another night in New York and coming back tomorrow to pack my things. Then I went off to find somewhere to live. It took the rest of the afternoon and I quickly discovered that the exaggerated claims of New York landlords rarely matched reality.

Places that were described as bijou apartments turned out to be shoeboxes. Stunning vistas of the New York skyline became views of an evil-smelling meat plant. Rooftop gardens were actually window-boxes.

Eventually, I found a place in Chelsea. It was a tiny flat in an apartment block, just a small bedroom, bathroom and a kitchen-cum-living room. But it was cosy and it had everything I required, with a rent of only ten dollars a week. I brought my luggage from the Y in a cab and unpacked my stuff. Later I would bring the remainder from Albany.

I now had a place I could call home and an address in Manhattan.

# 52.

My new job was even easier than I imagined. It boiled down to keeping the office of Brazil Bros ticking over smoothly. It meant massaging egos, wiping brows and providing a sympathetic shoulder to cry on. After a few weeks, I was amazed to discover I could do it in my sleep.

Untill recently, Brazil Bros had been a small, independent advertising agency but it had been taken over by a conglomerate called United Promotional Corporation. Jack Morrison had been the Senior Account Executive under the old regime, but the top management had been swallowed up in the takeover, with Jack the sole survivor. Now, he had been promoted to MD.

He was an amiable boss. His job was to liaise with the clients, who were mostly big food and drink companies, car manufacturers, fashion houses and the major retail stores in the New York area. Jack would draw up promotional campaigns which meant designing advertising and placing it with newspapers, radio, cinema and, increasingly, television.

It was a very stressful job but I never saw him lose his temper. He seemed to thrive on the work, and by-and-large, he left me alone. As long as the office was running efficiently, Jack was satisfied.

The twelve staff consisted of four graphic artists, two copy-writers, a couple of ideas men, two secretaries and a messenger boy. It was more highly strung than the Boston Symphony Orchestra. There would be long periods of intense creative activity and then war would break out. The artists would accuse the copy-writers of butchering their work. The copy-writers would retaliate by saying the artists were just a bunch of jumped-up prima donnas.

"What the hell do you think this is? The Mona Friggen Lisa? It's only an ad for baked beans, for Christ's sake."

A screaming match would ensue and I would be called on to intervene. It meant frequent trips to Bogie's, a cocktail bar up the street, where, over glasses of Long Island Iced Tea, I would attempt to unruffle the feathers and broker a peace deal.

But most of the time the diverse talents that made up Brazil Bros worked well together and the campaigns got launched on time. These usually involved lavish drinks parties at top hotels and smart restaurants, paid for by the clients.

They would be attended by well-known media celebrities and show-business people. Everybody got dressed up and had a good time. We drank champagne and got our pictures in the trade press. I always enjoyed the campaign launches, not least because they involved a bonus for each member of staff.

My three-month probation period came and went and nobody said anything, so I assumed I had passed. I thought it required some sort of token, so I treated myself to a nice lunch in an upmarket restaurant called Benny's Bistro, where I ate loin of pork stuffed with pate and drank a half bottle of bordeaux. I thought of my days in the River Restaurant and realised how far I had come.

I grew to love my job. Each morning I rose eager for the new day. For all the fights, I enjoyed being around creative people. They lived on adrenalin and I relished the buzz. I got that same buzz from the city itself; walking to work in the morning along the busy sidewalks or, at night, as the lights of Broadway flickered on. The city pulsated with life and I was part of it.

One morning in early December I got a call to the office. The tone was familiar, but I didn't recognise the voice.

"Hi, Stella. This is Kathy here. Remember me?"

"Who?"

"Kathy Brewster. We met at the Y."

Now I knew who it was: the blond woman who shared a table with me the morning I went for my interview.

"Of course. I'm sorry. I didn't recognise your voice. How are you?"

"I'm fine. I see you got the job."

"Yes. How about you?"

"Me too."

"So how are you working out?"

"Oh, you know," Kathy said, "making it, shaking it."

She was beginning to sound like a New Yorker.

"The reason I'm calling you, Stella, is that I'm researching an article on the advertising industry. And I thought about you."

"I think you want my boss. His name's Jack Morrison. I'll get him to call you. And, Kathy?"

"Yes?"

"Don't forget to give the company a plug. We could do with the publicity."

I heard her laughing on the phone.

"It's a deal. Hey, why don't we do lunch some day? Compare notes?"

"Sure. I'd like that."

"Well, get out your diary. Next Wednesday any good?"

"Next Wednesday's perfect."

"Okay. I'll see you in Mooney's at 1 p.m. It's at the corner of Broadway and 54th."

"You're very organised, Kathy."

"In this job, you've got to be."

*

Mooney's turned out to be a tavern that did bar lunches. I found Kathy sitting up at the counter nursing a hot port when I arrived. She was wearing a woollen hat, a coat with a fur collar and sturdy boots.

"Nobody told me about the weather in this city," she said. "In the summer, you fry, and in the winter, you freeze."

She held her arms wide and gave me a welcoming hug.

"What are you drinking?"

"I'll have a martini."

She put two fingers up to the barman and indicated her glass.

"So what's it like among the predators in the corporate jungle?" she asked.

"They're not predators. Most of them are pussy cats."

"Sounds like you're enjoying it."

"I am. How about you?"

"Happy as a pig in shit, if you'll pardon the expression."

We ordered lunch. As we tucked into plates of bacon and cabbage, I asked her where she was living.

"I've got an apartment in the Village. Well, it's not really an apartment. Just a couple of rooms and a kitchen. And it's not really the Village. More the fringe. But the rent is low and I can take the subway to work. You?"

"I'm not far away. I've got a place in Chelsea."

"So we're practically neighbours. We should see more of each other." She lowered her voice. "Met any nice men, yet?"

I hadn't. The nicest man I had met was Jack Morrison and he was already spoken for.

"I've been too busy. How about you?"

"Well, I'm seeing a guy. Bob Getz. He's a writer. He hasn't managed to get anything published yet but he's working on a novel. Social realism. It's about a kid growing up in Hell's Kitchen who wants to be a footballer."

"Sounds interesting."

Kathy shrugged.

"Publishing's tough. It's all a gamble. Bob's trying to cultivate a couple of people he knows. In the meantime, he works rewrite shifts in the *Post* to pay the rent."

"You like him?"

"Yeah, I guess so."

I looked at her. She seemed so happy.

"You've really found your niche, Kathy. It's obvious."

"Well, I guess I've just been lucky. Getting the job with the *Post* was a big break for me. You going to Albany for Christmas?"

"I don't think so. Christmas is a very busy time for us."

"We'll have to get together. I'll give you a call."

She finished her lunch and pushed the plate aside.

"Got time for another drink?"

"Afraid not. I've got to get back to work."
"I'll talk to you."

*

Kathy rang the following week as I was preparing for a meeting.
"Can you talk?"
"Sure."
"Okay. Here's the drill. I'm cooking dinner in my place on Christmas day. You're invited. Us orphans of the storm have to shelter together when all those married people are in the bosom of their familes. Take down the address."
I scribbled on a piece of paper.
"And Stella."
"Yes?"
"You don't have to bring anything. Just yourself and a bottle of wine. Okay?"
"Okay," I said and went off to my meeting.
The run-up to Christmas was hectic. We had three seperate campaigns to prepare and everyone was run ragged. On Christmas Eve, Jack took us for drinks in Bogie's and gave us our bonuses. I walked to St Patrick's Cathedral and heard Midnight Mass, then caught a cab back to my flat and went to bed.
I woke to the sound of bells pealing throughout the city. From my window, I could see the sky, dark and heavy with snowclouds. The streets that normally pulsed with traffic stood deserted. I had never seen the city look so peaceful.
I was glad now that Kathy had invited me. The thought of spending Christmas alone filled me with dread so I was looking forward to the lunch and the chance to meet new people. I found her flat easily enough. It was in an old Victorian house with iron railings and steps up to the front door. I arrived in a heavy coat and scarf, well-insulated against the winter cold and clutching a bottle of wine and a book.
I rang the bell and, a minute later, a voice shouted: "Hold on, I'm coming."

## STELLA'S STORY

The door opened and there stood the most handsome man I had
ever seen.

# 53.

His name was Joe Garvan. He was over six feet tall, with broad shoulders, dark hair and a smile that would steal your heart. He opened the door wide and grinned at me.

"Well don't just stand there, Stella. You'll freeze in the cold."

He brought me upstairs to the flat. It was warm and filled with the smell of cooking chicken. Kathy emerged from the kitchen, carrying a wooden spoon. When she saw me, she flung her arms around me and wished me a happy Christmas.

"You've met Joe already. This is Bob Getz. They're roommates."

A thin man with a goatee beard followed her out of the kitchen and grasped my hand. He had the serious look of those beatnik poets who were beginning to appear in the Village.

"Hi, Stella," he said. "Good to meet you."

I gave Kathy the wine and the book. She tore off the wrapping paper.

"Damon Runyon!" she exclaimed. "One of my heroes. How did you know?"

"Intuition," I said.

She kissed me.

"I just love Runyon. Now let's get our priorities sorted. You need a hot drink, right?"

"Right," I said.

She took my coat and Bob gave me a glass of mulled wine.

"You just make yourself comfy, Stella, while I get this damned dinner ready."

I looked round the flat. It was tiny, even smaller than my own, but she had decorated it tastefully and made the most of the space. She had

278

a sofa in the sitting room; shelves crammed with books and a couple of abstract prints on the walls.

Joe Garvan moved along the sofa for me to sit down.

"Kathy's told us all about you. You're Irish, right?"

"Yes."

"I'm Irish too."

I was getting used to this. Half the people I met in New York claimed to be Irish but at least his name sounded authentic.

"My father was from County Galway. You know it?"

"I know where it is but I've never been there."

"He was always talking about it. The way he went on, you'd think it was the Garden of Eden."

"Is your father dead?"

"Yeah. Died two years ago from lung cancer. He smoked two packs of Luckys a day. Even when the doctors warned him, he just kept right on."

"I'm sorry," I said.

Joe shrugged.

"Way I look at it, he had to die of something. I only got to know him towards the end. He didn't get on with my mother. She's Polish. They went their seperate ways when we were kids."

"Where does your mother live?"

"Over in Jersey. Small town called Lakewood."

While we chatted, I took an opportunity to study him. He had high cheek bones and deep blue eyes that twinkled as he spoke.

"What do you do, Joe?"

"I'm a gardener."

"Here in New York?"

"Don't look surprised. There are more gardens in this city than you might think. Next time you go up in a high-rise, have a look out the window and see how many roof-gardens you see. They all need someone to look after them."

He finished his glass and got another.

"You work for Brazil Bros?"

"That's right."

"You like it?"

"Sure. I love it."

"I don't think I could hack that. Stuck in an office all day. I need to be outdoors."

"Even in winter?"

Joe laughed.

"I guess every job has its downside."

We ate in the kitchen at a big pine table. Chicken with spaghetti in clam sauce. Kathy had prepared a bowl of salad and cut chunks of fresh Italian bread. We drank red wine and Bob talked about his novel. I felt sorry for him. He had sent chapters around but so far hadn't found a publisher.

"It must be very lonely," I said. "Working in your room all day on your own."

"Well, that's the writer's life. Look at James Joyce. Struggling for years in Zurich and Trieste. Living on handouts from people. But he believed in what he was doing and he produced a masterpiece."

Kathy stroked his arm and gazed admiringly into his eyes.

"You will too, Bob."

"The worst thing is when you get some damned publisher who doesn't understand what you're trying to do. Publishing's just a business now. The bottom line is sales. I had one idiot who told me there was no romance in the book. Can you imagine that? I'm writing about a kid growing up in a tenement slum in the West side and this bozo wants romance?"

Kathy produced a bottle of brandy and poured four shots. We drank a toast.

"To us pioneers in the big city."

We clinked glasses.

"To Bob's novel. May it be published to great acclaim and make him rich and famous."

"I'll drink to that," Joe said and poured another.

Kathy cleared away the food. I helped her wash up and then we adjourned to the living room. Outside, it had grown dark and wisps of snow were dropping like feathers from a leaden sky. She put a record on the gramophone. Ella Fitzgerald singing: 'This Can't Be Love'. Joe took my hand.

"Would you like to dance?"

I leaned my head on his shoulder and listened to Ella Fitzgerald singing about love. I was warm and content after the meal and the wine, and I felt happy. The four of us were together in this cosy nest while, outside, the cold wind drove the snow against the window pane.

I closed my eyes and felt Joe's strong arms hold me tight.

"Do you mind if I kiss you?" he said.

I didn't answer. I just put my face up to his and felt his soft warm lips against my mouth.

*

The office was closed for two days after Christmas. I took some leave I was owed and went up to Albany.

"Sounds like you're doing okay," Uncle James said when I told him about Brazil Bros. "Main thing is to take your opportunities. Half the people out there don't know what they're capable of because they never took the trouble to find out."

He took a cigar out of a box and skilfully cut the end off it.

"But be warned. New York's the toughest city in the world. Competition's so fierce that people get burnt up. That's the side of the American ethic nobody ever talks about."

Charlie Kettles seemed content. He was working hard at Mike Shanahan's garage and planned to move into his own house in the new year. Bridgie had already been shopping for furniture and the kids were enrolled in school.

"So you've decided to stay here?" I asked.

"Why not?" Charlie said. "Albany's a fine city. It's got everything I need. You can keep the bright lights, Stella. This is the place for me."

I tried to relax, staying late in bed, reading books and going to the movies. After the pace of New York, I found Albany strangely subdued.

But I missed the bustle and the honking traffic and the physical energy of the streets. Most of all, I missed Joe Garvan. At odd moments, I would find myself thinking about him and wondering what he was doing. After a few days, I got bored and wanted to return.

I rang Kathy, hoping she might mention Joe, but she just talked about the newspaper and Bob's book, and I hadn't the courage to ask about him. Uncle James and Charlie went back to work and soon it was time for me to return to New York.

Weeks passed and I was busy and I heard no more from Joe. But I still thought about him and often, in unguarded moments, my mind would drift back to the Christmas night when we danced at Kathy's flat.

January turned to February and the weather became bitterly cold. On the streets, the wind would come whistling up from the river and chill you to the bone. I wrapped in warm clothes and took the subway to work. One afternoon in March, as we were finalising our Easter campaign, the phone on my desk jumped.

"Yes?" I snapped.

"You sure sound hassled."

I recognised his voice immediately.

"Joe?"

"Yeah. Tell me you won't bite my head off if I ask you out to dinner."

# 54.

Every love story has a true beginning and that was ours. It was to lead to an experience so consuming that, even now, my skin tingles when I think about it. It would cause me to lose myself utterly in another human being, to care more for him than I did for myself, to flinch at the very mention of his name, to surrender myself so completely that sometimes I believed I had lost all hold on reality.

That first night, he took me to Del Rio's. It was a new restaurant off Broadway, only then beginning to gain the reputation that would see it become a favourite haunt of the fashionable set who hung around the theatres. A gilded palace with mirrors and chandeliers, a mock fountain splashed in the foyer. A smooth maître d' in a white tuxedo swept us across the floor to our table and delivered us to a waiter who presented the menus with a flourish so grand, you might think he was conducting an orchestra.

I ordered lamb with baby potatoes and asparagus tips and Joe had salmon in a white wine sauce with fettuccine. He asked for a bottle of Frascati and it came in a little silver ice-bucket with beads of condensation stippling the neck.

I wondered how he could pay for this extravagance but I was secretly delighted that he had gone to such lengths to impress me. Later, I was to learn that he had been saving for months, ever since the night we met. But that was Joe. He was a believer in the dramatic gesture and, when he wanted something badly, money never stood in his way.

We tipped glasses and he took my hand and gazed into my eyes.

"To the most beautiful woman in New York."

"You're fooling with me, Joe."

"No, I'm not. You don't think I bring every date to Del Rio's? This is for someone special."

"Well, thank you."

"Surely you've had other men tell you that you're beautiful?"

"Not men like you."

I watched as his face broke into that boyish smile that was to disarm me so many times throughout our relationship and cause me to forgive him, even when he did the most terrible things.

I can't recall too much about the meal; I was so distracted that food was the last thing on my mind. I remember more wine and much laughter, and the warm, contented feeling that made me believe nothing mattered any more, only this night. There was a band playing Italian love songs and Joe asked me to dance. When he took me in his arms and led me round the floor, I thought I could never be so happy again in my life.

Later, we called into a little bar on 46th Street for a night-cap. Joe ordered Manhattans and we sat at the counter and watched the neon lights winking along the avenue. He took my hand again.

"You know, I've thought about you every day since we met."

I was a little light-headed and his voice was like music.

"That's nice, Joe. You say the nicest things."

"It's true. I couldn't get you out of my mind. I thought if I tried hard, I would forget you, but it didn't work. I would wake in the middle of the night thinking about you."

"I thought of you too."

"Honestly?"

"Yes."

"That makes me so happy, Stella. You're so beautiful."

I sank my head on his shoulder.

"Please, Joe. Don't say any more."

"Why?

"Just tell me slowly. Don't tell me all at once."

He shook his head in wonder and turned to the barman.

"Two more, Mike. Make them doubles."

We left the bar at around 2 a.m. and caught a cab back to my place. I was half-hoping that Joe would ask to come in. I wanted this wonderful night to go on forever.

But instead he kissed me and said he would call. I stood on the doorstep and watched his cab speed away. Then, I climbed the stairs and got into bed, the memory of his last kiss still lingering on my lips. I fell asleep with thoughts of the glittering chandeliers and the handsome man who held me so close as we danced, I could hear his heart beat.

He rang the next day at 12.30 p.m. as I was going over papers at my desk.

"How are you today?"

I was thrilled to hear his voice again.

"I'm fine. And you?"

"Still thinking of last night."

"It was wonderful, Joe. How can I thank you?"

"No need. The pleasure's all mine. What are you doing for lunch?"

"I thought I'd grab a sandwich."

"There's a deli on the corner of 56th and Madison. How about I see you there at 1.30?"

"I'd like that."

"Good. I'll be there."

He put the phone down and I realised that I wanted to see him again more than anything else in the world.

He was sitting at a booth beside the window looking out on the street, wearing jeans, a sweatshirt, and a heavy lumber jacket to keep out the cold. As I snuggled into the seat beside him, he put an arm around me and kissed me.

"Are you hungry?"

"I think so. I only had time for coffee this morning."

"They do the most wonderful pastrami on rye here. Would you like to share one?"

"Sure."

The sandwich came packed with meat and provolone cheese. The coffee was dark and bitter, scalding hot. We sat together like lovers, eating in silence, just happy to be in each others company.

At last Joe said: "Why don't you call in sick and we'll catch a movie?"

"I couldn't, Joe. Do you want me to get fired?"

"Who's to know?"

"They're not stupid. And what about you? Aren't you at work today?"

"I took the day off. I can catch up tomorrow."

I kissed his cheek.

"I'd love to. But some other time."

He shrugged and finished his coffee.

"So, when will I see you again?"

"Tomorrow. You'll see me tomorrow."

*

I saw Joe every day for the next two months. For lunch, for dinner, for trips to the theatre, for walks in the park. I think I became obsessed with him. He rang me at all times of the day and night, waking me from my sleep, distracting me from my work. Always he was cheerful, always smiling that disarming smile. I don't think in those early days I ever saw him frown. Certainly, he brought a joy into my life that I had rarely known before.

It was inevitable that we would make love. I wanted it to happen. But I wanted it to be right, not a hurried rut or a drunken coupling. I picked my time, an evening when I knew he would be relaxed, and I arranged to cook dinner in my flat. I bought the ingredients in an Italian grocery: cuts of veal, artichoke hearts, salad, tomatoes, cheese, wholegrain bread, a litre of chianti.

After tidying the flat, I laid out the little table in the kitchen. I lit candles and found a radio station that played romantic music. Joe arrived at half-eight with a bouquet of roses, and we drank wine while I finished cooking the dinner. We ate by candlelight, listening to Frank Sinatra, and afterwards we danced.

Joe held me tight and kissed my neck. I felt his fingers fumbling with the buttons of my blouse, his warm, gentle hands caress my breasts. I closed my eyes and let the thrill of passion wash over me. He unzipped my skirt and I stood naked in the candlelight.

I was eager now. He took my hand and led me to the bedroom. Neither of us spoke. He kissed my mouth and I kissed him back, hungry for him. I felt the heavy weight of his chest press down on mine and then he was entering me and my body melted in a long lingering rush of pleasure.

# 55.

Joe was a passionate lover. He wasn't slow and precise like Jimmy Rickard. He was thrusting and hard and drove with fierce, quick strokes that had me screaming with passion. He made love like a man distracted, as if he was trying to divest himself of some terrible burden. His pleasure was almost like pain. At times it frightened me to see his face so contorted. And when it was over, he would lie on the damp sheets, his skin drenched in sweat and the nest of hair on his chest gleaming like silver.

That first time was a long night of pleasure. We eventually fell asleep about 4 a.m. and, when I woke, Joe was lying beside me, his breathing slow and calm like a baby's. I got up, put on the coffee and went into the bathroom to shower. When I returned, he was sitting up in bed, his eyes bleary from sleep. He watched as I got dressed.

"You've got the most beautiful body, Stella."

I smiled. I loved his compliments. They flattered and reassured me.

"You're not too bad yourself, Joe."

"You think so?"

"Sure. You're a handsome man."

"Do I make you happy?"

"Delirious."

"You make me happy too. We're made for each other, you and me. Do you believe in fate? Do you believe you're destined to meet one person and fall in love?"

"I don't know. I'm certainly glad I met you."

"I believe in fate. Even though we were born in different parts of the world, it was already decided that we would meet. Why do you think you came to Kathy's flat on Christmas Day the same as me?"

"Because I'd nothing else to do and she invited me."

I laughed. I was feeling light-hearted and gay. Outside the window, the sky was already dappled with light. I opened the curtains and the sun came flooding in. I went into the kitchen and brought Joe a mug of coffee.

"I've been thinking," he said. "If you're free on Saturday, I'll borrow a car and take you for a spin over to Jersey. Visit my mom?"

"Okay."

"She'd love to meet you. My sister and her husband live with her. We'll have a family reunion. You ever been to Jersey?"

I shook my head.

"You'll love it," he said. "Wait and see."

*

We started out early on Saturday morning. Joe had borrowed an old Ford from a friend. We drove through the Holland Tunnel into north Jersey, the radio playing country music, songs of broken hearts and unfaithful women, as I watched the little towns roll by with their neat wooden houses and white-painted gables. I looked at Joe, strong and handsome at the wheel, and felt so happy. I thought: if only it could be like this forever, I wouldn't ask for anything more.

We arrived in Lakewood before noon. Joe stopped at a liquor store and came back with a brown paper bag which he put on the back seat. Then we drove east along Squankum Road till we came to an old two-storey frame house. He pulled into the yard and sounded the horn.

A woman of about thirty came out, followed by a couple of kids in tee-shirts and shorts. The woman dried her hands on her apron and kissed Joe as he got out of the car. He helped me out and introduced me.

"This is my big sister, Amy. Amy, this is Stella. She's from Ireland."

"Oh, really? Just like Dad. You know Galway?"

"Yes," I said.

"That's where Dad was from."

"I know. Joe's already told me."

She was dark like Joe, with the same blue eyes.

"Come into the house," she said. "Mom's dying to see you."

It was cool inside. An old lady sat at a table in the kitchen, wrapped in a man's jacket. Her face was like wrinkled paper, thin with sharp, bony features.

She grasped Joe's hands and pulled him close.

"You never come to see me any more," she complained.

"Yes, I do. And I've brought someone to meet you. This is Stella. She's my girl."

She put on glasses and examined me. I didn't wait for her approval. I opened my handbag and gave her the scarf I had brought as a gift and the bags of candy I had got for the kids.

"Well thank you, Stella. Joe never brings me anything. He never even calls me on the telephone."

"Don't listen to her," Joe said. "I brought you a bottle of Jim Beam. You like that, don't you?"

He opened the paper bag and produced a bottle of whiskey, which she hid away under her petticoats.

"Jim Beam's all right. Helps me sleep. I hope you're taking care of him, Stella?"

"Joe doesn't need any care."

"You take my advice," the old lady sighed. "Men are worse than children. You gotta keep an eye on them. Else they get up to mischief."

"Fred's gone into town to pick up some things," Amy said. "You guys planning to stay the night?"

Joe shrugged.

"What do you think, Stella?"

It hadn't been part of the plan but I didn't want to be rude, so I just said: "Whatever you want, Joe."

"We'll stay. If it isn't any inconvenience, Amy."

"No. Mom's glad to see you. Stella can bunk down with Kitty and you can sleep on the couch. It's no big deal."

Amy's husband, Fred Stoat, came back at four o'clock in his pick-up truck. He was a small man of about forty, going bald. He was dressed in faded dungarees and a check work-shirt from his job as a handyman, fixing people's houses. He shook hands with Joe and I and we all sat round the dining table to eat a dinner of chicken, potatoes and sweet corn.

"How's business?" Joe inquired.

"So so. I've got enough to keep me going but not enough to make me rich."

"What do these people do about their gardens?" Joe asked.

"Tend 'em." Fred laughed. "Some of these guys put more work into their goddamned gardens than they put into their businesses."

"Yeah?" Joe said.

"Sure. I know guys who spend hundreds of dollars on fertilisers and lawn treatments just so their gardens will look better than the guy's next door. Why do you ask?"

"Just an idea I have."

"You thinking of going into business?"

"Maybe. Would it work?"

"I don't see why not. There's certainly enough customers out there."

We finished dinner and adjourned to the sitting room. The old lady wanted to know how Joe was getting on in New York and why he didn't come to see her more often. I was fascinated by his family but slightly resentful of the way they monopolised him. I wanted him to myself. But Joe didn't seem to mind. He chatted amiably about his work and his friends and life in the big city.

At eight o'clock, the old lady went to bed and the children followed shortly after.

Fred took a bottle of whiskey out of a cabinet and poured four shots. He got out a guitar and began to sing. It was mostly Jimmie Rodgers' songs about men travelling the railroads. He had a sweet voice and played well. We sat drinking whisky till it got dark and I began to feel sleepy. I'd been up early and had a long day.

At last, I said: "I'm going to bed."

Joe didn't seem to hear me. He was engrossed in the songs. I spoke more firmly.

"I said I'm going to bed, Joe."

"Sure. Okay."

He barely looked up as I rose and left the room, just lifted a hand and waved. Suddenly, I felt angry with him.

"Sing that one about the Mississippi," I heard him say as I closed the door and mounted the stairs. And then the guitar chords and Fred's voice beginning to croon.

*

Joe slept late the next day and when he appeared he was red-eyed and hungover. I was still angry with him for ignoring me the night before and I was growing tired of his family. I just wanted to get back to New York.

When we eventually left I sat in the car in silence, my anger festering. After a while Joe said: "Something biting you, Stella?"

"You didn't say goodnight to me, last night."

He began to laugh.

"Jesus, I'm sorry. I didn't think it mattered so much."

"You were more concerned about drinking with Fred Stoat than you were about me."

"Hell, I only see them a couple of times a year. You heard the old lady."

"It wouldn't have hurt you to kiss me goodnight."

He stamped his foot down hard on the brakes and we crunched to a stop in a layby. I got ready for an argument. He switched off the ignition and turned to face me.

"You're right. I was selfish."

He took me in his arms.

"I would never willingly hurt you, Stella. I love you more than anything else in the world. If I didn't have you, I don't know what I would do. I love you so much, I want you to marry me."

# 56.

I think I fell in love with Joe the moment I saw him. Some people don't believe in that. But I do. Within a week of going out with him, I was infatuated. I thought about him all the time. I would have done anything he said. If he had asked me to jump off Niagara Falls with him, I would have agreed. If that's not love, what is?

So, when he asked me to marry him, I didn't hesitate. I knew I had found the only man who mattered to me, the only man I could spend my life with. I saw no flaws in Joe, only goodness. I knew that people aren't perfect, but he was the closest to perfection I had ever met. Joe was kind and generous and handsome. He was warm and affectionate. He was humorous and he made me laugh. Just being in his presence was enough to make me happy.

He spent a hundred dollars on a diamond solitaire and took me back to Del Rio's for a celebratory dinner. When my colleagues in Brazil Bros saw the ring, they crowded round to admire it. One of the secretaries, Judy Muller, was particularly impressed.

"My God, Stella, that's some stone. This guy Joe? Is he a Wall Street broker or something?"

"No, Judy. Nothing like that. He's just an ordinary guy."

"Well he sure must love you an awful lot to buy you a ring like that."

Jack Morrison took me aside and congratulated me.

"Does this mean you'll be leaving us?"

"I don't think so."

"Well, that's good news. I'd be sorry to lose you, Stella."

*

Fixing the wedding date was only one of the many things to be decided.

But first, we had to find somewhere to live. It didn't seem to bother Joe.

"Why don't you move into my place? It's bigger than yours. And with two of us working, we'll save on rent."

"What about Bob?"

"He's already talking about leaving. He's looking for somewhere cheaper."

Joe's apartment was on East 57th Street. It had a large double bedroom and a roof garden that caught the sun all day. I would still be able to walk to work. The lease would have to be changed but that wasn't a big problem.

But these where small things compared with the one issue I had yet to face. The matter of Martin. When I parted with him, I made a decision to put him out of my mind and start my life afresh. I knew I would never see him again. The only links I had to him were my memories and the small mementoes like the picture I kept of his christening day.

Of course, it had been impossible. No woman can forget her child. At odd moments, Martin ambushed me and I found myself wondering how he was and whether he still remembered me. At times like these I would grow sad, cursing the fate that had forced me to give him away and thinking how things might have been if I had kept him. And then, I would chastise myself for reopening old wounds and try to put him out of my mind again.

I had never told Joe about him and now I faced a dilemma. I could keep silent about Martin and Joe would never find out. Martin was thousands of miles away. Nobody in America knew of his existence. But if I was going to marry Joe, I wanted to be honest, no secrets. I felt I owed it to us both.

I choose a Sunday afternoon. On Sundays, we often went walking in Central Park and later had dinner at an Italian restaurant that Joe liked on 72nd Street. It was a warm June day. The roses were in bloom. Families were playing baseball or having picnics on the grass. We found a quiet spot near the lake and sat on a bench in the shade of a silver maple. I took Joe's hand. I had been preparing myself for days.

"I've got something to tell you."

"Let me guess. You don't want to eat in Luigi's tonight? You want to go somewhere else?"

"No, this is serious. I want you to know it before we get married. I have a child, a little boy, back in Ireland."

I saw him start.

"How do you mean, Stella?"

"It happened years ago. I tried to keep him but I couldn't, so I gave him away for adoption. I wanted you to know about him, Joe."

I was trembling with anxiety.

"Who was the guy involved?"

"He was a soldier."

"Does he know about his kid?"

This was the hardest bit.

"No. I never saw him again."

"What was this guy's name?"

"Bud. I don't know his surname."

Joe turned to stare at me. I knew what he was thinking. I was a tramp. A woman who would go with a man she didn't even know.

I lowered my head.

"I just wanted to tell you so everything would be in the open between us."

I waited and then I felt his strong arms enfold me and his hands smooth down my hair. I felt his soft lips kiss my cheek.

"Oh, Stella. You poor, dumb jerk. Why didn't you tell me before?"

"I was afraid."

"You thought this would matter? You thought it would make me change my mind? I love you, Stella. I love you the way you are. For better or worse."

I was weeping now. I cuddled deeper into Joe's arms.

"What's the kid's name?"

"Martin," I said. "I called him after my brother."

*

We were married in August from Uncle James's house in Albany. It was a small wedding, just our immediate families. I had phoned home to tell Mammy and Daddy but it was impossible for them to come. Kathleen was heartbroken. She had started teaching now at a school in Enniskillen and was seeing a young man called Sean Fagan. She badly wanted to come. I promised to send photographs.

Bridgie was my bridesmaid and Bob Getz was best man. I wore a simple wedding dress of white satin. The staff at Brazil Bros sent a card and a wedding gift: a canteen of cutlery.

We had the reception back at the house. Uncle James spared nothing. We had champagne for the wedding toast and a cold buffet with turkey, roast beef, and lobster salad. Joe's mother sat in the living room and complained that he would never visit her at all, now that he was a married man.

Fred Stoat had brought his guitar and Bob Getz and him seemed to hit it off. They sat out in the back yard together singing Woody Guthrie songs and drinking Wild Turkey whiskey while Kathy Brewster listened attentively and the children ran around on the lawn.

The next morning, Joe and I drove down to Atlantic City for our honeymoon. We stayed at the Palladian Hotel, an old-fashioned place that was falling gracefully into decline. But it was comfortable and the restaurant served the best Louisiana gumbo I had ever tasted, cooked by an old Negro woman called Mamma Brown.

We lay late in bed and had breakfast in our room. We swam in the ocean and strolled the boardwalk with the day-trippers up from Philadelphia. I had my fortune read by a gypsy woman in a booth on the pier. She noticed my wedding ring and told me I would have six children, three girls and three boys, and they would bring me comfort in my old age.

At night we made love. I looked forward to those nights; Joe's strong, tanned body, his beautiful face, the coils of dark hair on his naked chest, the shudder of excitement that engulfed me each time he touched me. I gave myself to him with utter abandon. And when it was over and we lay entwined in the rumpled sheets, I would think: Surely I can never be so happy again in my life?

# 57.

The next eighteen months were bliss. I moved into Joe's apartment, up till now an untidy bachelor pad in need of a good cleaning. Together we redecorated it. We bought new furniture, painted the walls and ceilings, put up fresh curtains and laid down carpets. Soon we had the apartment looking proud. We invited Kathy and Bob over for a dinner party one night and Bob barely recognised his old place.

Sunday was the best day of the week. We rose early and had breakfast on the roof garden: hot coffee and doughnuts; or scrambled eggs, and fresh bagels which I got from the Jewish bakery at the corner of the street. We'd get dressed in jeans and runners and set off to explore the city.

I got to know New York that year of 1951. Joe's job took him all over the city so he was the perfect guide. We would ride the subway down as far as the Battery and walk back through the Bowery and Chinatown and Little Italy.

Stopping off to have a lunch of hero sandwiches and beer, we'd then set off again, walking till we were tired: visiting art galleries and museums, sitting in the little parks to feed the pigeons, or browsing through street markets and bookstores.

Every Sunday, we chose a different route; north into Harlem and the Bronx or south along First Avenue. We crossed on the ferry to Staten Island. We explored the East Village. We took the subway to Brooklyn. Joe brought me to bars with strange names: the Blue Fox, Banana Joe's, Good Time Charlie's, Sneaky Pete's. We would sit on high stools and order exotic cocktails.

Once, he took me to Coney Island and we rode the Big Dipper and paid fifty cents to see the Rubber Man. It turned out to be a swizz; just a skinny guy in bathing togs who did contortion tricks. He took me to cinemas and ball games where we sat on the bleachers in the sun and ate hot dogs and popcorn. By the end of that first year, I knew the city better than most people who had lived there all their lives.

Joe worked now for the Parks Department. He was occupied all year round, but certain seasons were busier than others. Spring was a particularly active time with planting and bedding and laying fresh lawns. So was autumn. There was a lot of pruning work to be done along with seeding and digging. All over the roof garden, he had laid out little pots and tubs with seedlings and cuttings which he would later transplant. I loved to sit there on a warm evening amid the roses, geraniums and sweet-scented stock, looking out over the city as far as the two rivers.

Joe's job allowed him to work as he pleased. Some days he did hardly anything; other days he would work for twelve or fourteen hours, come home exhausted and just tumble into bed. My job was more regular. It meant that sometimes we didn't see each other in the morning or at night; but we made a rule to always make time to be together at some part of the day. We would meet for lunch, or, after work, we'd head off to some nice restaurant for dinner. That period was one of the happiest in my life.

I had long ago mastered my job. Brazil Bros ticked over like clockwork. I kept the peace between the warring factions. Campaigns got launched on time. We built a reputation as a good firm to do business with. Increasingly, Jack Morrison came to rely on me and give me more and more responsibility. I loved the life and I earned good money: in 1951, my salary averaged eighty dollars a week.

But I was growing restless. Just as had happened back in Dublin, I found some of the old excitement going out of the job. I craved fresh challenges. Also, I knew that I would inevitably come up against the glass ceiling. Advertising was a very male profession, and not alone was I a woman, I was a married woman at that.

I could see that Joe, too, was getting bored; the career path in the Parks department was slow and bureaucratic. Opportunities were scarce. He liked his work but he was ambitious and already thinking of the future. So, I wasn't surprised when he announced one day that he was thinking of leaving.

"What would you do?"

"Set up on my own."

"Here? In New York?"

"Maybe. Maybe move to Jersey. There's plenty of business out there. I've been talking to Fred about it. I could set up as a landscape gardener. All I would need is a few hundred dollars for a truck and some tools."

"Where would we live?"

"We could buy a place. We could get a house in Jersey very cheap. A good house too, with a bit of land."

He smiled.

"We might need it, Stella. When we have children, they'll need space. This apartment is too small. Kids need room to run around."

"How much would we need?"

"Altogether? A thousand dollars?"

I had some money saved but it would mean borrowing the rest and taking out a mortgage. I thought of a house of our own and a big back yard; trees and birds and flowers and eventually, children.

"We could go over there this weekend and look around," Joe suggested. "See what's on offer."

We drove over on Sunday and by lunchtime we were in Freehold. It was a pretty town, bigger than Lakewood. It had a quaint colonial style; white gabled houses and old churches with pointed spires. It was March and already the daffodils were out. At once I liked it. It had a comfortable, neighbourly air; the sort of intimate place where people would look out for each other.

We ate at a diner and then went searching. All the real estate offices were closed, but we looked at the properties on offer in their windows. They had plenty of houses for sale, but nothing in our budget. We decided to ring in the morning and see what else they had on their books.

We returned by the back roads to get a feel for the place. They were mere dirt tracks, but they weaved through picturesque countryside: wide open fields, small farms, barns and silos and cattle grazing.

I was reminded of my childhood in Ballinaleck; Daddy and Michael and Martin saving the hay and milking the cows in the early dawn. And then on the bend in the road, we came upon a For Sale sign. Joe stopped the car and we got out.

The house was no bigger than a shack but it was surrounded by about an acre of land. It appeared to be vacant so we opened the gate and went in. As we approached, we could see slates hanging off the roof, broken windows and paint peeling from the doors. The small garden behind the house was overgrown. Weeds ran wild and briars trailed through the tangled undergrowth. The property looked as if it had been derelict for some time, abandoned to nature. But I could see that Joe was interested.

"I wonder how much they're looking for it?"

"It would need an awful lot of work, Joe."

"I could do that. Fred could help. And there's land for a nursery. I could grow vegetables and flowers. It's perfect, Stella. It's only fifteen minutes from Freehold and it's bound to come cheap."

The following morning, he rang the realtor. The house had belonged to an old lady who had died and was being sold by her son. He was asking for one thousand dollars. Joe offered eight hundred and the realtor came back later and said they would accept nine. Joe was excited now. We sat down at the table in the kitchen and worked out our finances. He calculated what it would cost to repair the house and buy a truck and equipment to start up in business. When he had deducted the money I had saved, we would need to borrow twelve hundred dollars from the bank.

"The repayments will be about forty dollars a month. It's less than the rent on the apartment," Joe said.

"Except I won't be working at Brazil Bros."

"Maybe you could commute?"

I had already thought about the long train journey to and from New York. It would involve leaving early in the morning and getting home late at night. I decided it was too much, I'd be exhausted.

"It wouldn't work, Joe."

"You're bound to find a job in Freehold. With your experience, they'd jump at the chance to hire you. And once I have the business up and running, we'll be well able to manage. It's a great opportunity, Stella. We have to go for it."

I knew he was right. It was time to quit the bright lights of New York. Time to settled down to a more peaceful life. Time to say Goodbye to Brazil Bros.

"All right," I said. "Let's do it."

Every weekend, Joe drove down to Freehold and worked on the property. Fred Stoat helped him and, bit by bit, our new home began to take shape. Joe rebuilt the house. He put in an extra guest bedroom, a new bathroom, a big modern kitchen and dining room, a sun deck and porch. The centrepiece was the sitting room with a large stone chimney and hearth.

He rotivated the land, laid a new lawn, and stocked the garden with roses, hydrangeas and flowering shrubs. When he was finished, the house had been transformed. In place of the tumbledown shack, there was now a fine modern dwelling that anyone would be proud of.

At the end of May, I gave notice to quit. Jack Morrison was shocked and begged me to reconsider. He offered me a raise. I told him we were moving to New Jersey and the commuting time was too long. Reluctantly, he agreed to let me go.

On June 27th, almost two years to the day when I began, I left Brazil Bros. We had a farewell party in Bogie's and the staff presented me with a voucher worth one hundred dollars.

I made a little speech. I thanked them for their loyalty and hard work and told them I would always remember the happy times we spent together. At eight o'clock, I slipped away. Joe had arranged to said my goodbyes. All that remained was to go.

He was waiting at the top of the street, our suitcases stowed in the boot of the car. I sat in beside him and he pecked my cheek. He fired the engine and headed west. Two hours later we were driving into Freehold to begin our new life.

# 58.

I was crazy about Joe and, since the move to Freehold, we made love all the time: at night in bed; in the morning; after dinner; out on the deck in the evening, as the sun went down, the heavy scent of the flowers drifting up as we coupled on the hard wooden boards.

Joe only had to touch me to make me want him. I loved everything about him: the set of his jaw, the colour of his eyes, the flat, tight muscles on his chest. I loved the way he walked and the things he said. I loved the way he shaved himself in the morning, standing naked in front of the bathroom mirror, his face covered in soap and the long ridge of his spine still damp from the shower. In those early months in our new home, I couldn't get enough of Joe and when we were apart, I thought about him all the time.

I got a job working in McCleery's department store in the town, at my old station behind the cosmetics counter. I still had my reference from Brown Thomas. The store was only a small place and the money was much less than I was used to. I got thirty dollars a week and no bonuses, but then I didn't have any responsibilities either, and the cash made a welcome contribution to the mortgage.

Joe threw himself into the landscape business. He bought a pick-up truck and had his name painted on the side. He hung a sign outside our house and got business cards printed up. He took out an advert in the phone directory and placed notices in shop windows. Work was slow to begin with, but as word spread, the business grew and, before long, he had more jobs than he could handle.

He did any gardening work that was demanded, and as a sideline, he grew vegetables and fruit on our land and sold the produce to stores as far away as Lakewood and Tom's River.

I bought a car and he taught me how to drive. I needed it to get to and from my job. Joe would get up early in the morning and load the truck with tools and equipment while I cooked breakfast. Then he would drive off to wherever the work was. In the evening, he would arrive home, his skin tanned from the sun, his hands dirty and calloused from the work. After he showered, we would eat dinner. In those early months, we mainly ate at home but sometimes, as a treat, we would go to an Italian place that Joe liked called Nico's where we would eat pasta with pesto sauce and drink Chianti wine.

I didn't miss New York and that surprised me. Freehold was a quiet place. By 7 p.m., the shops had all shut up for the day and the town was silent as a church. The evenings were so still that if a car went past on the road outside our house, you could still hear it, minutes later, phut-phutting away into the distance. But I was married now, and in love; all I wanted was to be with Joe. I would have followed him to the North Pole. Sometimes Kathy Brewster and Bob came down and spent a weekend with us, but I'd get the impression that they couldn't wait to get back to the big city.

I also kept in touch with Uncle James. Charlie Kettles was still working with Mike Shanahan but he had saved the money and was ready to go out on his own. They had moved out of Uncle James' house by now and bought their own place. I sent Mammy and Daddy wedding snaps and wrote to keep them informed of the news. They replied to tell me that Michael had got engaged and they were expecting Kathleen to follow suit any day now.

My life fell into a rhythm and I was content. We were paying off the mortgage on our own lovely house and Joe's business was doing well. I could see he was much happier working for himself. On Sunday afternoons, he would sit at the dining room table and do his accounts and, on Monday morning, he would lodge the week's takings into the bank. One day drifted into the next and before long it was autumn; the days grew shorter and the weather got colder as the leaves began to drop from the trees along the road. I got up one morning and realised I hadn't had a period for six weeks.

At first, I was shocked. The memories of the last time came flooding back. I was never late; my period was so regular I could tell the date by it. But our love-making had become so wild and abandoned that I had grown careless and the thought of pregnancy had never entered my head.

My shock quickly gave way to delight. This was the child we both wanted. This child would be loved and cherished. This child I would never have to give away. I was filled with such an enormous sense of satisfaction that I wanted to rush out at once and tell everyone I knew.

But I kept the news to myself for another two weeks and, when I missed my period for a second month, I made an appointment to see Dr Baldwin. He had a surgery off Main Street and I arranged to see him during my lunch break. An old-fashioned family doctor with rimless spectacles and a chubby face, he wore a tightly buttoned waistcoat that struggled to keep his bulging midriff from tumbling out of his pants.

I already knew the drill, so I brought a urine sample in a little medicine bottle with a screw-top stopper. He began by writing down my medical history and then he asked me about the date of my last period. He took my blood pressure and then he examined me. When he had finished, he asked: "Have you given birth before?"

I was startled. I didn't see how he could know.

"Yes," I said. "I had a child seven years ago."

His sharp eyes caught mine.

"Is the child all right?"

"Yes," I said quickly. "He's fine."

Dr Baldwin nodded and wrote on his note pad.

"Well, I can't tell you definitely till I've had the sample analysed, but I'll bet my boots you're pregnant. The results will take a few days to come back from the lab. Call and see me again on Thursday and we'll know for sure."

He smiled and shook my hand.

"I won't congratulate you just yet, and don't tell your husband in case it's a false alarm. But if I was you, Mrs Garvan, I'd start knitting baby clothes."

*

Three days later, it was confirmed. I could hardly contain my joy. I waited till Joe had come home and eaten dinner. He had taken to relaxing in the evening on the sun deck with a glass of whiskey. I went and sat beside him.

"I've got news."

"Oh," he said.

We had so little news that he probably assumed it was some tittle-tattle to do with the store.

"I'm pregnant."

The look on his face changed and, for an awful moment, I thought he was going to complain. Then he was out of his chair and hugging me in his arms.

"Oh, Stella. That's great news. That's the best news I've ever heard. When did you find out?"

"Today. It's confirmed. I'm six weeks gone."

Joe smacked his thigh.

"Well, I'll be damned."

He took the bottle of Old Crow and poured two shots.

"You know what this means, Stella? We're no longer a couple. We're going to be a family."

# 59.

With this pregnancy came morning sickness, terrible bouts of retching into the toilet bowl, so violent that I thought I was going to rip my guts out. I got them even when there was nothing left in my stomach to throw up except gobbets of green bile. The attacks would leave me feeling so weak that I had to lie down on the bed to recover.

Dr Baldwin put me on a course of vitamin supplements, little red tablets that I had to swallow after every meal. I had to see him once a month to monitor my progress. He weighed me and checked my chest and heart and took my blood pressure, writing it all down on his note pad and put it in my file.

I had to go to pre-natal classes with half a dozen other women where a young nurse with a pretty freckled face taught us the merits of breast-feeding, the necessity of sterilising baby's diapers, and the need to get regular exercise and maintain a healthy diet.

After a few weeks, the morning sickness stopped. I had decided not to tell anyone at work untill closer to the time, but as the months passed, I began to put on weight and it became impossible to hide. I went and saw old Mr McCleery, who couldn't have been kinder. He told me I could work till the baby was due and take up my position again after my confinement. He said if I wasn't feeling well to ring and tell him. He even transferred me to a job at the cash register so that I didn't have to stand all day.

Joe was very protective of me. He said I had to rest up and he took over the cooking and cleaning chores around the house. He cooked gargantuan meals that I could never finish. He made enormous salads from the garden and forced me to drink milk and eat cheese so that I would get a regular intake of calcium.

I felt sorry for him. He would come home in the evening tired and then start into cooking dinner. I could easily have done it; I still had plenty of energy and I felt guilty watching him doing all the work. But Joe insisted, treating me like an invalid, even stopping our love-making, although Dr Baldwin had told me it was perfectly safe up till the seventh month and that there was no reason why we shouldn't do it unless it felt uncomfortable.

Joe loved my pregnant body. He loved the way my breasts filled out and the nipples grew dark. He loved the way my belly expanded. In bed at night he would lie beside me and run his hands along my thighs and over my stomach and up to my heavy breasts. It was a beautiful, sensual feeling to have his hands caress me like that. It would get me aroused and, when he stopped, I would lie awake for a long time wishing he would take me and terrified of touching myself in case he'd know.

That winter was a cruel one. It started in November, cold days of wind and rain that lashed the window panes and made the timbers shudder. By December, it was snowing and Joe couldn't go to work. The bad weather continued past Christmas and into the new year. We would stay at home and bank up the big fire in the living room and watch game shows or read together by the fire.

I couldn't wait for the baby to arrive, and began counting the days. Dr Baldwin had told me it was due in the second week of May. I had the date marked on a chart in the bathroom and every morning I would score off another day. But, as the time edged closer and I got bigger, I began to grow tired of my condition and wished the waiting was over.

It was spring and Joe was busy again, rising at seven each morning to check the weather forecast before going to work.

One Saturday morning in March, he got up and turned on the radio as usual. I heard the announcer say more snow was on the way. Joe cursed under his breath. He looked out the window. The sky was dark with heavy, louring clouds.

"This damned weather," he said. "I have a job over by Brick, putting in a new lawn. I promised the guy I'd get it done today."

"It can wait," I said. "You can do it next week."

"I'm busy next week. I'm booked every day."

"Come back to bed."

But he was up now. He went down to the kitchen and I heard him put on the kettle. He came back with a mug of coffee and toast for me.

"Tell you what, Stella. I've got to go into town to pick up some stuff. Why don't you come with me? We can shop for baby things?"

I thought of the weather and the threat of snow.

"Leave it," I said. "We'll go another time."

"No, let's go today. It'll give us something to do. And we can have lunch in Nico's. A special treat."

I got dressed in a heavy coat and scarf and Joe wrapped up in his lumber jacket and we set off in the truck. Saturday was normally busy but today the town was almost deserted. Joe bought the equipment he needed and then we went to a store that specialised in baby goods. We looked at prams and cots. I thought they were expensive, but Joe was in a generous mood.

"What colour will we choose?"

"Something neutral. Maybe something dark that won't show the scratches too much."

"You expect it to get scratched?"

I smiled at his naivety.

"Joe, this is a pram. For pushing a baby around. Of course it's going to get scratched."

We chose a dark blue model with high wheels and a little parasol for shading the sun. We picked a plain wooden cot with pictures of rabbits and reindeers and a little hook for hanging toys. Joe paid for the goods and the assistant said they'd deliver them on Monday. Then we went off to Nico's for lunch. It was a fancy restuarant, with little lamps on the tables, starched linen napkins and a gramophone that played opera music.

Normally it was busy, but today there were only two other diners. Joe ordered minestrone soup and veal with taglietelle. I had chicken cooked with mushrooms and herbs. As the waiter turned to go, Joe called him back.

"Bring us a bottle of chianti."

Being pregnant, I had stopped drinking alcohol. I put a hand on Joe's wrist.

"None for me. A half bottle will do."

"Oh c'mon. This is a celebration. A glass won't hurt you."

He turned to the waiter.

"Bring us a bottle."

It came in a little straw basket and the waiter poured. Joe tasted the wine, then signalled for the glasses to be filled. I watched him drink it down and smack his lips.

"God, that hit the spot."

He refilled his glass. I took a sip from mine and waited for the food to come. It was delicious. Joe talked throughout the meal about the jobs he had lined up and the busy schedule ahead. He had work booked for the next two months with the prospect of more as the year progressed.

We had dessert and then coffee. Joe finished the bottle of wine and ordered an amaretto. He was in a happy mood now, but I was getting concerned.

"Why don't you wait till we get home? You've got to drive the truck."

He laughed.

"I'm perfectly sober. I could drive that damned truck from here to New York. Loosen up. You're like a cat on a hot tin roof."

But I didn't like Joe drinking and driving. There was always a danger of being stopped by the traffic cops and then he could lose his licence. I couldn't wait to get home. At last, we paid the bill and went out to the street. It was only two o'clock but already it was dark. The sky was the colour of night, heavy with black, threatening snow clouds.

I was glad to get into the truck. As we drove out of town, Joe turned on the radio and we listened to Guy Mitchell singing 'She Wears Red Feathers'. He beat his hand on the wheel in time with the music. I thought of the cosy fire that awaited us in the comfort of our own home.

The snow began to fall as we drove onto New Road and into the countryside, a few flurries at first and then heavy gusts that piled against the windscreen in thick layers like cotton wool. Joe turned on the wipers and slowed down. Visibility dropped to a few yards. I began to get anxious. I thought of having to abandon the pick-up and how we would get home, but Joe was determined. He drove with his head bent forward and his face almost pressed against the glass.

The road narrowed and we came to a junction. The snow was covering the windscreen as fast as the wipers could clear it off. I was fast regretting the stupid trip into town, and that I hadn't been sterner with Joe: if we hadn't gone to Nico's, we'd have been safely home by now.

A van seemed to come out of nowhere and was almost on top of us before we knew. I screamed at Joe and he swung the steering wheel hard to the right. I heard a crash of brakes and then the windscreen shattered. The truck spun out of control. I felt it bump and smash and turn over. My head hit the steering column and everything went black.

*

I awoke to bright lights and searing pain. I was in bed and Joe was sitting in a chair beside me. His head was bandaged and he was quietly sobbing to himself.

I became aware of a man in a white coat. His lips were moving but his voice seemed to come out in a whsiper.

"How do you feel?"

"Awful. Where am I?"

"Mercy hospital. You were in a road accident. You were nearly killed."

I looked at Joe but he didn't speak. I struggled to sit up in bed. The doctor was talking again. I could barely make out what he was saying.

"I have bad news for you, Mrs Garvan. You've broken some ribs. Worse than that, you've lost your baby."

# 60.

I couldn't believe the news. I was sedated most of the time and in those moments of lucidity, I told myself it was all a terrible nightmare. I couldn't believe that God would do this to me twice. Let me bear a child and then take it away from me.

I was devastated, and spent the first days drifting between shock and disbelief. When I slept, I had these terrible dreams. Monsters with horns and flaming tongues were trying to rip my baby from my womb. I would wake screaming and drenched in sweat, my cotton nightdress sticking to my skin.

Joe came to visit every day. He was as crushed as I was, and feeling guilty about what had happened. But I told myself it wasn't his fault. It had been an accident. The van driver hadn't see us with the snow. Nobody was to blame.

As I got better, he talked of other things. He was trying to take my mind off the death of our child. The truck had to be repaired but the insurance would cover that. In the meantime, the garage had loaned him another one. He had gone back to work and was busy again, trying to catch up with the time he had lost.

I envied Joe his work as I lay in that hospital bed with nothing to think of but the loss of my child. I had long ago given up religion, but now I began to pray. I asked God why he had let it happen; an innocent little baby that hadn't drawn a single breath in this world. I hadn't even seen the child. I didn't know what it looked like. The nurses had taken it away and buried it without even asking my permission.

The more I thought about it, the more depressed I became. I thought of my baby and all the wonderful things we could have done together as she grew up. I thought of the pretty dresses I'd have bought her and the ribbons I'd have put in her hair. I think I would have called her Anne, after my mother. I know Mammy would have liked that.

It got so bad that I would lie in bed all day and weep till the Matron on her rounds would shake me by the shoulder and say: "Snap out of it, Stella. Come on. You're never going to get better if you lie there all day feeling sorry for yourself."

The hospital chaplain came to see me. He looked more like a football player than a priest. He was tall and broad, in his mid-thirties, and wore an open-necked shirt and Levi jeans. He drew the curtains round the bed and sat down beside me to talk. He asked me where I came from and where I worked; it wasn't the sort of conversation you normally had with a priest, more like chatting with a friend. He told me about his work in the hospital and the parish he was attached to.

Then he said: "You're wondering why this has happened to you?"

"Yes, father."

"I can't tell you. Nobody knows why God allows these things to happen. It doesn't make any sense to us. But God never allows us to have more pain than we can bear. And sometimes pain is good. Sometimes it strengthens us."

"Did he do it to punish me?"

The priest looked shocked.

"Why do you say that?"

"Because I had another child and I gave him away."

"Oh no, Stella. God would never do that. Why did you give your child away?"

"Because I had no money and I couldn't care for him."

He was silent for a moment and then he reached out and held my hand.

"You must never think like that. What you did was for the best. You think it was wrong, but that's not how God sees it. Giving your child away was the most unselfish thing you could have done. You did it because you loved him. Now, you must let go of the past and look to the future. You and your husband are healthy young people. There's no reason why you shouldn't have more children."

313

We said a prayer together and when he stood up to go, I saw that his eyes were filled with tears.

But what he had said gave me hope. We would have more children. When I got out of hospital, Joe and I would start again. I would put what had happened behind me. Even if our baby was dead, I still had Joe.

On the second week, the physician said I could get up. I spent the time wandering round the hospital or sitting in the glass-covered sun lounge reading a book. I could feel myself getting better. My side was still hurting but my strength was returning. I began to look forward to my release.

The day I got out, Joe came to collect me in the car. As if by chance, the weather changed. The cold and rain gave way to brilliant sunshine and it was warm again. I sat in the car beside Joe as we drove the few miles to our house. He never mentioned what happened. It was as if he too had made a mental decision to put it behind him and start again.

A few weeks later, I returned to work. Mr McCleery had been to the hospital and brought me flowers and a book called *Thoughts for the Day*. He welcomed me back and put me working on the register again.

"You can stay here for a few weeks," he explained. "And then, when you feel strong enough, you can go back to your old job."

People were fantastic. They kept telling me how sorry they were about the accident. Alice Burns in the drapery department said her own sister had been involved in a similar collision at the very same spot three years before.

"I blame the traffic department. Why, they knew it was going to snow. The radio had been saying so all day. Why they couldn't have gritted that road in time, I just don't know. We're going to have to wait till somebody gets killed before they wake up and do something."

Nobody mentioned the baby. I was glad of that. I hadn't the courage to talk about it. But I knew they were thinking about it by the soft way they spoke to me and the kind things they said.

Joe and I began to make love again. He was gentle at first, as if afraid of hurting me, but gradually his old passion returned. As spring moved

314

forward into summer, the trees burst into leaf and the flowers in the back yard came ablaze with colour. I would wake in the morning to the sound of bird song.

Joe was busy all the time. He would get up early and be gone all day. In the evenings, after dinner, we would sit on the deck together and watch the light fading across the fields. Any spare time he had was spent tending the fruit and vegetables in our own garden or doing his accounts.

On the Fourth of July, we had the McCleery staff barbecue down at the Shawnee Lake. They decorated the place with red-white-and-blue bunting and put out tables. People brought their families and we had a cook-out. The adults sat on the sun-scorched grass and drank beer and wine while the kids played volleyball and swam in the lake.

It was a long, hot day typical of that time of year, and Joe was in fine form, looking forward to relaxing and meeting my colleagues. When we got to the lake, he undressed and plunged into the cold, blue water. He splashed around for a few minutes, then towelled off, popped a can of beer and began helping with the barbecue. I introduced him to old Mr McCleery and his wife Mabel. Joe shook hands with everybody and got right into the swing of things. I sat in the shade of a tree and watched. I felt pleased that Joe was enjoying himself.

We ate our food and someone produced a bottle of wine from an ice-bucket, and plastic cups. Joe filled his glass and knocked it back. A few minutes later, he had a fresh one. He began playing with the kids, carrying them on his back and horsing around. He seemed to be in giddy mood. The kids loved it. They chased after him, pulling at his shirt and shrieking with laughter.

But as the day wore on, something began to bother me. Joe always seemed to have a can in his hand. Every now and then, I would see him disappear into the woods. I presumed he was relieving himself. But each time he returned, he seemed to be more animated.

I grew concerned. My husband was getting drunk in front of my workmates. I hadn't seen him like this before and I was terrified that he would do something foolish and embarrass us. I decided to go looking for him, but he seemed to have disappeared. I started to panic. Mr McCleery saw my distress and came to my aid.

"I saw him five minutes ago," he said. "He was heading into the bushes."

Together we entered the woods. It was cool and dark and the grass was soft underfoot. Birds flew up as we approached. It took us five minutes to find Joe. He was asleep against a tree, an empty bottle of Old Crow hanging limp in his hand.

I felt my face flush red with shame.

"Let's see if we can get him up," Mr McCleery said.

He slapped Joe's face until he awoke and stared vacantly at us. He grunted something, then closed his eyes again, his head rolling forward onto his chest. It was obvious he was very drunk.

"We'll have to carry him," said Mr McCleery. "You think you can get an arm under his shoulder?"

We struggled to lift him up.

"C'mon now, fella," Mr McCleery said.

He steadied Joe and together we marched him out of the woods and back towards the lake.

"It's the heat," Mr McCleery said. "Heat and alcohol don't mix. Particularly whiskey."

I couldn't make any reply. I was distraught with shame. At the edge of the woods, another man saw us and came to help. We got Joe to the truck and put him into the cabin. People were standing around and staring.

"You want me to come with you?" Mr McCleery asked.

"No, it's okay. I'll get him home and put him right to bed."

I gathered our few possessions, got into the driving seat and started the engine. As I drove away, I heard a child say to his father: "What happened to that man, Dad?"

And the father's reply: "Shssh. It's nothing. Poor guy's just tired, that's all."

\*

The next day, Joe got up at lunchtime. When he appeared, he was bleary-eyed and hungover. He sat down at the kitchen table and poured himself a mug of black coffee. His hands shook as he drank it.

I didn't know what to say. I was still angry and humiliated from the day before.

"I'm sorry, Stella. I don't know what came over me. I just wanted to enjoy myself, that's all."

"That's why you stashed a bottle of Old Crow in the woods?"

Joe shrugged and made no reply.

"You embarrassed me, Joe. You shamed me in front of my colleagues. Everybody saw you. We had to carry you to the truck."

He just stared at me with a hang-dog look.

"I'm sorry, Stella. It won't happen again."

He sat there sipping his coffee and looking miserable and, despite my anger, I felt sorry for him. I flung my arms around his neck and kissed his face.

"Oh Joe, you big chump. Do us both a favour. Please. Cut down on the sauce."

And for a time, he did.

*

Every month, on a chart in the bathroom, I circled the date my next period was due, and as the day approached, I prayed that this time, please God, I was pregnant. But, inevitably, I would feel the pains in the pit of my stomach that told me the bleeding was about to start.

As the months passed and I failed to conceive, a desperation entered our love-making. It was no longer the carefree pleasure it had once been. Now it was purposeful and determined, almost mechanical. There was one objective. For me to get pregnant.

I read a book about fertility and discovered the times when I would be most likely to conceive. We tried different positions and I even changed my diet, but nothing happened. Regular as clockwork, my period arrived. Another cycle had passed and I was still without child.

I began to envy the young matrons who came into the store with their plump, well-fed babies, wondering if I would ever be like them. I pictured Joe and I growing old in our big house without the sound of children's laughter. As winter gave way to spring and on into another summer, and I was still not pregnant, my desperation finally turned into despair.

I went to see Dr Baldwin, who tried to reassure me, telling me to relax. We were both young. We were both healthy. I had conceived twice before, so what was I worried about? But I wasn't to be put off. I wanted an expert opinion and asked him to recommend a gynaecologist.

He referred me to a consultant in New York and made an appointment for me to visit him. It was a warm day in June. I wore a light dress and hat and took the bus. The man's name was Dr Max Ritter and his clinic was on First Avenue down near the East River. I sat nervously in his waiting room till my turn came to see him. He was a small man with grey hair and a serious, professional air.

Dr Baldwin had already sent him my file. He asked me some questions, then told me to undress while he examined me. He took X-rays and checked my blood pressure. The whole consultation lasted over an hour.

When it was completed, Dr Ritter put on his glasses and looked grave.

He said: "Mrs Garvan. I have to prepare you for bad news. Your uterus has been damaged. I suspect it occurred in the accident that caused you to miscarry your last child. In my opinion, it's highly unlikely that you will ever conceive again."

# 61.

The news plunged me into a depression. Dr Ritter's diagnosis was followed a few days later by a letter saying that the X-ray results confirmed his opinion. I couldn't bear the thought of a life without children, or face the long, lonely years that would surely lie ahead: barren, desolate, unfulfilled. My mind dwelled constantly on our dead child and on Martin, the son I had given away.

Life seemed bleak and dark and purposeless and for a time I could see no light or joy. But, after a while, I felt hope stirring again. Perhaps Dr Ritter was wrong. He was only one man. He was human and he could make a mistake. Like a drowning woman clutching at a straw, I returned to Dr Baldwin and asked him to recommend another doctor. This time, he didn't argue. He sent me to see a specialist in Philadelphia.

This man had a wide reputation and a record of success with childless couples. He was gentle and considerate. He listened patiently to what I had to say and took notes. I had three consultations with him and Joe had one. He sent Joe for a sperm test. He took more X-rays. But in the end, he had to tell me, sadly, that he couldn't find any reason to disagree with Dr Ritter's opinion. The likelihood of me ever conceiving again was so remote as to be virtually non-existent.

In my desperation, I began to turn against my husband. He had reacted to the news by starting to drink heavily again. Every evening, after dinner, he would sit on the deck and drink whiskey till it was time to go to bed. At first, I thought it was just a way for him to drown his sorrows, but it soon settled into a pattern and gradually it got worse. He would stagger up the stairs and collapse into a drunken sleep on the bed.

I dreaded those nights when I would lie alone in bed waiting for

Joe's stumbling footsteps on the stairs, his laboured breathing, his garbled speech, the sour smell of alcohol on his breath. It got so bad that I moved out of the marital bed altogether and slept in the guest room.

I hated to see him drinking, especially now when I needed him so much. It transformed him from a bright human being into a rambling, incoherent mess. I detested the way it made him weak, when he should be strong to share the pain for both of us.

I began to blame him for what had happened. I told myself if he hadn't been drinking that day of the snow, the accident would never have happened. He would have been alert. He would have seen the van. If he hadn't been drinking, our child would be alive.

My hostility for Joe began to grow and fester till it verged on hatred. I couldn't bear to be in the same room with him if he had been drinking. Eventually, inevitably, it led to a fight. We had never had a fight before; any small tensions between us had been easily overcome. I loved Joe so much in those early years that I was blinded to his faults and forgave him many wrongs. But this fight was a big thing and it left wounds that were to have lasting consequences.

It happened one Friday afternoon in September. It had been a busy day at the store and I arrived back at the house tired and irritable after driving from town along hot, dusty roads. I knew immediately that Joe was at home because his truck was parked in the drive.

I got the weekend groceries out of the car and made my way into the kitchen. The house was quiet except for the sound of the radio playing somewhere out the back. I left the groceries on the kitchen table and followed the music out to the deck where Joe was sitting in his rocking chair. He had a glass of whiskey in his hand. He turned to look at me and I saw at once that he was drunk.

"Hi," he said and waved an arm.

I felt a wave of disgust.

"Why are you home so early?" I said, coldly.

"I took a half day off."

"Weren't you supposed to be landscaping Murdoch's property over in Brick?"

Joe drained his glass and poured another one.

"So I was. But, hey, it was such a nice day, I decided to come home and enjoy it."

"You realise you won't get paid till the job is finished? We need that money, Joe."

"Relax," he said. "I'll finish it tomorrow. Guy's entitled to some time off now and again."

He smiled. A silly, lopsided grin that made him look like an imbecile. I felt my anger overflow at the way he was degrading himself. I walked quickly to the rocking chair and knocked the glass from his hand. It spun to the floor and shattered in tiny pieces.

He stared stupidly at me.

"What the hell, Stella? Why'd you do that?"

"Because I hate to see you like this. I hate to see you destroy yourself."

"Dammit, Stella! I'll drink if I want."

He stormed off to the kitchen and came back with another glass. He poured a shot and knocked it back, then poured another one, as if trying to provoke me.

"Don't do it, Joe. I'm warning you. You're going to wreck our marriage if you go on like this."

"Jeesus!" he shouted. "That's rich coming from you. You don't think maybe you share some of the blame? You've been acting like a goddamned lunatic these last few months. You won't even sleep with me. You drag me off to some quack to have my balls examined. And why? Because you can't have a kid. If you can't have a kid, Stella, who's fault is that?"

"Yours!" I screamed. "If you hadn't been drinking that day, the accident would never have happened. It's your fault I can't have a child. Your fault. You and that bloody drink."

He laughed.

"I was sober, Stella. The fault's all yours. The doctor said there's nothing wrong with me."

I felt my anger overwhelm me. He was laughing at me. And it was he who was responsible. That drunken idiot was the reason I would never have another child.

I flung myself on him, tearing at his eyes and his hair, gouging, biting, scratching. I hated him now, like I had never hated another human being. I beat him till I had no energy left even to raise my hand. He just pushed me aside and lifted the bottle from the floor and poured another drink.

"Fuck you, Stella!" he said. "You mad Irish bitch. How did I ever get involved with you in the first place?"

*

I couldn't sleep that night. I lay in bed weeping in helpless rage. In the four years of our marriage, Joe had never spoken to me like that. He had never shown me such disrespect. The kind, loving, generous man I first knew had turned into a monster, whose very sight now filled me with disgust.

I thought of packing my bags and leaving. But where would I go? And why should I leave? I hadn't done anything wrong. If anybody should have left it was Joe. He was the one had brought discord into our marriage. He was the one with the problem. I decided that tomorrow I would tell him. At last, I fell asleep as the first faltering lights of dawn began to creep across the window pane.

But when I woke, it was a different Joe who met me. Now, he was repentant. He brought me coffee and hot buttered toast. He had cleaned himself up and put sticking plaster on the scratches on his face. He had even cut a single, long-stemmed rose from the garden which he presented to me.

"Forgive me, Stella. Please. I don't know what came over me."

He had that sheepish, boyish grin that had disarmed me so often in the past.

"I apologise unreservedly. I take back everything I said. I love you, Stella. I don't know how I could live without you."

He was weeping now, begging my forgiveness. Immediately, I felt sorry for him. But this time, I was determined to be firm.

"You've got to see about your drinking, Joe. It's out of control."

"Sure. Whatever you say."

"I mean it. Your drinking is destroying our marriage."

"I'll do anything."

"There's a group meets in Freehold. Alcoholics Anonymous. I think you should go and talk to them."

He stared at me with shock on his face.

"I'm not an alcoholic, Stella. Alcoholics are bums, guys drinking at the back of the bus station. That's not me."

"I think you're an alcholic, Joe. Either you go to that meeting or you leave this house."

He went to the meetings. They were held twice a week in the Methodist church hall on South Street. Joe came home bubbling with enthusiasm. He had seen the light. He now recognised that alcohol was an addictive drug. He was determined to stay away from it by the simple step of taking one day at a time.

It seemed to work. He appeared to undergo a personality change. He went to work each morning, he helped around the house, he bought me little presents. He became the old Joe I had fallen in love with. And our marriage improved. I returned to the marital bed and we began making love again.

But this was not the love I had once known. Now it was hedged with caution. I was wary, watching Joe at parties or in restaurants in case he tried to slip a drink. The trust we had once enjoyed had been damaged and it would take a long time for it to repair.

Joe stayed sober throughout the winter and new year. I knew that Christmas would be a difficult time for him so we turned down invitations and stayed at home. We built a log fire in the grate and watched old movies on television. Joe seemed to be keeping his promise and I began to relax.

But it didn't last. The day came when I caught the smell of alcohol on his breath at breakfast. I challenged him and he denied it.

"Your imagining things, Stella. For God's sake, I was at a meeting only last night."

323

I studied his face for a sign. But he just smiled.

"Loosen up. I haven't been drinking."

"Swear!"

He put his hand up like a boy scout.

"I swear," he said.

I wanted to believe him. I wanted our marriage to continue. But I had learnt now that Joe could look at me and lie. And I knew I had smelt alcohol on his breath.

I waited till I heard the truck drive away from the house. Then I began to search. First the bedroom and bathroom, then the kitchen. All the hiding places I could think of were clean. I began to hope that maybe I was wrong, maybe it wasn't alcohol I had smelt at all. And then, in the bin outside the back door, convenient to the sun deck, I found a bottle of Old Crow. The cap was till loose where it hadn't been screwed back properly.

I kept my evidence till Joe had washed and eaten dinner. Then I produced it.

"What's this, Joe?"

The guilt immediately registered on his face.

"Looks like a bottle of whiskey to me," he said.

"You promised me."

This time there were no denials. At once he flew into a temper.

"What is this? My own wife spying on me? What sort of a wife would do a thing like that?"

"One who's been lied to. One who doesn't trust you anymore."

"Hell dammit!" he said. He brought his fist down hard on the table. "Sometimes I have a sip of whisky in the morning. It's to keep out the cold. You want to sit in that truck in this goddamned weather. It would freeze the balls off a statue."

I felt my heart sink. My eyes filled up with tears.

"You swore to me, Joe."

"I swore that I wasn't drinking. Having a sip to keep out the cold isn't drinking."

I looked at the bottle. Half of it was gone. "How much is a sip?"

"A tumbler."

I walked to the sink and poured the bottle down the drain.

"This is your last warning, Joe. You drink again, it's over."

*

Joe stayed sober for another four months. But all the time, he was edgy. He couldn't relax. When we were out together, I'd see him peering into bars as we went past. I prayed that he would stick to his promise but I had enough experience now to know that he might not succeed. Joe was in the grip of demons that I didn't understand. All I knew was that any day he could begin drinking again.

It happened in August. Another Friday night. Joe didn't come home for dinner. When it went past eight o'clock and I hadn't heard from him, I got worried. I rang the police in case something had happened. I got the desk sergeant, a man called Muldoon, and he told me there was no report of any accidents.

I was sure now that Joe was holed up in a bar somewhere. This time, I felt no anger, just a terrible sadness that my marriage was coming to an end. Muldoon rang me back at eleven o'clock to say that a man matching Joe's description had been seen drinking in a bar in Lakewood called the Lucky Nugget. He was in the company of another man and two women. I thanked him and put down the phone and went to bed.

He didn't come home on Saturday or Sunday. By now, I had given up hope. I didn't care what happened any more. On Monday morning, I got a call from the hospital to say that Joe was in the detox unit and was asking for me. He had been found unconscious at Shawnee Lake.

I knew what I had to do. I had rehearsed it so many times in my head. I called Mr McCleery and told him I needed a few days off work. I went to the offices of Crangle and Cox, Attorneys, in Throckmorton Street, and filed for divorce on the grounds of mental cruelty. I called a locksmith and got him to change all the locks on the house. I packed Joe's belongings in two suitcases and left them for him on the sun deck.

Then, I got in the car and drove north to Albany to stay with Uncle James.

# 62.

I have told you how our love affair began and now I am telling you how it ended. I'm not proud of what happened. It ended in a flood of alcohol and lies and recrimination. It ended with Joe drying out in hospital and being released and breaking into the house and getting arrested by the police. It ended in Room Seven of Freehold County Court with me being granted a decree of divorce. Joe didn't contest the petition. He didn't even show up in court. It ended with a barren woman facing a childless middle-age without a husband.

Love stories don't always end happily. For a long time I hated Joe and blamed him for what had happened. We could have had a good life together but his drinking changed everything. It was like a dagger at the heart of our marriage. I held him responsible for the death of our child and the fact that I could never again become pregnant. Distrust eats at the soul and that's what happened to us.

I kept the house and the furniture. Joe got the truck and the business. Half the mortgage had been paid off and I was able to manage. Joe moved into First Street with some floozie and I would hear reports of them drinking in bars and getting into fights. He was arrested a few times more and hospitalised again for drinking. I didn't care. I had blanked him out of my life. It was like reading about somebody in the paper. It didn't mean a thing to me. Then he disappeared altogether and somebody told me he had moved back to New York. I never heard from him again.

Some people who knew me felt sorry for me. My husband had turned into a drunk and run off with another woman. I had to tell

Bridgie and Uncle James but in my letters back to Ireland, I kept the news from my parents. I didn't think they would understand and I didn't want to hurt them. I tried to pick up the threads of my life and continued to work at McCleery's; it paid the bills and I enjoyed it, but I knew it was as far as I could go. There was no career ladder here for me to climb, no matter how good I was at selling lipsticks.

For a long time after my marriage failed, I withdrew from social contact. I worked. I shopped, I came home. I cooked the meals and cut the grass. In the winter, I watched television. In the summer, I rose early and did all my household chores before driving into town. It was a good time to be up. The birds would be out and the air was fresh and cool – a blessing on those long, hot New Jersey summer days.

Word that I was single soon spread around Freehold. I was thirty years of age. I got offers. Guys would come into the store and invite me out. I knew that men found me attractive, and the fact that I was divorced made no difference. If anything, I think it made them keener. After all, I was a woman with experience.

But I was cautious now and slow to get involved. I missed male company and intimacy. There were times when I would willingly have taken a man to my bed and made love. I wanted to feel a man's body close to mine; to wake up in the morning with a manly face lying next to me on the pillow. But I had been badly scarred in my relationship with Joe and I built a wall around myself to keep out pain. I settled into a routine that left no room for lovers in my life.

Charlie Kettles' business failed. He blamed it on bad debts. He got it into his head that business was better in New Jersey, that there was more money down here and people were more honest. Bridgie wrote and asked if they could come and stay with me for a while until Charlie found his feet again. I didn't really want them. Her kids would be a constant reminder of my own childless condition. But she was my sister and I couldn't very well refuse.

In the autumn of 1958, they arrived with their furniture in a hired van. I hadn't seen them for years and I hardly recognised the children, they had grown so much. At first, I found them tiresome. They were noisy and quarrelsome and they disrupted my routine. But eventually, I got used to them.

I gave Charlie and Bridgie the spare bedroom and bunked the kids down in the sitting room. Somehow we managed. They only stayed till Christmas. Charlie didn't hang around. He went off every morning searching for opportunities and eventually got a job as a mechanic in a garage in Lakewood. Soon after, they found a house and moved out.

I was alone again, and surprised to discover that I missed the company, the sound of voices in the house. There were times when I convinced myself that I was better off without children. I was free, I didn't have any worries. I didn't have the expense of raising kids. At work, I would hear people complaining about the scrapes their children got into, the concerns about their education, the fears for their future. I told myself I was spared all that. There was only me and I could do as I pleased. But in my heart, I knew it wasn't true. I knew I would have given anything to have a child.

As time went by, I realised that I needed to be with other people. There was a Ladies' Club in town and I decided to join. We met once a week. It was mainly social work; raising funds for worthwhile charities, holding bazaars and whist drives. But it got me out of the empty house and back into society again. It also introduced me to another man.

It was a Halloween Ball and I had been asked to organise the buffet. I liked this kind of job. It was largely a question of delegating tasks; someone to look after the cold meats, someone to take care of the salads and the coleslaw, someone else to take charge of the punch. It was the highlight of our year and we spent months preparing for it. A band had to be hired, a raffle organised, tickets printed, advertising booked.

The ball was to be held in the town hall and we expected several hundred people to attend. Our target was a thousand dollars to buy equipment for an infant school that had started up in the Mexican part of town.

I threw myself into the work with gusto. I enjoyed engaging my organisational skills once more. It gave me something to look forward to as I stood behind the Cosmetics counter in the store each day. It was to be a costume ball and I had chosen to go as a witch.

It wasn't very original – there were bound to be dozens of witches – but I was conscious of the social pecking order in the town and I didn't want to tread on any toes by drawing attention to myself. I knew that in these kind of situations, merging into the crowd was far the better course.

The day came. I left work at 5.15 p.m., went home and showered, then changed into my costume. By 6.30 p.m. I was at the town hall. The ball didn't begin till eight o'clock, so I made myself busy putting up the bunting and decorations, checking the sound equipment, making sure there were enough towels in the washrooms. Then I devoted myself to my special area of operations.

I had organised a big buffet: platters of roast beef and ham and cajun chicken and salmon and barbecued ribs. Bowls of salads, chopped peppers, marinated potatoes, curried rice. Little dishes of chutneys and pickled beetroot. Desserts of pavlova and chocolate layer cake and ice cream. And big jugs of punch. I checked cutlery and plates and paper napkins. Everything seemed to be in order. If nothing else, our guests would be well fed.

People began to arrive from 7.30 p.m. and at eight o'clock the band started to play. They began with a medley of Sinatra hits. Quickly, the floor filled up, till it was a mass of brightly costumed dancers: wizards, ghosts, hobgoblins and witches. I had been right about the witches. Everywhere I looked, I saw black pointed hats bobbing in the crowd. I was admiring the costumes when I heard a voice at my shoulder.

"For my money, you're easily the most attractive witch at the dance."

I spun round. A tall man in his late thirties was standing beside me. He was dressed in a badly fitting wizard's cloak. His face was familiar, but I couldn't identify it.

"Do I know you?"

"I hope so. You used to work with me."

"Jack Morrison?"

"That's right."

I recognised him now. It was my old boss from Brazil Bros in New York. He was plumper and there was a fleshiness about his cheeks.

"I thought it was you. When I saw you standing at the buffet table, I thought: I know that face. Hard to forget a good-looking woman, Stella."

"What are you doing here?" I asked.

"Working for Crangle and Cox."

"You're a lawyer?"

"That's right. I got fed up trying to convince suckers to buy products they didn't want and couldn't afford. So I studied at night school till I got my law degree."

"Don't you miss the buzz?"

"It's a rat-race, Stella. We're better off out of it. How do you like living in Freehold?"

"I like it," I said. "I'm a sales assistant in McCleery's. The department store."

"Your husband still in the garden business?"

"I don't have a husband any more, Jack."

I saw his face fall and immediately he began to apologise.

"I didn't know."

"That's all right. Just one of those things."

He looked at me for a moment.

"Yeah," he said. "One of those things."

# 63.

Jack called a few days later and asked me out to dinner. I felt I couldn't refuse. He was an old friend. But I wondered about him. What had brought him to Freehold? New York was where all the big law firms were. If he was building an alternative career that was where he should be.

He took me to a new restaurant over in Brick. It did lobster and steaks. It was a smart place, the sort of place you would go for an intimate evening, with little tables, crisp white napkins and candles. A band in evening dress played romantic numbers. It reminded me of Del Rio's, where Joe had taken me on our first date, and I suddenly realised that I hadn't been to dinner with a man since my marriage ended.

I ordered chicken and salad. Jack had a fillet steak with wild mushrooms and string beans. We shared a bottle of wine. He studied the list and ordered a burgundy. He seemed to know about wines.

"Here's to us," he said and we clinked glasses.

"What brought you to Freehold?" I asked.

He laughed good-naturedly.

"It's a long story. It would probably take a couple of dinners."

"No, seriously. I would have thought you would want to stay in New York. Freehold isn't exactly the centre of the legal world."

He lowered his eyes.

"There were good reasons, Stella. Like you, my relationship broke up."

Now it was my turn to apologise.

"Forget it," he said. "I certainly have. But I realised I needed a change of scenery. Besides, at my time of life, I prefer things a little quieter."

"You're not that old, Jack."

"I'll be forty, next birthday."

I studied him across the table. He was still a handsome man, with good clear skin and brown eyes. He had kept his hair, even if it was beginning to grey.

"What about you, Stella?"

"I'm divorced. Joe and I didn't get along. I don't think you ever met him, did you?"

"No."

"He was a decent guy. But you know how it is. People change."

"Any family?"

I shook my head.

We talked about the legal practice. There were six lawyers in the office and he specialised in conveyancing; buying and selling property.

"I plan to get out in a few years time. Set up on my own."

"Where do you live, Jack?"

"I'm renting an apartment over on Fulton Street. It's just a bachelor pad. But it suits me fine. I can walk to work."

The band started to play 'Mona Lisa'. Jack put down his glass and took my hand.

"Are you in the mood?" he asked.

*

We began to dine out together about once a week. Sometimes he came to the house and I cooked for him. I learned his story. He had been going out with a woman for six years and they were planning to get married. She was a commercial artist and very successful. A partner in a public relations firm, she owned her own apartment, drove a sports car and lived a wild social whirl.

"Her life was one long party. I couldn't keep up. I was studying for my law degree and trying to run Brazil Bros. She was boogying every night. Champagne cocktails and breakfast at dawn. I discovered she was seeing some other guy. He wasn't the first one, either. So I called it a day. When I got my qualifications, I checked out jobs. Crangle and

Cox were looking for a conveyancer. I thought: Freehold sounds like an okay town. And here I am."

I sensed that Jack was lonely. He was a sensitive guy, the sort of man who would hurt easily, and I suspected his experience had wounded him.

We became an item. He accompanied me to dinner parties and trips to the theatre and cinema. My friends were glad that I had found a partner again. Single unattached women can be difficult; hostesses are happier with couples.

Jack was a perfect companion: kind, witty, polite. He treated me like a lady, bringing me presents of flowers and candy. He would never forget an occasion like a birthday. But, in those early months, all we ever exchanged was a kiss. Making love was a big step. It meant making a commitment to Jack and I wasn't sure that I was ready.

It happened by accident. We had been out to see a movie and afterwards called into a little bar for a nightcap. It was a beautiful night. There was a big yellow moon hanging over the chestnut trees in the drive and the air was filled with the heady scent of stock.

Jack got out of the car and walked with me to the front door. As I took the keys from my bag, I fumbled and they dropped. Jack bent to pick them up and as he rose, his hand brushed against my breast. At once I felt a thrill of pleasure. He stood looking at me for a moment and then he took me in his arms and kissed me. I melted into him. I felt his hands move along my back, down to my waist and on to my thighs. I pressed harder against him.

He stood back and I opened the door and he followed me into the house. Neither of us spoke. We went upstairs to the bedroom. Jack undressed me in the moonlight, his mouth kissing my breasts, his hands caressing me till I was wild with passion. In quick movements, he shed his own clothes. I reached down and felt him hard in my hand. I was consumed with pleasure. I lay back with a sigh and guided him in.

After that, we made love several times a week. It had to be discreet. We made love on Saturday mornings when he would call to the house

333

for breakfast. We made love on Sunday afternoons when he would come over to help me with the yard work. We made love at night in Jack's apartment on Fulton Street.

I looked forward to our love-making. We were good together. I got to know Jack's rhythms and how he would respond. He was gentle and considerate, never selfish, always mindful of my needs as well as his own. The arrangement suited me. Now I had a job, a home and a lover, even if I had no children.

A few years later, Jack fulfilled his ambition to start his own law firm. The town had grown considerably and there was plenty of legal work to go around. He hired a young graduate called Henry Sharp and opened an office in Lenoir Avenue. In time I went to work for him as a legal secretary.

I had no experience but I learnt quickly. Jack paid for me to attend a course in legal studies and it gave me a grounding in the business. I ran the office, just as I had done when I worked in Brazil Bros. It was interesting and rewarding work and Jack paid me well. I was able to discharge the mortgage on the house and buy new furniture and a new car. I equipped the kitchen with the latest devices: a new cooker and extractor fan, a dishwasher, a big fridge-freezer.

I now had a busy round of social engagements: there was my work with the Ladies' Club, and legal conventions to attend with Jack. There were dinners, lunches and cook-outs, and vacations in Florida and Puerto Rico.

In this comfortable way, the time slipped past, one year gradually merging into another. I was happy with my life and its even tenor might have continued unabated had an event not occurred in the spring of 1965 which was to alter everything.

It was a warm day with just a welcome hint of breeze. I had been up early for a series of meetings and then I had to rush home to prepare a dinner we were giving for some important clients. I had just got into the house when the phone rang.

I took the call in the sitting room. It was a young man's voice and it seemed to be coming from far away.

"I'm ringing from Belfast," I heard him say.

"Yes?"

"Do you remember people called McBride?"

Immediately, I felt my heart skip a beat.

"They lived in Brompton Park? In Ardoyne?"

"Yes."

"What about them?"

"They're dead," I heard him say. "Do you remember a priest called Father Ambrose?"

"Yes."

"You had a child called Martin?"

Now the blood was pounding in my head.

"You gave him to the McBrides?"

"Yes."

"Do you know who this is speaking to you now?"

I could barely speak. I closed my eyes and saw again the little boy I had given away all those years ago in Belfast.

"Of course, Martin. It's you."

# 64.

After that phone call ended, I poured myself a stiff drink. I was stunned. In my head, I could still hear Martin's voice speaking to me across a void of twenty years. It was a voice I thought I would never hear. And he had sounded happy. That to me was the greatest joy. Oh the relief I felt! It washed away decades of guilt and self-recrimination. My son was happy and he didn't blame me for giving him away.

I sat in the kitchen and recounted the conversation, trying to digest all the news that had come tumbling out. Martin was healthy. He had a good life. He was working as a journalist on a newspaper. He had a young woman he was fond of. He had been to see Tess O'Neill and she, too, was well. Her boys were grown up now and had left home. Everything was positive. The one sad note was that the McBrides were dead. I thought briefly of the couple who had taken Martin. I felt no resentment now. They had obviously reared him well.

My thoughts were interrupted by another phone call. This time, it was Jack reminding me of our dinner party. I put on an apron and set about making preparations: washing vegetables, marinating meat, cooling wine. I just had time for a quick shower and a change of clothes when I heard the doorbell ring.

Our guests were two executives of a construction company who were planning to build a housing development on the outskirts of town. Jack was keen to woo them. If we landed the contract for the land purchase, it would mean a tidy profit.

I welcomed the men and their wives and led them into the sitting room. I offered drinks and put a Ray Conniff album on the record player. The men were bluff New Yorkers who had started life as bricklayers before setting up in business. Their wives were loud and overdressed. They all drank Manhattans and admired my house.

"Who built it?" asked the older man.

"My ex-husband."

"Guy work in construction?"

"No. He's a landscape gardener."

"Next time you're talking to him, tell him I've got a job for him." Everyone laughed.

Jack arrived at ten to eight and we sat down to dinner. I'd prepared smoked salmon and lamb cutlets. We finished with pecan pie and brandies on the sun deck. The conversation ran back and forth. I felt gay. I made witty remarks. I was the perfect hostess. But I couldn't wait for them to leave so I could be alone with my thoughts about Martin. They finally drove away at one o'clock. As he was leaving, Jack kissed me goodnight and said: "Stella you were wonderful. I can't remember when I've seen you so animated. I think we might be doing business. They want me to call them on Monday morning."

# 65.

Martin and I began to correspond. Sometimes we talked on the phone but mostly it was letters. I couldn't wait to see what he looked like. The picture, when it came, showed a handsome young man, tall and dark. He reminded me of my father when I was a child, coming in from the fields when his work was done, to wash himself under the pump.

Martin wanted to know so much. He wanted a lifetime in a few short scraps of paper. One of the first things he asked was if he had any siblings. I had to tell him no. I could hear the disappointment in his voice when he heard that word. And then I told him that Bridgie had children, so he had cousins, and that seemed to please him. I told him how I had tried to keep him and found it impossible; how I couldn't find work in Belfast and had to leave. I told him about my time in Dublin and coming to live in America. I told him of the photograph of him taken on his christening day, which I always kept beside my bed.

The correspondence went back and forth for weeks. And then, one day, the letter came that I had long been dreading. Martin wanted to know about his father. I agonised over that letter, thinking about it for days. What could I say? That I had only known his father for a couple of hours and could no longer even remember his face? That I didn't know his name?

I tried to reason with myself. I had told Joe, after all, why not tell Martin? But something held me back. Some pride or fear made it impossible for me. I wanted Martin so much that I was terrified of the truth. How could I tell my child I didn't know his father? What would he think? That his mother was a whore?

I took the coward's way out. In my next letter, I ignored his inquiry and talked about other things. But if I thought this would fool him, I was wrong. He wrote again in stronger terms, demanding information. I panicked and fell back on the strategem that had served me well before. I lied.

I told him his father had been my old boyfriend, Bill Dwyer. I gave Bill a whole new identity, saying that he had been an officer in the US Army who came from Chicago, and that we had lost touch during the war. That sort of thing had happened a lot. Women had got married after a whirlwind romance and never seen their husbands again. Put that way, it didn't sound so bad.

Throughout the time we corresponded, an idea had been forming in my mind. I wanted to see Martin again. I wanted to hold him. I wanted to talk to him face to face. Sometimes, I even had a wild thought that I could persuade him to stay with me, here in America. It would cause problems, for I would have to explain him to Bridgie and Jack, but I was sure I could find a way round it.

It was a hot day in June and the Ladies' Club had organised a fund-raising cook-out. I had volunteered to prepare the salads. I was in the kitchen when the phone rang. It was Martin.

He started in at once about Bill Dwyer. Now, he wanted to know what he looked like, if I knew his army number, if I knew how to find him.

I cut him short.

"How'd you like to come and stay with me for a while?"

"What?"

"We should really meet, Martin. I'd love to see you. And it won't cost you a penny. I'll send you the air fare."

"You want me to come to America?"

"Sure."

I heard him pause. A thought flashed into my head. Maybe I had been too rash? What if he should turn me down?

And then, he was speaking again.

"Oh, Stella. I'd love to. That would be brilliant."

I sat down at once and wrote a long letter to Martin with instructions about getting from the airport to the Port Authority terminal in New York and then catching the bus to Freehold. I wrote a cheque for the fare and placed it in the envelope with the letter. Then I drove to the post office and sent it by airmail.

It was ten days before I heard from him. He wrote to say he had to sort out a passport and visa but hoped to come in the last two weeks of July. With luck, I would see him in a few weeks time. I spoke to Jack and arranged to take some leave so that I could be with him.

I was busy at work; we had a contract to finalise for another developer and I had to prepare the papers. Then, I had to make a trip to Philadelphia for a legal conference. Martin rang to say that everything was organised now and he would soon be on his way.

Those last few days crawled by. I had a chart in my office at work and I marked them off. I was so excited, I could hardly sleep. I kept reminding myself of the momentous event that was about to occur: I was going to see again the child I had given away, twenty years before.

Finally the day arrived. I was up at 6 a.m. to get everything ready. It was another warm day. I rang the airport and confirmed the flight time and then I began to clean the house and yard. I couldn't settle because of my excitement. I aired the guest bedroom where Martin would sleep. I turned down the sheets, and made sure there was hot water. I was desperate to make the best impression. At 4.30 p.m., I left for the bus depot.

*

In the shade of the booking office, I stood and watched as the New York bus came groaning into the bay. I willed myself to remain calm, not wanting to embarrass him by doing anything foolish. Now that the moment had come, I was sick with anxiety. I waited as the passengers got off. Martin was among the last.

I recognised him the moment I saw him. Tall and dark, he stood blinking in the sunlight with a battered suitcase in his hand. As he turned, our eyes met. My heart leapt in my breast. He walked quickly towards me, put down his case and took me in his arms.

How can I describe the feelings that rushed over me in that

moment? I was holding my child again, the boy I had given away, who I thought I would never again see.

I closed my eyes and felt his hands trace the contours of my face.

"It's great to see you, Stella," he said. "We've waited a long time for this."

# 66.

In those first few days, I was fascinated by Martin. I had waited so long that I could hardly bare to let him out of my sight. It was as if I was terrified to take my eyes off him, in case he might suddenly disappear. When he was watching television or reading a book, I found myself stealing a glance at him, marvelling at the way he had grown into a handsome young man. I wanted to spend all my time with him and never let him go.

He was very taken with the house. He would wander around the rooms admiring the furniture and fittings, or stroll in the backyard among the trees and bushes that Joe had planted. I could see the curiosity in his eyes as he examined the kitchen gadgets, things he said he had never seen before.

He was particularly interested in the big television in the sitting room. It was a wide screen and he would sit in front of it in the afternoon, flicking between the channels to watch game shows and sports. I realised that he was seeing America through the same eyes as I had when I stepped off the RMS *Mauretania* in New York harbour in June 1950.

I was delighted. I took him to fancy restaurants and shopping malls, showing off because I wanted to impress him. But I was also making up for lost time. I wanted those two weeks to be perfect, so that he would remember them for the rest of his life.

In the evenings, we would sit on the deck at the back of the house and sip our drinks while I coaxed from him the details of his life. One evening I quizzed him about his career.

"Tell me about this reporting job. What exactly do you do?"

"I get the news to people."

"Is it difficult?"

Martin smiled indulgently.

"Well first you have to understand what news is."

"So tell me."

He began to expand. I could see he enjoyed explaining his job to me and I wanted to hear more.

"It's like this, Stella. People are always trying to push things at you. But really they're just looking for free publicity. The real news is the stuff they *don't* want you to know. You have to be able to tell the difference."

"Sounds interesting," I said.

"Oh, it is. But it can also be tedious. You have to check everything. That's the most important part. If you get things wrong, you might be sued for libel. The other thing is the pressure. You have to work fast. The clock is always ticking away."

"But you enjoy it?"

"I love it. It's the only job I want to do."

"I knew a reporter once. She worked for the *New York Post*."

I thought briefly of Kathy Brewster. I hadn't heard from her for years.

"That's a big paper," Martin said. "My paper is quite small."

"I think you've done well. You should be proud."

He shook his head.

"I've just been lucky."

"No. It's more than luck. It's down to hard work."

He smiled again.

"You're the one who worked hard, Stella. You arrived here with nothing and now look at the great life you've got."

When he said that I felt a wave of pleasure wash through me. I threw my arms around him and kissed him.

"Oh Martin, you really say the nicest things."

*

A few days later, I decided to take him to the shore. He could swim and

343

we could have lunch at a nice restaurant I knew. He was excited at the prospect of getting some exercise.

I packed our beach gear in the car and started for Point Pleasant. There was something I intended to say to him and I realised this would be a good opportunity. I still hadn't told anyone who he was and I was terrified that people might find out accidentally.

"Martin, now that you're my house guest, there are some ground rules we should lay down," I said cautiously.

"Sure."

"I don't want you answering the phone. If I'm not in the house and the phone rings, just leave it. Okay?"

"But it might be important."

"If it's important, they'll ring again. I'm very fussy about the phone. There's something else. If anyone asks who you are, tell them you're a friend visiting from Ireland."

He turned and stared at me.

"You mean nobody knows?"

"No. Why should they? This is something between us. There's no reason for everyone to know our business."

"But why don't you tell them?"

"Because I choose not to."

Martin lowered his head.

"Stella, you're not ashamed of me, are you?"

I started to panic. I realised I was handling this badly.

"Of course not," I said quickly. "It's got nothing to do with shame. I'm proud of you. But people talk too much. They love to gossip. Why should we give them something to talk about?"

We came to the shore. It was practically deserted. Martin got undressed and went into the water. I took a beach umbrella and a chair out of the car and sat down to read. He swam with strong, confident strokes way out beyond the marker buoys. I began to get scared. I heard the lifeguard blow his whistle and saw Martin wave and come back in again. He lay on his back and drifted in the sea, his face turned towards the sun. Eventually, he swam back to shore and dried himself.

I started to scold him.

"You shouldn't swim out so far," I said. "It's dangerous. You should always swim parallel to the shore."

He looked at me and smiled but I thought I could detect a slight edge in his voice.

"You know something, Stella? You sound just like my mother."

*

We went for lunch to Annabelle's. It was a classy place overlooking the shore. I had been there before with Jack. It was used a lot by the yachting crowd who frequented the marina just up the coast.

We ordered steaks and the conversation turned to my early life in Ballinaleck. I told him about growing up on the farm and coming to Belfast during the War and getting a job in the American Eagle.

He suddenly leaned forward, his eyes sparkling with interest.

"Was that where you met my father?"

"Yes."

"Tell me about him."

I blushed with confusion. I had been foolishly hoping to avoid this discussion and now that it had arrived I didn't know what to say.

"You don't want to know, Martin. Really."

"Of course, I want to know. He was my father, for God's sake.

"He's dead," I said. "Why don't you forget about him?"

Martin looked shocked.

"You never told me he was dead."

In my confusion, a lie slipped out.

"Yes, I did. In one of my letters."

"No. If you'd told me, I would have remembered."

"Well, he *is* dead. He was killed at the end of the War. Out in Europe somewhere."

"Where?"

I was unprepared for this and Martin's questions had me reeling.

"How would I know? Germany or Italy or one of those places. Wherever the fighting was."

345

"I want to hear about him Stella. What was he like?"

"I've told you already. He was an officer in the U.S. Army. He got me pregnant and before I could tell him, he went off to Europe and got killed."

"So he never knew about me?"

"No."

"Were you in love with him?"

"Of course."

He sat silent for a moment, slowly pushing the food around his plate.

"I want to trace him," he said. "Maybe he's not dead at all."

"He *is* dead. Why don't you just drop it?"

"The U.S. Army keeps records."

I felt a terror seize me.

"Why don't we talk about this some other time?"

He put down his knife and fork.

"Stella, there's something you should know. When I was trying to find you, people kept putting obstacles in my way. And now you're doing the very same thing."

I felt tired. I didn't want this argument to spoil our day.

I begged him.

"Please Martin. Just drop it. We'll talk about it again."

# 67.

A few days later, Bridgie came to visit. I had already told her on the phone that I had a guest. Naturally, she wanted to know who it was.

"You heard me talk of Tess O'Neill? The woman I stayed with in Belfast?"

"Sure," Bridgie said. "I remember her."

"It's one of her boys. He's visiting the States. She asked me if I would put him up for a couple of weeks. I could hardly refuse. She was very good to me back then."

The information just made Bridgie more keen to meet him.

"What's his name?"

"Martin."

"How old is he?"

"Twenty."

"Hmmmn," Bridgie said.

I was very nervous. I wondered if I could carry it off or if the whole thing would come to grief. I worried how Martin might react.

Bridgie arrived with one of her home-baked apple tarts. I already had the coffee pot on the stove. I introduced them and Bridgie shook Martin's hand. I could see her studying his face.

"How're you enjoying America?" she said.

"So far, so good," Martin replied.

"Stella looking after you? Showing you around?"

"Oh, yes. We've seen a lot."

"Feeding you well?"

"Too well," Martin laughed. "She stuffing me with food. I won't be able to get into my clothes when I get home."

"America's a fine country," Bridgie said. "It gave us all an opportunity we would never have got back in Ireland. How's your mother keeping?"

I felt my knees go weak.

"Who?"

"Your mother. Tess O'Neill. Is she keeping well? She was very good to Stella when she lived in Belfast."

Martin turned to me but I couldn't face him. There was an awkward pause.

"She's fine," I heard him say at last.

"That's good. She must be delighted for you, getting a nice vacation like this. Make sure to tell her I was asking for her."

"I will," Martin said.

"We talk a lot about the old country. It's all so long ago. But you never forget the past. The past never goes away."

Bridgie chatted as she always did when she came to visit, bringing me up to date on all the family affairs. Martin took a book and went out to the deck but every now and then I would see her staring at him, as if she was trying to make up her mind about something.

When she was gone, he came into the kitchen and I could see at once he was angry.

"Why did you make up that stuff about Tess O'Neill?"

"I had to explain you, Martin."

"But you didn't have to lie about me."

I tried to sooth him.

"Oh, for God's sake. You're making too much of it. It wasn't a real lie."

"Of course it was a real lie. Why don't you just tell the truth? Why don't you tell them I'm your son?"

I didn't want this argument. I tried to take his hand but he brushed me away.

"Please, don't be angry, Martin. If I told them the truth, they wouldn't be able to handle it. Sometimes it's better for everyone if you tell a little lie."

He rounded on me.

"It's not better for me. You told me you were proud of me but when Bridgie comes, you deny me."

"Oh no," I said. "It's not like that."

"Well what is it? I don't think less of you because of what happened. It's nothing to be ashamed of."

"I'm not ashamed of you."

"Then why don't you acknowledge who I am? If I had known you were going to behave like this, I would never have come."

He stormed out of the kitchen and down the back yard as far as the trees. I didn't know what to do. I just wanted everything to be good between us without all these questions about his birth. I waited a while for his anger to cool and then I poured a beer and brought it to him.

He looked at me, with hurt, resentful eyes.

I said: "I'm sorry, Martin. I love you with all my heart. It's just that people wouldn't understand."

# 68.

I could see I was making a mess of things and relations were deteriorating between Martin and me, so I decided to get him out of the house and take him for more trips. We drove all over the state, as far south as Atlantic City, starting out early in the morning and returning late at night. I tried to give him a good time, and I think these trips were a success as he stopped asking questions and the atmosphere between us improved.

I knew I would have to introduce Jack, so I invited him over for dinner one night. But I warned him in advance not to question Martin about his family. I didn't want a repetition of the disaster with Bridgie.

Jack arrived with a bouquet of roses and a bottle of Californian Chardonnay. I made Manhattans and we sat on the deck watching the sun go down behind the trees as Jack told Martin about the office and his legal work.

We ate a dinner of lamb with courgettes and potatoes at the big table in the dining room. Though I was desperate for the two of them to like each other, the talk merely limped along. Jack told a few funny stories at which Martin laughed but I wasn't sure that he fully understood. They chatted about baseball and politics and I could tell from the look on Martin's face that he was bored. About ten o'clock, Jack said he was expecting a business call at home and had to leave. I walked with him to the front door and kissed him goodnight.

When I returned, Martin was sitting in an armchair leafing through a magazine. I turned the radio on low and poured the last of the wine.

"Well, what did you think of Jack?"

"He seems a nice man. You're lucky to have a boss like him, Stella."

"Don't I know it? He's been very good to me. Did I tell you he paid for me to take a legal course so that I'd be more familiar with work in the office?"

Martin put down the magazine and turned to me.

"Why won't you talk about my father?"

His eyes looked cold.

"Who brought this up?"

"I did. Every time I raise the subject, you try to talk about something else. What are you trying to hide?"

I looked closely at him. Had he drunk too much wine?

"I'm not trying to hide anything."

"Then tell me about him. Maybe he's out there somewhere, waiting to hear from me, just the same way you were."

"No," I said quickly. "He's not."

"How can you be sure?"

"Because he's dead."

"Maybe he wasn't killed at all, Stella. Lots of people they thought were dead turned up later."

"He was killed all right."

"Where did you meet him?"

"Jesus, Martin. We've been over all this before. I met him at the American Eagle. He asked me to dance; that's how it began."

"What was he like?"

"Tall, good-looking. He was the most handsome man in the room. He swept me off my feet. You've got to remember, I was only eighteen."

"What part of Chicago was he from?"

"How would I know? All those places sounded the same to me."

"And his name was Bill Dwyer?"

"Yes."

He put down the magazine.

"Then why didn't you put it on my birth certificate?"

I was stung. I could see we were building up for another row.

"Didn't I?"

"No. The place for the father's name was left blank."

I tried to explain.

"You've got to understand. I was on my own, Martin. I was all mixed up. I didn't know what I was doing."

"What rank was he?"

He had taken an envelope from his pocket and was starting to make notes.

It was my turn to be angry. I stood up abruptly.

"I don't want to continue this conversation."

"Why not?"

"Because you're a guest in my house and you should remember your manners. I won't be interrogated in my own home."

\*

Why didn't I tell him what he wanted to know? How many times have I asked myself that question? The answer is: I couldn't face the truth. I was ashamed of what Martin would think of me if he learnt that there was no great love affair, that I had only met his father once and didn't know whether he was alive or dead. And I was terrified of what might happen if word got out among my family that I had a secret child. So I drifted along, desperately hoping to bluff my way through and avoid a confrontation with my son. And of course, this was impossible. The atmosphere between us turned sour. Every time we were together, I dreaded the subject of his father.

Bit by bit, I felt him slipping away. Our conversations became abrupt. If I touched him, he grew tense. If I tried to reach out to him, he pushed me away. He grew moody and resentful. Instead of sitting with me after dinner as he used to, he began to go for long walks, as if he couldn't bear to be in the same room. Sometimes he would be gone for hours and I couldn't relax till I heard his footsteps on the drive. Slowly, our relationship grew poisoned.

It all came to a head one evening in the second week of his visit. I had gone back to work. In truth, I was happy to be away from the house with its tension and silences. I got home shortly after six o'clock and began to prepare dinner. When I had everything ready, I went out to the deck where Martin was reading.

"Cocktail time," I said, trying to sound cheerful. "What will it be?"

He barely looked up.

"Whatever you like."

"Pina Coladas?"

"Sure. Pina Coladas will be fine."

I got the ingredients and the cocktail shaker and made the drinks. This had once been a happy ritual. Now it had become a dreaded chore. I carried the frosted glasses out to the deck and handed one to Martin.

"What sort of day did you have?"

He barely made a reply.

"Watched some sports on television. Read a couple of books."

"That was nice."

He shrugged.

"Only a few days left and then you'll be going home," I said.

"Yeah. That's right. Then you'll be free."

I ignored the remark. We finished our drinks and went in to dinner. Martin ate mechanically. He made no comment on the food and gave no sign that he enjoyed it.

"Have you spoken to your friends back home? You know I don't mind you making calls on the phone."

There was a sullen look on his face.

"I thought you told me not to use the phone?"

"No I didn't. I told you not to *answer* the phone."

"Oh. I must have misunderstood. I'm not allowed to *answer* the phone. That's in case people find out I'm here and start asking questions. Isn't that right?"

I didn't reply.

He sat back in his chair.

"Stella. Do something for me. Let me see that picture you have of me on my christening day. I'd like to see what I looked like as a baby."

I got up at once and wearily climbed the stairs to my bedroom. The photograph had always been beside my bed but, when Jack and I became lovers, I had put it away in a drawer. Now I couldn't find it. In the end I gave up searching, returned to the dining room and told Martin.

There was a look of triumph in his eyes and I realised immediately this was a trap. Martin must have been in my bedroom when I was out at work.

"You said you always kept it beside your bed."

"So I did. But it's not there now. I must have moved it. I'll have a good hard search for it tomorrow."

"Did you ever have it, Stella?"

I felt my cheeks redden at his cruel remark.

"What do you mean by that?"

"You made it up, didn't you? There never was any picture."

"Yes, there was. Tess O'Neill's husband took it."

"Tess O'Neill? That's the woman who's supposed to be my mother."

I said: "Martin. I try to be good to you. Why do you want to hurt me?"

He flared at me.

"Because you're living a lie, Stella. You want me here with you but you deny my birth. You try to pretend that it never happened. You won't acknowledge me to other people. You refuse to talk about my father. Don't you think I have a right to know who my own father is? Don't you think I have a right to be recognised and not passed off as Tess O'Neill's son? What are you ashamed of, Stella?"

I felt my eyes fill with the hot tears.

"I'm not ashamed of anything. But all that stuff is in the past. I've buried it. Why do you want to rake it up again?"

"Because I have rights. And you're not fooling anyone. They all know who I am. I can tell by the way they look at me. Everybody knows I'm your son. Even Bridgie knows."

I put my hand to my ears to stop his awful words.

"You're a selfish woman, Stella. You want everything your own way. You want my love but you aren't prepared to make the necessary compromises. It's not difficult. All I want from you is the truth."

He flung down his table napkin and walked out to the back of the house. I didn't follow. I just sat where I was. I knew now that any relationship we had was breaking up before my eyes. His voice kept echoing in my brain: *"The truth, Stella. All I want from you is the truth."*

# 69.

The following morning, Martin rose early. He came down to the kitchen as I was preparing to go to work. He didn't offer any apology for his remarks of the previous night. He poured a cup of coffee and buttered some toast.

"I'm going into New York," he announced.

"How are you getting there?"

"By bus."

"Enjoy it," I said. "It's going to be hot and crowded this time of year."

"So I believe," he said.

"Would you like me to drive you to the depot?"

"No, thanks. The walk will do me good."

He finished his coffee and put on his jacket and headed out the door. I watched him walk boldly down the drive and turn left for town.

He came back shortly after nine o'clock. The night was coming down and the dying sun cast long shadows across the lawn. When I asked if he was hungry, he just muttered something about eating at a Chinese restaurant in Manhattan. I didn't press him. I asked how he had got on and he mumbled some reply. He went into the sitting room and put on the television to watch a sports programme. I locked up the house and went to bed.

But in the morning, his attitude seemed transformed. I heard him singing in the shower. He sounded happy. I wondered what had happened during the night to make him change and felt a faint stirring of hope. Maybe he had got over his fight with me and we could be friends again.

He kissed my cheek when he came into the kitchen, then sat down at the table and rubbed his hands.

"I've been thinking, Stella. I'm leaving tomorrow. Tonight's my last night. Why don't I take you out to dinner?"

My spirits soared.

"That would be wonderful, Martin. But can you afford it?"

"Of course I can. I've set money aside for it."

"But you need your money. Why don't you let me pay?"

"Because it's my treat. And I won't hear any argument. We're going to dinner and I'm paying. End of story."

He sat at the kitchen table, looking relaxed and self-assured. I wondered at the way he had grown in confidence in a mere two weeks and how our roles had been reversed.

At work, I was in a gay mood. I couldn't wait for evening, for Martin and I to be together. I got home shortly after six and had a shower and changed into a nice dress with a little cotton jacket.

When I came downstairs, Martin had put on a suit and tie for the occasion. He had the cocktail shaker out and was making preparations.

"Manhattans all right?" he asked with a raised eyebrow.

"Manhattans are fine."

"I thought so," he said and poured.

He seemed to be in playful mood, so different to the sullen attitude of the day before. He raised his glass.

"Here's looking at you, babe."

"No," I said. "You've got that wrong. What Bogie actually said was: 'Here's looking at you, *kid.*'"

Martin smiled.

"All right. Have it your way."

We touched glasses and laughed.

He had booked a table at a new country and western restaurant off Main Street. There was sawdust on the floor and the waiters wore cowboy suits and carried imitation guns in holster belts. The menu was mainly steaks and ribs. I ordered chops and Martin had a T-bone. We drank beer.

I felt so happy. All around us laughing people were enjoying their meal. A man in a stetson hat sat on a little stage and played a guitar. Martin reached out to take my hand.

"Stella, I want to apologise. I'm sorry we fought. I'm sorry I hurt you."

"You know I've got that picture somewhere," I said quickly. "I've kept it for years. I'll bet the minute you're gone, I'll find it again."

I saw him shake his head.

"You don't understand. It's not about the picture, Stella. It's the fact that you won't acknowledge me. That's what hurts me most. And the fact that you won't talk about my father. You made a mistake when you were young. I don't think less of you because of that. But you shouldn't punish yourself for the rest of your life."

I looked at him. I wanted to tell him so that everything would be right between us. I wanted him to love me. But when I opened my mouth, no words came. At the critical moment, my courage failed.

Instead, I said: "Martin. This is our last night. Let's not argue."

He nodded his agreement.

"You're right, Stella. Let's talk about something else."

We listened to the music as we ate our meal. By ten o'clock we were home. I poured two nightcaps and we sat for a while watching television. I felt a terrible sadness take hold of me. Tomorrow, Martin was going back to Ireland, and I might never see him again. I regretted the stupid arguments. I wished now that all the days had been like this one, that we had been happy.

It came time for bed. I finished my drink and stood up. Martin kissed me goodnight and I slowly climbed the stairs. I undressed in the darkness and got in under the covers. Suddenly I was weeping. I wept for all the lost opportunities, for all the hurt and pain, for all the dreams I held that had been dashed.

*

The last day arrived. At seven o'clock, I awoke with a heavy heart and went downstairs to cook breakfast. Martin came in, looking subdued, his old suitcase in his hand.

We ate in silence. We could have been strangers. Eventually, it came time to leave for the depot. He put his case in the trunk and I drove out the dusty road for town. The New York bus was already waiting. I walked with him from the car and we stood awkwardly looking at each other. Now that the time had come, neither of us knew what to say.

At last, Martin took me in his arms and kissed me.

"Goodbye, Stella. Thanks for a lovely time."

"You'll write to me, won't you? You'll keep in touch?"

"Of course."

I clung to him.

"Promise me."

"I promise."

"Goodbye, Martin."

I felt sick with misery. He let me go and I watched him climb the steps of the bus. My heart was breaking. He sat at a window and the doors closed. I heard the engine start up and saw the bus move slowly out of the yard. It was all I could do not to weep. Martin sat with his face pressed to the window waving to me as the bus bore him away to New York and out of my life.

# 70.

I waited for a week before writing to Martin. I had no real news, so I filled the letter with tittle-tattle. It was basically just to maintain contact. I said I was already missing him and the house was quiet without him. I posted the letter and eagerly awaited his reply.

It didn't come. I told myself he was probably busy returning to work and picking up the threads of his life in Ireland. He would write when he had settled down. But as the weeks passed and I still didn't hear from him, I began to get uneasy. Perhaps he was ill or something had happened?

I wrote again. This time, I said I was concerned and urged him to write or call so that I would know he was all right. Every day, I watched nervously for the post, but there was no response. Now, I was definitely worried.

I decided to ring him at work. I chose a weekday afternoon when I knew he would be there. The phone rang for a long time before it was picked up by a woman. I asked to speak to Martin. She said he was out on a job and would be back soon. She took my name and number and said she would make sure he got the information. He never returned my call.

I made excuses for him. I clung to the hope that one day a letter would drop into my mailbox or the phone would ring and I would hear his voice again, apologising for the delay. That Christmas, I sent him a card. I picked it specially. It was a sentimental card which read: *From a Mother to her Son.* I told him I was sorry for what had happened and begged him to make contact with me. There was no reply.

Now, I could no longer make excuses. Martin was definitely avoiding me. I entered a long period of despair and self-blame, wishing

I had been honest with him and answered his questions. The consequences of telling the truth, no matter how bad, couldn't be worse than this terrible feeling of loss that haunted me day and night.

At last, I forced myself to sit down and write a long letter. It was hard for me to put it all down on paper. It brought back all the pain. I explained the circumstances of his birth. I told him I didn't know his father's name. I told him of the terrible shame I felt. I begged his forgiveness and pleaded with him to reply.

When I was finished, I felt better. I had finally rid myself of this awful guilt. I sent the letter by registered mail so I would know he had received it. I wanted desperately to be reconciled. Now, surely he would respond.

I couldn't wait. I counted the days. I had told Martin the truth and there was nothing left to hide. One morning, two weeks later, I saw the mailman turn into the drive and stop his van. He got out and walked to the front door. I was there before he could ring the bell. He handed me back my letter. It was unopened. Across the top had been written: RETURN TO SENDER. I knew now that Martin was never going to reply. He had broken off contact and I had lost him forever.

Jack must have noticed the effect all this was having on me. One day in April, when the chestnuts were bursting into leaf, he said: "Stella. You haven't been yourself lately. You seem depressed."

"It's the long winter," I said. "But now that spring is here, I'll soon recover."

"I've got the very tonic for you. I have to attend a Bar convention in San Francisco. How'd you like to come with me?"

I had never been to the west coast before. It would help to take my mind off Martin.

"I'd like that."

"Okay. It's done. I'll ring the hotel and book a double room. We leave in two days time. Start packing."

*

San Francisco was wonderful. I loved it from the moment we arrived:

the old-fashioned architecture, the hilly streets, the cable-cars and the bay. I loved the little shops and cafés and the laid-back atmosphere. Jack was at the convention for three days. I would attend the morning sessions with him and in the afternoons I'd go sight-seeing.

In the evenings, we would get dressed up and eat in some romantic restaurant; afterwards, we'd walk back through the streets to our hotel and make love.

On the last night, we went to Chinatown and ate in a Szechuan restaurant with a gaily painted dragon in the centre of the room. We drank wine and Jack gently took my hand.

"Enjoying yourself?"

"Yes."

"You know, I was worried about you for a while. You seemed to go into a tailspin after Martin left. It got me thinking. Why don't we do the right thing, Stella?"

"Meaning what?"

"Why don't we get married?"

His remark caught me by surprise.

"You're proposing to me?"

"Why not? I love you. Don't you love me?"

"Oh Jack. You know I do."

"Well, then? Why don't we make the logical decision and get married? You've got a house. I would save on rent. We'd be together all the time. And you'd have someone to talk to whenever you feel lonely or down."

I pushed my plate away.

"There's something you should know."

"Tell me."

"I can't have children."

Jack paused for a moment.

"That doesn't matter. I'll be taking you for better or worse. I'm a lawyer. I know what that means."

The wedding was a small affair. We were married in the town hall. Henry Sharp was Jack's best man and Bridgie was bridesmaid. Jack's parents came from New York and Charlie Kettles came with the children. The rest of the wedding party was made up of people from the office.

We had the reception in the Grand Hotel and at six o'clock we drove to the airport and flew to Fort Lauderdale in Florida. We spent a wonderful week. Jack hired a car and we went touring. A couple of times, he went fishing. The time passed quickly and soon we were back in Freehold. He moved his belongings into my house and we set up home.

We settled into the routine of married life. Our social circle expanded. We were invited to dinner parties and gave parties in return. We went on business trips together. Jack took up golf and persuaded me to join him. We were happy together and rarely disagreed.

I still thought of Martin. Occasionally, I would see a young man in a crowd who looked like him, and I'd find myself staring in anticipation. And then, I would have to remind myself that Martin was miles away, in another country. I supposed by now he was married and had children. I wondered what he told them when they asked about their grandmother.

The years passed and brought their share of tragedy. In November 1975, Daddy died. Bridgie got the news over the telephone from Kathleen. He had prostate cancer. I hadn't even known he was ill.

I thought of the strong man with the dark hair drinking pints in Donnelly's pub after the market and the warm smell of tobacco from his clothes.

I took a week off work and returned for the funeral. I hadn't been to Ireland for twenty-five years and everything had changed. There were British army checkpoints on the roads and the RUC station in Enniskillen was fortified with sandbags. I stayed with Michael and his family in the old house and stood holding Mammy's hand in the windy churchyard while they lowered my father's coffin into the ground.

Two years later, Mammy died. She was found dead in bed when Michael's wife brought her breakfast. This time, the news didn't shock me. I had been expecting it. Kathleen said that after Daddy died, she grew into herself. I thought how time had taken its toll on our family; my brother Martin, my father and now my mother. All resting together beneath the pointed spire of Ballinaleck church.

Bridgie's children grew up and one by one left to get married. I sat through three shower parties and three weddings one year after another. Charlie Kettles started talking of going home to open a pub in Ireland. I knew it would come to nothing. Bridgie had settled here and she would never go back.

Jack's law practice expanded and he hired more staff. Bit by bit, he withdrew from the business. He began to take more time off to play golf and relax at home. In December 1983, as the old year came to an end, he retired and sold the firm for a good price to Henry Sharp. That, along with his pension fund, meant the we were comfortable.

We passed our time growing old together – reading and listening to music, visiting our friends and taking trips to Florida when the weather turned cold. Jack played golf and I looked after the garden. It was a good life.

*

One afternoon in the summer of 1985, I was working in the back yard when I felt a sharp pain in my chest. I sat down to recover, feeling dizzy and out of breath, but the pain passed and I was fine again. Soon, I was able to stand up and carry on. I had been digging and I put it down to the physical exertion and thought no more about it.

Then one morning, a few weeks later, I woke to find that I couldn't open my right eye. Instinctively, I tried to reach my hand to my face but it wouldn't move. I stirred my leg but it too, was paralysed. I was in a panic now. My mind seemed fuzzy and disconnected from the rest of my body. I struggled to speak but no sound came.

I felt Jack stroking my hair.

"There, there," he was saying. "You're going to be all right. You've just had a turn, Stella. I'm going to ring now for an ambulance. You're going to be all right."

# 71.

When I woke again, I was in a bed in a room somewhere and a man was bending over me. He was wearing a white coat and had a shiny stethoscope hanging from his neck. My immediate impression was of whiteness: white walls, white sheets, bright sunlight. I felt like a fly caught in the centre of a great white web, unable to move. Gradually, I became aware of Jack sitting on a chair in the corner of the room.

I tried to speak but the words, when they came, sounded slurred. I realised that the man who was talking to me was a doctor. I watched his lips move and slowly the sense of what he was saying bore in on me.

"You're in Mercy Hospital, Mrs Morrison. You've had a stroke. You've suffered some damage. You're paralysed on your right side. But that may be reversible. We're going to carry out some tests on you and then we'll be able to chart a course for your recovery. But you have to think positive. Do you understand?"

I slowly forced my head to move.

"Good. How do you feel?"

I didn't reply. The effort was too much. And even if I could have spoken, what could I tell him? That the only feeling I had was a terrible despair, for myself and also for Jack. Poor Jack who would now have to nurse an invalid.

There followed long days of hopelessness when I raged against my body for failing me like this. I had always been active and now I was helpless as a child, depending on others to carry out the simplest tasks. I felt a terrible weight of frustration and anger. I began to pray again, to ask God to lift this burden from me. Privately, I believed I was being punished for my life. Why else had it happened? Surely God didn't do this kind of thing to people who were good?

I don't know how long I was in the hospital. Jack says three weeks, but to me, it seemed longer. They carried out tests on me and a physiotherapist tried to exercise my arm and leg. In the end they discharged me into Jack's care and he took me home and put me to bed in the front room.

My speech returned and my mind became lucid. But no movement came back to my limbs. Twice a week, the physio visited and worked on my useless arm and leg. She was a small woman but she was strong and determined. She showed no pity for me. She pulled and jerked till the perspiration stood in little beads on her forehead.

"We're not giving up, Stella, are we? We're going to get you out of this bed."

She would pull at my leg, bending and twisting it, as if by sheer force she could get it to work. But as time passed and there was no progress, I became resigned to the fact that I would never walk again.

An ambulance came to take me to the hospital once a week. They carried out more tests. They wired me to a machine and watched my heart beating on a monitor. Afterwards, the doctor and Jack would confer in quiet whispers. I had no need to ask Jack what they were saying. I could tell by the look on their faces that I didn't have long to live.

Throughout this ordeal, Jack never once complained. He washed me and fed me. He sat beside my bed and read to me. He cleaned the house and cooked my meals. Always, he struggled to be cheerful, urging me to think positive, to look on the bright side, not to give up hope. I had known for a long time that he loved me. But here, now, was the living proof.

The more I became convinced that I was dying, the more my thoughts turned to Martin and the unfinished business that lay between us. One day I said to Jack: "Do you remember Martin who came to stay with me from Ireland all those years ago?"

"Sure."

"I didn't tell you this but we had a row and he never forgave me. I wonder if it would be possible for someone to find him and tell him I'd like to see him again?"

"What's his surname?"

"McBride. He's a journalist. He works for a paper in Belfast."

Jack thought for a moment.

"You want to see him badly?"

"Yes."

"Okay. I'll ring your sister Kathleen and see what she can do."

I waited for a response and it was just like the long wait I had endured twenty years before when Martin had visited. I tried not to hope. I told myself that he could have moved or changed his job and Kathleen might never find him. And even if she did, he still might refuse to come. But it was impossible not to hope. Every morning when I woke, I prayed that God would send him. All through the long days in that darkened room, I waited for the news that Martin was coming back and we would be reconciled.

And then one afternoon, I heard the phone ring in the kitchen and Jack's footsteps hurrying to answer. He was on the phone a long time and eventually when he came into the room, I saw that he was smiling.

"He's coming," he said. "He'll be here tomorrow."

I don't know how I got through the next thirty hours. The next day, I got Jack to open the windows to let fresh air into the room. I asked him to wash me and comb my hair and put on my lipstick. He helped me into a pretty dress and propped me on the pillows. I wanted to look my best for Martin's visit.

I counted the minutes, watching as the sun went behind the trees and the long shadows crept across the lawn. Then, at five o'clock, I listened to the sound of the car driving away from the house as Jack went to the bus depot to collect him. An hour later he returned and I heard the key in the lock and voices speaking. And then the door of the room opened and Martin was standing there.

He was wearing a light gabardine coat. He looked tall and

367

handsome as I remembered him, but there were lines in his face and grey in his hair.

"Martin," I said. "Thank God you're back."

I reached out my hand and he approached the bed and held it. He pulled up a chair and sat beside me.

"How are you?" he said.

"Just happy to see you. Tell me what happened to you," I said.

He told me he was married with two children and had moved to live in Dublin. He had been promoted and was now a news editor. He was happy and had a good life.

I listened to his news and when he was finished, I said: "Martin. I'm sorry we fought."

He pressed a finger to my lips.

"Sssshh. Don't talk about it. It's past now. I've forgotten it."

"No. It's important. There are things I have to tell you. You asked about your father. I told you lies because I was too ashamed to admit the truth. I don't know who your father is."

I felt his hand tighten on mine.

"Stella, I already guessed."

"I thought if I told you the truth, you would have no regard for me, and I couldn't bear that. But I want you to know how it happened. We were at a party and I got drunk. I ended up in bed with this good-looking soldier. I don't even know his surname.

"I couldn't tell anybody. I couldn't tell my family. Bad enough to be pregnant but not even to know the father's name. It would have broken my mother's heart. I had to keep it a secret."

"Stella, you don't have to tell me this. It doesn't matter."

"No. It does matter. And I'm not finished."

I called for Jack and he came slowly into the room and stood at the door.

I said: "Jack. I want to introduce you. This is my son, Martin."

The two men looked at each other and Jack nodded.

"I'm pleased to know you, Martin."

I saw Martin's eyes fill with tears. He leaned across the bed and held me tight and kissed me. He buried his head in my breast. I felt his chest heave, like he was shedding some terrible burden.

"Thank you, Stella," he whispered. "Thank you so much."

*

Martin stayed for three days. He would come in the morning and read to me and we would talk about all the things that had happened since we last met. He spoke about his job and his family and the children. He would stay with me till evening when I grew tired and then he would have dinner with Jack and they would sit on the sun deck and drink whiskey. It made me happy that they got along so well.

At last, the time came for him to leave. He came into the room to say goodbye.

"I have to go now, Stella. My flight's at noon."

He took my hand.

"I'm glad you came, Martin."

"I am too. I'll keep in touch with you."

"And you'll come again? Next time you'll bring your family. I'd love to see my grandchildren."

He bent and kissed me farewell.

"Sure. I'll come again."

He turned and walked slowly out of the room and I heard Jack's car start up in the yard. I closed my eyes and something told me I would never see him again.

# 72.

I have almost finished now. I started this narrative six weeks ago, after Martin's visit. I wanted to leave him something that would explain my story to him. Perhaps, when he reads it, he will understand my life and know I am now at peace.

Every morning after breakfast, Jack sits with me and I dictate to him. He has bought a new tape recorder and I speak into a little microphone. In the evenings, he types it up.

My story is shared by thousands of women. I made a mistake and it followed me all my life. I know now I should have acted differently. But there is no one who can say they have led a perfect life. All we can hope for is to do the best.

I feel tired now. Recently, I have grown more weary. I seem to lack all energy. I think it is the drugs the doctor gives me. This afternoon, the physiotherapist will come and try to get me to walk. It is impossible but she never gives up.

I think I will sleep for a while. I will close my eyes and soon I will dream. I know what the dream will be and I welcome it. I will dream of Daddy coming in from the fields on a warm Irish day, his hands caked with dirt and his dark hair shining in the light. He will stop at the pump and wash himself. Then he will look up and see me watching.

He will turn to me and smile and say: "There's Stella Maguire. My wee angel. And when she grows up, she's going to break some poor boy's heart."

# Acknowledgements

A number of people have helped me in various ways with this novel and with my writing career in general and I would like to thank them: Marc Patton, Malcolm Imrie, Collette Hill, Ciara Considine, Edwin Higel, Fidelma Slattery, Lesley Keogh, Padriag O'Morain, Michael Farrell, Rose Doyle, Sean MacConnell, Doris Kelly, Joe Kennedy, Sally Mimnagh, Noel Costello, Mary Maher, Jim Cusack, Margaret Daly, Noel Hall, Maeve Binchy, Dick Ahlstrom, Georgia Memon, and, of course, my family, who have been a constant source of encouragement and support.